AFTER THE FALL

Also by Patricia Gussin

The Laura Nelson Novels

Shadow of Death

Twisted Justice

Weapon of Choice

Additional Novels by Patricia Gussin

The Test

And Then There Was One

Nonfiction by Patricia Gussin (with Robert Gussin)

What's Next...For You?

AFTER THE FALL

A NOVEL

PATRICIA GUSSIN

Longboat Key, Florida

ISBN: 978-1-60809-183-6

Published in the United States of America by Oceanview Publishing
Longboat Key, Florida

www.oceanviewpub.com
10 9 8 7 6 5 4 3 2 1

PRINTED IN THE UNITED STATES OF AMERICA

This book is dedicated to my brothers and sisters
Joanne, Don, Ed, Mary, and Terri

ACKNOWLEDGMENTS

I am so thankful to the Oceanview Publishing team for making this novel possible. Frank Troncale, who makes everything happen; David Ivester for his promotional magic; Emily Baar for assistance in all aspects of publishing; George Foster for the brilliant cover; Bill O'Connor for his design skills; Kirsten Barger for her passion for accuracy. And, a special thanks to my editor Ellen Count.

Above all else, the hugest thanks of all to my husband, Dr. Robert Gussin.

After the Fall is the fourth Laura Nelson novel and completes the series. I am grateful for the help from so many over the span of time from *Shadow of Death* through *After the Fall*.

AFTER THE FALL

CHAPTER ONE

"Mr. Parnell, I'm a surgeon, not an administrator."

"And I'm a pretty good judge of character and talent," Paul Parnell told Laura. "You have to give me that. I handpicked Fred thirty years ago, and now he wants to retire and get some use out of that yacht he gave Christina for their fortieth anniversary. You're our choice to replace him."

Dr. Laura Nelson sat between Parnell, Keystone Pharma chairman of the board, and Dr. Fred Minn, vice president of research, at a well-appointed table at the Fountain Room of Philadelphia's Four Seasons Hotel. Laura had assumed dinner to be a gesture of appreciation for her research on their new drug, Immunone, and her recent appearance at the FDA Advisory Committee hearing on their behalf. Now it was clear—they were trying to recruit her.

As Parnell spoke, Laura admired the fit and fabric of his charcoal gray suit with the thinnest of stripes—but why not spend money on clothes? Paul Parnell was a billionaire and a mega-philanthropist, as well as a Nobel Prize recipient.

"Not a yacht, a forty-foot Sea Ray," Minn said. "First on my agenda is a trip to New Zealand."

"On your Sea Ray?" Laura couldn't imagine the frail man negotiating that journey.

Minn chuckled. "No. By air. I have twin grandchildren there whom I've never even seen." Minn looked his age at sixty-seven, a small man with a neatly trimmed gray beard, intelligent blue eyes, and a ready smile.

"I have twin daughters," Laura said, glad for the diversion. "Are yours boys or girls?" She normally did not mix business with family, but she needed a gracious way out of this hard-sell recruitment situation. She loved surgery; couldn't imagine life without an operating room. She loved her job as chief of surgery at Tampa City Hospital and head of the surgical department at the medical school. An office job was out of the question.

"So much for twins," Parnell said. "Among my grandchildren, I have two sets. What does that have to do with Laura becoming vice president of research? Look, Laura, I've followed your career ever since that epidemic you got yourself into in Tampa."

Seven years ago, Keystone Pharma had provided an investigational drug, ticokellin, which had saved innumerable lives, including that of one of her twin daughters. Yes, she did owe Paul Parnell and Keystone Pharma a debt, but did she owe them her career? Her heart began to race just thinking of that epidemic disaster...

"I've briefed Paul on the role you played in organizing the clinical trials for Immunone," said Minn. "You recruited the most influential heart-lung transplant surgeons across the country, designed the protocol, guided the statisticians, presented at the FDA—the whole nine yards."

"It's been a real pleasure working with you, Dr. Minn, and your team, and collaborating with other heart-lung transplant surgeons, but I'm *not* a clinical pharmacologist. I'm *not* an immunologist. I'm *not* an administrator—"

"How can you say that?" Parnell interrupted with his wide, charming smile. "You're the head of the surgical department of a major university, a department that has fared very well in your hands, judging from the NIH grants you pull in."

The conversation went round and round. Laura said "no."

Parnell and Minn said "yes." Appetizer, main course, pecan pie with coffee.

"Will you promise to think about it?" Parnell concluded.

"I need you to say 'yes,'" Minn said. "I promised my wife. Once Immunone is approved, we're off to New Zealand. And Paul won't let me go until I have my replacement."

"You think about our offer, Laura," Parnell said, pulling a folded sheet of paper from his jacket pocket, handing it to her. "This summarizes the elements of compensation. Salary, bonuses, stock, stock options, health benefits, use of the company aircraft, moving expense reimbursement, that kind of thing. Now, I'm heading to my room. Sales meeting's here in the morning to get our reps all fired up about Immunone."

"I'm spending the night in the company apartment on Rittenhouse Square," Minn said. "Snow's forecasted for tonight, and I want to walk there before it starts."

"Are you staying in the hotel tonight, Laura?" Parnell asked.

"In town," she said. Not, *I'm staying with my boyfriend*—or whatever a woman her age calls the man she's seeing. "I have an early flight home to Tampa."

"Hope the snow holds off," Parnell said.

"And the ice," said Minn.

"Back to the sunshine tomorrow morning," Laura said as she bid good-night to Parnell, collected her coat, and walked with Minn to the front door.

"Taxi?" the doorman inquired, his voice muffled by the wool scarf that all but covered his lower lip.

"Yes, please." Laura sniffed the frigid air, wondering if the subtle smell was that of impending snow.

Minn stayed by her side as the doorman stepped to the curb to hail the lone cab lurking across the street. The frail older man seemed swallowed up by his thick cashmere coat. Why wasn't he wearing a hat?

"You go along before these conditions get worse," she urged. "Better yet, let's share the cab."

"Don't be silly, I'm just a block away." With a wave, Minn headed for the sidewalk.

As Laura reached to open the cab's door, the rumble of a motor starting up distracted her. In the eerie lighting outside the hotel, she could make out a vehicle, an older-style Jeep, across the street, maybe a half block away. Dark green or camouflage, or maybe black. On the roads tonight, a Jeep seemed an appropriate vehicle. As she climbed into the cab, she saw the Jeep pull out into the street.

"Where to, ma'am?" her bearded, burly driver asked.

Laura hesitated a moment, her attention on the Jeep, now accelerating.

"Ma'am? Where do you want to go?"

"Sorry. 1900 Delancy Place," she said. "I know it's not that far, I'll pay double."

"Too far to be walking in those high heels, ma'am," he said with a chuckle. "And here comes the snow."

Laura leaned back into the seat and opened the window for just a second so she could feel an icy flake on her hand. She'd moved from Michigan to Florida twenty-one years ago, never missing winter at all.

During the brief ride, Laura's mind drifted to a disturbing message from a man who had called her office in Tampa after she'd left for Washington, DC. A man claiming he was assistant to the mayor of Detroit, whom she knew to be Coleman Young. His name was Lonnie Greenwood, a name Laura did not recognize. His reason for contacting her: his son had cystic fibrosis and needed a lung transplant. Fine, that's what she did: lung transplants. Then he'd specifically stated that she be "reminded about Johnny Diggs." Johnny Diggs had died twenty-five years ago at the age of eighteen. How did she know this? She had pulled the trigger on the gun that killed him. *Could this Lonnie Greenwood know? Impossible!* With a force of will that had served her well in the past, she closed off that compartment of fear. Focus on the here and now.

The here and now jolted her back with a skidding approach to the curb at Tim's place.

"Careful on the ice, ma'am," the cabbie said as she paid him. Before Laura stepped into the condo building, she stood for a moment, letting the white flakes caress her face, tasting their crispness on her tongue.

CHAPTER TWO

Parked along the curb down the street from the Four Seasons Hotel, Jake Harter was positioned just right, ready to fire up and go. He'd hung around the bar of the Fountain Room long enough to watch the headwaiter present the bill to the dinner party, then he'd slipped out and headed to his vehicle. He didn't need to kill the old man, only seriously disable him, but once the Jeep made contact, the outcome would be out of his control. Steel and g-forces on flesh and bone.

Jake pulled the black knit cap over his crew-cut, salt-and-pepper hair. The temperature had plunged, but what was that for a tough former Marine? He hunched further down in the olive-drab Jeep, the vehicle that had been through a lot of years with him. He had nothing personal against Fred Minn. Matter of fact, he admired him. The guy was a straight shooter, pretty much a novelty in the pharmaceutical industry. But retiring the old guy was now necessary, a temporary solution as he finalized his ultimate plan.

Keystone's drug, Immunone, must not be approved—at least not yet. Dr. Minn, the mastermind behind the approval process, knew every detail about that drug. Without him, the company would scramble for direction. That would give Jake the time he needed.

Jake watched as the doorman held the door for the woman,

Dr. Nelson, and the hatless gray-haired man with the stooped shoulders, Fred Minn. A cab immediately pulled up to the Four Seasons entrance.

Shit! If Minn got in that cab, tonight was a loss.

As Jake watched, only the woman climbed into the back seat. Okay. Good. He started the Jeep, noticing for the first time how loud it sounded. Just as Jake had anticipated, Minn turned right, heading away from the hotel. A short walk down the deserted sidewalk and he'd be on 18th Street. Just a few steps after that, he'd reach Cherry, cross at the light, and take a right, heading to Keystone's corporate apartment in that high-rise on Cherry Street, less than a block away.

Bad night like this, there wasn't much traffic in Logan Square, and that made Jake's job a lot easier. Cherry was a one-way street heading west, so he had an unobstructed view. Minn would have to step off the curb onto Cherry, his left side exposed. Conditions were perfect—no other pedestrians, no traffic, a moonless night, and snow obscuring the ground. Jake took one last look. Any sign of a cop and he'd abort the mission. Wait for the next opening.

Nothing suspicious. Go!

The Jeep shot forward in a direct trajectory. The man reacted, turned, his chest exposed to the oncoming vehicle. The impact was direct, flinging Minn onto the adjoining sidewalk. Jake felt and heard a thump, but had no time to glance back. The puny guy was either dead or a bag of broken bones and crushed organs.

Jake sped on, just a few blocks west to 22nd Street. The Jeep was the lone car on the road. A right on 22nd would take him to the Vine Street Expressway. With ease, he merged with the few cars heading east toward the Delaware River. At this time of night, a five-minute shot to I-95, his route back home to Rockville. As the Vine Expressway took him over the Ben Franklin Parkway, Jake glanced furtively off to the right for signs of police activity.

No tail. He drove with caution, attracting no attention, fitting in among the lanes of scant traffic. Somewhere on the way home, he'd pull over, reattach his own Maryland plates, and lose the Pennsylvania plates he'd lifted from a car in an off-airport parking lot. He'd check out the Jeep body. The vehicle already had its share of dings, but any damage from ramming the old man could be covered up by a tussle with a tree trunk.

Snow started to accumulate on the drive back home to Rockville, and Jake kept to the speed limit. He'd had a tense day at the office, trying to dampen his agency's enthusiasm for Keystone's new drug. The FDA Advisory Committee yesterday had been overwhelmingly positive. For the first time in his project management career, an advisory committee had wholeheartedly endorsed a drug, pressuring the FDA to approve it expeditiously. As the assigned FDA New Drug Evaluation manager for this project, Jake had organized the public meeting. He'd tried to insert as much pessimism as possible, but once the pro-approval frenzy started, Jake knew he'd have to come up with a new plan to slow the approval process. By chance, in the elevator on his way out of the FDA Parklawn Building, Dr. Fred Minn, Keystone's key scientist, and his consultant, Dr. Laura Nelson, were discussing their dinner appointment for Sunday night in Philadelphia. Perfect timing: get rid of Minn.

He was ready now for his next step, but Karolee might not go down so easily.

CHAPTER THREE

Laura and Tim Robinson met when they were in medical school in Detroit. That'd been twenty-five years ago. Laura had been married. Tim had been, and still was, single. They'd reconnected on and off ever since Laura's husband, Steve, died fourteen years ago. A long-distance relationship since Laura was chief of surgery in Tampa and Tim a pediatric heart surgeon in Philadelphia. But a relationship that had progressed from platonic, to intimate, to romantic, to what? Love? Could that even be possible for her?

Now, as they snuggled on Tim's living room sofa, each with a brandy snifter in hand, Laura told him about her dinner meeting with Paul Parnell and Fred Minn.

"You wouldn't believe Keystone's agenda," Laura told Tim. "They want me to be vice president of research. *Me.* I almost laughed in their faces, but they were dead serious."

She set her drink down and lifted her blond hair off the collar of the bulky robe that Tim had lent her. "Imagine me wearing a suit every day. A big office in the Executive Suite. Jetting off in the company plane. Of all the perks, that definitely would be my favorite."

Laura looked up at Tim, expecting an incredulous grin. No grin. A serious, concerned expression, instead.

"What did you tell them, Laura?"

"I told them 'no-way.'"

"Why?"

"Because I don't want to be a bureaucrat."

"You should think about it. Think about the influence you'd have in developing new drugs that would save thousands of lives. Right now, when you operate, you have a direct impact on several patients' lives a week. But when you develop a new drug, like Immunone, you'll save so many more patients who would have died from organ rejection."

"Tim?" Laura said, reaching over to tousle his rust-red curls. "Of all people, you should know what it's like to be a surgeon. There can be no better career. I take out diseased lungs and insert new ones. That's what I do. I'm good at it."

"But you did enjoy organizing that big clinical trial for Immunone, right?"

"Sure, but the company did most of the organizing. I just helped out. Gave them advice when they needed it. Convinced all the other surgeons to come on board."

"I rest my case, babe. You did a hell of a job."

Laura was about to say something, but stopped when she felt Tim lean into her, lift her face to his and kiss her. The kiss lasted quite a long time, the longest and best kiss she'd had for way too many years. And it made her feel dreamy and sexy and... *I'm a forty-eight-year-old woman for God's sake...* But she did not pull back. After the longest time, Tim pulled her even closer and whispered, "Will you marry me, Laura?"

She froze. Didn't say anything. Couldn't breathe. Couldn't look up at him.

Time passed. He finally said, "Laura, did you hear me?"

"I did," she whispered.

More silence as she struggled for what to say. She'd suspected that someday Tim would ask her to marry him. He'd hinted at it. He'd joked about it. He'd even clowned around with her kids about it. They loved "Uncle Tim"; he was like a surrogate father—albeit long distance and occasional.

"And?"

"Tim," she said, her eyes meeting his. "I've been single for so long, raising five kids on my own. I don't know if I would even be a good wife." She didn't know if she even wanted to be a wife ever again. Sure, she'd thought about having a partner. When the kids were younger, she worried that she owed them a father figure. But she'd gone it alone, and now they were grown and launching their own separate lives.

"What about you, Laura? You've always been there for your kids. But what about you? You and me? You must know I've loved you for a long, long time. Maybe since that trip to Montreal when we were surgery students."

"You were dating my best friend back then," she reminded him. "And I was married."

"Yes," Tim said.

Laura wondered whether he knew more about what else happened to her on that fateful trip to Montreal. The falling snow outside, now huge flakes, reminded her of that snowbound experience twenty-three years ago.

In silence, they stared at the window, the ledge covered with white fluff. Tim took her left hand and gently rubbed her ring finger. She'd put away the ring long ago, without regret. *What would it be like, married to Tim?*

"I love your kids, Laura, and I think they like me, but it's not about them. This is about you and me. Do you love me? There, I've asked you. The question that scares the life out of me."

Tim, the entrenched bachelor, scared? *Scared that I might say "no?"*

In the silence, she wondered, *Do I love him?* Truthfully, she didn't know. She'd never allowed herself to indulge in thoughts of love. Maybe she did. But one thing was sure. She couldn't hurt him. Tim had been there for her whenever she needed him. Back when her son Patrick had needed heart surgery. Back when her daughter Natalie had nearly died. She *had* to say something. "Yes, Tim, I do love you. I really do."

"Then marry me."

"Can you give me some time to think about it? I mean, you caught me by surprise. I'm a little overwhelmed."

"Let's finish our brandy and then go to bed."

Yes, go to bed. Over the past few years, Laura had gradually slipped into an intimate relationship with Tim. When she visited him in Philly. When he visited her in Tampa. They never slept in separate beds anymore. Yes, sleeping with Tim every night would be beyond wonderful. But marriage? Giving up her freedom? Giving up her surgical practice in Tampa? Giving up the department chair she'd worked and fought for?

Nestled in the crook of Tim's arm, hearing his soft, regular breathing, Laura tried to relax, to just give herself time to consider Tim's proposal. Tomorrow she'd be back on her own in Tampa, facing the usual round of problems that crept up in her absence. One problem, especially. That message from Lonnie Greenwood.

CHAPTER FOUR

Jake had planned to return to his home in Rockville, Maryland, after he sped away from what was left of the old man in Philadelphia.
Lights off, he'd park the Jeep in his driveway, let himself inside, and
hunker down. His wife was away and, for all appearances, he'd have
spent the night home alone. But as Jake got closer, he found himself
diverting off course. With Karolee away, he could spend what was
left of the night with Addie. Tonight, of all nights, he needed her.
Reaching Addie's apartment in nearby Bethesda, he took the elevator to the fourth floor of the high-rise. He tapped on her door with
his fingertips. Tonight was not a night to draw attention to himself.
Open the door, Addie.

No response. Should have made a key for himself. Jake
knocked and waited, knocked again. Addie was a light sleeper.
Certainly she'd hear him.

The door across the hall opened a crack. "What's going on?"
The voice was cranky and he couldn't tell if it was male or female.
"It's the middle of the night. Give it up. Go away."

"Shit," he muttered, turning, keeping his back to the crack.

Then Addie's door opened. Her hand grabbed his coat sleeve
and pulled him inside.

"It's me, Addie," he said. Unnecessary. Who else would it be?
"I tried not to wake you."

"What are you doing here?" Her eyes blazed and her words

sounded cold, unwelcoming. "You woke my neighbors. I don't need anybody gossiping about my night life. You know that—"

"I couldn't sleep, I needed you." Jake held out his arms for her, but she backed away. Her lustrous black hair hung wild and wavy, her skin a rosy bronze, her breasts peeking out from under a flimsy pink negligé. Jake could not resist a grin. When it came to sexy and expensive adornments, Addie definitely enjoyed Western culture. How could she go back to a burka, covering her beautiful face, exposing only those soulful, dark eyes.

"What about your wife?" Addie took another step backward. Normally, his wife worked late into the evenings with Jake needing to leave Addie to be home when Karolee returned.

Tonight Jake didn't want to discuss his wife. Not at this hour. Not after what he'd just executed.

"Karolee went to Florida to see the granddaughter. Baby's two weeks old already."

"I can't believe you're a grandfather. And not a good one. You should have gone with your wife."

"I want to be with *you*. She'll be gone for two days. We'll have two days and two nights."

"Why didn't you tell me earlier? What time is it, anyway?" She answered her own question. "Two-thirty in the morning."

Addie's English was near perfect, her voice naturally husky, and with her lingering hint of an Arabic accent, she sounded very sexy. He hadn't planned to have her tonight, but—

"I'm awake now," she announced. "I need to talk to you. You didn't call me after the Advisory Committee on Friday. I waited all day yesterday and today. But no call. Why? Is something wrong? I expected you to call and tell me what the FDA decided to do, and when."

"Addie, not tonight. I'm beat." Jake took off his coat, hung it in her entry closet, and started toward her bedroom. "Let's—"

"Something must be wrong." Addie edged in front of him, blocking the doorway. "I know the committee voted to approve Immunone. So what's happening? I need to know when the approval will come through. My family wants me back in Iraq, but I want to wait for the approval, to collect my share of the money Replica will owe me."

"Addie, please, let's get some sleep." Jake squeezed past her, brushing against her breasts. *Maybe more than just sleep,* he thought, starting to unbutton his shirt.

"Things are getting worse for my country every day. The United Nations just sent the ninth inspection team in. This time looking for centrifuge components to produce enriched uranium. What if they find something bad? Could I be deported?" Addie paused to take a breath. "Immunone's approval is so important to me."

"It's important to me too," Jake said, now undressed, moving toward the bed. Addie followed him, and he took her hand, eased her down beside him, stroking her thigh as they sat, waiting for her to stop her rant so he could kiss her.

Addie sat beside him, but did not stop. "Despite tearing the country apart, they haven't found anything, have they? Now they're focusing on this centrifuge bullshit."

"Addie, would your father approve of your crude language?" Jake wanted to distract her from the return-to-Iraq theme.

"Bullshit?" she said. "No, and he wouldn't like 'fuck' any better, and if he knew that you and I were fucking, he'd have to kill you, and maybe me too. That's why you cannot be careless like this. You could have called. Not good that you woke the old lady across the hall. Everyone knows I'm a Muslim. I'm expected to live up to Muslim standards."

"Standards?" Did Addie seriously think she could go back to Baghdad, live like a Sunni woman, stripped of her basic human rights and all the Western privileges and conveniences and independence she enjoyed here?

Addie stood up, facing him. "Yes, Jake, standards. And one of them is respect. And when you ignore my questions, you are not giving me respect."

And she actually was talking about returning to the Muslim culture, where respect for women was nonexistent?

"I ask you again: where is the FDA with Immunone's approval? Tell me."

Jake stood to face her. "Addie, you know I can't reveal—"

"What? Your precious confidentiality is more important than me?" She turned her back on him, her thin shoulders hunched over. "I thought you loved me, Jake."

I do love you, Addie. I am doing this all for you. So we can be together.

Once the Immunone NDA—New Drug Application—was approved, Addie would return to her family and her Muslim culture. *Unless she was a married woman.* But first, he needed a divorce from Karolee. And that would be most unpleasant. So much better for Karolee to meet an untimely death. A death he'd been contemplating, a death now critical to his plan.

Jake had first met Adawia Abdul when she'd represented her pharmaceutical company, Replica, at an FDA meeting to discuss the approval of the drug Immunone. As a project manager at the FDA for twenty-five years, he'd heard hundreds of pharmaceutical pitches, but never one so stunningly brilliant, and never one delivered by a woman so overwhelmingly beautiful. As soon as the Replica entourage had left, he'd run her credentials. PhD in molecular biology, University of Michigan, Iraqi national, age thirty-four.

A project manager at the FDA is responsible for pulling together the components of a New Drug Application. You could do his admin-type job adequately with a bachelor's degree, but Jake was not adequate, he was damn good. Easy for him to make an excuse to contact Dr. Adawia Abdul to ask for data clarification and so forth. Initially, he suggested they meet for coffee so he could explain the FDA process. Of course, fraternizing with employees of the pharmaceutical industry was forbidden, he knew—an inherent conflict of interest. After that first coffee, listening to her scientific rationale for the drug's mechanism of action—not understanding that much of the complex biotechnology—listening to her talk of her country, her Iraqi family, he fell under her spell—magically, immediately, passionately. This was the woman he'd dreamed of, needed, must have at all costs.

Jake stepped to Addie, gently turned her around, led her back toward the bed, sat her down, and blotted her tears with the hem of the sheet. "Okay," he said, sitting next to her, taking her hand, "even though it's late. I will…"

Adawia Abdul had grown up in Baghdad, the daughter of a medical researcher with prominent political connections to the Iraqi regime. She had a younger sister Farrah, married now with two little boys. Despite Islam's restrictive position on women, Adawia had been sent to America to get a PhD with the key condition that she return to Iraq to work in a government laboratory. But after graduate school, Adawia had convinced her father she needed more experience, and she headed off to Bethesda as a scientist in a start-up pharmaceutical company, Replica. While there, she discovered the mechanism of action of Immunone and its chemical analogs. In appreciation of her contribution and to entice her to stay, the cash-poor start-up gave her 5 percent of the company. It wasn't worth much back then, but now that Keystone Pharma had acquired Immunone, the value of Replica stock had skyrocketed. The good news: when Adawia was able to cash out, she'd collect $7.5 million. The bad news: she'd return to Iraq.

Jake grabbed a pillow, stuck it behind his head, and pulled Addie over, curving his arm around her. "Addie, you know FDA Advisory Committees are just that, they advise. They don't approve. I can tell you the FDA still has a lot of questions. Mostly about safety. They're talking about more data. More clinical trials." This was all a lie, but he had to quell the elation that predicted the 100 percent positive vote of the Advisory Committee would translate into a speedy approval. Certainly, the loss of Dr. Fred Minn would slow the company down as they struggled to address the drug safety questions he would manufacture for them. Jake may not have the clout of a medical review officer, but he controlled the project data; it would be no big deal for him to misplace or even tamper with the files.

"No, we don't need more trials," Addie stated, removing her hand from his. "Dr. Nelson presented all 500 patients receiving Immunone and another 500 on the placebo control. Double-blind. The patients treated with Immunone had a 70 percent reduction in rejection. Seventy percent. That's huge, Jake. You know that. And no side effects."

"The FDA is always leery of results that look too good to be true, Addie."

Jake felt her edge away from him.

"Maybe they think someone cheated? Or they just don't believe the data?"

"Look, it's late," Jake said. " I'll find out more when I go in tomorrow. We have to get some sleep." He reached for her, pulling her down next to him, pressing his body to hers, breathing in her exotic scent. "Everything will work out."

CHAPTER FIVE

Monday, February 17

The beep of Tim's alarm clock woke Laura at 5:30 a.m. She hadn't slept well, her mind doing flip-flops, one moment dwelling on Tim's proposal—how it would feel being married—did she want to be married—did she love Tim enough to spend the rest of her life with him? The next minute trying to imagine herself directing pharmaceutical research, walking away from the surgical career she loved—would it be possible to work for Keystone Pharma and still do surgery on the side? Her answer to that, a clear no. Surgery required total focus, at least the way she practiced it. There'd be no having it both ways. What would she tell Tim?

He had leaned over to turn off the alarm and, when he rolled back, he pulled her into the crook of his arm. "Get any sleep, babe?"

"Not much. Too much to think about." But, she could have Tim *and* surgery. That is, if she moved to Philadelphia. Or, if he moved to Tampa. *Would he be willing to do that for her? Would she be willing to move for him? Maybe.* She'd lived in Tampa for twenty years, raised her children there, but they'd all moved. Her son Mike, a lawyer in Philadelphia, and her twin daughters, med students at the University of Pennsylvania. What was left for her in Tampa?

"What about you?"

"No. I think I've always known I would ask you to marry me.

I just never knew when. Should have done it years ago. But you know what? I'm glad I blurted it out last night."

"Tim, I still can't wrap my mind around getting married. You took me by surprise. I mean..."

"You promised me you'd think about it, Laura. But right now, I've got to get you up and out of here or you'll miss your plane. Or can I convince you to stay?"

Laura snuggled closer to Tim's warm, inviting body, placed a light, playful kiss on the curly auburn hairs on his chest, and pushed herself to a sitting position. "Wish I could stay longer," she said, glancing out the window. "Not looking forward to facing the elements out there. I believe you call that white stuff snow."

"Looks like we got a good three inches during the night. Treacherous driving conditions on top of that ice. Just one more reason to delay your flight." Tim was sitting now, and he grabbed both of her hands in his. "We have a lot to talk about, Laura. Could you delay going back until later in the day? Even better, tomorrow?"

Laura considered her day. She did not have a case on today's operating room schedule, but she did need to prepare for tomorrow's hospital staff meeting. As usual, she'd be presenting the surgical department's morbidity and mortality statistics. Maybe she could get a colleague to pull the report together for her.

Another look out the window told her: too risky. If this weather continued, she might not be able to get out of Philadelphia.

"I know that look of yours, Laura. I'll go make coffee. You take a shower and get dressed, but I'm coming to Tampa next weekend, and it won't be for the weather, it'll be for you."

Laura had stepped out of Tim's shower, a very manly one, devoid of the myriad of hair products she kept stashed in hers, when she heard Tim's voice at the door.

"Come in," she said, not bothering to pull the towel around her naked body. *What a difference a marriage proposal makes,* she thought with a sly smile.

"Mike," Tim said, holding out the phone. "Wants to know if you'd like him to pick you up, drive you to the airport. I told him I have a town car on its way, but if he wants to see you off…"

Laura took the phone. "Hi, Mike." She listened as her son repeated his offer. He could swing by Tim's, pick her up, take her to the airport, all in time for him to arrive at his Center City law office.

"Too complicated, honey," she said. "I'm exhausted just listening to the itinerary. Not that I don't want to see you. I have some interesting stuff to tell you." Laura glanced up at Tim, winked at him. "Some personal; some professional. But it can wait."

"Mom, what's going on? Now you have me curious."

"Tell you next time. Okay, honey? And thanks for the offer to pick me up. I really appreciate it, especially in this crappy weather. Gotta go. Don't forget to check in with your sisters every few days."

"Those girls are twenty-four years old, Mom. But you know I will. Love you."

As Laura handed the phone back to Tim, he beamed. "You going to tell your kids about us getting married, or do you want me to ask their permission?"

That look worried Laura. It seemed too optimistic, too final. Final was nowhere near her reality yet.

"Neither," she said before the chime of the bell interrupted.

Tim partially closed the bathroom door and went to answer the front door. "Came a bit early for your passenger, Dr. Robinson." Laura could hear a man's voice. "Conditions are slippery out there. I'll wait in the car, just wanted you to know I was here."

"Be down as soon as I can," Laura called. "Can I have that coffee to go?"

Laura emerged from the bedroom dressed in a red-and-gray-patterned wool dress cinched at the waist with a gray belt, and wearing three-inch red heels with the Ferragamo emblem. Her blond hair hung collar length, and she'd made no attempt to tame the waves. She chose to wear glasses; no time today to deal with her contacts.

Tim was waiting by the door, her red winter coat in one hand, coffee container in another. "Lady in red," he said, glancing at her feet. "But not too practical for a day like today."

"Before you say, 'I told you so,' next time I come to Philly, I'm investing in some boots."

"Babe, you should take off those heels. Change into your sneakers."

"I just have to make it to the car. Once I get dropped off at the airport, the sidewalks will be shoveled. Right?" Laura looked down at her feet. "Should have packed flats. I have only myself to blame. Never was a Boy Scout—"

"I'm taking you shopping myself," Tim said, "for some big, furry boots."

Laura pulled on the coat, buttoned the top button, and ran her fingers over the stubble on Tim's unshaved cheek.

"Until next Saturday in Tampa," Tim said, taking one of her hands in his. "I love you, Laura. I want to spend my life with you."

Interrupted by the driver who'd come for her bags, Laura and Tim exchanged a kiss, then he placed the travel mug of coffee in her hands.

"Better get a move on," the driver said. "Gonna be slow going on these roads."

"I'm ready," said Laura, following him out Tim's door, onto the elevator, and then out into the elements.

CHAPTER SIX

MONDAY, FEBRUARY 17

A sense of abandonment swept over Tim as the elevator door closed behind Laura. Like his life was walking away, leaving him an empty shell. He'd asked her to marry him. After all those years of thinking about it, agonizing whether it was the right time. And now he'd gone and done it. What would be her response? That favorite Corinthians 13 quote came to mind. About the only biblical quote he knew: *"Love bears all things, believes all things, hopes all things, endures all things. Love never ends."* For a time, he stood at the door to his apartment, until jarred back into the moment by the paper delivery man. A hefty man, who covered the prime addresses in Center City and probably made as much money as any academic surgeon.

That trivial economic speculation started him thinking about where he and Laura should live. He'd already decided he'd move to Tampa. All Children's Hospital in St. Petersburg would be happy to have him. But what would Laura want now that her kids were no longer in Tampa, but, rather, clustered about Philly? Mike permanently, the twins in med school. Kevin an architect in nearby Princeton, and Patrick in grad school at New York University, an hour's train ride away. If Laura joined the staff at the University of Pennsylvania as a thoracic surgeon, would she be okay not being chief?

"Paper, sir," the carrier said. "Bad news. Hit and run right outside the Four Seasons."

Tim wasn't in the mood for news, bad or otherwise, so he accepted the paper, murmured a "thanks," and went back to his cup of coffee on the kitchen table. The snow was still falling, not enough yet to close the airport, so Laura's flight should get off okay.

He'd asked the hospital not to schedule any early cases, knowing Laura would spend the night, but now he found himself with extra time. He opened the *Philadelphia Inquirer.* On the front page he saw the headlines: "Keystone Pharma Vice President of Research Struck Dead Outside Four Seasons: Hit and Run. Dr. Fred Minn, sixty-seven years old..." The coffee in his mug slopped over the rim as his hand trembled. Minn was one of the men Laura had had dinner with last night. Tim checked the article for the time of the incident: 11:00 p.m. Frighteningly close to the time Laura had left the hotel. God, it could have been Laura. The Corinthians verse replayed in his mind.

Tim reached for the telephone on the kitchen counter. He needed to call Laura. To tell her what happened. Obviously, she'd had no idea. She had one of those clunky cell phones. Hated using it, but with her job and her kids, she needed to stay connected.

The phone rang. And rang. Why wasn't she answering? By now she'd be off in the cab, her purse nearby. Tim hung up. Tried again. Same result.

How would Laura react to Fred Minn's death? She respected him, admired his scientific discipline, enjoyed working with him on the Immunone clinical trials, but she wouldn't consider him a personal friend, close enough to come back to Philly to attend his funeral. *How selfish can a guy get?* Tim chastised himself. Now that he'd finally declared his love for Laura, he wanted her beside him. *All the time.*

He tried calling her on her mobile phone again. Same results. Nothing. *She must not have charged the battery,* he thought, as he gulped the last of the tepid coffee and headed to the shower.

Then he heard someone pounding on his door.

Tim opened the door, at first not recognizing the man whom

he'd just seen leaving, toting Laura's suitcase. Gone was the friendly attitude, the easy smile. Replaced by a wild look of panic.

"Dr. Robinson, the woman who just left. She took a bad fall. I had my service call an ambulance. I left her out there. A neighbor's with her. Thought you should know. I gotta get back down."

"Laura?" Tim asked, but the man was gone.

Tim bolted after him, but the elevator had already left. He took the five floors of stairs at a run, sprinting through the lobby toward the automated front door.

He dashed through the door the instant it opened and found himself facing a black town car surrounded by a small crowd. At first, he did not see Laura lying crumpled next to the passenger door near the rear wheel. Until a crimson red coat against the white snow caught his eye through the bent figures who'd gathered to observe a prone woman on the icy ground.

"Laura," he called out. "Are you okay?"

A tall, middle-aged man in a sweat suit responded. "I stepped out of my building to check the weather, and I saw it happen. The woman reached for the back passenger door, and she went down. Hit really hard. I could hear the crack from over there." He pointed to the door of the next building.

Tim knelt at Laura's side. She appeared to be curled up, asleep, on top of the two inches of fresh snow. Except for the rivulet of blood staining the snow beneath the right side of her head. When Tim looked closer, he could see that her right lower arm protruded at an awful angle. "Call an ambulance," he shouted, forcing himself not to try to shake her awake. For a moment, even the trauma basics escaped him. The ABCs: airway, breathing, circulation.

"Dr. Robinson, I am so sorry." The driver knelt beside Tim. "I told her I'd get the door, but I had to move some things around in the trunk, and she didn't wait for me. Dispatch has an ambulance on its way. Should be here right away."

That was a good thing about living in Center City, Philadelphia. The ERs of four teaching hospitals all within minutes away.

Tim heard a woman's voice call out, "I hear the sirens now. Thank God."

So far, Tim had done nothing other than take Laura's pulse at the right carotid artery in her exposed neck. Normal breathing, normal pulse. He wanted to turn her over, but was afraid to move her. What if she had a neck fracture? He was a pediatric cardiologist. His trauma experience dated back to medical school. He called her name. Nothing. She was out cold. Blood seeping out from under her head was expanding the red stain, but not at an alarming rate. Blood loss he did know how to assess, and this was minor.

Tim, jacketless, was still kneeling beside her when the paramedics' van pulled up. The female driver stopped behind the town car. Two male paramedics jumped out, one almost slipping on black ice obscured by fresh snow. The driver stayed inside behind the wheel as the two men pulled a stretcher out of the back, adjusted the height, and wheeled it to Laura. Tim frowned. The ambulance was sent from Hahnemann University Hospital, not the University of Pennsylvania, which would have been his preference, where her daughters were residents. But Hahnemann was a fine hospital, and speed was of the essence.

"Sir, do you know the woman?" asked one of the paramedics, who now knelt beside Tim, assessing Laura's condition as he spoke.

"Yes. She's Dr. Laura Nelson. She was visiting me from Tampa. Was on her way home."

The second attendant had joined them. "She's a doctor? Wow, she took a bad fall."

Tim stood, his teeth chattering, trying not to shake with cold and concern as the two men worked wordlessly to secure Laura's neck in a cervical collar, then carefully unfolded her from her twisted shape on the ground.

"Hurry," Tim heard himself say. "Get her to the hospital."

"Gotta splint the arm. And the hand looks deformed." When Tim followed the younger paramedic's gaze, his heart fell, almost stopped beating. Laura was right-handed; her right hand was her livelihood. His clinical impression: that hand was beyond repair.

"Lift," the paramedic said, kicking aside the plastic cover of Laura's coffee container. They placed her on the stretcher and steered toward the ambulance in a jerky motion as they navigated the snow and ice. "You going with us, sir?"

"Yes," Tim said. He started to shake, violently now, and the limo driver took off his coat and placed it over Tim's shoulders.

"No," Tim started to say.

"Least I can do, Dr. Robinson," the driver said, his arm around Tim as he climbed into the ambulance behind the stretcher. "Godspeed."

CHAPTER SEVEN

The Monday morning media had been glowing in their praise of government and industry working together for the common good, blah, blah. Jake headed to his windowless office at the behemoth FDA Parklawn Building on Fisher's Lane in Rockville, Maryland. He was prepared to block, in any way he could, the wave of enthusiasm he knew would overrun his department following the Immunone Advisory Committee meeting. The FDA likes to look good and they did when their medical officers and Keystone Pharma's doctors and consultants all went for fast-track approval on this life-saving drug for organ transplant recipients.

Addie did not subscribe to newspapers so Jake had to wait until he got to work for a chance to check the *Washington Post*. He wanted to see the headlines about Dr. Fred Minn's fate—whatever the outcome. With Keystone Pharma now about to launch a blockbuster drug, for sure, the Minn incident would get much more media attention than it would have only a week ago.

Jake grabbed a coffee and a paper as he passed through the Office of New Drugs staff lounge. You weren't supposed to remove the newspapers from the break area, but he needed privacy. Reaching his office, he closed the door and spread the paper out on his cluttered desk. Second page: "Keystone Pharma Scientist Struck Down in Philadelphia: Doctor Fred Minn Victim of Hit and Run." Minn had been pronounced dead on arrival at

Jefferson Hospital emergency room. So he *had* killed the old man. The article went on to expound on Minn, his career, Immunone's likely approval. Paul Parnell, Keystone's chairman of the board and former CEO, was "shocked and saddened." As well he should be.

Working for the FDA is what you make of it, Jake knew. The vast majority of his coworkers put in their time. Show up. Stay eight hours. Take long breaks. Drink free coffee. Eat out of brown paper bags, skip the government cafeteria food. Go home. What happens in between, no big deal. Plug in the numbers. Give your bigwig bureaucrats what they seem to want. Come back the next day. Collect paycheck. Get pension.

But for a few, the job was about power, or perceived power. Everybody thinks the bigwigs make the decisions at the FDA. Not true. Any lowly reviewer in the trenches could throw a monkey wrench in a drug approval, or could raise a fuss about a food substance, or could initiate a hygiene concern. Pretty much at will. If they were so inclined. Which most weren't. Most just showed up, followed standard operating procedures, and went home.

Until now, Jake had been with the majority. Do the job. Go home. But today, he would join the small percentage who got off on using their FDA power to manipulate the outside world. And the outside world under the FDA's economic influence was vast. The FDA regulates 25 percent of all consumer expenditures in the United States. That's a lot of money, and that's a lot of influence for one individual—a seemingly lowly bureaucrat—to parlay.

Jake would not be using his position to exercise any measure of global power, but only as a means to keep Addie in the United States. Despite pressure from her father, she was determined to stay employed at Replica until she came into that Immunone windfall. Jake would have made her an honest woman by then. The Muslim religion had no problem with divorced men, but they wanted their woman pure and untouched until they were properly married. At least that was Jake's understanding. He was no expert on Islam, but he supposed he would become one once he and Addie were joined in marriage. Would he still be considered an infidel? Even if he converted?

Jake stuffed the *Post* into his briefcase, opened his door, and gazed out into the hall. His coworkers were pouring in, and he wanted to pick up on the morning chatter: Friday's Advisory Committee and the Fred Minn hit and run last night. But two overarching problems needed his urgent attention. One, he'd get started today on undercutting Immunone. And two, Karolee. She'd surprised him by taking off from her big-money executive chef gig to go to Miami to visit their first grandchild, a two-week-old baby girl. Hard to imagine his haughty wife as a granny. Jake smirked at the thought. And how was Granny's visit going? Their son's wife couldn't stand Karolee, and the sentiment was mutual. Mark should have moved farther away than Miami.

Jake was still sitting at his desk when a colleague poked his head in the cubbyhole office and announced, "Jake, get your butt to the conference room. Meeting's starting now."

Jake arranged his papers, grabbed a fresh, lined yellow pad, and made his way down the hall to join the rest of the team from the Office of Drug Evaluation III. He took the last vacant seat at the rectangular conference table as Agency Deputy Director Sid Casey began to address the attendees. His mood seemed even more jovial than usual. "Jake, my man," he started, nodding his way, "great show last Friday. You guys pulled it off. Even the *New York Times* had kudos for the Agency. Now, how long has it been since that happened?"

"Forever," a voice called out.

"So now we get down to the real work. Putting the approval package together. Jake, as project manager extraordinaire, you take the lead. That'll free up the medical reviewers and pharmacologists to finalize their sections. Work with Drug Safety to make sure the adverse event monitoring is tweaked to collect as much new data as possible."

"Will do." Jake already knew how he would quash all this optimism. Before coming in, he had requested all the data on the deaths that had occurred during the Immunone trials. No matter how safe a drug is, patients always die on drug trials. Sometimes they get hit by a truck. Sometimes they take a stray bullet. Some accident occurs that's obviously not drug related. Other times they rupture an aorta, throw a blood clot, develop pneumonia, commit suicide. Who knows: drug related, or not? These cases are more difficult to decide. Did the drug increase the blood pressure, coagulate the blood, weaken immunity, cause depression? If one such incident occurs, it's considered an isolated incident. More than one triggers doubt, and doubt translates to delays.

The director continued, "...drug like Immunone is a tricky synthesis. Chemistry, Manufacturing and Controls—you CMC guys—gotta be all over this Immunone process. We're in the honeymoon period now, boys and girls. Any minute, doctors and patients are going to be clamoring for this drug, so make damn sure Keystone can make it in scaled-up quantities." He pointed to Jake, now sitting at the far end of the table. "Those validation reports have to be letter-of-the-law. No cutting corners. No rest for the wicked. Jake, that's all on you to verify. Okay? Understood? Questions?"

Jake had planned to broach the subject of doubt. Doubt about the status of the death evaluations, but he thought better of it. So much attention had been directed his way, basically the entire coordination process. He'd have plenty of time to "stumble" onto the unfortunate "discovery" that critical data was missing relative to the thirteen deaths that had occurred during the clinical trials.

When the team was dismissed, Jake thanked the director for the confidence he'd placed in him. Then he went back to his office to call Addie. He'd tell her the meeting did not go well. There were complications. Serious problems with Immunone that were confidential and being kept out of the media.

CHAPTER EIGHT

A dull pounding reverberated in her head. Indiscernible voices drifted. And in the background, a beeping, like a heart monitor. A familiar, yet irritating odor. Starched stiffness covering her. Pulsating pain ran from her right shoulder all the way to her hand where it was even more intense. Laura tried to open her eyes, but the effort seemed too much. And when she tried to turn her head, the pounding in her head became a jackhammer. So she lay still, eyes closed. Where was she? How did she get there?

As Laura lay motionless, she heard her son Mike's voice, "Kevin's meeting Patrick at the train station and coming right here." The reality of place began to register.

All three of my sons coming here?

"Mom should be at Penn." Laura recognized the bossy voice of her daughter Nicole. "I say we move her."

"She's got a concussion," Natalie said. "We can't move her yet. Even though I think we should once she wakes up."

All five of the kids?

Mike's voice, "I know you're both med students at Penn, but Hahnemann is a great hospital. They had Mom's MRI results before I even got here."

Concussion? Hahnemann? Penn? MRI? Despite the throbbing sensation, Laura forced her eyes open. She couldn't see much more than a white ceiling. Yes, she was in a hospital. The beeping sound was a monitor. The smell, antiseptics. The pain, real and severe. A sensation that her whole right side was suspended.

She was about to try to make a sound, try to communicate, when Natalie said, "Tim's calling in the best hand surgeon in the country for the reconstruction."

"If only I'd insisted on picking her up this morning," Mike said, "none of this would have happened."

"Stop, Mike," Nicole's voice, "she fell on the ice. That's nobody's fault. Let's just concentrate on cheering her up when she wakes up. Okay?"

I fell? I have a concussion? That accounted for the intolerable pounding. Laura tried to focus on her kids' conversation but failed, drifting into a cocooned half sleep, grateful that when she stopped concentrating on the voices, the pressure in her head subsided.

***

Laura awoke to the sounds of her children disagreeing, but could only catch snippets, didn't know if she was dreaming. Then memory returned, unwelcome, ominous.

An attempt to speak resulted in a pathetic muffled sound. How long had she been out? Sunlight streamed in the lone window...

"Mom, you're awake." Her daughters spoke over each other.

Laura tried to sit up, but with a massive spike of pain on her right side, collapsed back against the pillows. She squeezed her eyes shut. Something was very wrong. *Try to isolate the pain.* Her training was starting to kick in, only this was not a patient, this was her body, and this was more pain than she ever could have imagined.

Immediately, Laura felt hands on her, so many hands reaching out to her that she couldn't muster the concentration to count. Her kids' and Tim's, all easing her back against the pillow.

Tim's voice came through. "Laura, you've had a fall. You hit your head pretty hard. On the ice."

She looked from worried face to worried face. Even moving her eyes made her feel dizzy, disoriented. She did realize she had an intravenous line in her left arm, taped to a padded board. But something horrible was wrong with her right arm. The pain on her right side was excruciating. Worse than the raging thunderbolts in her head. She had to find the source, but moving her head sent shock waves through her brain.

"Mom, you're going to be okay," Natalie said. "Just lean back, okay?" Her med student daughter practicing bedside manner.

Laura ignored the increased throbbing in her head to twist as far to the right as she could. That's when she saw the contraption that suspended her arm, as well as the bulky dressing that enveloped her arm from just below the shoulder to her hand. She was not an orthopedic surgeon, but she'd seen enough trauma to recognize that she must have fractured her hand or her wrist or both.

"What's wrong with my hand?" Laura gasped, her voice raspy. She tried to raise her head. Couldn't. Her head stayed on the pillow.

A gaunt, blond doctor in a white coat had walked into the room. He stood for a moment with no facial expression, observing, before addressing them. "Mom's awake, I see. Now if you'll let me inside your inner circle, I'll do a quick neuro assessment."

Laura hated when doctors talked about their patients in the third person, and antipathy brought with it sharper consciousness. She wanted to say: "How about starting like this. 'Laura,' or 'Doctor Nelson, I see you are awake. I'd like to examine you.'" Stepping toward her, he did announce that he was Dr. So and So, a neurosurgeon. Not a neurosurgeon she'd want operating on her.

Tim and the kids stood back as the doctor brushed aside her bangs and inspected her head. Then he put her through a series of tests to check her mental status, her cranial nerves, her motor skills, and her reflexes. Laura tried to comply, just wanting him out of there so she could insist that her family tell her what was wrong with her hand.

"Mom has a hairline skull fracture, a brain contusion with

minimal swelling, no localizing lesions," the neurosurgeon reported. "She should be okay, but we'll do a repeat CAT scan tomorrow." Then he nodded toward Laura's bandaged appendage. "How we doing here?"

I don't know about you, but I'm doing poorly.

"Thank you, Doctor." Tim terminated the consultation, guiding the man by his elbow to the door.

The kids had surrounded her again when Tim pushed his way into the middle of the pack.

"Okay," Laura said, looking from one stricken face to another. "Who's going to tell me?"

"Laura, you've just regained consciousness. You were out for almost thirty hours. Your head must hurt terribly. We can get you pain medication—"

"I have an awful headache. But, tell me. What is wrong with my *hand?*"

"You fell on the ice. Just outside my apartment," Tim said. "Next to the limo. You went down hard, hit your head. You must have tried to break the fall with your right hand."

Laura could feel her face twist into a grimace, and she must have let out a groan because Patrick moved in closer and said, "Mom, let's go over this later. Okay?"

"Now," Laura said. "Please."

Tim continued. "Your hand took the brunt as well as your wrist. Several bones are fractured. There's some nerve injury."

Laura knew the damage must be severe. Why else would all the faces around her look so terrified? A fractured hand, a wrist, no big deal. *Unless you are a surgeon.*

"You've already had stabilizing surgery, but you're going to need a top-notch hand surgeon. We have one flying in from Denver. We all assume Philly's the mecca of medical care, and turns out the best guy is in Denver."

"Lots of ski accidents," Kevin said.

"The specialist will be in this afternoon," Mike said. "Then we'll know more, but right now you should get some rest."

"We all waited for you to wake up, Mom," said Nicole, "and now we all want you back to sleep."

A gray-haired woman in a blue-patterned uniform came through the door with a prefilled syringe on a tray. "Your pain meds," she said, glancing up at Laura's elevated right arm. "You're going to need this, honey."

Laura—chief of surgery at Tampa City—relegated to "honey." And yes, the pain was excruciating, and she did welcome the offer of relief.

CHAPTER NINE

When Laura awoke in the late afternoon Tim and all five kids were there. Her family was strangely subdued, each looking to the other, no one having much to say. The pain in her head had abated, but her right hand and her whole forearm felt on fire.

A nurse came in, offered pain meds.

Laura refused. She had to know what was happening before she drifted off to la-la land.

"Dr. Nelson," a booming male voice intruded. "Good. You're awake. I need you awake to explain what's going on."

Laura blinked, her vision hazy. She was almost blind without her contacts or glasses, but the person was tall, had a lot of dark curly hair, and wore scrubs.

"I'm Dr. Matt Corey," he explained, his voice still loud, yet kindly. "I'm here from Denver. I specialize in hand injuries like yours."

Yes, she'd injured her hand in a fall. And she'd hit her head.

"I don't beat around the bush. The fall fractured the radial styloid; you have a proximal avulsion of the abductor pollicis longus and the extensor pollicis brevis."

Laura felt tears spilling. She looked into Dr. Corey's eyes. She saw compassion and respect. He was giving it to her straight. She translated, mentally: wrist shattered; muscles and tendons connecting the bones in the hand to the forearm torn out of their insertions; small bones in the hand crushed.

But the hand specialist was not finished. "We could repair most of that, but..." He hesitated. Laura thought she could hear Tim and all the kids holding their breath. *But what?* "You're developing compartment syndrome. Around the thenar space. The specialists here took you to the operating room, did a fasciotomy, decompressed the space, tried a K-wire, but there was too much ischemic tissue damage—"

"Dr. Corey, you are telling me my hand will no longer be functional." Not a question, a statement of fact.

Tim and her kids gathered in closer, and Laura felt every heartbeat exaggerate the drumming ache in her head and tear at the overwhelming pain in her hand.

"Dr. Corey, I thank you for your honesty," she managed before the tears started overflowing, "and for coming so far on such short notice." She couldn't hold back, couldn't remember when she'd cried in front of her kids. Maybe never. Maybe when their father died.

"I'm sorry, Laura," Tim said, grabbing a handful of Kleenex.

"I'll be okay," Laura choked out through the tears. "But could you ask that nurse to come back. I'd love some pain meds. My hand hurts like hell."

CHAPTER TEN

Jake left the FDA early on Tuesday afternoon. He'd had a busy day strategizing, networking, planting problems for Immunone, the wonder drug. Keystone Pharma was well respected among FDA staffers, having few detractors, so he couldn't count on applause when he detonated his Immunone-bashing plan. Not a problem, because he was at the center of the data collection process and could arrange for data to disappear. Twenty-five years at the agency, you knew all the nooks and crannies, all the hiding places, physical and electronic. Today, he would set the stage. Tomorrow, he'd implement. But tonight, he'd enjoy.

After leaving the FDA, Jake stopped by his house to gather a few items of clothing. He planned to arrive at Addie's in time for them to have a nice dinner out before a night of sizzling sex. He was fifty-five years old but performing like an eighteen-year-old. Sexual prowess was not a problem. The anticipation of Karolee's return, the menace of Addie's Islamic family, the conflict of interest concerns in their jobs—despite three potential strikes against them, Jake and Addie were unstoppable.

As Jake pulled into a rare empty spot in front of Addie's building, he felt an overpowering sense of wonder. Yes, fifty-five years old and crazy in love with a thirty-four-year-old Arab beauty. And the most wonderful part was that she loved him too. They may have three or three hundred strikes against them, but Jake had been a Marine. Marines win.

Jake had arrived early. Addie wouldn't be home for another hour. So he lowered the car seat, leaned against the head rest, and drifted off to sleep.

He woke up to a pecking noise on the driver's side window. For a moment, Jake didn't know where he was. The sun had set, leaving him in a dark, moonless night. Then someone leaned over the windshield, gesturing to him. Addie. He'd been in a deep sleep. He tried to shake it off, reaching for the lever to adjust the seat upward, and motioned her to get in on the passenger side.

"What are you doing here? What if somebody sees you?" she asked, opening the door, tossing her briefcase on the floorboard, and climbing in.

"It's dark. Nobody's going to see me, Addie. You worry too much."

"Did you hear the really bad news?" she asked, black eyes flashing in the dimly lit interior.

Jake shook his head. With Addie, bad news was usually about the deteriorating situation between the United States and Iraq, and the UN's hunt for weapons of mass destruction.

"Dr. Minn from Keystone Pharma died. He was hit by a car Sunday night in Philadelphia. My family thinks Washington is dangerous for me, but Philadelphia and Baltimore are worse."

Jake refrained from saying, *What about Baghdad?*

Addie didn't stop to take a breath. "What does that mean for Immunone? Dr. Minn was the key researcher. Will this slow down the approval? What if—"

"Addie, stop! I told you there were problems with the drug. I'm sorry about Dr. Minn, but it shouldn't matter." By all means, Dr. Minn out of the picture must matter.

"It's too cold to talk in here," Addie said, grabbing her briefcase, noticing Jake's overnight bag in the back seat. "Good. You brought your things. You're staying all night?"

"Yes, my darling, we have the whole night. Just the two of us. After a nice dinner, we'll—"

"We can't stay out here. People will see you. Like that old lady did last night. My father can't find out that a man stayed overnight with me, it's against Islamic law. You Westerners will never understand."

"I can look out for myself, and I can take care of you. You worry too much. Now let's go upstairs, decide where to have dinner."

Addie got out of the car and they walked together to the elevator, took it to her floor, and proceeded to her apartment. Jake noticed how she kept her head down, eyes averted. That would change once they were married. She'd hold her head high, proud to be with him.

When they got inside, Jake noticed a letter sitting on the table by the door. Addressed to Dr. Adawia Abdul; the return address, an indecipherable name and a street address in Dearborn, Michigan. When she went into the bedroom to change, he picked up the envelope, looked inside, finding a letter written in what he assumed was Arabic script.

He was still holding the letter when Addie emerged, dressed in a clingy, beige pants suit, a sheer blouse underneath that exposed the lacy bra he'd bought her at Victoria's Secret. Addie loved racy, if not outright sexy, clothes, a habit he was happy to indulge.

"Who's this from?" Jake asked.

"My father," she said.

"From Dearborn? Michigan?"

"I have a contact there. My family sends mail through him. Father thinks it's safer that way. Paranoid, maybe, but with the US-Iraq situation, you can't be too careful."

"Why should he worry? Your father's not a radical anti-American, is he?"

"Of course not, but he wants me home. I've tried to explain about the big payment I'll get if I stay until Immunone's approval, but he doesn't care. Leave now, he insists; he doesn't want me in an enemy country. My father has always supported Saddam Hussein's regime. He's in the inner circle, privy to whatever happens with the UN inspections. America is the enemy now."

Jake had never asked Addie about her father, what he did for a living, about his political loyalties. He knew she loved and respected both of her parents, missed them a lot, but he'd never probed for more. Now, her possessive old man was trying to take Addie out of his life. Well, that wouldn't happen.

"They didn't find any uranium, "Addie said. "Iraq is a sovereign nation. Why can't they leave us alone? Wasn't one invasion enough?"

"Aren't they, the Bush administration, worried about biological and chemical weapons?"

"My father says it's primarily about uranium, nuclear material and facilities. The latest team is going to focus on Mosul."

"Sorry, Addie, my geography is lousy. Where's Mosul? Close to Baghdad?" In truth, Baghdad was the only Iraq city name Jake recognized. That would have to change. He'd pick up a guide book. Or were there any? Did people actually travel to Iraq for anything except military business or peacekeeping missions? Or war reporting?

"Mosul is in northern Iraq, close to where they produce Al Jazeera TV. Jake, do you realize that this will be the tenth International Atomic Energy inspection? My father says Dick Cheney's behind this IAEA bullshit. My people call him a monster."

"*Bullshit?* American slang becomes you."

"I tell you, Jake, I live like a Western woman here. Nice clothes, makeup, drive a car. But in my heart, I'm Iraqi. And I must return. My father needs me back, and very soon. That's why you have to do something to get Immunone approved. I don't want to leave all the money behind. I worked hard for Immunone. I deserve that money. Someday, I might need it. So, please, do everything you can to get Immunone approved fast."

Did she really think he'd facilitate sending her back to Baghdad? "What if you don't go back?" he asked. "How in the hell—" Jake managed to stop. *How the hell could you want to go back to a shit hole like that?*

Jake stood, still holding the letter; the Arabic script seemed to taunt him. Was she telling the truth? Or did she have a boy-friend back home? If she returned, would her parents commit her to an arranged marriage? He dropped the letter on the table where he'd found it. "Everything will work out. Let's go grab something to eat. How about Djaje Shawarma?" He knew he'd butchered the pronunciation. "That'll make you feel better. We can talk there about Immunone. Okay, Addie?"

"You don't like Arabic food," she said. "But I will feel better after some sambousik, lamb this time."

"I'm okay with their rotisserie chicken." The one dish on the menu that Jake could stomach.

"Djaje Shawarma," she said. "Okay, let's go." She grabbed her coat and a bright magenta scarf. "I'm wearing what I have on. You'll want to get out of the suit. Wear a sweater and slacks. It's a casual place."

"I'm okay," Jake said. Dinner was the least of it; the main event would be their amorous evening.

***

As he and Addie settled into the booth in the small restaurant, Jake reminded himself to avoid the heavy-duty subject of Immunone's anticipated approval. The seeds of doubt he'd planted at the FDA after the team meeting today needed time to germinate. Before he left for the afternoon, he'd generated a memo questioning the ad-equacy of the data on the clinical trial deaths they'd received from Keystone Pharma. Before pushing the "Send" button, he'd eradi-cated several backup reports from his paper files and from the elec-tronic files that he controlled as project manager.

That seemingly innocent memo would send the medical reviewers into a tailspin. No doubt, they'd "remember" seeing the extensive reports Keystone *did* submit, but they'd be unable to find them in their database. Jake had a key to the depart-mental offices, and tomorrow he would get there very early and search the reviewers' paper files. The electronic files were his domain. All electronic records could eventually be retrieved,

he knew, but he didn't think it would come to that. Most likely, requests would be made to Keystone to resend the reports.
That would take time, especially with Dr. Minn gone. Once
they were received and the data reconciled, they'd chalk it up to
clerical error. Happens all the time. Expected to happen in any
bureaucracy.

But tonight, as they waited for their food to arrive, Jake
struggled without success to keep the conversation light. Addie sat opposite him, her black eyes simmering with anger.
When he reached across the table for her hand, she pulled it
away. "I don't want to chitchat. I want answers, Jake. First,
when is your wife coming home? Is she suspicious about us?
What if she finds out? She can ruin everything. For me, my
job. Your job."

"Karolee could care less. Too busy with her damn restaurant. Truth is, she surprised me, going to see our son and the baby.
Mark moved to Miami to get away from her, but—ha! ha!—
foiled by the evil mother."

"You told me your son and your wife don't get along. Too
bad. And what about that baby, your granddaughter, don't you
want to see her?"

"Yes. When I see my granddaughter I want you to be with
me, as my wife." There, Jake had said it. Marriage.

Addie set down the flatbread she'd been munching. Jake
could see her features transform. Pretty became grim. She enun-
ciated her words clearly through gritted teeth. "You keep saying
you'll divorce her. When, Jake?"

Addie had no idea that divorcing a woman like Karolee would be like descending into hell. All those things that
had attracted Jake to Karolee when they'd met at college now
tormented him. She had family money she'd parlayed into a
trendy Bethesda restaurant, a money machine. Aggressive, de-
manding, loud, opinionated, domineering. That was the con-
sensus. He would add paranoid and downright stingy. No
limit on what Karolee could spend on her hair, her clothes, *her*

house. But let him overspend his share of their income and all hell broke loose.

No, you don't divorce a woman like Karolee. Far too difficult navigating the legal system. He'd simply terminate her. Combining the skills of a Marine with his project management ability, he'd come up with a plan. And—happy thought—he would finally get his hands on her money. Even though Karolee was always threatening, he didn't think she'd made a will. She despised her daughter-in-law, so she wouldn't leave her wealth to Mark. Baby Amanda was far too young to be considered, so it would all default to him as her husband.

"Soon, Addie," Jake said. "I'm getting the papers drawn up. She'll be away until Friday. I'll get it through court quickly. Then we can be together." A pleasant thought slipped into Jake's mind: with Karolee's money *and* Addie's, he'd be a truly wealthy man.

"Addie, I want to marry you. I'll do anything for you."

"I don't know, Jake." He watched the anger dissipate, replaced by a spark of hope, but then frustration. "I'm really worried about my family. Do you think the government people you know could get my family to the United States? I mean, if things get really bad there?"

"I can work on it," Jake said, as if he had contacts in the State Department. He'd now taken her hand, was squeezing it.

"I'm so confused," she said. "I want to stay here. Maybe if we get married, I can. I won't be a disgrace to my family. But I would be a disappointment. They want to pick my husband, a Muslim, of course."

"Addie, if you want me to—"

"But first," she interrupted, "I have to get that money from Immunone. Tell me. Now. What is happening?"

Jake couldn't dance around her demand. As soon as the waiter laid out the spicy Middle Eastern food, he told her about the "problem." FDA couldn't find key data. Now, with their lead researcher dead, he didn't know how long it would take Keystone Pharma to respond to the missing data requests. He was making it up as he went. But, in reality, Jake Harter was in the perfect position to make data disappear to fit his needs. He needed to keep reminding himself of that.

Addie stopped eating as he explained. Her face was set in stone, but no tears. As Jake enjoyed his tender, slow-cooked, expertly seasoned chicken, she sat in silence, staring at him over the plate of lamb she'd barely touched.

CHAPTER ELEVEN

Laura awoke to dusk settling on Philadelphia. She must have slept about five hours. Before she spoke—before they even knew she was awake—she counted all five adult kids. And Tim, of course. Tim, who had proposed to her. Had that been only two nights ago? Would he still want to marry her now that her career was over? Tampa City Hospital would let her stay on as chief, at least for a while, supervising, strategizing, administrating. But sooner rather than later, they'd replace her with a hotshot surgeon who had two good hands.

The pressure in Laura's head had scaled down to a dull thud like a severe tension headache. She'd had her share of these, a single mother with five kids and a brutal job. She could deal with the headache, but not the fiery pain raging from her right hand to her shoulder. Dr. Corey, the hand specialist from Colorado, told her that compounding the fractures, she had compartment syndrome. Translation: disastrous tissue damage. Pressure rapidly builds up in the small compartments, creating an inflammatory cocktail that eats away at tissue and destroys nerves. They'd done a fasciotomy to relieve the pressure, so her hand had been carved up and splayed out under the bandages, with the result being unbearable pain.

She couldn't hold off too long before asking for more pain meds, but Laura did need to release Tim and let the kids go back to where they belonged. She'd insist that hanging around made no sense.

"I'm okay, everybody." She turned her head and opened her eyes as wide as she could. "But not for long. My hand is killing me, and I'm going to ask for pain meds."

Kevin bolted up. "I'll get the nurse, Mom." He headed for the door.

"Not yet, Kevin. Sit back down. I have something to tell you."

"You okay, Mom?" Patrick asked.

No, I'm not okay. "I'm going to be okay," Laura said. "Look, guys, I know my hand is injured beyond repair. I have no illusions about what that means. I'm not going to be able to operate in the future. Okay? I get it. I'll be okay with that." *Or will I?*

"How can you be sure?" Natalie interrupted. "Dr. Corey said that—"

"I *am* sure. Let's just all accept this. I need a fresh start in my life. Once I get out from under this god-awful pain."

Kevin was on his feet again, "Mom, I don't want you to suffer like this." His eyes traveled to her bandaged, elevated arm. Of all her kids, he was the most squeamish. Took a lot of teasing from the medical siblings who enjoyed freaking him out with details of blood and gore.

"Not yet. I have a request—all of you."

"Whatever you want, Mom," Natalie inched closer to the bed, adjusted the sheet. Laura did not have the heart to tell her that any miniscule impact sent flames down her arm. The twins may be med students, but they still had a lot to learn about pain—as did she. Only with Laura, that education would be first person, real time.

"I want you all to go home. Patrick, back to your classes in Manhattan. Kevin, back to Princeton and your architect practice. Mike and Natalie and Nicole, back to work. You're local, so you can come visit tomorrow night. I think I'll be a lot better by then, less pain. You can keep Kevin and Patrick up to date."

"No way!" Patrick and Kevin tried to keep their decibel levels reasonable. "We're staying." Patrick spoke for both.

Laura felt her strength dwindle as the burning pain from

her arm spread across her chest and into her abdomen. "Kids, this is not a suggestion. It's a serious request. You know how much I love you, how much I appreciate your being here, so I hope you understand when I tell you I need some time. To process this...catastrophe."

She hadn't wanted to describe events that way, end with that word, but isn't this what she was facing? She had worked so hard to be a surgeon, sacrificed so much, and now...

"Okay, Kevin," she said as she looked around at the stricken faces, "please go get the pain nurse. Never thought I was such a wimp, but I really need that stuff."

Kevin returned, following a nurse carrying a prefilled syringe. As the analgesic infiltrated the IV tubing, the kids all gathered on the opposite side of the bed, thankfully not leaning in to touch her.

"If that's what you want, Mom."

"We love you."

"Get well soon."

Tim waved them off so they didn't kiss her. They left as a group, blowing kisses.

The drug started to take its blissful effect, but not before she heard Tim say, "I'm staying right here, Laura. With you. No matter what." Drifting off, Laura realized she'd not sent Tim away with the kids. *What did that mean?*

She was out before she could tell herself the answer.

CHAPTER TWELVE

Jake almost left his apartment without checking the messages on the answering machine in the kitchen. Halfway out the door, he'd felt a weird twist in his gut.

Other than quick stops to pick up extra clothes, he hadn't been home in three days. Not since his trip into Philadelphia on Sunday. He'd spent his free time and his nights with Addie, and now was absolutely determined to spend every possible moment with her for the rest of his life. She made him feel young, vibrant, whole. Sum it up in a word: happy. A word he hadn't thought to use for longer than he could remember. And now he was looking forward to two more nights of sensational lovemaking. Or so he thought, before Karolee's messages—she was coming home early. *Today*. She told him to pick her up at the airport at four p.m.

Six messages starting at five last evening. One at eight. At nine. At eleven. At midnight. At one a.m. Each one louder, angrier. Seems their son Mark and daughter-in-law had asked Karolee to leave. Claire, a mini-bitch herself, ordered Karolee, the bitch-of-all-bitches, out of her house. Now wasn't that the pot calling the kettle black? And when Karolee called home and didn't find her husband, her obscenities blasted through the answering machine.

"Fireworks tonight," Jake said aloud. His stomach clenched,

but only briefly, till opportunity began to replace dread. This explosion of Karolee's may offer him just the excuse he'd been looking for—an appropriate time to confront her, to parlay her anger into what he wanted: a divorce. But a surge of reality quickly replaced any sense of optimism. Jake was an ex-Marine, but when Karolee flew into attack mode, his only strategy was avoidance. "Yes, ma'am" her and go off to work during the day, hang around the house at night when she'd be at her la-de-da restaurant. Go to bed before she got home. Leave in the morning before she got up. That was an MO he could handle. Until now. Addie had changed everything.

Jake needed to reconfigure his day. At work, he'd planned another delicate manipulation of the Immunone data files that only he could do. Jake did not believe Keystone Pharma had an understudy to replace Minn in the pivotal Immunone approval role, so losing one day shouldn't screw up his plan.

Jake had to concentrate only on Karolee from this moment until her touchdown at the airport. His stomach again seized, and a wave of acid shot up his esophagus. Acid reflux. He'd call in sick; an attack of severe gastritis.

Unpleasant as it was, he needed to talk to Karolee at Mark's house. Find out her arrival details. Jake gritted his teeth for the call. His excuse for last night? He didn't have one. He'd make one up as he listened to her opening round.

Mark answered. "She's pissed, Dad, off the wall this time. Didn't think things could get worse, but they did. Why didn't you pick up when she called you last night?"

"Where is she now?" Jake asked. He hoped to hell she was in bed, that Mark could let him know her travel arrangements.

"Still asleep. Kept us up most of the night with her ranting and raving. Baby in the house is noise enough. We don't need a crazy grandmother. The woman smokes like a chimney, and you know how that sets off Claire. Passive smoke for the baby. Mostly, Mom took the smokes outside. But not happily. That was the root cause of the first row she and Claire had, until

Claire lost her cool when she found Mom smoking in the guest room. Gotta say, I stick by Claire on this issue. Bad enough I'm gonna have shitty lungs based on Mom smoking when I was young."

"The smoking, that's why she decided to leave?" Jake asked. Karolee was one of those women who would never stop smoking. Don't even ask her about it, she'll bite your head off. And her daughter-in-law, a zealous anti-smoking advocate.

"Oh boy, Mark, not a great week for the new dad, huh?"

"Claire insisted that Mom leave after that incident. Made me do the honors. Put me at the top of the shit list—until you didn't answer the phone last night."

"Maybe I should speak to her," Jake said, trying to take back the words even as he uttered them.

"Oh no, Dad, not after that rant last night. Don't ask me to wake her up. We're going to let her sleep as long as possible. Then I'm assigned to take her out for a late breakfast before dropping her at Miami International. I had to take off work. No way I could leave her with Claire."

"Should have moved farther away, son."

"Listen, her Delta flight gets to National at 4:10. I'd suggest you be there, Dad, with a helluva good excuse."

"I'll be there," Jake promised. *And I'll have more for her than just an excuse.*

"Mom did do something for the baby though. She set up a trust for Amanda's education. Knowing how she hates Claire's guts—well, I was blown away. A hundred thousand bucks. That's a side of Mom I never saw. The generous side."

Uncharacteristic, for sure. "Hmm," was all Jake could come up with. Karolee scored high on the miser scale. Was a grandmotherly side of Karolee coming through? Jake leaned against the kitchen counter. At least the baby girl was too young to recognize the words Karolee had yelled into the phone last night, but weren't infants sensitive to tone of voice? Karolee's would have been terrifying.

After the call to Mark, Jake methodically erased the answering machine messages. Not really sure if police had a way to restore deleted messages, he'd just get rid of the machine altogether. Anyone wants to know, he'd say it's broke. Why hadn't he thought of that when he was talking to Mark? Should have told him the damn thing was out of commission, that's why Karolee's calls had not been picked up. Shit, did any of this make sense? Phone machines working, not working? He had no time for fine points. Jake could push paper at work, but at his core, he was a Marine. Marines deal in physical punishment. His move would be fast and final.

Since meeting Addie, Jake had fantasized endlessly about killing Karolee. Now the fantasies were morphing into solid plans. Only the details had yet to solidify. He couldn't get that song "50 Ways to Leave Your Lover" out of his brain. He was leaning toward a quick, effective kill mode. The killing part didn't faze him whatsoever. He was prepared. He was a Marine. He had an arsenal. He'd kept in shape.

Karolee was five foot three, a hundred and ten pounds.

Before last Sunday night, Jake had killed twice. Never in combat, he conceded. In Vietnam, he'd worked communications, far away from the battle fields, but his first kill had been a fellow Marine, a disgrace to the uniform. Happened outside a house of ill repute in Saigon. By mistake, Jake had walked into a client room as the asshole was brutalizing a very young Vietnamese girl, beating the shit out of her. Jake had backed out, bringing no attention to himself. Leaving the brothel, he'd waited. When the guy staggered out, Jake struck him in the solar plexus, shoved him into a dark corner, and slipped his Gerber Mark II out of its sheath and slit the bastard's throat. Took less than a minute. No man—especially a Marine—should beat up a woman. He considered that kill righteous. There had been no repercussions.

Second time, maybe not so righteous. Ten years ago, he'd taken out a brawny, mouthy guy who cheated him at cards.

Repeatedly cheated. Jake had drowned the drunk at the guy's own fishing camp. Again, no repercussions. He'd covered his tracks.

Sunday night, his weapon had been his Jeep Cherokee. Did the job. Another clean kill. For Karolee, he wouldn't need a two-ton machine.

This time, more important than weapon of choice was crafting a plausible scenario surrounding her death. That was the trick, a feasible plan: hit-not-miss—ready to go in seven hours.

What if: He feels better this afternoon and goes to the office, hell-bent on his important Immunone project. But he starts feeling really sick again and nods off at his desk. Only wakes up at four-thirty—too late to pick up my wife, he tells his colleagues; she'll catch a cab home from the airport.

At the airport: He pictures Karolee at the arrival gate, looks around for him, more agitated, royally pissed—he's not there! She takes the escalator to baggage claim, hauls her luggage off the belt, still no Jake, gets more pissed. She finds a pay phone, calls home. No answer. No answering machine to record her royal tantrum.

Her timing: a half hour to get luggage, make calls, grab a cab; a forty-five minute trip home, more for bad traffic. Karolee walks in the door at quarter past five, give or take.

His timing: couldn't leave work too early, people would take note. Their house was fifteen minutes from the FDA along a route where traffic moved predictably well. Stay in his office until a quarter till five. Create a diversion on his usual route home. Traffic delay to support his story that I got stuck in the traffic jam caused by…fill-in-the-blank.

Jake had made himself a mug of instant coffee. At the kitchen table, face in his hands, fingers pressed against closed eyes, he concentrated. A bomb? A fire? A hit-and-run? A fallen tree? A broken water main? Live electricity? A load of whatever dumped in the middle of the street? An escaped convict?

A headache derailed his train of thought. Jake's doctor had

warned him he was borderline diabetic. Was he experiencing hypoglycemia? Maybe he should get something to eat.

Two pieces of wheat toast, a hunk of cheddar, and slugs of orange juice later, Jake sat back down. He would defer the question of how to cause a traffic delay and focus on what he had to do before going in to work in the afternoon.

Now it was 9:30 a.m. Plenty of time to get set up. This phase would be easy. He made a list: Go through each room of the house. Take items of obvious value. Leave a burglary mess everywhere. Take the loot to the dumpster behind the gym across town where he'd been a member. Break a window to document the burglar's entry... Jake kept writing until he had two single-spaced pages of action items. Like the project manager he was, he sorted them chronologically, worked out a complicated time line. Done, except for the diversion component that would alibi him from the time he left the FDA to the time he arrived home to find Karolee...

Keep that on the side for now. He'd been in situations before when the answer popped up at the last possible moment. Now he had to get moving on his action list.

CHAPTER THIRTEEN

In Laura's place, Tim hoped he'd be as brave as she was. Laura had opted for on-demand pain relief rather than continuous infusion of pain meds. She said she didn't want to live in a narcotic fog. She was accustomed to control, didn't abdicate it easily. Neither would Tim, under the circumstances.

He napped on a narrow cot set up in the far corner of her hospital room. Even though her condition was listed as stable, she needed care on an hourly basis. Besides routine vital signs, nurses checked her intravenous lines, changed her dressings, and monitored her pain.

Each time Laura stirred throughout the night, Tim instantly awoke. A skill left behind from his training, all those thirty-six-hour call schedules. Drop off to sleep in an instant. Wake up on demand. On each occasion, he pressed the button for the pain nurse. Compartment pain in the hand is excruciating. She'd need a long course of pain meds; narcotics, unfortunately.

Once during the night when Laura's pain started to break through the drugs, she seemed particularly agitated. As she awoke, she murmured a man's name. Not Tim. Not the name of her dead husband Steve. But, *David*.

Tim's heart plummeted.

What else could it mean? So, Laura has been seeing another man. No wonder she didn't say "yes" when he'd asked her to marry him. How could he have been so stupid not to know? To allow himself to think that they'd had an exclusive relationship?

But Laura had seemed to want him there with her. She'd dismissed her kids, but not him. And, he'd promised the kids he'd stay with her. Yes, even if she did have another guy, he vowed to see her through this. The accident happened in front of his house. If only he'd gone down to the car with her, been there to stabilize her on that black ice.

At eight in the morning, food service brought Tim a tray. Typical hospital food, no different here at Hahnemann than at CHOP—Children's Hospital of Philadelphia—where he was the senior cardiac surgeon, trained under the best, C. Everett Koop, who made it to surgeon general of the United States.

Tim picked at the soggy scrambled eggs, nibbled the crispy bacon and the fresh orange slices, but mostly he appreciated the hot, caffeinated coffee. Laura was a true caffeine addict. She needed it to jump-start her breathing in the morning. He'd tease her about refilling her cup nonstop, marvel at how she could drink coffee just before she went to bed. Even if she wasn't suffering from a concussion, she'd have a headache from caffeine withdrawal. How long did caffeine withdrawal symptoms last? How do we know if her headache is related to the concussion or the caffeine withdrawal? Tim mentally slapped himself in the face. *How stupid can you get, obsessing over Laura's simple caffeine headache when she faced horrible pain in her hand as well as the loss of her career?*

"Tim," Laura's muffled voice told him they both were awake. "You still here?"

"I am," said Tim, setting down his coffee cup.

"Is it morning? Wednesday? With these meds in my system, I can hardly think."

"Yes. Wednesday. Looks like it'll be brighter than yesterday. Philadelphia could use a little sunshine in February. We're not spoiled like you Floridians." Talking small talk to Laura when her whole life was at stake? For a moment, Tim wondered about his competence to deal with adult patients; his patients were children, babies mostly. A nurse's voice interrupted Tim's insecurity.

"Dr. Nelson, you slept about sixteen hours. Do you need another dose of pain meds?"

"No," Laura said, "not yet, but thanks."

The nurse turned to go, and Laura said, "Tim, I have to think. About what I should do with my life. I can't be groggy. I have to call my office..."

"Hey," Tim pointed to her elevated arm. "Just try to be as still and quiet and as pain free as you can. You don't have to deal with anything else right now."

"A doctor advising 'be still'? You're supposed to say, 'Move around. Get up and out of bed. Prevent blood clots.' You know, the way we force our patients to function through the pain."

When she attempted to ease herself upward without moving the suspended right limb, Tim rushed to Laura's side. "Easy. Let me help you."

The grimace on her face and her panting breaths signaled her level of pain. Tim gently urged her forward so he could tuck in a pillow to support her back. She was quiet for a moment, then rewarded him with a wan smile.

"Thanks, Tim. You know—about our last night, when..."

The night when she did not say "yes."

"Laura, we can talk more when you feel better." But did he really want to talk? Was he ready for her to tell him about another man? About *David*?

"No. I want to say this. I understand if you want to change your mind. Under the circumstances, I mean. So much has changed..."

Tim bent over to kiss her dry lips, moving carefully so as not to jiggle anything that would threaten her suspended arm.

"What's going on in here, kids?" They were interrupted by Laura's hand surgeon, not Dr. Corey who'd already returned to Denver, but the orthopedic specialist on staff at Hahnemann, Dr.

Hanover. He entered, trailed by a cadre of medical residents and students.

"Neuro has cleared you, Dr. Nelson," he said with a forced smile. Tim knew what would come next. Ambulation. Hydrotherapy. Physical therapy. Pain piled upon pain. The goal: to salvage as much function in the hand as possible. Laura may not be able to use a scalpel, but working hard with an occupational therapist, she could relearn to pick up a coffee cup, cutlery.

"I know that it's hard to appreciate right now, but you are fortunate to have an uninjured alternate hand. You're going to get good in the near term at using your left hand. Believe me, so many hand injuries are bilateral. Burns are the worst."

For Tim, this guy's use of the words "fortunate" and "lucky" in relation to Laura was inappropriate, at best.

"I appreciate everything you're doing, Dr. Hanover," Laura said. "Please, could you give me some idea of how long I'll be in here?"

"Far too early to say." He turned to his entourage. "This patient is a surgeon—"

Tim could feel the collective intake of breath as sets of eyes stared upward at Laura's hand.

"Our chore today is to take her to the operating room to debride the wound. Assess the tissue viability. Then decide on a physical therapy plan."

"Is that necessary?" Tim knew his question came out like a groan and tried with little success to keep his tone professional. "Back to the OR?"

Before the doctor could respond, Laura said, "Well, there'll be an anesthesiologist in there."

Laura had a point. She wouldn't feel a thing as they probed her mangled tissues with a scalpel. Bit by bit, they'd scrape away dead tissue so new tissue could grow back. Problem was, how much of that new growth would be scar tissue?

Dr. Hanover spoke as much to his entourage as to his patient, "We debride surgically as often as necessary; once we see healthy tissue, we'll debride mechanically." He turned to the student on his right, a tall, thin young man in a short white coat. "What other debridement methods can we use?"

The young man reminded Tim of himself twenty-five years ago. "Chemical and autolytic." The student hesitated before adding, "And live maggot debridement?"

Dr. Hanover grinned. "Not to worry, Dr. Nelson, no maggots for you, although maggot therapy is approved by the FDA. Mechanical therapy with wet to dry dressings should be adequate, provided we get all the necrotic stuff out." He turned to Laura. "And that we will do, Dr. Nelson, in the operating room."

Laura nodded her appreciation, but Tim could read her concern over the agonizing pain she'd face when she emerged from anesthesia. Laura had been right not to want her kids hanging around. What good would it do for them to see her suffer? *I will be here for you, Laura. I will try to earn your love.*

***

Later that morning, after Laura's debridement procedure, Dr. Hanover assured Tim that the surgery had gone as well as could be expected. How many times had Tim himself used exactly those words to tell anxious parents their baby's condition was guarded?

"We think we got most of the debris. We'll go back in tomorrow, and if all looks clean, move to mechanical. We'll use pulsed saline at the bedside. Lots of pain, which we'll manage with parenteral narcotics." Dr. Hanover shrugged. "Gotta go see more patients. Your wife will be back in her room soon." He turned to go, but turned again to Tim. "You are her husband, aren't you?"

"Fiancé," Tim said. "Fiancé" just came out of his mouth, like saying it aloud would make it true.

CHAPTER FOURTEEN

Jake lurked behind the front door of his home, back pressed against the coolness of the hall mirror, waiting. Calm had replaced frantic planning. He mentally reviewed his checklist. He'd settled on the means and on the weapon—a Smith & Wesson Saturday night special with a suppressor. He'd won it in a in a card game and it had no identifying markings. The basis of his uncomplicated plan: KISS. Keep It Simple, Stupid. Karolee arrives home by cab. Unlocks the front door. Walks into a robbery in progress. Takes a bullet to the chest. Point black. Two bullets—just to be sure.

Jake's busy morning had been productive. The rest of his scene staged. He'd selected the burglar's entry point and he'd gone through the house to make the home invasion look realistic. He hadn't armed the alarm. "Never do when I'm home alone," he'd tell the cops. He'd rummaged through Karolee's jewelry and picked a few expensive pieces to report as missing. Jake wanted to keep Karolee's more valuable pieces for Addie, but he couldn't take the chance. He'd put the chosen pieces in one of her jewelry bags, close it securely, and drop it in a public place. If whoever picked it up turned it in, great, he'd get it back. If not, he wouldn't fucking worry about it.

As soon as he'd made that decision, the traffic diversion idea he needed came to him suddenly and clearly. Ingenious scenario: on his way from the FDA to his house, his Jeep breaks down.

He'd get it towed to a garage, hang around until it was fixed. Alibi established, he'd head home and literally stumble on his wife's corpse.

The plan in place, all he had to do now was hope her flight landed on time. He figured when he didn't show at the airport, Karolee would grab a cab. He didn't think she'd try to call anyone else for a ride. Karolee was not high on patience, wouldn't want to wait the extra time for someone to get to the airport. By the time she stormed in through that door, she'd be pretty blind with rage.

Jake straightened at the sound of a car door slamming. His senses on alert, his gun at the ready, Jake stepped back behind a partially open closet door. From there he'd be hidden from view as she stepped inside. He checked his watch. Twenty after five, only a few minutes after his estimate. Jake heard the key turn in the door, could see the door move. Karolee kicked it open with her boot. Her head was turned so she faced the street as the cab pulled away.

"Fuck," he heard her say as she wrestled her suitcase over the doorsill.

Jake suspended his breathing as he waited behind the door for her to shove the luggage inside the entryway, let the door slam, and click the bolt into place.

"That asshole bastard better—"

"Good afternoon, Karolee." Jake had planned to just shoot her, but the temptation to relish the look on her face proved too much. As he spoke, he extended his arm with the gun, locking his aim on the second button on her camel-colored cashmere coat.

Her gaping stare registered a quick progression of her disdain, then disbelief, then shock. Her cowhide messenger-style bag slid off her shoulder. As the weight of it hit the ground with a thud, she did not shift her gaze, kept it locked on Jake. Before she could say a word, he shot her point blank in the chest. A lethal shot, but he shot her again.

CHAPTER FIFTEEN

Dr. Adawia Abdul sat in the small office off her lab at Replica, perplexed and perturbed. She must talk to Jake about Immunone. Ever
since the Advisory Committee last Friday, he had been evading her
questions about the drug's status. She'd attended the meeting, sitting in the first row seat Jake had secured for her, even though she
and Jake had to conceal their relationship. The Advisory Committee of outside experts in organ transplant surgery, academicians
primarily, had been tasked by the FDA to review the data on Immunone's safety and efficacy, both data as prepared by Keystone
Pharma and as prepared by FDA reviewers. After listening to the
company's and the FDA's prepared presentations, the committee
responded to a list of questions compiled by the FDA.

A titular chairperson conducted the meeting, but Jake, as
the FDA Immunone project manager, ran the show behind the
scenes. He had selected the questions, chosen the order of presentation, controlled the timing, and compiled the notes. He had to
know everything. So why wasn't he telling her?

No one was more pleased than Addie with the meeting
outcome. The FDA panel of consultant scientists clearly indicated the drug should be approved. Naturally, the company scientists did too, but of all the presenters, Addie thought
Keystone Pharma's consultant, Dr. Laura Nelson, made the
most compelling argument. A transplant surgeon who led the

Immunone clinical studies, her data highlighted the number of lives that would be saved if the drug were approved. Her message: the transplant process is so arduous for recipients and donors that when the body rejects the organ, failure amounts to tragedy. Immunone decreased the chance of rejection, according to Dr. Nelson's studies, by more than 70 percent. The thought made Addie shiver with pride. Immunone was *her drug*. She'd discovered it when she was a grad student at Michigan, and she'd nurtured it through its development at Replica until Keystone Pharma acquired all rights for an insane amount of money.

Addie was impressed by how well Keystone had done by Immunone. For the last year it had been their number-one priority, and they'd convinced the FDA to fast track it. She had every reason to feel optimistic, yet she didn't. There was something Jake wasn't telling her. He acted like he was trying to protect her, to shield her from bad news. She wondered if it had anything to do with the death of Dr. Minn, the Keystone scientist who got killed last weekend? But how could it? The FDA had all the data. All that remained was the final approval.

Addie glanced at the clock on the wall. Almost five. Jake's wife would be away for two more nights. She'd better get home before he got to her place. She didn't want him lurking outside her apartment, attracting the neighbors' attention. She started to pack her notebook in her briefcase when a business card fell out. She picked it up, turned it over: "Dr. Laura Nelson, Chief of Surgery, Tampa City Hospital."

During the break at the Advisory Committee meeting, Addie had approached the attractive doctor, introduced herself; they'd exchanged cards, and Dr. Nelson had encouraged her to call if she ever had any questions about Immunone's performance in the clinical studies. Addie had considered her offer most generous, and she would have liked to talk to her longer, but the FDA committee chairman had interrupted.

What about calling Dr. Nelson? Would she reveal whether there could be any problems with Immunone? No, better wait to see what Jake had to say. She'd put more pressure on him tonight—like female spies did in espionage movies. Jake may be old, but he was a sex machine. If something were wrong with the Immunone approval process, she'd find out tonight.

CHAPTER SIXTEEN

"Hey there, sleepyhead." Tim stood at Laura's side, gazing down on her. "About time you woke up. Never had such boring company."

Laura drifted into consciousness as the sky outside her lone window displayed muted shades of orange. Sunset comes early in February in Philadelphia, earlier than in Tampa. She must have slept the entire afternoon. What day must it be? She tried to raise her head just a fraction, pleased that at least her head did not throb.

"Still here?" Her voice sounded raspy and weak but, she hoped, not unappreciative. Truth be told, she'd never been so grateful to see anyone.

"You kicked out your kids, but not me." Again, that smug grin. "But I did have to promise to call them the minute you woke up."

The last thing she remembered was being wheeled into the operating room; the pain in her hand was agonizing, but not to the excruciating point she had feared. "Tim, can you help me sit up? And before you talk to the kids, can we talk?"

"Are you okay? Your pain, do you—?"

"I don't want any pain meds. Not now."

Tim added a pillow, gently elevated her head to a forty-five degree angle, careful to stabilize her right arm.

"You can't imagine how good that feels, just to sit partway

up." Laura inspected her IV line. "Guess I'm getting my nutrition. Foley catheter, so no bathroom trips. What's to complain about?"

Tim puttered around, arranging pillows, straightening her sheets, adjusting her thin blanket. Finally, she said, "Please, Tim, will you sit down?"

He pulled a chair up to the bed opposite her elevated right arm. "Laura, I did promise—"

"They can wait," she said, reaching with her good hand to touch his.

"Dr. Hanover was in not long ago," Tim said. "You were out cold, but he checked the wound—"

"How did the procedure go?" she asked.

Tim glanced upward at her suspended, heavily bandaged hand. "The surgery went well. As far as they could tell, they got all the necrotic tissue. They don't think they will have to go back in. They'll keep you pumped up on antibiotics. Physical therapy later. Overall, good news."

Laura knew it was. If the necrosis had not been controlled, she would have lost her hand. But good news was relative, wasn't it? Her right hand would remain attached to her arm, but even with rigorous physical therapy, it wouldn't be able to do much of anything. Not enough to sustain her career. She'd made up her mind. She'd take the Keystone Pharma job. No reason that a hand injury would affect an administrative job. A head injury, another story, but her thinking was clear, concussion symptoms waning.

"Tim, I want you to be the first to know. I'm going to take that Keystone vice president job."

Tim stood up, went to the window, his back to her.

Laura's heart sank. She had no illusions about Tim's commitment to her under these new circumstances, but she hadn't anticipated this degree of desperation to escape his recent marriage proposal.

When he returned to her bedside, tears filled his blue eyes.

"Tim, I…I can do this on my own, I'm—"

"Laura, I'm sorry, I'm just so overjoyed, I can't—"

"Tim? Are you okay?" Laura pulled back her words. Had she totally misjudged his reaction? He was not trying to back out?

"I'm more than okay, Laura, but please, please tell me this means that you and I will be together. I want that more than anything else in the world. More than I've ever wanted anything. Much, much more. More than I can even imagine wanting. For the first time in my life, I've been praying. First, that you'd be okay; then, that you'd be with me."

"Tim?" Laura felt tears gathering. Tears of what? Guilt, that she'd been so lacking in comprehension? Guilt, that she'd so underestimated his love for her? Guilt, that he'd be stuck with a maimed wife? "Tim?" she repeated.

"I want to take you in my arms," he said, "but that wouldn't feel so good for you."

When Tim leaned in, brushing tears from his eyes with the back of his hand, he rewarded her with the most glorious smile before he gently placed his lips on hers.

At that exact moment, Laura knew. Her tears had nothing to do with guilt. They reflected a flood of love. A love that pushed aside disappointments of the past, insecurities that had consumed her all those years.

"Tim," she sighed, "I love you."

"Laura, please marry me," he said.

"Yes, Tim, I will," she said, tears dampening her hospital gown. With her good hand she grabbed Tim's and clutched it fiercely.

An aide hesitated at the door, hoisting a tray. "Dr. Robinson," she said, "a VIP dinner from the kitchen."

"Thanks. Over here," he said, easing his hand out of Laura's to clear a space on the bedside table.

The aide glanced at Laura. "Dr. Nelson, are you okay?" she asked. "Do you want some dinner too? Your orders say you can have whatever you want." She pointed to the beef short ribs and mashed potatoes.

"Not sure I'm up to that yet," Laura said, smiling through

lingering tears. "But maybe..." she hesitated, maybe she could try some broth. But the pulsating pain in her hand reminded her she'd have to learn to eat with her left hand. "...Jell-O," she said, a less risky first attempt. "And champagne."

"We don't—"

"Just kidding," Laura said. Champagne would have to wait until she was off potent narcotics. "Tim, get started. Please, eat."

"I've had no appetite since I've been here, but suddenly I'm ravenous. Does happiness do that to you?"

"I'm actually looking forward to Jell-O!"

"After I eat this, though, I'm going to call the kids. I promised, and I'm a man of my word."

You are, Tim Robinson, and I'm one lucky woman.

"Can we tell them?" Laura asked, a grin spreading across her face as she recognized the giggle in her voice.

"I need to have a talk with them," Tim said. "Ask their permission. The old-fashioned approach."

"They're my kids, not my father. Are you going to ask him?"

"Forgot to tell you. Your parents did call to check on you. Said they'd call back. I'll ask your dad when—"

"I'm an old-fashioned girl," Laura said, "but I think I'm old enough to forgo that formality."

The Jell-O was a long time coming, and Laura had to ask for pain relief before it arrived; however, she insisted on half the dose. When the kids did arrive that evening, they'd notice a big difference. And they'd be thrilled for her, she knew.

She fell asleep with a smile on her face.

CHAPTER SEVENTEEN

Jake left by the back door and retraced his steps to Mack's garage along the fence line that separated adjacent back yards in his neighborhood. Lined with mature trees, leafless now, but still large enough to give Jake plenty of cover as he maneuvered from tree to tree. The distance took five minutes, just as it had when he'd left his friend's garage, stealthily moving to his house. Mack played poker with Jake at the local Veterans of Foreign Wars post. He also drove a Jeep Cherokee, only his was dark blue, close enough to olive green in the dusk that was falling around Rockville. Mack used to brag that he never locked his doors, so Jake borrowed the space for the half hour that he'd needed shelter. Mack would never know. Wouldn't care if he did, unless, of course, he knew what Jake had done during that half hour.

Earlier, Jake had backed into Mack's garage, and now he simply had to open and close the manual door and drive normally into the moderate traffic. Gloves would prevent fingerprints, but unlikely that cops would connect Mack's garage to Karolee's murder. The gun was another matter. He'd chosen it from the collection of firearms he'd amassed over the years. Jake's fishing and card-playing buddies knew he had a gun collection, but none were familiar enough to know a piece was missing. When it came to police questions about his guns, he'd try to avoid disclosing that he kept them in a secure gun compartment. He didn't have a concealed-carry permit, but so what. The Smith & Wesson would not be missed, nor could it be traced to him.

First order of business: empty the gun, wipe it down, get rid of it. He'd already chosen the location in Croydon Creek; fast and easy to drop the gun where the thick muck would hide it forever. This time of year, the locals had no interest in the creek, and Jake's disposal attracted no attention. A dull career as a project planner had its satisfactions. Usually plans worked—as planned.

Five minutes later, Jake pulled the Jeep into the clearing he'd chosen, off the Twinbrook Parkway, a busy thoroughfare leading north from the Parklawn Building where he worked. Five minutes into his usual drive, ten minutes away from his house, the site offered a secluded spot as well as proximity to a middle class neighborhood where he could ask for help and get it. He went to work immediately. Opening the Jeep's hood, using asbestos gloves, he quickly severed the serpentine belt with industrial-sized scissors. He cut the snake-like, ribbed-metal belt into six pieces and stuffed them in a heavy plastic bag. The ground was frozen, so forget trying to bury the pieces. He cinched the bag and tied it around his waist, under his heavy jacket. Made him look like he had the start of a potbelly, something most men his age carried around. He'd ditch the bag in the first available dumpster on the way home.

Jake rehearsed his story: his beloved Jeep overheating all of a sudden, his complete ignorance about cars and panic at the red light flashing on the dash. No antifreeze with him. He does know enough not to drive when that hot light is on, so he waits, but the engine was still just as hot after a good thirty minutes.

The account sounded good to him, so he left the vehicle, hood up, and headed through a sparsely wooded area to the neighborhood about a hundred feet away. He stopped at the first house with a light on. He came out of the shadows, stood under the porch light, and knocked on the door.

A sturdy white man about his own age answered. "He'p ya?"

"Car broke down off Twinbrook. Sorry to bother you, man,

but could I use your phone to call a garage or a tow? Think I'll need a tow."

"Yeah, come on in. What you got?"

What I got? Jake stood, perplexed.

"What the fuck's wrong with your car, man?"

"Don't know. Heated up. I waited fifteen minutes, you know, for it to cool down. Tried again. Red light still on. Tried again. Twice. But the engine's still too hot to drive. Don't have any anti-freeze in the vehicle. It was getting dark—"

"I'll take a look, man. I got some antifreeze if that's all it is. You get a tow, fuckers'll rob ya blind." He grabbed a heavy, black-and-white checkered coat and led the way out, stopping in his garage to grab a container of antifreeze, going back in again for an industrial-size flashlight.

"Can't thank you enough," Jake mumbled. This was working out better than he'd expected. Two layers of alibi. This Good Samaritan and the eventual tow-truck driver.

Jake led the way to his vehicle. "Here it is."

"Fuck, man, not smart to leave the hood open. Neighborhood's not bad, but—"

"Should have known better," Jake said. "Hope nobody walked off with any parts."

Good Samaritan reached into a jacket pocket and pulled out the large flashlight, shined it onto the exposed engine block.

"Fuck, man, you ain't got no serpentine belt. Shit, no amount of antifreeze gonna do shit. You need a new belt, man." He bent further into the engine with his flashlight. "Damn thing's completely off. No wonder the engine light was on."

"Yeah, went on a way back. Thought it would be okay, then got worried."

"Good thing, man. Serpentine must have shredded and shed over the last few miles maybe. Like I said, it's gone now. Funny thing," he said with a sniff, "I don't smell nothin'. Should be stinkin' like a son a bitch."

"Serpentine?" Jake asked, trying to shift away from the tell-tale lack of odor. "That have something to do with overheating?"

"Hell yeah. It's a continuous belt that runs the alternator, water pump, compressor, air pump, you name it." Jake was glad he wore a tie to match the image of a wimp who didn't know shit about cars.

"All that?" Jake asked. "Hey, thanks, buddy. Never was into car engines." Careful, Jake warned himself. He'd taught his son a fair amount about engines. Or tried to, he corrected himself. Mark had no mechanical talent.

"Yeah, that belt breaks, you do lose all that shit."

"Shit," Jake said. "Guess I'll need a tow after all. Can I use your phone?"

"Sure thing. I could fix it for you if I had the right tools and the part, of course. Sorry I don't, so lock this baby up and come back with me to make the call. Fuck, man, it's gonna cost ya."

"Yeah, well, thanks for trying. What's your name, by the way?"

"Barker, man. Frank Barker."

Jake ran through his memorized action list. All accounted for, except for repeated phone calls he'd make from the garage to get hold of Karolee and tell her he'd had car trouble. Even though he'd disabled the answering machine, the cops could check the garage's phone records. No doubt they'd appreciate a dutiful husband's attempts to update his wife.

CHAPTER EIGHTEEN

Based on the lower dose of narcotic Laura was taking, Tim figured she should be awake by early evening and happy to see her family. He'd suggested all the kids arrive at seven-thirty. She'd been a good mom to those kids. Not an easy job with three boys, two girls, and no husband.

Laura's husband had died fourteen years ago under traumatic and rather mysterious circumstances. Something secret and bad had happened between Laura and Steve. Something, since Tim had only had a peripheral glimpse of their lives, to which he'd not been privy. Just before Steve was killed, their youngest son Patrick had needed emergency heart surgery, which Tim had arranged at Children's Hospital of Pennsylvania. Whatever had happened between Steve and Laura, Tim believed it had something to do with Patrick. He'd pondered this over the years, wondering if Laura would ever tell him, but, so far, not a word. Would that change now?

Laura's nurses had produced a case of cosmetic products, and Tim had watched as they fixed her hair and cleaned her face with magical pads that left her looking much fresher. The girls noticed right away, and when Nicole said, "Wow, Mom is looking great," Laura promptly opened her eyes.

Tim literally held his breath. Had Laura meant what she said?

The girls adjusted the angle of her bed and her pillows while they all chatted about how much better she seemed.

"I have news," Laura said, her tone cut though the chitchat. Instant silence.

Tim risked a breath.

"Tim and I—" Laura stopped to flash him a smile, while he scrutinized the young faces as each of the kids sputtered, "What?"

"—are getting married."

For Tim, time stood still, until all the faces turned to him in one major grin.

"When?" Kevin was asking him.

Tim had no idea.

Laura looked up. "When, Tim?"

"As soon as you break out of here? In my opinion," he added, "we've already waited too long."

"Really, Mom, are you sure?" Natalie asked. "I mean, it seems so sudden, and you just had that concussion and—" Natalie turned to Tim, "Oh my God, Uncle Tim, I didn't mean... It's just so..."

Tim and Natalie had a special relationship ever since he'd stayed at her side when she'd been critically ill several years ago. He'd earned her trust and she'd never let him down. Tim knew that. And he'd always loved that Laura's kids called him "Uncle."

"Are you okay with this? I mean, I was going to ask your permission, each one of you, but your mom just blurted it out."

The three boys shook his hand, slapped him on the back. Said things like "great news," "about time," "welcome to the family," "we still get to call you Uncle Tim?"

So far, so good. Eventually, would they want to call him...Dad?

Tim had arranged six chairs around Laura's bed and, once they'd all settled down, Natalie and Nicole directed the chatter into the what-to-wear theme—long dress, short dress, white or not.

Tim saw the boys exchange exasperated looks, but he could not erase the grin on his own face. Until Mike asked in an elaborately casual tone. "What about your job, Mom?"

Laura, always the pragmatist, seemed relieved to get back to solid ground. She was a beautiful woman, always well dressed, but with little interest in fashion. "Right. My job. I have to quit my job. But I have an offer. Here, in Philadelphia. Won't need my hand."

Just like Laura, Tim thought. Matter of fact. Move forward.

"A job? Here?" Nicole's turn to ask, her tone a shade skeptical.

"Keystone Pharma. Vice President of Research."

"That's wonderful," Natalie said. "You'll be living close to us. At least until we finish med school—"

"Keystone—" Mike said. "Mom, did you know that doctor who was killed?"

"Killed! But who—?"

Tim had not told Laura about Dr. Fred Minn. Her condition, in his opinion, not exactly compatible with shocking announcements.

"Tim?" She looked at him for an explanation.

"Laura, you've been so ill... Fred Minn died last Sunday night."

"Fred Minn?" Laura's eyes widened in shock.

"Something terrible happened when he left the dinner with you Sunday night. He was struck by a vehicle that was leaving the Four Seasons. His injuries proved fatal."

"It's been in all the papers," Patrick said. "They don't know who did it or why."

"Fred was a wonderful man, a brilliant doctor, looking forward to retirement with his wife. Paul Parnell wanted me to replace him... Oh, that's just so sad." Laura hesitated, then added, "Tim, do you think this would change their objectives?"

"Not at all. Paul Parnell stopped by yesterday to ask about you. He made me promise to have you call him as soon as you're able to think about their offer. They're very anxious to recruit you, Laura."

"Good. I'll call tomorrow and accept, but I feel terrible about Dr. Minn." Laura's expression saddened momentarily, then she forced a grin through the pain, through the uncertainty of a new career. "Okay, kids, you're going to be stuck with me in Philadelphia."

They all chatted a bit longer until Tim suggested Laura get some rest. As soon as the kids had left, she rang for the nurse to insist that they take out the urinary catheter so she could use the bathroom, and that they discontinue her intravenous and step her down to oral pain meds.

CHAPTER NINETEEN

Addie had fussed over a dinner of Jake's preferred Western dishes—roasted chicken, potatoes au gratin, steamed green beans—and she had bought a pecan pie for dessert. But now it was after nine o'clock, and no Jake. They'd usually eat between seven and eight, then move on to the bedroom. Jake seemed to really care about her, but what were her feelings for him? She didn't know. She'd had little experience with men.

Addie had arrived in the United States at age twenty-one, gone straight to Ann Arbor, where she'd spent six years earning a PhD in biochemistry. A Muslim woman in a country where she knew no one, she at first detested the US with its wealth and evil ways. She thought she could tolerate the place long enough to obtain a respected advanced degree. At home in Iraq, Addie and her sister and mother wore the burka. On coming to America, she'd decided to adopt a simple scarf head cover, long-sleeved shirts, and skirts covering the knee. After a week, she'd shed even the scarf and started to spend the limited money she got from home on clothes. Later on, when she became a laboratory assistant under a research grant, she spent her pay on more fashionable clothes and her coveted collection of shoes. She saw no reason to impose Islamic dress code restrictions on herself when living in the West. She needed to appear the professional scientist that she was; didn't want to provoke distrust or trigger racial prejudice.

The fusion of Addie's scientific brilliance with a generous dose of luck resulted in her discovery of the family of compounds that had produced Immunone. When Replica licensed Immunone from the University of Michigan, they hired Addie as their principal scientist. Replica, a small start-up pharmaceutical company, had recognized the potential blockbuster drug, and they realized they needed her expertise to move it through development. They couldn't pay her a mega salary, but in what must seem to them now like a reckless move, they offered her 5 percent of any subsequent sale of Immunone at the time of its ultimate approval. The math: Keystone Pharma had paid $150 million for Immunone; Addie's payout would be $7.5 million. *Once the drug was approved.*

But the money was still some way off, and the pressure from her father in Iraq was building. He wanted her home, had an important job waiting for her in Baghdad. Her mother never had wanted her to leave Iraq, and had protested her father's efforts to endorse Addie for the coveted United States university slot. Why couldn't Addie, like her younger sister, marry the man of her parents' choice, live in her husband's family's house, have children? Addie loved her mother and her sister, missed them terribly, but could she ever be like them, genuinely unperturbed by the restricted freedom imposed by the Islamic culture?

During Addie's childhood, her father had been a microbiology research scientist at the University of Baghdad. She grew up sharing his love of science. He had encouraged her, against her mother's counsel, to study in America, and when she'd pleaded to stay to work as a scientist, he'd reluctantly agreed. He himself had never been to the States, never visited her here. Unthinkable during Operation Desert Storm and now, because of the United Nations inspection teams' insulting scrutiny of Iraq, combined with his failing health, he never would. Maybe that's why he was now adamant that she come home. She'd explained repeatedly about the money she would collect when Immunone was approved. He hadn't seemed impressed. Iraq had enough money with its oil.

She would obey him, but she wanted to wait until she got the money. In the United States, even though she was a woman, the money was due. She was quite sure that she'd get it, but had no idea about how long it would take to be paid, even after Immunone was approved. Or in what form she'd be paid: cash or stock or some annuity payoff? And what about US taxes? Could she even get the large sum out of this country? She didn't know a thing about finance. Her salary went straight into her bank account and she wrote checks. She'd never needed to send money home. Her family was well off by Iraqi standards.

A knock at the door interrupted her worries. Finally, Jake. She needed to give him his own key, but was she ready for that? She liked him. He treated her with respect.

"Jake!" She started opening the apartment door. Only it wasn't Jake. At the door was a vision from her past.

"Badur?" The man who'd mentored her for the first few months after she got to America. A fellow Iraqi student at the University of Michigan. About ten years older. Not a scientist. A business major.

"Adawia." His baritone voice was unmistakable. And he looked no different than when they had first met twelve years ago. Well, maybe some gray at the temples, but no wrinkles and no weight gain. But she knew she still looked good too.

"Expecting somebody?" He glanced at her sexy nightgown ensemble. Still blocking the doorway, she tightened the draw-string belt around her waist. "Or is he already here?"

Addie considered Badur Hammadi westernized, but finding her dressed like this would exceed his benevolent tolerance. What was he doing here? And thank Allah that Jake had not yet shown up.

"Come in, Badur." Addie held open the door. "No one's here."

"Dressed like that? But you do look beautiful. Time for you to marry, Adawia."

"Sit down," Addie said, now hoping against hope that Jake would not show up. "I can make you some tea."

"Whiskey would work," he said. "Let's not pretend we don't

drink alcohol. We both know better than that. I've followed your progress, you know."

She did not know. She hadn't seen him since she'd left Ann Arbor, six years ago.

He sat on her sofa, glancing about, looking for what? He rose when she returned with two old-fashioned glasses half full of Jim Beam. "Want ice? Water?"

"Neat is fine. Can I use your bathroom?"

Shit. She only had one, and Jake's toothbrush and toiletries were sitting right out there to be inspected. She pointed to the bathroom door.

"Adawia, let's not fool around. I know you have an illicit relationship. Jake Harter, a middle manager at the FDA, but right now in quite a strategic position. I have to give you credit for seducing him."

Addie was impressed that Badur had lost the last traces of the Arabic accent that still had marked his speech when she'd last seen him. But what was he telling her? He knows all about her? They'd had no connection whatsoever...

"Surprised, dear one?"

"Badur, I just don't know what to say."

"Dru. They call me Dru," he said, going into the bathroom. "Sounds more American."

Is that why Jake called her 'Addie'? He wanted her more American? Why not? Americans hated Iraqis since the war. Did she even belong here? What if the United States attacked Iraq again? Would they revoke her green card?

"Do you think about home much, Adawia?" Badur asked, as he settled back on the sofa and reached for the glass of whiskey.

"Yes, I miss my mother and my sister. And I've never seen my nephews. Yes, I do."

"Are you loyal?" he asked.

Loyal to what? Addie took a moment to move a magazine off a chair before sitting down with her drink. "Badur, I don't know what you mean."

"I'm called Dru, remember? To your country. To your parents. To Islam."

"Yes, I am loyal. I never forget I'm Iraqi and I'm a Muslim. Maybe I'm not perfect." She gestured with her glass. "But neither are you."

"Big difference, dear one. Or have you been in the West too long to remember the place of the woman in Islam?" Badur nodded toward the bathroom. "Your father and your brother would have to kill the man who had his way with you. Jake Harter would be murdered, his balls chopped up into little pieces."

Addie cringed on cue. But Jake prided himself in being a Marine. Would he be frightened away by the men in her family? She doubted it.

"You've been in the land of the infidel for twelve years, Adawia, and now it's your time."

"My time for what? Dru, why are you here? What do you want from me?"

"Let's just say I'm your financial advisor. I'm going to tell you what to do with the money from that drug you developed." He must have detected her blink of surprise. "Yes, I know about that too."

"You know, I've been thinking a lot about that, the money, I mean. The company owes me 5 percent of the selling price to Keystone Pharma—seven point five million. And that's to be paid when it's approved. And I think that's getting close and—"

"You *think?*" Dru's deep voice interrupted. "I heard it was a done deal."

"Me too," Addie said, "but I get the feeling there may be some kind of issue."

"I have been following the business news carefully. There's been no hint of a problem. Keystone's stock is skyrocketing. Since they are a public company, they'd have to disclose a problem with a drug that big."

"It's just a feeling," Addie said. "Maybe just a premonition."

She should have kept her mouth shut. Now she'll be dragging Jake into this.

"Your boyfriend?" Dru demanded. "He said there's a problem?"

"Not exactly. He just—"

"When are you seeing him next?" Dru was on his feet now, pacing.

"I don't know. He may come tonight. Thought he'd be here by now."

"Where is he? Call him."

"I can't. He must be home. I can't call him there. His wife—"

"How does he manage to sneak over here if he's married?"

"His wife is out of town for a few days. Usually he does not stay here. She works late and he leaves me before—"

"Call him. I need to know the timing."

Addie checked her watch. It was just after ten-thirty. "I'm not sure—"

"Do it. Tell him you have to see him. Tonight."

A woman's voice answered at Jake's home with a simple "Hello." Addie had never called his home number. She assumed it was his wife.

"Is Jake Harter there?" she asked.

"Who's calling?" the voice countered.

Addie hung up. What was she going to say? "This is Dr. Adawia Abdul with Replica Laboratories. I need to obtain some confidential information from your husband about Immunone."

"I couldn't just leave a message," she informed the staring face from her past.

"A lot is at stake here, Adawia. Not just your family, but mine too. Unlike you, I did marry and I have two young sons. Let me look at your Replica contract. Get it. Now."

Addie did not understand the Badur-turned-Dru's cryptic charge, but her need to get rid of him before Jake arrived seemed more urgent than her desire for answers. She retrieved a copy of her Replica employment contract from her briefcase and handed it to Dru. He was a banker; in fact, she'd always planned to contact him for advice about investing the money.

When Dru finally left, Addie locked the door after him. She tried to recall their relationship back in Ann Arbor. He'd been supportive, nonjudgmental; she, the appreciative mentee. Nothing more. No strings seemed attached. But who was this new Dru? Could she trust him?

"I don't need either of you," she said to no one. Jake, a coward, plain and simple; the wimp couldn't muster the guts even to call tonight. Dru, suddenly reinserting himself into her life.

Addie stormed into the kitchen. She yanked the chicken out of the oven and dumped it, splattering drippings on every surface near the garbage bin.

CHAPTER TWENTY

Jake pulled the Jeep into his driveway. He left the motor running, climbed out, and slammed the door behind him. Heading to his mailbox, he glanced about, but it was too dark to tell if any of his neighbors were watching. He hoped they were. After retrieving his mail, he returned to the Jeep, got back in, slammed the door again, and continued up his driveway. He parked in his usual space just outside the garage, got out, and for the third time, slammed the Jeep's door shut before approaching the front door to his house, turning the key in the lock, stepping inside.

He realized he was holding his breath and, only when he saw Karolee lying lifeless, exactly as he had left her, did he exhale a sharp breath of relief. Jake had rehearsed the actions of the caring husband in shock when he discovers the bloody corpse of his wife sprawled on the entryway floor of the family home. The Good Husband kneels, fumbles to feel her neck for a pulse, getting blood on his shirt cuffs. Then he takes action. And that's what he does. Jake barges out of the house, running to the house across the street, pounding on the door of neighbors he knows only by sight, yelling for them to call 911.

And that they do, handing him the phone to clutch in trembling hands to blurt out that his wife has been shot, that he thinks she is dead. He acknowledges the dispatcher's instructions to stay right where he is, to not go back inside his house.

Sirens screaming, lights rotating, the cops and the ambulance arrive. Jake makes a show of trying to barge into his home, but police officers keep his frantic efforts at bay. Finally, a female officer politely pulls him aside, offers her condolences, confirms that Karolee is dead, possibly of a gunshot wound to the chest. To establish cause and means, she explains, the medical examiner will investigate and confer with detectives. Jake summons the dramatically correct blend of shock and grief as the scene plays out, just as television viewers have a right to expect.

Three detectives usher him inside his house via the back door. They interview him in his kitchen.

Question: How had Jake found his wife?

Answer: Almost tripped over her body.

Question: Exactly when had he found her?

Answer: At eight fifty-five, approximately. Hadn't checked his watch. Just before he called 911.

Question: Where had he been before coming home?

Answer: At work. Car stalled out on the way home. Had to get it towed to a garage. Lucky they could fix it. Grabbed something to eat at McDonald's on the way home.

Question: Where had she been?

Answer: Expected home from the airport, having visited their son and new baby granddaughter.

All the logical questions. Then they released him to call his son before escorting him to his bedroom, suggesting that he grab a few personal things. The property was now a crime scene.

Naturally, they listened in as he dialed Mark's Miami number.

Mark's wife answered.

"Claire, it's Jake, is Mark home?"

"He just got the baby down, and he drifted off to sleep on the couch. I don't want to wake him. Did she get home? Please tell me she's not stuck in Florida anywhere."

"Karolee made it home." Jake struggled to make his voice sound shaky. What he felt was triumphant. "But please wake up Mark, it's important."

Claire sighed. "Okay, if you say so."

Mark sounded groggy. "What's up, Dad?"

"Your mother, she's dead. I don't know how to say it any easier. A break-in at the house—They shot her in the chest—"

"You did pick her up?" Mark asked. "Then how—?"

"I didn't go into the office today until late. I had the most god-awful gastrointestinal thing all night and most of the day. When I did go in, well, I hate to admit it, but I nodded off at my desk. That sounds lame, I know."

"But I told you her arrival time."

"Yes, I know. 4:10 p.m. I did know that. I planned to be there, but—"

"Mom's dead?" Mark repeated, maybe for Claire's benefit. If she reacted, Jake didn't hear it. No love lost there, but Mark sounded really upset.

"I've got to go now, Mark. The police are here."

"Okay, Dad, I'll be there tomorrow. I can't get out tonight, but first thing tomorrow. Don't know about Claire and the baby. Up to her. But I gotta be there. Call me, Dad, if you hear anything else, and make sure the police find out who did this. Maybe we didn't always get along, but she was my mother..."

Shit. Jake hadn't counted on Mark coming to town, possibly even with his wife and baby. Jake had enough going on, didn't need that distraction.

He desperately needed to talk to Addie, but couldn't risk contacting her. She expected him at her place tonight and would be pissed when he didn't show up. But wait until she found out why—he was free—free to marry her! Jake wondered how long he'd be under investigation—a suspect, he guessed—as the cops searched for Karolee's killer. How long could he stand being away from Addie?

Now, his priority was a place to spend the night. He decided on a motel near the FDA.

For the next week he'd have a helluva management load: keep Immunone in limbo, unapproved; contact Karolee's lawyer about her affairs; *cooperate* with the cops with the murder case; plan the funeral; and most importantly, make sure Addie was okay.

CHAPTER TWENTY-ONE

Laura carefully timed her call to Keystone Pharma, holding off until that fleeting moment when the effect of her pain meds would be minimal and yet her pain not too overwhelming. When she spoke to Paul Parnell, she wanted him to hear in her speech and voice only alertness and competence. She needed to sound credible when she proposed showing up for work in just four days.

Her years of experience in dealing with severe pain, anyone's pain but her own, were less than useful now. But she did understood the pharmacology of narcotics, that there was a trade-off: the relief of debilitating pain means mental impairment. She needed mental clarity and had set a schedule to stop taking all narcotics. Sunday would be her last dose, no matter what, so she could start work at Keystone this Monday with a clear head. A new job with new challenges should help keep her mind off her damaged hand. Later, when she felt more in control, she'd go back to Tampa to wrap up her professional and personal life there.

She'd been awake that morning when Dr. Hanover made rounds. He'd declared her much improved. Ready for a simple sling to replace the apparatus that hung her arm from a pole on her bed. That meant she could ambulate without assistance, a huge improvement. Just after that assessment from Dr. Hanover,

Tim left the hospital to attend a staff meeting at CHOP. Laura was glad to see him start paying attention to his own professional life.

When Laura dialed Paul Parnell's direct number, he picked up immediately. After expressing her condolences for Fred Minn, and after accepting "get-well" wishes, she asked whether the VP job still was available. Across the line, she heard a loud sigh of relief.

"Thank God, Laura. Yes, it is. When can you start?"

"Monday," she said, waited until he expressed disbelief, and answered, "Yes, I am sure. I can start Monday."

"You don't know how much better that makes me feel," he replied. "Losing Fred in such a traumatic way... Well, Laura, we'll bring you up to speed on Monday. Right now, I have to focus on Fred's funeral tomorrow. But would it be okay if I sent over Barney McCoy, our VP of human resources, to work out the employment package? It will be most generous, I assure you. Oh, I can't tell you how pleased we are. And to help sweeten the bad news about your resignation in Tampa, Keystone will donate a million dollars to their surgical department in your name."

"Mr. Parnell, that's far too generous!" Laura did feel an urge to procrastinate about those difficult calls to Tampa City Hospital and the medical school.

"We're colleagues, Laura. Paul, the name is Paul. And Barney can come by the hospital today. How does early afternoon sound?"

After hanging up with Paul Parnell, Laura dialed her number at Tampa City. Before calling anyone else, she needed to tell the news to Eileen Donovan, her secretary of fifteen years. Next, she'd inform the CEO of Tampa City and the dean of the medical school; Parnell's offer of a million dollars should make the news easier to take, and relieve any anxiety about replacing her with a skilled—and able-handed—surgeon.

Laura and Eileen shared an emotional moment; the older woman knew all her kids, knew all her idiosyncrasies. She'd been

Laura's support system. Through some tears, she poured out her good wishes. Laura would miss her and their relationship. They were saying extended good-byes when a kid in a white coat looking no older than her daughters stepped into her hospital room.

"Have to go," Laura said. "Heading off to a physical therapy session. Better described as a torture session."

"Before you hang up, Laura," her secretary slipped back one more time into her habitual role, "did you ever return Mr. Greenwood's call?"

No, she hadn't.

"Mr. Greenwood," Eileen reiterated. "Lonnie Greenwood, with the Detroit mayor's office. The man with the son who needs a lung transplant? He left you that cryptic message. He called again, and I told him I gave you the message, but that you were hospitalized in Philadelphia. Hope that was okay?"

Laura felt her heart start to twitch. After the fall, she'd completely forgotten about that ominous message. The cue that took her back to the darkest corner of her life. Johnny Diggs. Her mind must have wanted to keep that corner buried. She thought it *had* been buried since her discussion with Detective Reynolds, the day she left Detroit—twenty-one years ago.

"I will call...Mr. Greenwood," she promised.

She had to call the man, Laura knew. She had to find out about his link with Johnny Diggs. Did it pose a threat to her? To all she'd become since...? But not now. She had unavoidable misery to face. She had insisted on immediately starting physical therapy on her hand, knowing it would be pure torture, but would expedite getting back to as close to normal as she'd ever get.

"Okay, Dr. Nelson, time to rock and roll." Her young therapist managed a brave grin. "I'm going to take your arm down, leave it in a sling at heart level. Our aim is to get function back in the hand. Not going to kid you, it'll be painful and will take a long time. Dr. Hanover wants you medicated to the greatest extent possible."

Laura had wanted to tough it out, but before they had

progressed much in the exercise routine, she asked for medication. Her injured hand was being stretched to the agony
threshold. She wished she had made those calls to Tampa, but
they would have to wait. As would Lonnie Greenwood from
Detroit.

***

Laura awoke to three voices, two familiar and one she did not recognize. She willed her eyes open, checked the position of her hand,
now lying laterally on her chest, bandaged, but no sign of the un-
wieldy trapeze apparatus. The hand hurt like hell, but nothing near
the torturous pain inflicted by her therapist.

Mike was saying, "Mom is tough. The whole team of us can't
keep her down. Her doctor wanted her hand suspended for a few
more days, but as you can see—"

"I don't like people talking about me while I'm under the influence," she interrupted him. "How about giving me a hand—no
pun intended—in raising this bed out of invalid mode. No, second thought, I'll just find the button and do it myself."

"No, I'll do it." Tim was at her side, already adjusting the angle of her bed.

"Laura, you have a visitor," Tim said. "Barney McCoy from
Keystone Pharma. You were expecting him?"

Shit. She'd forgotten to ask the staff to wake her up. What
had Paul said? Barney McCoy, early afternoon?

"What time is it?" she asked, looking up at the sixtyish man
in the herringbone suit, striped tie, and skeptical smile.

"Oh, Dr. Nelson, I'm so, so sorry. Paul Parnell said—"

"I'm just glad you're here, Mr. McCoy." And she was, but she
looked a wreck, and now without the Foley catheter, she had to
pee. How could she hold this guy off until she could pull herself
together?

"Mom, it's one-thirty." Mike came to her rescue. "I've been
here for an hour, skipped lunch. Mr. McCoy, why don't you come
down to the cafeteria with me? I'll get a sandwich, you can grab a

coffee while I give you the real scoop on my mom. As her eldest son, I know all her secrets."

And he did too. Well, most.

"Great, Mike," McCoy said. "And, Dr. Nelson, I'm ready for all your questions about the company. We can go over the paper work, and if we're all in agreement, you'll be a Keystone employee by this afternoon. But one thing, you have to call me Barney. You too, Mike, and Dr. Robinson."

"Okay, Barney, and I'm Tim."

Laura smiled. "Laura, Barney."

Tim helped her to the tiny bathroom and stayed to watch her urinate. She tried to remember if Steve had ever watched her pee. She thought so, but it had been a long time since she'd had a husband.

"We might as well get married," Tim said, "now that we've gotten that intimacy over with. Seriously, Laura, when should we?"

As a Catholic widow, Laura had no impediments to a church marriage, but now that she'd made the decision to marry Tim, she wanted to skip the formalities. "Let's get our license the instant I get out of here. And—"

"What about City Hall?" Tim said, settling her back into bed.

"Perfect. That building is so intriguing."

"I happen to know the William Penn up on top is the tallest statue on any building in the world."

"It's such a beautiful old building."

"The largest municipal building in the country. Over seven hundred rooms."

"You seem quite the expert, Tim, and just which one of those seven hundred rooms shall we pick for the occasion?"

"What occasion, Mom?" Mike interrupted, Barney in tow. "The occasion? Hope you two don't mind, but I told Barney your big news."

"Congratulations," her new colleague offered.

Crap. She'd let the wedding banter with Tim distract her from combing her hair and putting on some lipstick. While in the bathroom, she'd glanced at herself in the mirror. An unkempt disaster. She'd never hire anyone who looked as awful as she did.

"You've never been good with family secrets, Mikey, at least with this family's." Laura enjoyed his blush at his little-kid nickname.

Mike came to her bedside and kissed Laura's cheek. "Sorry to go now, Mom. Good to see you so spunky. Call me if you need a lawyer—we don't want Keystone putting anything over on you."

As soon as Mike left, Laura decided to forget about her hair and get down to the contract. She needed to settle this employment business before her next round of therapy later in the afternoon. And, she had the Tampa calls to make.

"Okay if Tim stays?" she asked.

She was rewarded by Tim's biggest grin. *This marriage thing might be just what she needed.*

"Of course." Then Barney outlined an employment package that so exceeded her expectations, she and Tim could only stare at one another. Big pharma was living up to its reputation.

CHAPTER TWENTY-TWO

THURSDAY, FEBRUARY 20

Jake spent all day Thursday morning at the Rockville City Police Station. He answered one intrusive question after another; none a surprise except one. He'd prepared for the relationship probe: he and his wife were as normal as a couple could be after thirty-one years of marriage; not much spark these days but mutual respect; a son, married, living in Miami; wife had her job; he had his; no social life since she worked nights in her restaurant; he had a day job. Same-old-same-old, day to day. No, she had no enemies, not unless there were issues at the restaurant he didn't know about. No, he had no enemies either. Neither of them brought their work problems home. No money worries. His salary was adequate. She had a good income from the restaurant she'd started with family money. Nothing they wanted they couldn't afford. Your average American dream—well, maybe not Hollywood style. Until some common criminal took Karolee's life.

When they got to his alibi, his timeline stood up well. He knew they'd check Frank Barker's story, the Good Samaritan, and, of course, the garage where he'd waited for his new serpentine belt. They asked if he'd made any calls. Yes, three to his home to inform his wife he was delayed. Yes, he had assumed she'd take a cab. The events flowed logically, no hiccups. They said they needed to do an inventory of the household goods. He scheduled a walkthrough with them later in the afternoon after he picked up his son at the airport. From the beginning, burglary had been the motive; Jake had broken into Karolee's jewelry box, smashing the lock, scattering the less expensive pieces. He'd already told them he believed that her most valuable jewels were missing.

The surprise question had been about a phone call to the house last night.

They told him that at 10:50 p.m. as the crime scene was being processed, Officer Lois Sweeney had picked up a call on the Harter line. The female caller asked for Jake Harter. She hung up without identifying herself.

Who would be calling at that hour?

"No name? Did she leave a contact number?" Jake asked the detective. Of course, he wanted to ask if the woman had an accent, but then Addie's accent was almost imperceptible. Could they trace the call, another question he wanted to ask, but couldn't. Instead, he just shrugged. "No idea. Can't say I get many late-night calls from women."

"Someone from your job? Working at the FDA, you guys must get all kinds of emergencies. People getting sick on bad food, stuff like that?"

"No," Jake said, "not in my line of work. I deal with new drugs not on the market yet. Rare that we have some kind of after-hours emergency. Yeah, sure, I work late plenty, but, no, in my department, we don't get calls of that nature."

Jake did not want the cops sniffing around his work. He had enough problems there trying to manipulate records and data. What he needed now was the cops off his back so he could keep after Immunone. Too much time was being wasted. Today with the detectives and his son Mark. Tomorrow at the funeral home, picking out a casket, clothes for her body, and a burial site. Karolee in all her foresight and so-called wisdom had not made a single plan in the event of her death. Could he just have her cremated? No, Mark would expect him to do it up fancy for Mom, never mind that his son had just thrown the woman out of his own house. The guiltier Mark felt, the fancier he'd want the funeral. Guilt does that to people. Plus, Jake had to play the grieving husband. Convincingly.

And Addie? If only he could contact her. But she must have heard about Karolee's murder in the news. Surely, she'd know that soon they could be together. Forever.

CHAPTER TWENTY-THREE

Tim had been with Laura on Friday when she'd made the calls to Tampa City Hospital and the university. She resigned outright; told them straight out that she'd never operate again. That her decision was best for them, best for her. Stoic. Not a quaver in her voice. But Tim knew the toll it was taking. Laura had worked so damned hard for how many years to make chief of surgery—while raising five kids!

When they met, she'd been a med student. Even back then, her passion for surgery had absorbed her. The surgical residents used to obsess about her; the only woman in the class who had kids—she had two when she started and five when she graduated. While other students struggled to get through, Laura breezed along, collecting more than her share of honors. Tim remembered blushing at how the guys used to take odds on whether she breast-fed or not. No one ever found out, including him. Would he find out now? One thing for sure, he'd never share that tidbit with those other jokers.

He could now sum up his own behavior back then in one word: disgusting. He'd never had a monogamous relationship, had a few mini-affairs, and a lot of one-night stands. For twenty-two years now, one of those misadventures still haunted him. One involved Rosie Santangelo, Laura's friend. He and Rosie had endured a tumultuous relationship, neither of them committed to any definition of faithful, but in Laura's view, he and Rosie were a couple. When he'd propositioned Laura at a surgical conference in Montreal, she'd rebuffed him in no uncertain terms. Of course, he had been drunk. And, she was married with four kids.

Tim had shown up at Laura and Rosie's graduation, bringing a bouquet of roses for Rosie, but really he'd wanted to see Laura one last time. And he had, but the circumstances had turned tragic that day. Over the ensuing eight years, Tim had thought of Laura relentlessly, couldn't shake his infatuation with her. Although he'd cleaned up his philandering approach to *amour,* he hadn't transformed into an ascetic. Now at fifty years of age, Tim had to admit to himself that even with the variety of women he had dated, he'd never been "in love." How could he have been, he now realized, with Laura *always on my mind.* Just like that song.

After graduation, Tim's next encounter with Laura had been a phone call. Fourteen years ago. Laura, frantic. Urgent. Her nine-year-old son Patrick had been diagnosed with a cardiac tumor. She had begged him to get Dr. Koop at CHOP to operate on her son. He had, Tim assisting Koop with the surgery. Successful, as judged by Patrick's subsequent athletic feats.

About that time, Steve, Laura's husband, died, and Tim saw Laura only rarely until about seven years ago when he arrived in Tampa just as Natalie fell prey to a heinous act of bioterrorism. He'd been there for Laura when she needed him most and, since then, their relationship had progressed from friendship to intimacy. But never had they broached the subject of a life together. He'd wanted to as his love for her deepened, but their careers and her kids seemed too daunting a barrier. Only now could he harbor more than hope.

Over the weekend, Tim wondered if it had been pure selfishness on his part to encourage Laura to work in a drug company. Would she miss patient contact? The exhilaration that came with a successful surgical cure? Could she handle the bureaucracy? Get real, he told himself. If she could handle a department of surgical prima donnas, she could handle research scientists. And besides, she was no longer able to operate.

Now it was Monday morning, Laura's first day at Keystone Pharma. They'd sent a limo to pick her up. This time Tim did escort her to the car, making sure she was comfortable inside. Laura had kept her vow to stop all pain meds except for Tylenol with codeine. She still needed to keep her arm elevated. She'd find a way to work in physical therapy. So off to work they'd gone. He to his job. She to hers. A normal work routine. He'd alerted the surgical secretaries to find him if she called, but she hadn't. He'd picked up dinner on the way home—a rotisserie chicken, mashed potatoes, a mixed salad.

She returned from her first day at Keystone late that afternoon, and they dined early, topping off their meal with peppermint ice cream. Laura seemed upbeat, wanting to talk about their future. Tim's reservations started to slip away. Laura was going to be okay.

"Should we live here in your apartment?" she asked. "It's small, but none of the kids live at home anymore. Like they say, 'Less is more.'"

"Nice location if you're a city dweller, but you'll be working in the suburbs; that'll be a long commute," he said.

"Once I sell the house in Tampa, maybe we can buy a bigger condo? Here in Center City, Philadelphia?"

Tim was touched by her deference. As if she had to ask his permission! Whatever she wanted would be just fine with him. "That'll be a forty-minute drive to Montgomery County."

"A reverse commute. Shouldn't be so bad; besides, I'll be traveling a lot, and this is much closer to the airport."

Not a pleasant thought, Laura traveling, but Tim reminded himself that he had to give her space. He'd never had a wife before so he didn't know what to expect or how to react.

"You sure you want to sell the Tampa house? You've lived there for twenty years. Kids all grew up in that house."

"No problem," Laura said. "Matter of fact, I've wanted out of that place. Too many memories of Steve. Couldn't do it though, because of the kids."

He remembered all the photos and mementos she displayed in the Tampa home. "Laura, you've done a fine job, preserving his memory for the kids. Things must have been rough for you around the time he died." Tim didn't want to bring up bad memories, but he did want to know more at last, about the mysterious—apparently dire—circumstances of Steve's death.

They were sitting by the fire in the living room, nestled together on the oversized sofa. A long silence. Tim suspected she'd once again stonewall. He'd accept Laura with her secrets, but he did long for a relationship where there was no such need—on her side, either. Reconciled to sticking with safe topics, he asked, "Any surprises at Keystone?"

"Met a million people. Kept getting lost looking for the bathroom. But, Tim, about Steve, I think I better tell you. I think it's time. You want to hear?"

Tim gulped. *Did he? Yes, he'd always wanted to hear. But now was he sure?* "Laura, you needn't—"

"Yes, but you're going to be my husband, and I want you to know. Once you do, you might change your mind."

Tim faced her, pulled her closer to him. Her green eyes were wide, the pupils dilated as if in fear, and tears started to trickle down her cheeks. *Shit, now I've made her cry.* But she read his mind.

"Tim, ignore the tears—just listen?" She rushed on. "When you came up to Traverse City to take Patrick to Philadelphia in the medevac plane, you walked into a catastrophe."

Tim had known that something must have happened between Laura and her husband, but his priority had been getting her son to CHOP and onto the operating table.

"Remember when you and me and those other surgical residents went to Montreal for that international conference?"

"Laura, I have never forgiven myself for my uncouth behavior. I knew you were married. I'd had too much to drink. Every time I think about it, and I have thought about it more times than I care to count, I can't believe I was such a consummate ass.

And you know what? I've never even apologized. Well, I will now. I am very sorry."

"Yes, you had had a few drinks," Laura said. "I wasn't insulted. I was more concerned about you cheating on my friend Rosie."

"That blizzard," Tim said, feeling a little bit off the hook for his boorish behavior. "And you never making it out the next morning. We couldn't find you. I was so damned worried about you. Are you still upset that we left without you? We were on the surgical schedule, and if we hadn't gotten back, Dr. Monroe would have had our—"

"I was with Dr. Monroe," Laura said.

"You were with...?" He must not have heard her. Laura Nelson, third-year medical student, mother of four little kids, wife of Steve—*with* the venerated chief of surgery, *the* Dr. David Monroe?

"Tim, I've never told anyone. No one."

Tim felt himself inch away from Laura. He needed more space. Her tears, now copious, had soaked the neckline of her t-shirt, and he groped in his pocket for a handkerchief and wordlessly handed it to her. He had wanted to know the truth, but had not expected what then would have been a scandal—still was a bombshell. She had rebuffed his advances. Now he finds out she was sleeping with Dr. Monroe? Tim tried to remember if Monroe had been married. Oh yeah, it came back to him, the socialite wife, picture always in the *Detroit Free Press* for supporting one charity or another.

"I know you must hate me, and I should have told you before we spoke to the kids about getting married."

Was he supposed to ignore Laura's serious sobs? "Laura, I don't care," Tim said, reaching toward her, pulling him close in his arms. "I guess I'm shocked, yes, I have to admit. For two seconds. Look, that was how many years ago?"

"There's more." Laura's complexion had lost every trace of color. "Patrick is David's child." Laura all but choked on the words she left for last: "David is dead because of me."

Tim knew his whole future with Laura would hinge on his reaction. But how does one react to a double blast like that? He'd known that back in Traverse City, when he'd picked up Patrick for transport to Philadelphia, that Steve had cruelly rejected an innocent nine-year-old child facing major heart surgery. But he'd had no inkling of why—and now he did.

And then Steve had been killed. And Tim had pushed the Laura-Patrick-Steve drama into remote memory. So Steve had discovered Laura's secret. Tim held Laura's eyes. His voice did not quaver when he said, "Laura, what's past is past. We have the future. You and I. And your kids. Our future. Together."

He felt her body go slack and, for a minute, he thought she'd fainted. But when he folded his arms around her, he felt her erratic breaths as her tears started to subside.

"Steve never knew about David," she said in a small voice, straightening up, looking back into Tim's eyes, now moist with his own tears. "But when I gave blood, he did find out that, genetically, he was not Patrick's father. Until then, he and Patrick had the idyllic father-son relationship, just as everyone said."

"But Patrick obviously remembers the good stuff, thanks to you."

"All the kids missed Steve, but Patrick the most. Ironic, huh?"

"That must have been tough on you. What did you tell Steve—about the father?"

"I told Steve I'd been raped." Laura looked as if she might elaborate, but instead she dropped her eyes.

Told him she'd been raped?

"Laura, please believe that I love and respect you for telling me this." Tim tilted her head upward so their gazes met. "And you can trust me to tell no one."

"Thank you, Tim. I don't deserve you. I'd understand if—"

"Okay if I ask one more question, just to clarify what you said about Dr. Monroe's death?" Tim could never think of Dr. Monroe as *David*. "Dr. Monroe was shot by a young punk at your graduation. Remember, I was there to congratulate Rosie.

Dr. Monroe was standing over by your family." Tim hesitated at the memory—he specifically recalled that the chief of surgery had been holding Laura's baby. *His own baby.*

"What could you have had to do with that random murder? That had nothing to do with you."

"I don't know," Laura said, her tears only a trickle now. "But, Tim, what am I going to do about Patrick? Should I tell him? He's twenty-two years old. Doesn't he deserve to know? And the other kids? Especially Mike, he has to know something horrible happened to make their dad treat Patrick that way. Mike was four-teen—old enough to—"

"Laura, that's a lot to think about right now. We can face that together. Down the road. In the meantime, let's just move on. I'm grateful for your honesty. I don't think we should dwell on the past. Okay?" Tim tilted her head, their lips met, and the kiss they shared cemented their love.

As Tim cleaned up the kitchen after dinner, Laura sat at the counter, composed now, recounting her first day at work. She'd met her staff. Too soon to form an opinion of them. Losing their beloved Dr. Minn had shattered the soul of Keystone's research department.

"It's going to take time," she said.

"Anybody you know? That you'd met during the clinical tri-als or getting ready for the Advisory Committee meeting?"

"I got to know the VP of regulatory affairs pretty well, and the medical director, and a few of the physicians. When I did the trials, the clinical research associates and the medical monitors came down to Tampa to scour through all my records. Never met such sticklers on detail."

"I've done several drug trials, beta blockers in kids, new anti-biotics. One from Keystone Pharma, the analogue of the one that saved Natalie during that epidemic. Picowell is the brand name. But look at me, telling you this, you use Picowell all the time in thoracic surgery."

Once he said this, Tim reached over to touch her intact

arm. "I'm sorry," he murmured. She would no longer be doing any surgery.

"Tim, stop it. Stop trying to be sensitive. I'm in a new career now. I want to focus. I don't have time to worry about my old one."

"They're going to have a hell of a time replacing you in Tampa."

"I just hope they go with Ed Plant for chief of surgery. I'd trust my research and my patients to him. But it's not my problem," Laura said with finality. "I have to focus on getting to know my research department. I've never had five hundred people reporting to me. How will I ever learn their names?"

"If that turns out to be your worst problem, you'll be in good shape."

"You know, Tim, I think I might actually like this job. I sense everybody's commitment to developing new drugs that will help so many people."

Tim started up the dishwasher and turned to take Laura's elbow. "Let's get to bed early," he said. "Sounds like you're going to have a busy day at work tomorrow, but don't forget your PT appointment at Hahnemann in the afternoon."

"I forgot to tell you that Keystone arranged to have my therapist come out to the company. They've set aside a private room off the huge workout area they had designed and built for the employees."

In the bedroom, as Tim pulled back the comforter, Laura said as an afterthought, "I did have one strange phone call today."

Tim peeled back the sheet and patted her side of the bed. She sat, cradling her arm and continued, "Well, maybe it wasn't that strange, but a young woman I met at the FDA Advisory Meeting called. She's a research scientist at Replica, the company we bought Immunone from."

Tim suppressed a grin at her use of "we." Laura's transition from top surgeon to corporate management seemed to be on track.

"What did she want?"

"That's just it, I'm not sure. She tracked me down through the hospital in Tampa. Didn't even know I was at Keystone until somebody in my old department told her. Said she wanted to know what was happening in the approval process of Immunone. That she needed this information. That the FDA wasn't keeping her updated."

"No surprise there," Tim said.

"The FDA never keeps anybody updated, I told her. She seemed surprised, as if she deserved to be in the approval loop."

Tim helped Laura remove her blouse. "Is she a medical doctor or a researcher?"

"Researcher. PhD. Sounded naïve about how the US regulatory system works. About confidentiality barriers between industry and government. Didn't seem familiar with the concept. Must be different in her country."

"She's not American?"

"No. She's from a Middle Eastern country. Iraq? Iran? Pakistan? Based on skin color and a very slight accent, but I could be wrong. A beautiful woman though, and if she had something to do with discovering the Immunone series, definitely brilliant."

"How'd you leave it with her?" Tim asked.

"Oh, another reason why I think Middle East. Her name: Adawia Abdul. I left it that we will hear from the FDA on the FDA's timetable. I did advise her not to contact the FDA, especially the upper brass, that they don't appreciate end runs from anyone in industry."

Tim had removed Laura's blouse and bra, and slipped a sleeveless nightgown over her head, letting it drape over her shoulder. "One day on the job and you're an expert on FDA strategy. You're right though. I've been in enough drug and device company meetings to know that. Now, lean back, and I'll pull off your pantyhose."

"Tim, thanks, but I think I can manage with one hand."

CHAPTER TWENTY-FOUR

Karolee's funeral had been on Monday, the earliest Jake could arrange after the authorities released her body. The ceremony fell short of what Karolee would have expected, but Jake didn't have the inclination or the energy to put on an extravagant event. She had no religious affiliation, neither did he, so the services took place at the local funeral chapel and interment at the historic Rockville Cemetery, former site of F. Scott Fitzgerald's grave.

When Mark's wife arrived with the baby, she'd volunteered to select Karolee's burial outfit. How ironic. Claire's taste was nothing like Karolee's; Claire chose the only dumpy dress Karolee owned. When Jake had the sense to reach out to Karolee's business partner for help in selecting music for the brief service, the restaurant offered to host a post-cemetery luncheon in her honor. A nice gesture for the many Karolee admirers who wanted a free meal at the trendy Limelight Bistro. Jake was relieved of any duties beyond the basics, not that he had any such intentions. His sentiments: Good-bye, Karolee, and good riddance. Now, about the will?

Jake and Mark met with Karolee's attorney the following morning at nine o'clock, to talk about transferring her assets and filing death documents. Jake and Karolee filed separate tax returns, neither consulting with the other. His as a government employee was so basic he could handle it with an online tax program. Hers required a tax attorney. Karolee ran the Limelight Bistro business; her co-owner Max Scarpetti ran the kitchen. From the beginning, his wife had been secretive about her financial affairs, keeping her own counsel, her own bank account, and only rarely did she share her hefty income with him. They split normal household expenses fifty-fifty. He hated that she had thousands left over for stylish hair, expensive clothes. He got by month to month. Any leftovers funded his monthly card game and fishing excursions in the summer with a few pals.

Jake salivated when he thought about Karolee's bank account. It would be all his now. At least he assumed it would. He'd never bothered with a will and neither had she. Now, as he and Mark gathered around her tax attorney's desk, he wondered whether he should offer Mark a token of the inheritance. He was their only child, and now he had a child of his own, the scrawny, irritable baby Amanda. He hoped they'd leave with the baby tomorrow morning. He couldn't take much more all-night, high-pitched crying. Had Mark ever been that aggravating? Jake didn't think so.

"Jake, Mark," the lawyer said, as soon as a round of coffee had been served, "Karolee had a will that I will now read."

"You must be mistaken," Jake interrupted. "Karolee didn't have a will. She would have told me." Jake looked at Mark, whose face betrayed nothing.

"I have the document, gentlemen. Written only three weeks ago. Signed and notarized. I've been after her to draw up a will for years now, and all of a sudden she decides it's time. Makes you wonder whether she had a premonition, doesn't it?" The graying lawyer with the sad, baggy eyes, pointedly studied Jake.

Shit. Had Karolee somehow found out about Addie? Jake's mind sorted through the possibilities, not coming up with any specific incident. Say she had, did she tell her lawyer? Would he be bound to confidentiality? Would he go to the police?

"Well, I digress. The tenets of her will are simple. Her interest in Limelight Bistro goes to her business partner, Max Scarpetti."

That's gotta be a million-dollar value, maybe two, Jake figured. *Shit. Had Karolee had something going with Max?* They spent hours almost every night together. Made sense, didn't it? About the same age. Only Max was married. But so was Karolee. Married didn't mean monogamous. What's good for the gander—

"Her stock portfolio and bank accounts are willed to her son, Mark. Except for a million dollars held in trust for Amanda Harter, a minor."

Karolee had more than a million dollars saved up? And she wouldn't buy him diddly-shit. The miserly bitch got what she deserved.

Jake watched Mark's eyes light up and, at that moment, he hated his son. Hate was a strong word, resented was closer.

What about me? What do I get for living with a mean-spirited bitch for thirty-one years?

The lawyer droned on, but there wasn't much to listen for. Not much else left. The house they owned jointly. All household goods would go to him. Karolee had willed him her BMW sedan.

"How much do I get after the baby's portion is taken out?" Mark asked, probably in anticipation of Claire's first question.

"This will all have to go through probate," the lawyer said. "The estate taxes will be significant, but I'd say at least another million, Mark, when all is said and done."

"A million dollars," Jake said aloud. "A million fucking dollars."

"Dad, seriously, you didn't know about the money? You look, well—stunned."

Karolee's lawyer studied him. Would he tell the police that Jake Harter seemed genuinely surprised he didn't get his wife's estate?

"Not surprised at all," he lied. "Your mother knew I'd be fine with my job and the house. What more do I need? She knew I disliked everything about the restaurant. And now that you have a child, Mark, it makes sense. I just didn't think we'd lose her for many, many years to come. Just tragic. That's what still has me stunned."

And when Addie and I get the Immunone money, I won't need your measly million.

"Well, do what you have to do to probate this will. I have a job to do and must get back to work. Mark, I'll see you at home tonight."

"Dad, I'm leaving this evening. Claire and I and the baby. We have a direct flight to Miami. We'll be sleeping in our own beds tonight. I'm sorry, but we thought we were an imposition, and the baby needs her familiar surroundings."

"Suit yourself," Jake said, rising to leave, heading for the door without as much as another nod toward his son. His heartbeat accelerated. For the first time since Karolee had been shot, he'd be free to see Addie. Or would he?

CHAPTER TWENTY-FIVE

Addie realized Jake could lose his job if the FDA found out he'd been sharing information about a drug evaluation. Until the last week, he'd been her pipeline into the agency's deliberations on Immunone. But why had she heard nothing since he'd left last Wednesday morning and not shown up that evening?

For months she'd been able to follow, step by step, as the pharmacologists and the toxicologists cleared it, as the results of the clinical trials came in even better than she'd dared to hope. She knew the Chemistry, Manufacturing, and Controls—the CMC section of the NDA—sailed through the FDA department best known for nitpicking and stalling.

Had she been using Jake for her own purposes? Addie asked herself. The American concept of confidentiality was difficult to fathom. She did appreciate the risks he took, but so did he appreciate the rewards she gave him. Fair exchange.

He'd pursued her and she'd enjoyed his attention. His crew-cut hair was turning gray, but he was muscular, kept himself in good shape, working out in a gym, lifting weights. He wasn't a tall man, was her height, actually, five foot nine, but attractive, well dressed, and he treated her well.

She used to fantasize about what it would be like to live with Jake in a stable relationship. She was thirty-four, Jake fifty-five. Did the age gap matter? She didn't think so, but now that he was a grandfather? Jake kept telling her he loved her. Whatever that meant. Addie had never been in love. She'd dated a few men, always cutting off the relationship when it started to get serious. She may not dress like a conservative Muslim woman, but she was one—and until Jake, a virgin. She'd always known that someday her parents would force her—force may be too strong a word— into an arranged marriage. She dearly loved her parents, always had assumed she would follow their wishes and accept their choice of a husband.

She couldn't explain how it had happened with Jake, and she'd certainly never imagined a man could be so passionate about sex. But the truth was, she'd thrown away twelve years of virginity in America only to start up an affair with Jake. *What impact would that have if a future husband expected a virgin?*

Addie learned of the brutal murder of Karolee Harter only when she'd arrived at work the next day, Thursday morning. An outsider to American gossip, she never paid much attention to the chatter around the coffee machine. That morning she'd been particularly uninterested, having slept little after Badur's/Dru's visit. All night long, she'd tried to figure out what he'd wanted, and how she was going to keep him and Jake from crossing paths. She was filling her cup with water for tea, when her colleagues' conversation made her jerk her mug so violently that she spilled hot water onto her other hand and on her pantsuit jacket.

"Addie, are you okay?" They all seemed genuinely concerned.

"What did you say about Jake Harter's wife?"

"Let me take that mug. You'd better put ice on your hand." The woman closest to Addie reached out to steady her and to take the cup out of her hand.

"I'm okay," Addie said.

A young male technician turned to scrutinize her. "Guess you don't read the papers, Boss. Mrs. Harter was out of town, and when she arrived home, she walked into a robbery. Whoever was in there must have shot her. They say she was dead when Jake Harter found her."

"Jake found her?" Addie echoed, immediately hoping "Jake" didn't sound too familiar.

"Yeah, but she'd been dead—what'd it say, a couple of hours by then?"

So that's why he hadn't shown up. He'd been at his house with the police. When she remembered she had called his house, her knees started to buckle. The woman who'd answered must not have been Jake's wife.

Her colleagues started to dissipate, returning to their respective labs, but when Addie lingered, the young tech beside her asked, "Did you know Mrs. Harter?"

"I never met her," Addie said. "Of course, I know Jake Harter from the FDA."

"Oh," said the tech, as they headed for the lab. "I thought you may have had a social relationship with the Harters."

"Why would you think that?" she said, afraid to ask, but needing to know if someone knew about her and Jake.

"No reason," he said, "just thought I may have seen—"

"His position at the FDA," she interrupted. "You know how important he is to Immunonc's approval, and how crucial that approval is to Replica. That's all I think about, getting that drug approved."

"I can attest to that, Dr. Abdul. Nobody works harder than you do. The rumor mill says your share will be a whole lot of money. No wonder you're so worried about the Harter murder. You know, they always look at the husband. What do you think?"

"What I think is, let's get to work."

From then on, Addie had refused to be drawn in to any speculation about what happened to Jake Harter's wife. She'd been tempted to go to the funeral, to stay in the background, just to make eye contact with Jake, to signal that she needed to talk to him. But she couldn't risk a public encounter. Surely, there'd be police lurking around. Would they be looking for her? Because of that phone call? Could they track the number to her apartment?

Addie had made one other desperate attempt to find out what was happening with Immunone. On Monday, she'd called Tampa City Hospital to talk to that nice woman doctor she'd seen at the Advisory Committee meeting, Dr. Laura Nelson. But to her great surprise, she'd been told Dr. Nelson now worked at Keystone Pharma. Since the only phone number she had for Keystone was Dr. Minn's, she tried it. A voice answered, "Dr. Nelson's office." Addie identified herself and asked to speak to Dr. Nelson and was told to hold. While she waited for Dr. Nelson to pick up, she felt a pang of sadness. Poor Dr. Minn. Two deaths in her world in one week, unpleasant coincidence since both related to Immunone and, worse yet, each potentially could slow down the approval: Minn, a key player, dead; Jake, distracted because of his wife's death. Even though, Addie had to conclude, he wasn't *close* to Mrs. Harter.

Dr. Nelson had been cordial on the phone; pointed out this was her first day on the job at Keystone; she knew Addie was the inventor of the drug; respected her; appreciated her. Bottom line for Addie: nothing.

Badur/Dru had insisted that Addie determine the probable date of Immunone's approval. He'd demanded the legal papers pertaining to the payout she'd get from Replica once they got the funds from Keystone Pharma, and she'd given him a copy of the contract. Dru was a finance man, and she hoped he'd be ready to facilitate the transfer process to get the money into her hands. Only it would never get to her hands if Immunone's approval was delayed and her father summoned her.

After Dru left her a week ago, she'd slept little, trying in vain to account for his sudden intrusion. How had he known about her and Jake? How could she keep him and Jake from crossing paths? Addie considered her reality if she returned to Baghdad. Did she have the faith to go back and live in a place where an Islamic woman's status was as low as that of animals in the field?

What if she married Jake? His wife was dead, so no waiting

for a divorce. If he embraced Islam, would her father approve? After so-called Desert Storm, Iraqi and American relations kept deteriorating. Ten waves of the invasive IAEA inspections. The harder they look, the more they come up with nothing, but George W. Bush's obsession about nuclear weapons in her country made him seem determined to bring Iraq to its knees. As an Iraqi—especially one whose family has ties to Saddam—she could lose her green card and be sent home. Marriage to a US citizen could keep her here for as long as she cared to stay.

Addie couldn't get much accomplished that day, and she sensed her co-workers' concern, overhearing, "What's the matter with Addie?"

Her technician again asked her if she was okay.

CHAPTER TWENTY-SIX

For Jake, Thursday morning couldn't come soon enough. He'd set up a meeting on Immunone at 11:00. He'd asked the two medical officers responsible for the drug's review to attend: Dr. Karl Hayes, the young Turk who'd done most of the actual review; Dr. Susan Ridley, the senior reviewer who'd been around the block a few times, a lazy woman who would take the easy way out rather than make the effort to determine the real deal.

To set the stage for the meeting, Jake had dropped by his office late Tuesday after the meeting with Karolee's attorney to issue a brief memo to Karl and Susan. In it, he expressed his concerns about missing laboratory data. He wanted to plant the seed, even though he wouldn't return full force to the FDA until Thursday.

To play the proper grieving husband, he stayed home Wednesday. All day long he paced, anxious to get back to work, anxious to be with Addie, but needing to play it safe. The cops might stop by for more of their endless questions. Prior to the funeral, he'd had two lengthy sessions with the Rockville detectives in their office. He was convinced he'd done a decent job playing the distraught, traumatized husband. Married thirty-one years. Now desolate. "At least I have my work," he kept telling them. "My important work at the FDA has meaning. It's what will get me through this tragedy."

Now, preparing for his meeting with the medical officers,

Jake laid out on the small conference table two copies of a PowerPoint presentation. The top page showed a tabulation of Immunone adverse reactions. Next, a compilation of the most serious adverse reactions, displayed according to body system. Each report had three columns: active drug, placebo, and statistical difference. Under these reports was a tabulation of all deaths; beneath that, a one-page report on each of the thirteen deaths that had occurred in the clinical trial.

Karl was the first to arrive, rushing toward Jake, flinging his arm around his shoulder. "Jake, we didn't expect you in this week. I told Susan I'd cover for you. Help put together reports, that kind of thing."

When Jake tried to pull away, Karl gripped his arm and squeezed. "I'm so sorry, man, about your wife. Who could have done such a thing? Any leads on—"

"No, nothing. I can tell you that it's very frustrating—"

"Jake." They were interrupted by a tall, sturdy woman, with frosted gray hair hanging in an old-fashioned pageboy. "You sure you should be in? I mean, there must be so many things to take care of, I can't imagine." She paused. "Or did you come in to say you needed some time off? I could understand, but we'd be short-handed at a critical time. We're sitting on the imminent approval of Immunone, and I don't need to tell you, the role of the project manager is key."

"Don't worry, Susan, I'm not taking time off. I need to work to take my mind off poor Karolee. Every time I think about that monster who took her life, I just fall apart. No, I want to be here."

Susan relaxed, took a seat at the table, reached for Jake's information packet.

Karl released his grip, and Jake took the seat at the table across from Susan, leaving to Karl the chair by the second stack of papers. "By the way, thank you again, both of you, for coming to her service. It meant a lot to me."

Both reviewers nodded politely, eyeing the stack of papers in front of them.

"I asked for this meeting first thing when I got back," Jake said, "because I'm worried. Worried about the Immunone safety report. Something doesn't seem quite right."

Two sets of quizzical eyebrows rose, and Jake continued, "I kept thinking about the deaths that occurred in the trials. Yes, we had a write-up on each, but something's nagging at me: where was the supporting information? The company is obliged to send the source documents, the actual hospital reports—"

"Come on, Jake," Susan said, "Karl reviewed all that. Right, Karl?"

"Yeah, sure. Where are you going with this, Jake?"

"You know it's my job to make sure all the data is compiled properly."

"Yes, but—" Susan started to push back her chair.

"In front of you, you have the adverse reactions tabulations. Overall AR Report, the Serious AR Report, and the Death Reconciliation Report. I am concerned there are discrepancies as well as missing data from the latter."

"Something missing in the Death Report?" Susan asked, tossing her pageboy-styled hair. "Impossible."

Here's where Jake had to tread carefully. He needed these two reviewers on his side. He could not afford to challenge their competency. He had to make them believe there was foul play that did not involve them. That they were the innocent, hoodwinked victims.

"When I went to collate the deaths, I found the individual reports, but the support documents were missing."

"I've been a medical reviewer for twenty-seven years," Susan said. "I go back to the Middle Ages when we didn't collect support data. So what's the big deal? We've got the reports. They look good. Active drug outperforms placebo in safety. What more do you want?"

Jake gulped. He wasn't expecting his point to be simply brushed aside.

Then Karl spoke. "Susan, source documents are critical to quality control. Before we had them, clinical investigators could simply make up data so they'd get paid by the drug companies. Blatant fraud. I've seen the case studies."

"Bullshit," Susan said. "You reviewed that data, Karl. You signed off. You'd never sign off without crossing all the i's and dotting all the t's."

"That'd be dotting the i's and crossing the t's. Never mind." Karl frowned at Jake. "Susan's right. I did check the backup. I reviewed the hospital reports. The works. Everything was in place."

"Let's just get this damn Immunone approved so we'll be out of the spotlight," Susan said, looking ready to get up and walk out. "We've got a backlog of drugs that have a lot of legitimate concerns waiting for review."

"Look, you two, I'm just doing my job. There's nobody who wants to get Immunone behind us as much as I do." Jake knew he had to kiss up to Susan while he kept Karl on his side. Susan and Karl were medical doctors, and when it came to drug approvals, they called the shots. Yay or nay. He was a project manager, a paper pusher. He facilitated, he didn't decide. "Our backlog is crushing, so I agree with Susan, but I couldn't live with myself if I failed to bring this strange, even suspicious, finding to your attention."

"For God's sake, Jake, you're that concerned?" Susan flipped through the pages of the document.

"Not wanting to waste your time, I put this information package together." Jake gestured to the stacks and turned on the overhead projector.

"Shit, Jake, your wife was just murdered and you went to all this trouble?" Karl glanced at Susan. "Of course, we'll go through this with you."

Jake dimmed the lights and proceeded with his presentation.

Susan and Karl's eyes glazed over when he presented the adverse reaction charts. Again. The data were tabulated according to the systems in the body. Jake had highlighted several line items in the cardiovascular category: arrhythmias, tachycardia, long QT syndrome, nonspecific ECG changes, high serum potassium level, low serum potassium.

"We've reviewed all this how many times?" Susan said. "The Immunone group is no worse than placebo."

"I know. I'm underscoring these values for perspective. Setting the stage."

Susan flipped to the next page. The severe reactions—those causing hospitalization or permanent injury. Again, Jake had highlighted the cardiovascular system. Again, there was no difference between the active drug, Immunone, and placebo. Jake pointed it out to preempt another Susan outburst. "Turn to the Deaths," he said, when she tossed her head again.

"Okay," Karl said, "but I can probably recite these details in my sleep. Phase Two, one death on Immunone, two on placebo. Phase Three, three on Immunone, seven on placebo. Pretty powerful evidence that the drug needs to be approved. The sooner the better. More transplants every day. Imagine how many lives will be saved once Keystone Pharma moves into kidney and liver transplants."

"Their strategy to go with lung transplants rather than kidneys has always baffled me," Susan said. "Like, why go for the smaller market, not the much larger one?"

"They figured we'd approve a drug for the lower incidence procedure with limited data," Jake said. "Now, let me point out the problem here. Take a look at the four deaths in the active treatment group." He flipped from the tabulated death report to individual narratives summarizing the circumstances of each patient death. One page per patient who died during the clinical trial.

"Yes?" Susan asked. "I've seen these. Karl wrote them."

"The source documents are missing," Jake said. "The hospital records surrounding the time of death."

"Can't be," Karl said, riffling through the pack. "Compliance always checks on them. They have their checklists."

"I can't find them. I wanted to double-check the blood chemistries. Especially potassium, as we have an arrhythmia and an ischemic stroke. I was looking for long QT syndrome."

"What are you saying, Jake?" Susan said, head bent, scanning the reports.

"Long QT syndrome?" Karl asked. "You're not a physician. What do you know about prolonged QT?"

You're not a physician. How many times over his career had Jake heard this demeaning line? Second-class citizen. That's all he'd ever been. Little jerks like Karl lording it over him. It'd be fun causing him to squirm when the integrity of his report was brought into question.

"Look, I've been to enough advisory committee meetings, heard enough cardiology consultants, to know potassium plays a role in fatal arrhythmias. Torsades de pointes is a known side effect for several drugs. I want to be sure we had the potassium levels at the time of death. And the actual electrocardiograms."

"You sure went out of your way, Jake," Susan said. "Unusual for you."

"Only curiosity at first. It wasn't until I couldn't find them that I became alarmed. I didn't want you to make an approval decision without knowing this."

"Shit," Susan said, "I don't need this grief. This is a hell of a good drug."

"Just give me some time to track down the documents. Keystone Pharma must have duplicates. Then we'll know for sure the fatal event had nothing to do with torsades. If there's a connection, we can still approve the drug, just put in a warning for long QT." Jake would take his time contacting the company. And with their key scientist dead, the company in disarray—Yes, it will take some time. As much time as Jake needed it to take.

"Susan," Karl said, "Jake may have something here. I mean, better we identify this now. Get the warning on the package insert and not have to endure the criticism that we missed something. Right?"

"Shit," she said, glaring at Jake. "You're a pain in the ass." She flung the package of papers onto the table, got up, and stalked out of the conference room.

"Karl," Jake said. "I'll work to get the documents."

Karl stood, neatly stacking Jake's reports and tucking them into his folder. "Let's just hope those documents support my summaries," he said. "If we have to go back to an advisory committee, it's my head on the chopping block."

"I think they'll do the job, Karl—unless—" he shook his head in frustration, "there's something more sinister going on."

CHAPTER TWENTY-SEVEN

Laura had stopped taking narcotic analgesics, unwilling to surrender to their mind-addling effects, and was paying the price. Excruciating pain, radiating from her hand all the way up her arm to her shoulder. She'd given lectures on pain management, about all the different nerve tracks and where they ended up in the brain. About how to describe pain: crushing, throbbing, stabbing, lancinating, searing, burning. Right now, she could claim all of the above.

She'd just finished a torturous hydrotherapy session in a private treatment room on the premises of Keystone Pharma headquarters. Her young male therapist had recommended acupuncture, and she had agreed to a session before her scheduled therapy on Monday.

Waiting alone in the treatment room for the worst of the painful impulses to abate, she thought about the rest of her day and the approaching weekend. The chairman, Paul Parnell, was to officially introduce her to the rest of the board of directors at an informal, after-work cocktail party in the boardroom. At just the thought that Tim would escort her, Laura felt a smile break through her grimace.

During the last two weeks, as she'd struggled with her crushing injury, totally changed career paths, and began a new job, Tim had become her rock. She wondered how she could have survived without him, aware and amazed that he pervaded her every thought. Even as she sat here, waiting for the pain to diminish to a tolerable level, she could feel his presence, always at one with her. Laura treasured her independence, would never sacrifice it, but this sense of interdependency just felt natural. She didn't remember ever feeling this with Steve. Maybe in the beginning, but she didn't think so. What she had with Tim, she knew she would treasure forever.

On her way to her office—a work in progress while the decorator and his assistants swarmed the space, clearly delighted to depart from manly office furnishings as they envisioned a rose-and-peach-colored décor—Laura stopped for a word with her new secretary. The woman had been devoted to Dr. Minn, and Laura hoped she could eventually fill his shoes. Back in Tampa, her secretary for fifteen years knew all her idiosyncrasies, knew all her kids, knew most of her secrets—but not all.

The thought of Tampa reminded her of Lonnie Greenwood, who'd called her at Keystone yesterday. Again, leaving a message. Said he was back in Detroit. Needed to talk to her urgently. Wanted to remind her that he was a friend of the Jones family. *What will the Joneses do if they find out I killed one of their own? Would it matter if they knew Johnny raped me at knifepoint, threatened my life?*

"Dr. Abdul called you again." Back in the moment, Laura, listened. "Was very insistent you call her back. The one from Replica, the company that discovered Immunone. Dr. Minn thought very highly of her."

"Yes, I know who she is," said Laura. She caught the woman staring at her bandaged hand, still supported in a sling.

When would they stop gaping at her disabled hand?

Another annoyance. Everyone here assumed she knew nothing about Immunone. She'd been the lead clinical investigator, probably knew more than most in the building. "I'll call her back," Laura said, moving toward her office.

"Dr. Abdul, this is Dr. Nelson."

"Thanks for returning my call, Dr. Nelson. I hate to bother

you, but have you heard anything about Immunone's approval? I tried calling the FDA, but no one returned my call."

"Dr. Abdul, I told you, they don't want industry calls."

"But the FBI called me today. I got worried. Thought something was wrong."

Laura thought she meant FDA, not FBI. Why would the FBI be involved? She said nothing, waited.

"I'm not an American citizen. Oh, I have a green card. Everything legal, but I don't understand. In your country, can the FDA and the FBI and the CIA work together? Anything to do with the DEA, even though Immunone is not a narcotic? Not even close in its pharmacology."

"Whoa," Laura said. "You have me confused. What did you say about the FBI?"

"Not really FBI, the police, but aren't they the same?"

Laura didn't intend to advise anyone on law enforcement. "It can be complicated," she said.

"Dr. Nelson, I'm scared. I got a call from the police. They want to question me about the murder of Jake Harter's wife. You know who he is? He's the FDA man in charge of Immunone. I must know what is happening at the FDA. You speak to these people. You can find out."

"But why do the police want to question you?" Laura asked, the pain in her hand diminished now to a level that allowed her to think. And the woman was wrong about Jake Harter; he was not in charge. He was the project manager, not a medical officer.

"I called his house," the woman said. "I called his house the day his wife died. They must have traced my call. So they know."

"They know what?" Laura asked, perplexed, getting annoyed.

"That he was...I can't tell you. Can you call him? Jake Harter?"

Jake? She called his home? Could this woman be having a relationship with Harter? A real no-no. A flagrant conflict of interest. As a foreigner, the woman may not know it, but Harter's job would be on the line.

"No, I can't do that, Dr. Abdul," Laura said. "And you

should not call him either. As for the police, my only advice is to answer their questions truthfully." Laura remembered her brief conversation with the attractive Middle Eastern-looking woman at the FDA advisory meeting. She'd had beautiful, dark brown eyes, luxuriant black hair, and a distinctive, husky voice with almost no accent.

"They want to talk to me tomorrow. At the police station."

Why was she telling her this? She hardly knew the woman.

Laura could hear muffled sobs. "Don't worry," she relented. "Call me back on Monday if there's any connection between the police questions and Immunone. Okay?"

"Oh, thank you, Dr. Nelson," the woman said between sniffles.

How would I feel in a foreign country if the police wanted to question me? Bad enough when you're in your own home town and have a husband to support you.

Laura concluded the strange call, returned a few more, then headed up the handsomely curved flight of stairs to the board-room to meet her fellow Keystone board members.

CHAPTER TWENTY-EIGHT

The spouse was always the prime suspect, and Jake realized it'd take some time before the dust settled, and Karolee's case slipped into oblivion. He knew he'd be in for more police questioning, but he hadn't expected cops at his door at nine o'clock on a Saturday morning. Didn't government employees take weekends off?

He'd already talked to a mix of detectives. He'd repeated his story ad nauseum, should have recorded it so he could flip on the tape for them. Today he opened the door to the two lead detectives working Karolee's murder: Detective Nathan Booker, senior of the two, a skinny, balding black man with a hyperactive nervous demeanor; Detective Calvin Finley, pudgy, pasty-white, with a lazy let's-make-this-quick-and-easy approach.

He would invite them in, offer them coffee, nothing else. Everything in the house was stale or spoiled. Karolee, being in the restaurant business, had managed their food chain. *How many years had it been since he'd seen the inside of a supermarket?*

Once the detectives left today, Jake would decide whether or not it was safe to contact Addie. He missed her more every day, wanted to tell her about his role in Karolee's death, but, of course, he wouldn't.

"Come in, Officers," he greeted them.

"Mr. Harter," the older cop said. "Remember me? Detective Nathan Booker, Rockville PD. My partner, Detective Calvin Finley."

"Yes, I remember you both," Jake said. "Let me take your coats."

Jake left them standing as he hung both outer garments in his hall closet, the one just beside where Karolee's body ended up, and the one leading to his gun cabinet—which the crime scene techs had not discovered. The crime scene residue was all gone now, thanks to the cleaning crew the Limelight Bistro had sent to restore order to the house.

Booker and Finley wore suits, button-down shirts, no ties— maybe in deference to the weekend. Booker's suit was pressed, his shirt crisp; Finley looked like a slob in his baggy suit and a wrinkled graying-white shirt. Neither wore a smile.

"Sit," Jake suggested, his demeanor perfectly relaxed, cooperative. "Would you like coffee? I was about to make some."

They nodded a yes, and Jake was glad for the diversion. Thankfully, coffee was the one kitchen chore he could manage. "Sugar? Milk?"

"Neither," said Booker, the skinny, elderly one.

"Both," said the younger, overweight Finley.

Jake left them in the living room while he took his time brewing the coffee and locating powdered creamer.

"You've been back at work, Mr. Harter?" Booker said. "The FDA. Seems rather soon, but I hear in the news an important drug for organ transplants is about to get approved. You involved in that?"

"I am," said Jake, not sure whether he should highlight his key role or let it slide.

"I have two daughters with PhDs from Howard. Biochemistry, both of them. Just finishing up. One works in a drug company, discovering new drugs like the one you're working on. The other just got hired as a research scientist at Georgetown. Gotta admit, I'm proud of those girls. Since I caught this case, and since you're in the drug business, I've been asking them some questions. So I'm up on that new drug, Immunone."

Great. A detective who does his homework.

"Well, don't worry. I'm not going to grill you about your job. I know all that's confidential. Working in the government sector, you have to be careful about everything you say. Right, Calvin?"

Detective Finley had slumped back into the chair, but hearing his name, he rubbed his eyes and sat up.

"My young partner here has a new baby at home. Doesn't get much sleep."

"Yeah," Finley said, "so let's get this over with, Booker. You want to start or what?"

Booker sat back. "Why don't you lead off? I'll jump in if I think of something."

Finley went over the whole scenario. Went over the timeline. Twice. When did Jake leave work? When did his car break down? How long did he wait before getting help? Did he ask anyone else for help before Frank Barker? How long did it take the tow truck to get there? Jake knew they'd have verified all the timing with the Good Samaritan, the phone company, the tow truck company, the garage, maybe even McDonald's where he'd stopped for a Big Mac and fries.

Finley had just asked what time Jake found the body.

"Eight forty-five, eight fifty, about that time," Jake said.

"You trip over her?" Booker interrupted. "Or what?"

"Uh, what?" Jake said, needing time to think. *The lights. What had he told the cops about the lights? Had the porch lights been on? Yes. Had the hall light inside been on? Shit, he couldn't remember what he'd told them before. He'd only trip on the body if the lights had been off.* "Not exactly trip. I didn't fall down, but my shoe bumped...her head."

Yes, her head had been facing the front door.

"So did you see her the moment you stepped inside?" Booker asked.

"Not really. I must have been distracted. My foot touched her first." Jake lowered his head, made himself sniffle. "Look, Detectives, I'm trying to be as helpful as I can. I want you to find out who did this to Karolee, but to relive finding her, this is so difficult. Hard realizing I'll never see her alive, that she's gone—"

"Yeah," Finley said. "Just doin' our jobs. Gotta be rough, losin' your wife this way."

"We do intend to find whoever murdered your wife," Booker said, "and get a conviction. Now, who is Adawia Abdul?"

Jake felt his face change. Involuntarily, but noticeably. Both sets of eyes boring into him. *Bingo?*

"Dr. Abdul?" Jake repeated. Of course, he'd be expected to know her. She'd attended the early FDA meeting on Immunone. How much to tell them? Why had they introduced her?

"Yes," said Finley.

"And she's...?" Booker prompted.

"She's a research scientist at Replica Laboratories. She came to the FDA meetings on Immunone before Keystone Pharma took it over."

"How well do you know her?" Finley asked.

Why were they interested in Addie? For a moment, terror struck. Had Karolee found out about Addie? Had she told someone? Left some record? Knowing Karolee, the vindictive bitch could have hired a private investigator. Were there pictures of him and Addie in some PI's report being circulated within the Rockville City Police Department? For a moment, Jake let his thoughts drift from his own predicament to Addie's. What if those incriminating photos got back to her father in Iraq? Addie would be shamed. Maybe banished from her family. Maybe that would be good, Jake thought, letting a faint smile creep across his face. Daddy disowns her, he marries her, they keep her Immunone money.

"I saw her last at the FDA Advisory Committee I organized. Friday, February 14th," Jake said.

"Why would she call you at home on Wednesday night? The night your wife was killed?"

Addie called him the night he killed Karolee? She knew Karolee was out of town and she'd expected him to spend the night at her apartment. He hadn't showed and she'd called him? Made sense. She had no way to know the cops had taken over his house, made it a crime scene. *Addie, you really screwed up.*

Jake shook his head. "Don't know," he said. "Something about the drug I'm working on? It came out of her lab."

"Does she do this often? Call you at home. At night?"

"Certainly not," Jake said, a shrug of his shoulders, an appearance of nonchalance.

"Realize that we'll check phone records," Booker stated.

Jake took account. Karolee routinely scoured all their bills, all their records, so he'd never called Addie from home. To his knowledge, she'd never called him. He'd called her occasionally from the FDA, but usually he used a pay phone to connect with her, make their plans. Same with Addie. She'd call from a phone near the Metro on her way to or from work. Usually. He'd had to reinforce with her a few times how they had to avoid any appearance of conflict of interest. How important it was for both of them. Each time, he'd faced a why-all-that-nonsense look. The detectives probably would find calls to him from her home or her office to his office. How many he didn't know. He'd have to explain them away.

"Dr. Abdul is not an American citizen," Jake said. "She's unclear on why she shouldn't just call the FDA and get an update on her drug's progress."

"What's her interest?" Booker asked. "Her company sold the drug to Keystone Pharma."

"The way I understand it, when the drug is approved, she gets a milestone payment. That's all I know. I had to stop her from giving me confidential information. I don't know if what she's told me—or was going to tell me—is public or not, but I didn't want to hear it." To emphasize the point, Jake put his hands over his ears.

Finley let out a low whistle. "The plot thickens."

Stupid remark from a stupid cop. Jake had to steer this conversation away from Addie.

"Look, I'm not sure why she'd call me. This is all speculation. What can you tell me about Karolee's murder investigation? You must have suspects. Somebody breaks into my house, kills my wife—"

Booker held up his hand. "We're working on it. Following up all leads. Brought in the Montgomery County PD for back-up. Trust me, Mr. Harter, your wife's murder is a high priority."

"And we'll interrogate this Adawia Abdul," Finley said, checking his watch. "See if she leads us in a new direction," Finley said.

"More coffee?" Jake asked, glancing at three empty cups.

To his relief, Finley stood, waited for Booker to do likewise. "Thank you, Mr. Harter," Booker said. "We'll be back. You're our strongest link to Karolee's last moment in life."

Jake retrieved their coats and, without another word, they left.

CHAPTER TWENTY-NINE

Twenty six years ago, Badur Hammadi and his twin brother Malik had been selected to attend a prestigious private high school, and then sent to study finance on scholarships to the University of Baghdad. Their mother moved, all expenses paid, from a hovel in the slum where they'd been born, to a lovely garden apartment in central Baghdad. Badur still could recall how they had to learn to use the appliances in their new kitchen.

The brothers had excelled, graduated at the top of their class; their mother had been proud and, for a brief few days after their graduation, happy. In school, they had led as carefree a life as two young men could in turbulent political times in Iraq, paying little attention to their benefactors, military types who made periodic visits to their mother's home. While trying to focus on their education in finance, they couldn't help but be drawn into explosive political discussions. They steered as neutral a path as possible, wanting to avoid trouble, and stay as far away as possible from the bloody coups and mass executions. As much as they could, they ignored the escalating tension between the Arab Socialist Union Party and the Ba'athist leader Saddam Hussein.

Two days after the boys' graduation, while they waited their government job assignments, an aggressive military contingent arrived at their home. There, an officer read their orders. Malik

would be inducted into the civilian wing of the Ba'ath Party—
the party Saddam would take over within the next three years.
Good. But when Badur's fate became clear, the mother's smile
disappeared, and then she collapsed. The party was exiling him to
America, perhaps planting him there for future use. That had been
twenty-one years ago, 1971.

Twenty-six hours ago, Badur had said good-bye to his wife
Shada and his two sons, seven-year-old Ali and four-year-old
Sam, at the British Airways departure gate, Detroit Metro Airport. That had been Thursday night and three flights—a stopover
in London and another in Amman—before the Royal Jordanian
Airlines plane landed at Saddam International Airport. He'd never been able to sleep on planes or in airports, nor did he function
well when sleep deprived.

During the trip, he'd been plagued by the recurrent ping-
pong game that more frequently played in his head. The Middle
East. North America. Back and forth. Iraq. The United States.
Although a naturalized United States citizen as of five years
ago, "Dru," as he now thought of himself, had never severed his
strong ties to his homeland. Ties of love and devotion: his widowed mother and his twin brother Malik. And ties of indenture.
Dru had never been given a written copy of the orders read by
the officer twenty-one years ago in his mother's apartment. But
he needed none. He had memorized every detail then and there,
in 1971.

"Badur Hammadi," a gruff male voice caught Dru's attention
as he approached immigration. "Come." A man of few words spoken in clipped Arabic. Dru wondered how his Arabic sounded
now that he'd been in the West for so long. He and his brother
would have to compare accents. When they were young, no one
could tell who was speaking, Malik or Badur. No one called him
"Dru" back then. Even now when calling home, he had to caution
his wife not to slip and call him "Dru." He wouldn't be surprised
if nickname use was against some Islamic law.

His escort hiked up the wrinkled brown pants that were slipping down his hips, and said nothing. Dru started to veer toward the lone immigration booth. "No," the man said. "Come." No immigration process. This was a first.

"Where are we going?" he asked in Arabic.

No response.

"To my hotel, I hope," Dru hoped this guy got the point. "Long trip. I need sleep."

Nothing. Dru noticed the sole on one of the man's shoes flapped when he walked. With no choice but to follow, Dru glanced around at his surroundings. He was one of few civilians. Soldiers with machine guns and menacing facial expressions filled the terminal. Dru had flown in and out of this airport before, and other than the military presence, he didn't think it looked much different than it had before last year's Persian Gulf War, the one triggered by Saddam's invasion of Kuwait. The whole thing—Operation Desert Storm—had lasted less than two months, but the residual public relations disaster was incalculable, to say nothing of the financial impact. Just four years before that, Saddam had come off an eight-year war with Iran. A brutal conflict with dire losses. The name "Saddam" means "he who confronts," and whoever named the baby who someday would be president of Iraq must have consulted a seer.

But what did Saddam want with him? Why had he summoned him to Baghdad in these worst of political times? The regime had always kept him secluded, a one-man cell in the heart of the Muslim community in Dearborn. A naturalized US citizen successfully assimilated into Western culture and structure, a respected banker at Chase Manhattan. The last time he'd been called to Iraq had been ten years ago, and that had been to wed Shada, the woman selected for him by his handlers. Thoughts of Shada made Dru smile. He hadn't chosen her, but there was not a woman on the face of the earth he'd rather have for his life partner.

Exiting the terminal, Dru's escort led him to a nondescript, gray sedan parked immediately within the security zone of the terminal. They had top clearance, so apparently this was not to be a social visit, an opportunity to see his mother, reconnect with his brother. The escort opened the back door for Dru, closed it, and took the front passenger seat. Without a word, the driver pulled into sparse traffic and proceeded past the multitudinous security checks with the mere flash of a plastic card. Dru had bypassed customs, all security checkpoints. Not what he'd expected in post-Gulf War Iraq. His American passport had gotten him to London, but there he'd been given a Jordanian passport to use on the flight to Amman and then to Baghdad. As far as US Immigration knew, he was in England. The US had closed its embassy in Baghdad in 1991, and were not likely to reopen it any time soon. Dru was on his own in his native and now volatile and violent country.

The airport was located in Abu Ghraib, a suburb about twenty miles west of central Baghdad. The route, however, did not lead into town where Dru had anticipated a hotel at least, or perhaps even a stay with his aging mother. Dru had dozed for a few minutes, his body slumped against the door nearest him. He jerked awake when the car came to a stop within sight of a palatial building. Must be dreaming, he thought, blinking. Then the realization hit. Radwaniyah Palace, the Presidential Complex. A place he'd never been to, never wanted to go to—the nest of Saddam's family of vipers.

His silent escort opened his door before he'd righted himself from his brief sleep, and Dru all but fell out of the vehicle. He caught himself and, despite his fatigue and the forced march between two mute men, he couldn't help but ogle the gleaming structure, the elaborate landscaping, the glitter of gold as the massive front door opened to reveal even more splendor.

"They're waiting for you," his escort said, breaking his silence. "Come."

Dru jolted to full alert despite sleep deprivation. He complied without comment, blinking as they passed by floor-to-ceiling windows revealing an immense pool with fountains spewing crystal clear water, the whole area surrounded by luscious palm trees and beds of massed flowers layered in vibrant colors and intricate designs. He had a good fix on Iraq's finances and a pretty good idea of Saddam's family wealth, but he could not have imagined such opulence. Again, like thunder, the question struck: What do they want with me?

Dru had heard about Al-Faw Palace within the Radwaniyah complex and its companion on the property to the south: Victory Over Iran Palace, still under construction. Both edifices bordered a huge manmade lake. A lake stocked with Saddam's famous bass. Dru caught glimpses of the water as they continued down the marble-lined Radwaniyah corridor. He could imagine the extended Hussein family's Jet Skis buzzing over the azure-blue glassy surface.

When his companions stopped suddenly in front of gilded double doors, Dru forced himself back to reality. He was in Saddam Hussein's palace—one of his hundred or so palaces; one of the eight palaces declared off-limits to the UN inspection teams. And when the door to the small, elite conference room opened, he faced two of the most dangerous men in the world: Qusay Hussein and Hussein Kamel. The former, Saddam's son, and responsible for Iraq's indescribably brutal "security." The latter, Saddam's son-in-law, responsible, Dru knew, for Iraq's notorious weapons of mass destruction. Nuclear, chemical, biological, you name it. Saddam's powerful public relations machine had not deluded him.

Dru mentally writhed in the reality of coming into face-to-face contact with these vicious Iraqis. Lack of sleep must have dazed him, as he hadn't noticed the frail, elderly man who sat between them. The old man spoke first, his voice shaky and fragile, "Badur, I believe you know my daughter?"

Asleep or awake? Which?

"Go!" Qusay dismissed the two men who had picked up Dru at the airport and made sure his journey from Detroit ended here, in this small conference room. Dru reminded himself he had spoken to no one, seen no one but these two since touchdown. "Sit!" Qusay ordered.

Dru took the only empty chair at the small square table, across from the older man. Should he ask him what he meant? *You know my daughter.*

Hussein Kamel preempted him in loud Arabic. "Hammadi. We don't have time to waste."

"This is Jamail Abdul," Qusay spoke next. "Adawia Abdul's father. You are the woman's handler. We want her back in Baghdad. Immediately. That is your assignment. We brought you here at great expense and risk to deliver your orders. Directly. No middleman nonsense. You deliver the woman." For emphasis, Qusay pounded the table with his fist.

"She'll come if you explain I am very ill," the old man spoke, out of turn. "Tell her I need her. Since colleagues have disappeared, my program is at risk. The infidel inspections here are driving us underground."

"Okay, Jamail, enough," Qusay said. "Are we very clear here, Hammadi? You get Jamail's daughter back to Iraq now. Same way you came. Through Jordan. False passport. Use your resources. Get her here. Now."

"Dr. Abdul is..." Dru struggled to find his voice, to speak in Arabic. "Dr. Abdul is about to come into a very large sum of money. But she must be employed by her company in order to collect it. Millions—"

Kamel stood, his face inflamed. "Do we look like we need her fucking money? I need my bio program. Now. Get the fucking whore over here!"

Dru watched Jamail's face pinch at the insult to his daughter, but the old man didn't protest.

"Hammadi—these palaces here, my father has dozens," Qusay said with a smirk. "There'll be a new one soon: Victory Over America. I have money everywhere in the world and can buy whatever I need. And now my brother Kamel needs a replacement for Jamail. Get her. Immediately."

Both tyrants got up to leave. Qusay stormed out without a word, leaving Kamel to say, "You have one hour with Jamail Abdul. He will instruct you as to what to tell his daughter. You will return immediately to the States to accomplish your mission."

"My mother?" Dru asked. "My brother?" Ten years since their last reunion. His mother was well into her sixties. He had family matters to discuss with his brother. He'd promised Shada that he'd see her sister, give her the letters Shada could not risk mailing.

"Not today," Kamel snarled. "One hour for Jamail, then plane back. Your mother's and brother's fates depend on you. Same as your wife's and sons' in America."

Dru watched the clock ticking on the wall as he sat back down to deal with Addie's father. He didn't trust himself; he was exhausted to the point of total body pain. Don't let your mind wander. Stay focused. Your life and everybody's you care about are on the line. No screwups.

"Son, I have much to tell you in one short hour," the old man began, as he edged his chair as close to the table as he could, and gestured for Dru to do the same.

"I don't understand," Dru began, running fingers through his black, disheveled hair.

"Just listen to me." Dru was sure the casual gesture of Addie's father's hand moving to his mouth had a meaning. The walls have ears. He glanced upwards; discreetly disguised cameras too.

Dru positioned his chair at the edge of the table, bringing him so close to the old man that he could smell acetone on his breath. Didn't that smell mean severe illness?

"I know about my daughter Adawia. I know she's smart, she's made a name for herself among the infidels. I know about her Western ways. I know how she's desecrated the family name by her whoring. But none of that matters. I am dying. I need her here to take over my research."

Poor Addie. She and Dru—by proximity—were in deep shit. Dru had known Addie's father was an important research doctor in Baghdad, that his political alliance was with Saddam. He had not realized he was a player in Iraq's bioweapons program, that he worked closely with Hussein Kamel, second cousin of Saddam and his son-in-law as well. Since Dru had been exiled to America twenty-one years ago, all his connections to the homeland had been tightly managed by the Iraqi Intelligence Service, doled out strictly on a need-to-know basis. He wondered if Addie knew the depth of her father's involvement in his country's infamous biological warfare. Did she have any inkling?

"What do you want me to do?" Dru asked, sucking in his breath.

"The UN has been everywhere, looking for where we make the biologicals. Anthrax, Ebola, Clostridium, Brucella, others. Looking for the missiles, the warheads, the gyros. They won't find them. Buried too deep." The man started to cough, pulled out a ragged cloth, spit into it. Dru held his breath until the hacking ceased. "So many of my good scientists are dead. Some to infection, most to the regime."

Had he heard correctly? "The regime?" he questioned.

"You need to know this, son, so you can convince my daughter. The man you just met, Hussein Kamel, is the head of the biological and chemical programs, but Uday—Saddam's oldest son—is the mastermind. That man is paranoid. Eliminates anyone who wavers in any way." Addie's infirm father stared fiercely into Dru's eyes, held the gaze for too long. Dru understood the message. One woman or one more family would be trivial to Saddam Hussein's sons.

"So, Dr. Abdul, you want Addie, I mean Adawia, to take your place?"

"They want her. Uday and Kamel. She's a woman, I tell them." He started to wheeze. "Not suitable. But they insist. You have to get her here. I need to pass my knowledge on to her. There is no one else they trust."

"Did you know about the drug she developed? That she's about to come into a good deal of money? Millions?" Dru knew it to be $7.5 million, but wasn't sure he should disclose the amount.

"Do you think money matters to them?" The old man gestured at the opulence of even this incidental room. "This palace and many just as lavish. That money means nothing."

To Addie, the money meant eventual freedom. Dru had planned to advise her on how to get it out of the United States. How to secrete it from the Iraqi government. And in the mix, he'd take plenty for himself. Money he needed to get his family to a safe place, beyond the reach of the bloodthirsty Iraqi regime.

The old man looked up at the clock. "We have only fifteen minutes. Let me give you information to tell to my daughter."

Dru nodded, leaning back just a fraction in his chair. Stay alert. Listen. Many lives are at stake. He blinked at that reality. His life, his family's, Addie's family. But what about all the lives that would be taken? Hadn't Saddam and his ruthless sons gassed more than 5,000 Kurds and unleashed any number of other chemical and biological weapons?

"Tell Adawia we need her expertise to proceed with our program."

"Dr. Abdul, I don't understand. Your daughter's research is in immunology, transplant rejection."

"My daughter has a PhD in biochemistry from the University of Michigan. As a doctoral student there, she worked on an analog of the drug for antirejection of organs. That analog has properties to protect against infection caused by certain biological organisms. We want that protection in our hands before the infidels discover the potential."

A knock on the door interrupted. The same two men, driver and escort, appeared.

"Time," the escort said, his Arabic guttural.

"Son," the old man struggled to stand. "Get my daughter here immediately." His breath was ragged. He had to clutch the edge of the table to steady himself. "I have much to teach her. I am ill, but her mother and sister and my grandson are—"

Someone grasped Dru's arms from behind, propelling him past the old man, through the office door, and, in an extreme hurry, out of the Radwaniyah Complex.

CHAPTER THIRTY

"Tim, when you asked me to marry you, I had no idea you were a gourmet cook."

Laura had always struggled to keep her weight under 130—close to normal for a five-foot-five woman—but with Tim's culinary skills, she'd be fighting an uphill battle.

"Artist," Tim corrected, looking up from the cutting board where he had prepared various herbs. "Never follow a recipe. I'm a food impressionist. Just call me Monet of the kitchen."

"Can I do anything? I feel incompetent just sitting here watching." Not that she could do much with a useless hand. But even with two surgically adept hands, she'd been a disaster in the kitchen.

"You're making me a little nervous. Why don't you run along and study those charts and graphs bulging out of your briefcase."

"Between the drug development critical path spreadsheets and the drug safety pie charts and the endless organization charts, I don't know where to start. But Tim, I can't get into any of that, not tonight."

This was the night they'd decided to tell Patrick about his father. His biological father. They both agreed he needed to know. They'd tell him together. He'd be at the door any minute, and Laura had all she could do to keep it together. Why had she waited until her son was twenty-two? How many times had she rehearsed what she'd say? How could she make him understand? Patrick was the most grounded of all her children, well balanced. But could he forgive her for what she'd done? Would he forgive her for hiding the truth for so many years?

The bell rang to Tim's apartment, their apartment.

"Laura," Tim said, putting down the shallow dish of lamb chops marinating in his special concoction, "Patrick will be okay. He just needs to know the truth."

She felt fine tremors across all the muscles in her body as she rose from the high stool at the kitchen counter and headed to Tim, kissed him on the cheek, then went to open the door for Patrick.

"Mom," he said, rushing in, holding out both arms for a hug. "Oops, how's the arm?" he asked, pulling back.

Wiping his hands on a dish towel, Tim joined Laura at the front door, and Patrick turned to give him a man hug. Taking off his trench coat, Patrick looked around. "Anybody else here yet?"

Laura held out her good arm for his coat, but he said, "Still finding my way around here. Where's the coat closet?"

Laura felt her pulse race. Patrick looked so much like David Monroe. The same lanky frame, hazel eyes with brown specks, light brown hair. Some gray had shown up by then at the temples. When Patrick was born, David had been forty-one; had he survived, he'd be sixty-three now.

"Who all's coming? Can the girls get out of that residency prison they're in?"

"Nobody, honey," Laura said. "Tonight, it's just you."

"Only child—there were times when I was growing up that I wished for that. The youngest, always getting kicked around. But when they all left for college and I had two years of just you and me, Mom, I missed the sibs. No offense, but, well, you know how busy you were."

Laura turned to Patrick with such a stricken look that he corrected himself, "Not that you weren't there for me. Quite the opposite. Busy as you were, you made more of my games than any other parent on my baseball team. It's just that you weren't so good when it came to pickup football or basketball. After Mike and Kevin left, I was on my own."

"I missed each one of you when you went off to college, but none more than you, Patrick, my baby."

"Sure, that's what you tell us all. 'You're my favorite kid.'"

Laura led Patrick into the kitchen and they each took a stool at the counter. "What's for dinner?" Patrick asked. "Tim, are you cooking?"

"You kids have a lot to learn about your future stepfather," Tim said with a grin. "I'm multitalented, as you will soon find out."

Laura loved the relationship Patrick and Tim had developed over the years. Patrick had been nine when Tim arranged and participated in his heart surgery, old enough to remember Tim's professional and personal support.

"Lamb chops and my special au gratin potatoes, broccoli, and a chopped salad are on the menu," Tim said. "Does it meet with our guest's approval?"

When should she tell him? Before dinner? During? After? Tim said he'd follow her lead, support in any way he could. *Can I do this?*

Tim's informal dining room was a cozy alcove off the kitchen that overlooked Center City. The table had been set for three, and Patrick wandered over to peer out the window. All of a sudden, he'd gone quiet. Always perceptive as a child, did he suspect something was up?

When he returned to the kitchen, Laura was about to ask Patrick if he'd like a glass of wine—Tim would freak if she offered beer, Patrick's beverage of choice, with the epicurean menu.

"Okay, Mom, what's wrong?" Patrick interrupted the surface tranquility. "I've been your son too long not to know that when you single one of us out for an 'invitation,' there's a chance we might not exactly be in your good graces. Right?"

Laura looked to Tim, who bent over his baking dish of potatoes, checking whether the cheese was bubbling adequately.

"Or, is it you, Mom? Something to do with your health. Your hand? But if so, why not tell us all? Together?"

"Tim?" Laura asked. "Can you take a break? I'd like for us to talk to Patrick."

When Tim turned to face her, she saw a look of disbelief cross his face. It took her a moment to realize that to Tim, interrupting his culinary preparations was earthshaking, at least. After a brief pause to regain his composure, he said, "Of course. Just give me a minute." Tim adjusted a few dials on the stove, pulled out a stool at the kitchen counter, and nodded to Laura.

"Patrick, you're right. We—I—do have to talk to you. To tell you something I should have told you long ago. But something I was afraid—ashamed—to tell you."

Laura laid her good left hand on Patrick's right arm and turned her gaze toward him. *I can't do this! How can I tell him I cheated on Steve?*

She felt hot tears flood her eyes. She blinked them back. This was not going as she planned. But then, she had to admit, she'd had no plan. Blurt it out: that had been her plan.

"Mom?" Patrick asked, "What's wrong? Are you okay?" He looked to Tim. "What's the matter with my mother? What is she talking about?"

"Laura?" Tim said. And to her wonderment, just hearing Tim's voice fortified her to go on.

"Patrick, I still don't know how to tell you," Laura said, voice quavering, "but it's about your father."

"Dad?" He'd turned to face her, but she still had her hand on his arm as if holding him there, preventing his escape, his leaving her life forever.

"Steve," she said. "Steve was not your biological father." Laura felt the trickle of tears on her cheeks. "That's why, when you were a little boy, going off to have surgery in Detroit, that's why he didn't come. He had just found out. He was upset..." Laura gripped her son's arm tighter, holding on to him. Please, God, make Patrick understand.

Patrick stared across the counter at Tim. "You." An accusation, not a question.

"No!" Laura said. "No, no. Not Tim."

Patrick's tone had a sharp edge. "But you know all this?" His eyes met Tim's.

Tim said, "I knew something had happened between your mother and your dad back then. But until your mother told me just recently, I never knew the details. You were nine years old and needed emergency surgery. We had all we could do to get you to Philadelphia. I never asked your mother, though I had no idea what had sent your father into such a rage."

"Mike and Kevin know," stated Patrick. "They told me when I was a kid. That my dad was—"

"I am so sorry, Patrick." Laura turned toward her son, attempting an embrace that her mangled right arm would not allow. She felt Patrick pull his arm out from under her hand. He inched his stool away from hers. A sob escaped. "I want to tell you," she managed to say, "everything."

And so, she told him. About how she and Steve had problems in their marriage. How she'd fallen in love with a surgeon who had wanted to marry her. But he'd never known he was Patrick's father, until... She faltered.

"Until he died," Tim said, "when you were still a baby, Patrick."

"I refused to leave Steve," Laura said. "He was a good father to you boys. And after he died, you still were too young to understand, and I never told you. I'm sorry, so sorry."

"Sorry," Patrick echoed.

But Laura was not sorry about David. She was not sorry to have David's child, Patrick. Only sorry she had to tell her son that she had strayed, that she had been unfaithful to her husband, that she had broken her marriage vows.

"Who was the guy? My biological father. What is his name?"

"David Monroe," Laura said. Whenever she said his name, she felt a twinge in her chest. She detected a note in her own voice that she hoped Tim would not pick up on. "And, Patrick, you have met...a relative."

"What?" Patrick shot back, shoving his stool violently backward. "What the fuck!"

This was a first. One of her children deliberately using the f-word in front of her. They all used it when they didn't think she could hear—even the girls—but to her face, never.

"Who, Laura?" Tim asked.

Shit, how could she possibly have forgotten to mention this to him. Now was Tim doubting her too?

"Yeah, Mom, who do I know who may be my what? Cousin? Uncle? Aunt? Grandparent?" Patrick got up, went to the refrigerator, selected a beer, sat back down beside her. "I mean, this is too much..."

Laura looked sideways at her son. She had three sons and two daughters, and honestly could say she had no favorites. She adored them all. Would do anything for each one of them. But in the here and now, Patrick required all the love she could muster. She needed him to forgive her.

"Are you going to tell us or not?" Patrick stared across the counter now, at Tim. "Doesn't seem your soon-to-be-husband knows either." Something she'd never heard in Patrick's tone, sarcasm bordering on surly.

"Paul Monroe," Laura said, turning to face him, to gauge his reaction. "Mike's friend from Notre Dame."

"Shit," Patrick said, his head in his hands now. "Mike's buddy from Notre Dame. The one who came to the house on winter breaks. His brother is Scott Monroe, the Yankees catcher. Used to get us spring training tickets. That Paul Monroe?"

Laura kept silent.

Patrick lifted his head. "What's his relation?"

Laura looked across at Tim, who eyed her curiously. "He would be your blood cousin." Trying to stifle a new surge of tears, she continued, "David had a brother, Nick. He and his wife had four sons and they adopted a daughter."

"Have you met them, Laura? Spent time with them?" Tim's questions.

Laura bit her lip. She would not lie. She'd never been formally introduced to Nick Monroe, although she'd seen him at David's funeral, which she'd attended with Patrick in her arms. He'd communicated once through an attorney, but that didn't count. "No," she said. "I enjoyed Paul when he stayed with us, but that's it. Mike did mention that Paul's mother died a couple of years ago."

"And Scott Monroe's injuries took him out of baseball last year, that much I know," said Tim.

"Shit, when Paul and I played pickup baseball," Patrick said, "I was playing with my fucking cousin!"

Laura could never express the collage of feelings that surged in her whenever David's nephew and Patrick's cousin, Paul Monroe, had stayed at her place. Everyone but she innocent as to Patrick and Paul's family relationship. No one else but she picking up on the hazel eyes, the identical hairline, the chestnut brown hair, Patrick's cut longer than Paul's.

"What do Mike and Kevin and the girls know?" Patrick finally broke the silence.

Laura looked across at Tim for encouragement, but he simply nodded. She knew she'd shocked Tim with her disclosure about David. When she'd been a student and Tim a surgical resident, the rumor of a medical student and the chief of surgery having an affair would have been rejected as unbelievable. Not an affair, she reminded herself, one night. One glorious night.

Laura answered her son, "Nothing. I never discussed it with them."

"Well, Mom, Mike and Kevin told me when I was a kid: that I was not a real Nelson; Dad didn't want me because Mom was a—well, I can't even say the word. What was I supposed to think? If you'd explained all this, I wouldn't have had to deal with that crap for all these years."

"I am sorry." Laura could not contain her tears, and she picked up the nearest napkin to swipe her cheeks. "Patrick, what can I do to make up for all the pain I have caused you?" Laura had had no idea her older sons had tortured Patrick about his paternity. Or what Steve had told them about her. He had been vicious back then, and vindictive.

"I don't know, Mom. This is too much for me. I can't stay here tonight."

Patrick stood, and Laura and Tim with him.

"Please, Patrick. You know how much I love you. I just didn't know how to tell you. I was scared. I didn't want to hurt you."

"Tim, I'm sorry about dinner. This is too much of a shock."

"Know what you mean, buddy. I was pretty blown away too. But now that the truth is out, we have to deal with it, try to put the past aside, move forward."

Patrick collected his overnight bag and his coat and headed toward the door. As he reached to open it, Laura put her arm around his waist. "Please, Patrick, forgive me," she pleaded.

Patrick turned abruptly. "One more question. How did he die? My biological father, this David Monroe?"

He was killed by a bullet intended for me. But she did not say that. "A disturbed young man shot into the crowd at my medical school graduation. The bullet killed David instantly." *The instant after he'd realized that the baby in her arms was his own.*

And this was, in fact, the Detroit PD's version of David's murder. They, in turn, shot the killer dead. Laura had never been questioned about any relationship between her and the shooter. But there had been one—Snake Rogers had come after her that day. And now Lonnie Greenwood was threatening to reopen that whole nightmare scenario in her life. What did Lonnie Greenwood know and what did he want? How long could she put off returning his call?

"What the fuck?" Patrick exclaimed. "My biological father and the father I grew up with, both...murdered? This is too much..."

He pulled open the door, and had one foot in the hallway before he turned. "Mom, this is truly a shock to me, but I want you to know that what I said about Mike and Kevin—that wasn't quite true. I did hear Mike talking to Kevin once about how weird Dad got when I had that operation. I think Mike might know. But even if he did, you should know all your sons better. They would never taunt me with something so hurtful."

Laura felt a weight lift. Patrick had wanted to hurt her, but in the end, he couldn't.

"But are you going to tell them? The other kids? Or do you want me to tell them that I'm just their half-brother?"

"No, I should tell them," she stuttered. "But how?"

Patrick turned back from the hallway. "We should tell them," he said, "so there will be no more secrets. But right now, I need time to think about what you told me, to figure out what this means to me. I cannot imagine the effect right now. Whether my life will be different or impacted in some way. I'm sorry, but I have to go."

"Where will you stay? You can't go back to New York to-night." Always the anxious mother, especially with your youngest.

"I'm twenty-two years old, Mom. And Tim, again, sorry about dinner." And then with a hint of a grin, Patrick asked, "And while we're at it, Tim, do you have anything you want to reveal?"

"Uh, no," Tim said. "I've led a simple life. Always a bachelor."

But not celibate, Laura knew. But that was more than Patrick needed to know about Tim.

One of two horrible secrets that had haunted Laura for twenty-three years, now was in the open. The other was not marital infidelity, but murder. As much as she yearned to tell Tim, she'd decided against it. But the wild card that could change everything was Lonnie Greenwood and the call that she'd so far left unanswered.

CHAPTER THIRTY-ONE

SUNDAY, MARCH 1

Jake had rehearsed all night long different versions of what he'd tell Addie today. "Addie, I want to marry you, now." "Addie, I want to marry you, but we have to wait until the police stop investigating Karolee's murder." Like a scene in a Broadway play he'd once seen. "Addie, I killed Karolee so we'd be free to marry." "Addie, I will convert to Islam if that's important to you."

Convert to Islam? Would that mean no alcohol? Like he could do that! So he'd be like all the other religious hypocrites. Talk the talk; not walk the walk. The only other requirement he knew—besides not eating pork—was he'd have to kneel down and pray to the East. But maybe that was really just a myth? Jake had never seen Addie on her knees on a prayer rug. Maybe women needn't bother. They weren't worth much in the Muslim world. But they had to follow the rules.

Awaking from a restless sleep, Jake checked his bedside clock. Nine thirty. He hauled his legs over the edge of the bed. He'd be late for work and he had so much to do. Then he sank back into the pillows. Today was Sunday. A day with great promise. A day he and Addie would cherish forever. Their engagement day. Sometime during the night, during all that back-and-forth with himself, he'd decided to contact Addie today, to declare his love, to propose marriage. Once they were married, she'd be able to stay in the United States. Her family would not be shamed. She'd come into her money from Immunone. They would be able to live anywhere. Screw Karolee and her goddamned will. He and Addie will have more money than that miserly bitch ever could have imagined.

Jake showered, dressed in gray slacks and a light-blue striped shirt, and went to the window. Clear bright skies, a good omen. He decided to stop for coffee and breakfast on his way to Addie's. Optimism always boosted his appetite.

After feasting on eggs, bacon, and pancakes, Jake pulled up to a parking spot on the crossroad by Addie's building. Before getting out, he hesitated for a moment, wishing he'd stopped for flowers. Addie loved roses. He imagined the smile that would break out on her gorgeous face. Nothing like the smile a diamond ring would bring. But the ring would have to wait. He wanted a huge stone, an elegant cut, one appropriate for her imminent status as a woman of wealth. When Jake did climb out of the car, he saw her at once; Addie, walking briskly toward her building. How perfect.

"Addie," he called, rushing to her side.

She picked up her pace, ignoring him.

Jake increased his stride and reached to take her arm.

"Stop it." She shook off his arm and marched forward.

Jake did not want a scene. Soon enough, he and Addie would no longer bother about who saw them in public.

In silence, side by side, they covered the distance to the door of her building.

"I'm coming in with you, Addie," Jake said.

"No, Jake, you didn't even call me. I mean nothing to you—"

"Addie, not out here." He reached over to put his hand on her shoulder, exhaling with relief when she did not brush him aside. With a nudge, he urged her inside and followed behind her as she stalked ahead to the elevator.

Addie unlocked the door to her apartment and let Jake enter behind her. Once she had bolted the door, he snatched her from behind, turned her around to face him and drew her into in his

arms. Before Addie could utter a sound, Jake covered her mouth
with his, kissing her, burying his fingers in her long black hair.
His heart accelerated as he felt her voluptuous body melt in his
arms. She felt so perfect, so angelic. He had missed this woman so
much. Never again would he be separated from her. Still locked in
an embrace, they stumbled into her bedroom, onto her bed, and
into blissful passion.

By late afternoon, sated, Jake and Addie showered, and she
made a light lunch that they brought to the coffee table in the living room. "I still have some of that white wine," Addie said, going
back into the kitchen. "I almost threw it out, I was so mad at you."
She poured a glass for each of them.

They sat side by side on the sofa, tentative, sipping their
drinks, neither one eager to start a difficult conversation. Jake
knew Addie was upset and thought it best for her to speak her
mind, then he would preempt with his proposal. *And don't forget
to go over what she told the police about calling my house that night.*

"Jake, why didn't you call me?"

"I love you, Addie. So much that I had to hold back. My wife
was murdered. I couldn't let you be drawn into it."

"I don't understand," she said, stroking his thigh with her
delicate hand. Addie had only a sketchy idea of American justice.

"Addie, I want to marry you," he said, taking her glass, setting
it down and kissing her. "Will you marry me? Here, wait a minute." Jake stood, then knelt and took her hand. "Marry me, Addie.
You love me, don't you, Addie?"

Still on his knees, he waited. When Addie slowly opened
her eyes, he was gazing directly into them. What he saw perplexed Jake. Shock? Fear? Concern? Not the unadulterated
love he'd envisioned. She covered her mouth with her hands as
he stood. Before he sat back down at her side, he stared at her
for a moment. He couldn't read her body language. Jake felt a
jolt of rejection. Then as Addie leaned into him, turning to take
his face in her hands, he relaxed. Tears—of happiness?—rolled
down her cheeks.

"Addie?" he prompted.

"All last week I did not hear from you. I'm frantic about Immunone. It must get approved. Nobody will tell me. You did not call me. I felt alone, abandoned. Like you did not care about me."

"Addie, Addie, please. I love you. I want you for my wife. I just had to let the police investigation cool down."

"They talked to me, you know. About a call I made to your house. I know I'm not supposed to call, but your wife was away...I didn't know she was dead, that the police were there."

Jake had hoped to put off that conversation till later, but now he'd get it over with. "What did you say to them?"

"A woman answered. I thought it must be your wife. I just asked if you were there. She said no, so I hung up."

"That's all?" Jake asked, relieved.

"Then."

"Then?"

"The police were here. Twice. Detectives Booker and Finley. They left their cards. They were here yesterday. They'd traced the number. The police can do that in Iraq too."

"Addie, I told you never—"

"All I said is that I needed information about my drug."

Shit. If the FDA found out he had a relationship with a drug company employee, he'd be fired outright. How far would Booker and Finley go with this? Would they trace it back to the FDA? Interrogate his boss? Others in the department? He'd always been careful where he went with Addie. Had he messed up? Had someone seen them out together?

"So, do they know? About you and me?"

"I don't think so. They seemed nice, for police officers."

Okay, Jake thought. He'd say, "Look—this woman is a foreign scientist, not a DC bureaucrat, she's not up on conflict of interest. Somehow she got his home phone number and called. Inappropriate, yes, but, different culture and all that, what could he do?"

Jake wanted to forget all about Karolee and the murder

investigation. He had to convince Addie they should get engaged now, but secretly—only tell her family. Wait a few months for the police to shelve his wife's murder. Meanwhile, if her father knew she was engaged to be married, wouldn't he stop pressuring her to return to Iraq?

So many uncertainties. Jake's job might be project management, but when it came to managing his own life right now, he was in a mess. At least Karolee was out of the way. And Dr. Fred Minn's role in the Immunone approval eliminated. But the Immunone approval schedule was becoming a double-edged sword. The options: 1) Fast approval: Addie gets the money, stays in the US during a secret engagement—best case; 2) Fast approval: Addie defers to her father and returns to Iraq, despite this secret engagement and never returns—disaster; 3) Deferred approval: Addie stays employed in the US long enough to get her money—still the safest bet. Dr. Minn did not die in vain.

Addie interrupted this analysis, pulling Jake back into the moment. She was telling him that some guy had come to see her. An Iraqi named Dru.

"Dru?" Jake repeated. "Sorry, I'm not following."

"The night I called your house, he was here with me. He insisted I call you. Wanted me to tell you to please get Immunone approved quickly. He said he'd be back, but I haven't heard anything more from him."

"Who is this Dru guy?"

"He was my mentor, I guess you'd say, when I came to the University of Michigan. I had a research fellowship so I didn't need money for tuition, but he'd check to make sure I had a decent place to live, enough money to get by. A go-between. Connected to the Republic of Iraq and my father."

Jake realized how little he knew about Addie's ties to Iraq, her family's status there, her religion, the politics, the anti-West sentiments.

"So what did this Dru guy want?" Jake wanted off this topic, too, and back to talking about their life together.

"He's a banker and he'll help me manage the Immunone money. He seemed anxious. I know my father wants me back in Iraq, but I don't want to go until I collect the money. Jake, that money is my freedom. My insurance policy. You don't understand how they treat women in my country. Women intrinsically have less value. If I have that money put away, even if they exile me, I'll be okay. Security, but..." She stopped talking, stood up, and started pacing back and forth in front of the sofa. "...I think I can trust Dru..."

"Addie, you can trust *me*. You're going to be *my* wife. Together we'll figure it out." Jake patted the sofa beside him. "Now, come. Let's talk about you and me, my love."

"You make me feel safe, Jake." She snuggled next to him again. "And now that your wife is gone, do you really think we could be married? I used to dream about it, but never—"

"Yes, Addie, yes, yes, yes."

"Can I tell my family?" Jake saw a cloud come over Addie's face. "But they'll consider you an infidel—"

"Yes, you can tell your family." Jake beamed, glowed, kissed her hand. Addie and he would be together. That's all he wanted. "I'll convert to Islam if that would make you happy."

"You will?" Addie's dark eyes widened.

"Gladly," Jake said, confident that such a transition would be trivial. "But there's only one thing, my love. We have to keep our engagement a secret for now—except for your family. The Rockville police have to close out the investigation of Karolee's death."

Jake saw the disappointment in her eyes. "For how long?" she asked.

"Until they find out who killed her." Jake so wanted to say, I killed her, Addie. I killed Karolee so I could be with you. "But we can wait so long as we know we'll be together for the rest of our lives. Besides, until Immunone gets approved, we cannot have a public relationship, or people will think I've given the drug special treatment and that would cause serious delays."

"I don't think that's right," she protested.

"So will you marry me, Adawia Abdul?"

"Yes, I will, Jake Harter."

CHAPTER THIRTY-TWO

The conference door opened. Clutching papers in both hands, Louis Sigmund headed to his seat at Laura's first staff meeting. His jaw tightly set, the VP of regulatory affairs, distributed a sheet of paper to each member of her management team, and said, "Bad news about Immunone. We just got a fax from Jake Harter. The FDA is questioning the deaths in the trials."

"What?" Win White, the medical director, was on his feet. "They fucking can't. We've been all through that," he shouted. "They have every detail. That data is as clean as it gets."

"Let's just all read the fax," Louis suggested. As they did so, lots of sighing.

Does this type of thing happen frequently? Laura wondered, having read the accusation that Keystone had not provided accurate supporting clinical data about the patients who had died in the clinical trial. *Or was this unusual?* She scanned the team's faces: expressions of disbelief all around. She was way out of her experience zone. Was this a mere hiccup in the drug approval process, or was this the kiss of death? She knew the clinical data cold. But she did not know the inner operations of the FDA. She'd have to rely on Louis, and he appeared devastated—not a good sign. *Why hadn't she paid more attention when Fred Minn had tried to explain how the FDA worked?*

The FDA Advisory Committee had gone so well, but now

as she reread the fax, the FDA claimed Keystone Pharma had held back key information. The tone was accusatory, like they'd presented fraudulent data, tried to mislead the FDA and the committee.

"This is bullshit!" Win's voice ricocheted off the paneled conference room walls. "How dare they insinuate we held back data. We gave them more backup than they required, more than they asked for. I'm going to call that son-of-a-bitch Harter. Demand to speak to the medical reviewers, tell them to get their heads out of their asses. Come on, Louis. Now. We call them now. Goddamned Susan Ridley and Karl Hayes. They've seen that data. They have to be out of their minds..."

Oh, yeah, this is what her predecessor meant when he said Win White had a temper and had to be insulated from any situation requiring diplomacy. A brilliant clinical scientist and strategist, Win was not one to put on public display. Fred Minn himself had played the public persona of the medical department, but now he was dead, and she had to figure out how to handle this explosive situation.

Paul Parnell had explained that the market had already factored in the imminent approval of Immunone, had calculated the financial upside of such an important drug. Now, even the hint of a problem with the approval would send Keystone's stock plummeting. *Holy shit,* and she had planned to take the company plane and fly to Tampa to get her affairs in order there. Now she was in the midst of a disaster. First, the medical director had to be tamed, but her head of regulatory affairs couldn't control his colleague's outbursts. Nor did any of her staff members make a move to intervene. Mel Greenberg did try, but Win hammered him. "Hey, it was your people who put all those charts and graphs together, did all the fucking statistics. You know goddamned well I'm right, Mel. Come on, back me up here."

Laura flashed on years of testosterone-driven tirades from prima donna surgeons. "Win, will you sit down? Please. We need to work this out. Who are the key players?" She looked around, and pointed her finger to three of them while answering her own question. "Win, medical; Louis, regulatory affairs; and Mel, information management. First, as you know, we need to keep this FDA communication strictly need-to-know. We will analyze it, decide what to do, and get this handled. We're going to crisis management mode."

Her staff looked at her quizzically. Like, what would she know about crisis management? Well, she managed one hell of a crisis seven years ago—a life and death biological threat. Watch her deal with a mere administrative crisis. "Mel, Win, Louis, set up your operation in this conference room. Mel, get in the necessary communication devices. I'll operate out of here too. We share all information. All communications come from this room. No lone rangers. No loose ends. All decisions are made by me, once we as a group consider the options. Everything coordinated in this room as of this instant. The rest of you, business as usual for your departments, but stay on call twenty-four hours a day. The issue is confined to medical right now, but be ready in case we need you."

Stunned faces confronted her, but chairs pushed back, papers were gathered.

"Before you go, I want you to know that I, personally, know this medical data. I've reviewed it meticulously. Personally talked to each principal investigator who reported a death."

Laura nodded to Win, "You're right to be angry. I am too. I don't know what's behind this accusation, but we have to take it seriously. We will methodically refute it. Point by point." Laura looked at Mel. "Your people compiled and audited all the source documents. We presented a comprehensive package." She watched tension drain from Win's and Mel's faces, and the panic in Louis' eyes turn to determination. A manager supports her people. Surely, that had been Fred Minn's practice too.

"If the FDA is picking an area to criticize, at least it's one I know well. Thank goodness they didn't attack toxicology or chemistry; there, I'd be at a loss. So let's go forward." She announced that she needed to brief CEO Paul Parnell, that she'd be back shortly. "In the meantime, Louis, please draft a response that says we're addressing all the FDA's concerns. Tone should be polite, conciliatory—right?" She and Louis exchanged knowing looks.

On her way to the CEO's suite, Laura couldn't help but think of Patrick and how he was doing. Her motto—compart-mentalize—worked most of the time, but before diving headlong into the machinations of the drug approval process, she had to call Lonnie Greenwood in Detroit.

CHAPTER THIRTY-THREE

"Jake Harter."

"Sid Casey for you. Please hold." Casey was acting director of Drug Evaluation and Research, one of the six major branches of the FDA.

Jake tensed for two long minutes, waiting until the man himself came on. He'd never had a call from anyone this high up.

"Jake, I have a press conference in Manhattan today. The usual: what's the FDA doing about getting lifesaving drugs approved faster? I'd like to use Immunone as a positive example. Can I say the approval is imminent? Will you have it signed off by the end of the week? I'm calling you directly since you control the process flow."

So the higher-ups don't have a clue. Yet. This morning, Jake had dropped off a copy of Friday's fax to Susan and Karl. He'd not marked the fax urgent, hoping for low-priority treatment and delayed progress up the chain of command. Apparently, the ploy worked. Jake would have to break the news now.

"Dr. Casey, I need to inform you of something that may—"

"I'm in a hurry, Jake. Will the approval clear by the end of the week or not? I want to use Immunone as a promising example of how we are all working together toward a common goal. You know the rhetoric."

"I found that some clinical data is missing, sir. I sent a fax to the company asking for clarification. There's no way this can be cleared up this week."

"You can't be serious? A problem with the approval? Why wasn't I informed? Our public relations people are working with Keystone on press releases. I don't have to tell you that this is a high-profile case. Press coverage of the Advisory Committee, an all-time high; our reviewers had no reservations; the committee gave the green light. What are you trying to tell me?"

"I just discovered missing medical backup in the death cases." Jake knew that the word *death* would give this man pause. He put it out there and waited.

"I want to see you and the medical reviewers first thing tomorrow morning. I want to be briefed on every detail. This puts my press conference in shambles. First thing in the morning. In my office. All of you."

Jake had waited until late on Friday to fax Keystone the document advising them that key documents were missing from their Immunone submission. The report referenced complicated statistical analysis that would take time for their statisticians to decipher.

He'd sent the fax on his own initiative, not bothering to check with the medical reviewers. Karl Hayes had taken a vacation day and Susan Ridley had indicated no interest when he'd brought the matter to their attention. He'd taken that for a green light to make demands—bordering on veiled accusations—of Keystone Pharma. Whatever it took to slow things down. Win White, their medical director, had an anger management problem. Maybe he'd blow his stack. Cause a major diversion by challenging the FDA. Something that would piss off Susan and make Karl go all self-righteous. Jake would take a back seat, support his medical reviewers, deny having seen the records in question, delay resolution long enough to keep Addie in the country.

Today, Jake reclined in his office chair, sipping coffee, waiting for the first salvo from Keystone Pharma. He'd waited all day yesterday, anticipating that he'd be getting a call Monday morning as soon as they ripped the fax off the machine. Win White would go into a rage, and Jake would be on the receiving end of his fiery temper. But nothing.

Jake set down his coffee mug when his desk phone rang. An inside line. Had Keystone's CEO gone directly to the commissioner? He wouldn't put it past Paul Parnell. Why did big drug companies refuse to believe that calling the commissioner is the kiss of death? Nothing pisses off an FDA reviewer more than a company going over their head. The FDA is not like private industry, where the power resides at the top. No, here at the agency, the power emanates from the lowly medical reviewers—Susan and Karl in this case. A supervisor's attempt to overrule a medical reviewer would set up a liability risk that even the FDA commissioner found unacceptable. No one tampers with the lowly reviewer.

CHAPTER THIRTY-FOUR

Jake had called Addie last night to tell her he was bringing Indian food take-out. He didn't stay long—just long enough for food and sex. He'd explained to Addie they had to be careful. Only twelve days after his wife had been murdered. The police were snooping around their relationship. He had to be home at night—alone—in case he was under surveillance.

"Surveillance?" The word alarmed her. In Iraq, men under surveillance disappeared. She'd known of many. Scientists who had worked with her father, friends of her family. Though her parents gave her little information about what was happening at home after the Gulf War, she learned about conditions from her sister, Farrah, on the rare occasions she received a letter. Addie hadn't seen Farrah since her last visit home four years ago. If only she could sit with her, tell her about Jake and his marriage proposal. Farrah may be younger, but she was married and a mother. She would tell her honestly whether Jake would be accepted in Iraq, even if he did convert to Islam. Or whether they'd always be outcasts.

Jake had tried to reassure her, explaining that husbands always are suspect after a wife's murder. Addie shuddered whenever she thought about Karolee's violent death. Shot in her own home. She'd considered America safe—compared to Iraq—but her confidence had suffered. Who had killed Karolee? And why? A robber, according to Jake. But something about the way he'd said it caused her doubt.

And now, as she sat at her desk, trying to concentrate on yesterday's research results, she again puzzled over why, when she had asked Jake—multiple times—about Immunone, he kept evading her? Each time she implored him to tell her what was happening at the FDA, and explained how urgently she needed to know, he'd repeated, "It's in the approval process." What does that mean? she wanted to scream. What was Jake not telling her?

Something was wrong and Jake didn't trust her. Why were Americans in business so obsessed by confidentiality and conflict of interest?

And the implications of Jake not trusting the woman he wanted to marry? Does he love me? Do I love him? Should I marry him?

She was interrupted by a phone call. "Dr. Abdul," she answered, hoping it was Jake calling to say he'd stop by again tonight.

"Adawia, it's Dru. I have to see you."

"I'll get out of work at five," she said. "Want to meet for a drink somewhere near my office?" She didn't want him at her apartment. Didn't want a Dru-Jake scene. Dru knew about Jake, and she'd told Jake about Dru. Still...

"Now. This is important. Your place. Come home immediately. I'm there now."

"I can't leave work. The Immunone approval will come any day now—"

"No." Dru's tone sounded threatening. She'd known Dru for twelve years. He'd always been polite and easygoing.

"Now."

When the line went dead, Addie grabbed her purse and the uneaten half of her sandwich. She'd finish it in the car on the way home; she'd stay just long enough to hear Dru out so she could be back for a three o'clock meeting. But on her way to the door, she turned back to her desk. Dru would want an update on Immunone. Since Jake refused to tell her anything, she'd call Dr. Nelson. She didn't want to bug her, but she'd been so nice before, and Dru's tone of voice sounded dire.

Parking spots were hard to come by, and Addie parked on the street, two blocks away from home. As she approached on foot, she saw Dru pacing back and forth in front of her building.

"Dru," she said, walking up to him from behind, touching his arm. He appeared bedraggled, not his usual, buttoned-up businessman look.

Addie almost lost her balance as he pivoted toward her, both arms extended as if he intended to strangle her.

"What's the matter with you?" She took two steps backward.

"Let's go inside."

Dru said nothing on the ride up the elevator to her floor. Once inside her door, he announced, "We have to talk."

"Okay." She led him to two chairs, an end table between them. "Have you had lunch? You caught me during mine. I finished it in the car, but I'd be happy—"

"No. Let me get to the point. Tell you what you need to do."

Addie bristled. This was the United States. Men didn't tell women what to do.

"I was summoned to Iraq last week. To the Presidential Palace."

Addie felt her heart contract, a long squeezing sensation, followed by lightheadedness.

Dru continued, "I met with your father—"

"You did?" She brightened. Word from home was rare since the Gulf War. Then she put it together. The drastic change in Dru's demeanor—a meeting with her father. "What's wrong? My mother?" Her mother had terrible asthma, and the pollution in Baghdad was worsening. Her father had tried to get her to move to the country, but she wouldn't leave the city without him, and he had his research work.

Dru stared at her, and she repeated, "My mother. Did you see my mother?"

"No. I didn't see her. Neither was I allowed to see my mother or my brother."

Addie couldn't imagine going all the way to Iraq and not even seeing your own family. She knew that Dru had a twin brother and two small nephews, whom he'd never seen.

"Qusay Hussein and Hussein Kamel were there. With your father."

"They were?" Addie's lightheadedness returned, and she slumped back in her chair, for a moment, unable to breathe. Qusay was portrayed as a monster in the Western press, and he was equally demonized among Iraqis. Kamel was Saddam's cousin and son-in-law, the primary target of the United Nations' frenzy to find weapons of mass destruction. Weapons she couldn't fathom: chemical, biological, nuclear. Yes, she knew Iraq had them. But, no, she didn't want to think about them.

Dru waited a moment. "They gave me one hour with your father. He is terminally ill, Addie. I'm sorry."

Addie's eyes filled with tears. "Oh, no, please God. I want to see him. Did he say what is wrong? If we could get him over here, maybe—"

"He needs you in Baghdad, Adawia. Now. Qusay and Kamel demand it. By demand, you know what I mean. A threat of the highest order. You must go. Immediately."

"I want to see my father." Addie fidgeted in her chair. "He's been wanting me to return to Iraq for a long time. I've always promised my mother that I would return, but one thing always led to another and—"

"I have booked a flight. You will leave Friday."

"Three days from now. You must be kidding!"

"I will take care of everything," Dru continued. "You just have to be on that flight. DC to London, where you'll be handed a new passport, a new identity, which you'll use to get to Amman and on to Baghdad."

"No way. You know I can't leave until Immunone is approved. You're the one who explained all the details of my contract with

Replica. As long as I am still employed by Replica when the FDA approval milestone payment of one hundred fifty million dollars comes in, I get five percent. Seven and a half million dollars. Once I have the money, I'll be secure. And there's something else. Jake Harter asked me to marry him." Addie couldn't help but flash a smug look. A look that vanished as Dru continued.

"Adawia, forget about marrying an infidel. They'd kill him. But here's the reality from Baghdad—if you don't show up there by the end of this week, your family, and my family, will be eliminated. Outright. No trial. Simply disappear."

"Dru, you're exaggerating, blowing this out of proportion. I know that after the Bush war, the military has clamped down, but—"

"There is no law, no security, anymore. Take this seriously, Adawia. I am afraid for all of us. So much so, that I already have hidden Shada and my sons. I took care of that the moment I returned. But those in Iraq: my mother and my brother and his family, your mother and your sister and your nephews. You know what Qusay will do with them. I faced him eye to eye. His brother Uday and Hussein Kamel are desperate for you to continue your father's work. They think they can trust you. That you owe them your allegiance."

"Why me? They have research scientists."

"Not many are left. And few they can trust. Qusay has had many eliminated. You know the extent of his paranoia. He's at the root of innumerable disappearances. You can be sure that destroying your family will be a simple order."

"And you, Dru? They will make you disappear too?"

"Yes, and you. Their reach in America is extensive. You have no choice in this, Adawia."

"And my father's work?" she asked. Deep down, she'd always known, but had never asked.

"I didn't go into that. But your father said he has much to pass along to you. Techniques. Locations. Supplies. Said you were a well-trained scientist and could carry on his legacy."

A legacy of mass destruction. Could she do this? At a time when the United Nations kept sending in wave after wave of inspectors looking for evidence of Iraq's programs in bio, chemical, and nuclear terrorism. The ninth and current IAEA inspection focused on nuclear: uranium enrichment centrifuges and heavy-water production facilities. So far, nothing, nor had they found evidence of anthrax and the other bio pathogens that obsessed George Bush. Uday and Kamel would have taken all that underground, perhaps to Saddam's palaces, which remained off limits to the inspectors 'For security reasons.'

Finally. Payback for her superb education, twelve years of comfortable living. And right as she was on the verge of becoming a millionaire, a woman of substance, a woman with choices. Deep down, Addie had always known it would come down to this, but she'd managed to suppress it, to carry on, ignoring the specter of future demands. And here she was, facing psychological warfare of the purest nature: should she not comply, a sure and painful death for all whom she loved. She thought of her father, a gentle man, a brilliant scientist. Had her father's participation as a scientist in Saddam's preparation for mass murder been coerced, just as hers surely would be?

CHAPTER THIRTY-FIVE

A marathon sleeper ever since her medical training, Laura now had become an insomnia victim. Eyes determinedly closed, she saw an album of troubling images. Patrick, pale with shock—she'd not heard from him since her Sunday night confession. If she found a way to tell the other kids about his paternity, would the beautiful, devoted family vanish from her life? Tim, his smile looking a bit forced, asked her at least once a day to set a wedding date. Why did she keep changing the subject? Was it David Monroe, resurfacing a generation later like a faded snapshot?

When she tried to pry her mind away from her personal problems, Immunone squeezed in. She never should have taken the job; she was in way over her head. She could see Paul Parnell's unusually hard look...Immunone files, pages and pages, fluttering...

But her personal and professional problems paled in the shadow of Lonnie Greenwood and his ailing son, Johnny—named for Johnny Diggs, whose face was as real as ever—the face of the nightmare that played in high fidelity in her head.

"Dr. Laura Nelson?" the woman who'd answered at Mayor Coleman Young's office had said, "Yes. Mr. Greenwood instructed me to interrupt him if you called."

Laura shivered under her blanket as she heard the conversation yet again, in her head. What did this man know? Could he destroy everything? Her family? Her professional status? Could she go to jail? She knew there was there was no statutory time limit for murder.

A deep male voice had answered her call to Detroit. "Dr. Nelson," Greenwood said, "I am aware of your bad accident. And that you are no longer at Tampa City. I saw you on television answering questions in Washington about the new drug. Actually, I was in DC myself to consult with former Mayor Marion Barry. I left a message that my son has cystic fibrosis and is in dire need of a lung transplant. Because of your reputation, I wanted you to do the surgery, and to use that new drug you tested—"

When he'd paused for a breath, Laura said, "As you know, I no longer am able to..." She hesitated. For the first time outside her family and her immediate colleagues, she'd spoken her new reality... "operate."

"I do realize that," he said. "But can you still help my son?"

So far, no mention of Greenwood's connection to the Jones family in Detroit. "I'll do what I can. My colleague in Tampa, Dr. Ed Plant, is extremely capable, and the drug I was testing should be approved very soon."

"What if it isn't?" he asked. "My son is twenty-three years old. He's in bad shape. I don't have to tell you how ravaging cystic fibrosis can be. I was in Tampa with Mayor Coleman Young to meet with Mayor Sandra Freedman. She started talking about the study at Tampa City Hospital, talked about you. Your name rang a bell. Found out you did your medical training at Detroit City—and that brought up some painful memories. Did you know the Diggs brothers, Anthony and Johnny? Lived on Theodore Street?"

Anthony, my first patient; Johnny, just eighteen when I took his life... Self-defense, she had to keep reminding herself. What would the charges be if she were prosecuted now? Second-degree murder? Manslaughter? Laura had been accused of murder once, found innocent, but she'd never been arrested for the one she *had* committed. All who had known are now dead or at least so she'd thought. What does Lonnie Greenwood know? How do I respond?

He'd have access to Detroit archives, obviously. She decided truth was the safe option. "Yes," she said. "And I do know the Jones family. Still in touch with Stacy and Lucy." The Diggs brothers' sister Stacy, and Lucy, their mother.

"Will you help Johnny, Dr. Nelson?" Greenwood asked. "My son, named after my buddy, Johnny Diggs. His mama took Johnny to live in Tampa when he was just a baby and I was still a thug—before I got rehabilitated, treated for post-traumatic stress from 'Nam."

"Yes," Laura said, "I'll do what I can. Since I now work for Keystone Pharma, I can fast-track a compassionate IND—investigational drug approval. I'll work with Dr. Plant. I'll need your son's medical doctor's name, all his records, he'll have to make an appointment with Dr. Plant. I can facilitate all this, Mr. Greenwood, if you and your son decide—"

"Please," the man said.

They discussed how she could exert her influence to get Johnny Greenwood into the Tampa lung transplant program, despite the long waiting list for a lung.

The conversation over, Greenwood thanked Laura, without another word about his insights into their shared Detroit contacts and experiences. Her curiosity was on overdrive, but tempered by the reality of what was at stake. She'd been blackmailed once about her role in Johnny Diggs' death. Was this just a more sophisticated attempt?

Lonnie Greenwood's son needed Immunone. That led her back to the missing Immunone data. How could problems at the FDA be so endemic that they lost important data? Over the years, she'd heard endless grumblings about how slow they were, about the caliber of their scientists, and on and on, but she'd always attributed the pharmaceutical industry's dissatisfaction to the disparate responsibilities and accountabilities of the two groups. The FDA to protect the public by controlling the approval of new

medications; the pharmaceutical industry, to develop safe and effective medications that enrich their shareholders and also save
lives. A fundamental check and balance system she'd felt worked
reasonably well. But until last week, she'd been a member of neither cohort. As a medical practitioner, she and her patients had
been the beneficiary of the drug developer and of the governmen-
tal drug-approval process. Now she found herself squarely on the
side of the drug developer.

***

By the time dawn broke, Laura had decided to call the FDA directly
instead of going through Louis Sigmund, her VP of regulatory affairs, as protocol would demand. During the "honeymoon" period
of her new job, she'd not be expected to know all the "rules." She'd
also personally call Jake Harter, the Immunone project manager. If
she could shortcut the bureaucracy, maybe she could nip this missing data issue in the bud. The data existed. She'd seen it ready for
submission. But what if Keystone Pharma had slipped up and neglected to submit it?

Before leaving the office last night, she'd issued an all-hands
priority memo to make replicate copies of all the clinical data relevant to deaths in the Immunone trials. Copies should do. If not,
would they have to go back to all the clinical trial sites and relocate
the source documents? That would take time and an army of Keystone staff. Oh, but, she had copies of those documents in her hospital office in Tampa. Had her office already been taken over by her
successor? And who was that successor? Ed Plant, she hoped.

For the first time in their overnight relationship, Laura got
up before Tim. Managing well enough with one hand, she made
coffee and set out the Cheerios that Tim ate every morning with
bananas and brown sugar. Ten-grain toast for her with apricot jel-
ly. Cranberry juice for both.

"Good morning," she called as Tim joined her in the kitchen.

Before he could respond, the phone rang. "For you," she predicted, picking up the handset and handing it to Tim. His first

case today was a complicated valve repair on a critically ill, two-month-old baby from Saudi Arabia.

"Oh, hi," Tim said, "No, we're up. She's right here." He gave back the phone to Laura, mouthing, "Mike."

"Hello?" Over the years, Laura had trained her kids to wait until mid-morning to call her—just in case she was having one of those rare opportunities to sleep in.

"Hi, Mom."

"Everything okay?" Laura asked.

"Hope so," Mike said. "Patrick stayed over Sunday and Monday night. Came from Tim's—I mean—your place Sunday. He was pretty shook up. He left early this morning for New York."

Had Patrick told Mike? Hadn't they left it that they would jointly tell the other kids?

Mike paused. When Laura said nothing, he continued, "When I asked what was going on, he just said, 'Ask Mom.' So I'm asking you, what's up?"

"Oh, Mike," Laura said, giving a sidewise glance to Tim, now pouring his cereal from box to bowl. "I had a talk with Patrick, a long overdue discussion. I'm afraid what we talked about upset him."

"Go on," Mike said when Laura stopped.

"I'd rather tell you in person," she said.

"Can you just tell me what it's about? Patrick did say to ask you. That's all he said. Even when Nicole came over yesterday, that's all he said. Now you have the whole family's attention. You know what a big-mouth Nicole is. Both Natalie and Kevin called me last night. I couldn't say much because Patrick was still here."

Laura wondered why they hadn't called her.

Mike said, "All three of them are afraid to call you. They think that you must have diagnosed him with some terrible disease—Natalie even mentioned AIDS, but that's—"

"No," Laura said, firmly. "Nothing like that, Mike."

"Mom, I'm Patrick's big brother, and I'm trying to figure this out. Just be honest, does it have to do with Dad?"

"Mike, you and the family need to know what this is about. But I need to work this out with Patrick. When he's ready—"

"Then call him. He knows we're all speculating. Think about it; I'm old enough to know what this is about. I was fourteen when Dad was shot; right after he refused to go with Patrick for the emergency surgery. Mom, I know you know that I know. So it's up to you to clear this up with all of us. I don't know the details, but I do know Patrick is not Dad's son. I've never discussed this with Kevin or the girls, but I've known since the year Dad died, and I think it's time for you to be honest with us all."

"Okay, Mike. And thank you," she managed to say, in a voice that shook.

She related her conversation to Tim and promised she'd call Patrick that day. Tim suggested they all get together for the weekend. He would attempt another home-cooked dinner. Laura nodded her assent. She packed up her briefcase, kissed Tim goodbye, and headed to the waiting limo. She skipped her morning slice of toast.

***

Laura's commute from Center City, Philadelphia, to Keystone's offices in Montgomery County took forty minutes, enough time for her to organize her day. First on her agenda would be a call to the FDA project manager in charge of Immunone. In fact, not wanting to risk her staff telling her that the drug company vice president calling FDA staff was not kosher, there were protocols for such communications, she placed the call from the limo phone.

"Drug Evaluation. Immunology. Jake Harter." Good, Laura thought. No need for phone tag.

"This is Dr. Nelson. Keystone Pharma."

"Yes?"

A note of wariness in Harter's tone reminded her that the man's wife had been murdered since she'd last seen him at the advisory meeting. "I want to offer my condolences on the loss of your wife." How many times had she delivered a version of this message over her career as a thoracic surgeon? Too many. The throb of pain in her right hand reminded her that future occasions would be limited. She was a paper pusher now, not a surgeon.

"Thank you, Dr. Nelson. And let me tell you how sorry I am about your injury. I know you are at Keystone Pharma now. That must be quite a change from the operating room and research labs. The pharmaceutical industry is a far cry from academia. Right?"

"I have lots to learn, that's for sure, but I have a great staff. I must admit, though, filling Dr. Minn's shoes is not going to be easy. He was beloved by his Keystone colleagues."

"A great loss, indeed," agreed Harter. "He seemed to be the pivotal force in R&D at Keystone. I assume Dr. Win White will be taking over Immunone. I haven't had much experience with Dr. White, as Dr. Minn usually attended the FDA meetings in person."

Laura cringed at the thought of Win White, with his volatile temper, interacting with the FDA. A surefire formula for disaster, despite the man's clinical and strategic brilliance. "No, Mr. Harter, I will be handling Immunone. And that's why I'm calling, to respond to the fax you sent. About your problems locating the source documents related to the deaths in the clinical trials."

Laura heard a sharp intake of breath. "But you just started."

"True, but I know the data. I've personally reviewed each case. I have seen the reports that contain the specific information you list as missing."

"Look here, Dr. Nelson. I have been in this project management job for twenty-five years. You have been in your job for what—a few days? When I say we do not have the data to adequately assess the safety of a new drug, I think I know what I'm talking about."

Definitely off on the wrong foot, Laura wished she'd waited longer for the missing records to be documented so she'd have them in front of her now as she laid down this challenge. Now she'd jumped the gun, assuming this would be an easy call to clarify a misunderstanding.

"Mr. Harter, I was not implying anything controversial, just that the information you need does indeed exist. It's all been submitted to you, but in case you are having difficulty locating it, Keystone is pulling it together. And once we have it, we'll send it by express directly to your attention at the Parklawn Building in Rockville. Right?"

"If Keystone plans to send me any documents, Dr. Nelson, I suggest you go through Dr. Louis Sigmund. He's the head of regulatory affairs at your company. He's the proper person in your organization to call me. Don't bother with a carrier. It'll only get lost. Louis knows that. He knows the proper way to deliver documents to us."

Laura had not expected this dressing down. She was the head of research at the third largest pharmaceutical company in the world. And an FDA project manager had just told her to fuck off. Yes, there was a lot about working with the FDA that she didn't understand. *You should have followed protocol, Laura.*

"I see," she said, not wanting to capitulate, not wanting to burn any bridges, just wanting to get that data into the FDA and put this whole mess to bed.

"I expect it will take some time—if you have the data—to pull it together and get it back to us. Then, of course, we'll have to review it, verify it. That all takes time, Dr. Nelson."

When Laura had presented at the FDA Advisory Committee, Mr. Harter had seemed pleasant enough as he flitted about distributing reports, seeing to the needs of the FDA medical staff, the committee members, and the presenters from Keystone Pharma, herself included. So why was he now coming off as such a self-righteous, negativist jerk? At the conclusion of the meeting, the FDA reviewers, the committee members, and the various spectators—including the media—had been upbeat and optimistic. Laura especially remembered the exotic young woman from Replica, the scientist who had discovered Immunone's drug category and who had called her yesterday trying to get information on the drug's approval. Hadn't she seen her deep in conversation with Jake Harter in an alcove off the meeting room?

"Thanks for your time, Mr. Harter," Laura said. "Just so you know, I personally went over the data you're looking for with your department's medical reviewer, Dr. Hayes."

"He's the junior reviewer here," Harter said. "I hope he didn't misplace it if he did have it in his possession."

"Tell him not to worry, Mr. Harter. I have replicate copies of everything in my office in Tampa should Keystone have any difficulty locating the data, which I'm sure they won't."

Silence met this statement, and Laura said a simple good-bye. She could have heard a mumbled "shit" on the other end, but it could as well have been her own expletive as she slammed down the phone.

She had to tell Louis Sigmund about her unorthodox call, and as soon as she arrived at Keystone, she headed straight to his office. His secretary informed her that he was in a meeting with his staff, going over budgets. "I need to see him now," she said. "My office."

The elderly woman peered up over her half glasses. "Now," she repeated. "You want me to interrupt his meeting?"

"Now," Laura confirmed, heading back to her office. She guessed that the gentlemanly Dr. Minn did not make such demands. And normally, neither did she, but she'd just dug herself into a hole with the FDA. Wait until Paul Parnell found out his new hire had doomed the gazillion-dollar Immunone approval.

Louis arrived momentarily, toting a monogrammed leather binder. "Laura. Is something wrong?"

She figured anxiety must be written all over her face. One thing she was not: a good poker player.

"Yes, Louis. Let me tell you what just happened. Please, sit down."

They sat across from each other at her conference table. He opened the binder to a lined yellow note pad, but didn't pull out a pen.

"Immunone?" he guessed. "I've been waiting all day for information from Science Information. Impossible that we never submitted the data. Nothing like this has ever happened. I can't—"

"Yes, Louis, I need to talk about Immunone. I haven't heard whether Medical and Information Management have what we need or not. We can head to Mel Greenberg's office after this."

"Good idea," Louis jumped up, hesitating when Laura remained seated.

"I called the FDA," Laura said.

Louis reseated himself with a thud, as incredulity crossed his face. "You did?"

"I spoke to Jake Harter. The project manager."

Louis nodded. "Not a bad guy," he said, "as project managers in the agency go."

"He was quite hostile," Laura knew she had to be honest. Sugarcoating wouldn't help.

"I'm not understanding," Louis said.

"I called to tell him that I'd personally reviewed the death cases. That I reviewed them all with Dr. Hayes." Louis' expression was skeptical. "Karl Hayes, one of Immunone's medical reviewers."

"Yes. Of course I know him," Louis said. "He's the junior reviewer under Susan Ridley. They had to have reviewed the death cases."

"He was most unreceptive. Defensive, I guess. Told me all communications needed to come from you. Pretty much put me in my place. Then I told him that I have replicate reports in my Tampa office—former Tampa office."

"Laura, I know you meant well, but the FDA has certain expectations. Communications have to go through channels. Regulatory affairs manages document transmission and advises on all FDA matters. Otherwise, things get out of control, and these one-on-one interactions cause misunderstandings. That's what happened here. I'll give him a call. Smooth things over. Depending on when we have a data package ready, I can hand deliver it. I work with these project managers all the time. It'll be fine."

"I'm not sure, Louis. He seemed belligerent. Maybe he just doesn't like me. He said he assumed Win White would be taking over Immunone."

"Trust me, Laura, Jake Harter detests our medical director. They're like oil and water. He did, however, seem to respect Fred Minn. Maybe it's just you taking his place—"

"Perhaps, but I'm not backing down for the time being. Keep me posted. Today's Tuesday. If Mel has any trouble finding what we need, I'll fly to Tampa."

"Let's go check Mel's progress in locating that missing data. Better that it come officially from Keystone than from your Tampa office."

But Laura would go to Tampa. Tonight. She had to arrange for Johnny Greenwood's lung transplant.

CHAPTER THIRTY-SIX

Addie called the department secretary at Replica, told her she'd left early, she was ill. And she was ill. After Dru left she'd vomited the contents of her stomach, then dry retched over and over. Now she sat with a cup of tea, and her stomach so far had not revolted.

How to deal with Dru's message? She'd known the day may come, but so abruptly? Give up forever the independence she'd come to take for granted?

What were her options? Did she have any? Or did she have to submit—as Muslim women had done over the centuries?

Addie didn't waste time on that question. The answer: submission.

All that was left to her now were the logistics.

Would it still be possible—one way or another—to get the $7.5 million? Stash it somewhere? Keep it in America? Open one of those offshore accounts? She knew that certain Iraqis had huge sums of money in foreign accounts all over the world. Saddam and his sons and sons-in-law were experts at exploiting the global financial system.

Dru was a banker, but when he'd mentioned the money to her father, he'd dismissed it as inconsequential. And Dru, who seemed so anxious for her to collect the Immunone money, now seemed disinterested. Dru was so scared that he'd put his wife and sons in hiding. Addie admitted that her years in the West had made her a capitalist. Under capitalism, if you worked hard, you were rewarded. Well, she'd worked hard, was ready for her reward. Could she simply walk away?

There has to be a way, Addie kept telling herself as she rose to make herself another cup of tea. What am I going to do? Then she thought of Jake. His proposal of marriage. Could that be her way out? What if they were secretly married before her flight on Friday? Could a husband collect for her? In Iraq, husbands controlled their wife's finances.

She knew that in America they'd need a state license, so she called the State of Maryland to ask about marriage licenses. She was transferred to a woman who grudgingly provided the requirements: picture IDs for both; for Jake, a death certificate for his wife—had to be certified; she'd need her green card; no blood tests; waiting period—two days, or to be exact, 48 hours; cash money up to $85. You had to go to the circuit court. She copied down the addresses of the ones she thought far enough away from Rockville but within an hour or so drive. If they got the license today—there was still enough time—they could be married on Thursday.

Next, she needed to call Jake at work, something she never did. She remembered the trouble she'd caused by calling him at his home the night his wife was killed right there in his house. Could he get in trouble with this call too?

As she picked up the phone, Addie's hands started to tremble. She set it back down. Did she have everything figured out? Her job: she needed to be employed by Replica when the approval milestone for Immunone was finalized. That she couldn't control. Maybe Jake could, but he had not been forthcoming. The thought had never occurred to her before, but could she take a leave of absence from Replica? Tomorrow, she'd go to Human Resources, tell them her father was critically ill—the truth, if Dru could be believed—request a medical condolence leave, or whatever they called it—maybe for a month. By then Immunone would certainly be approved, and Jake, as her husband, could get the money and invest it for her. He might have to resign at the FDA because of their conflict of interest paranoia, but with that kind of money, so what?

Again, she reached for the phone. One more consideration shook her resolve. Jake—could Jake be trusted? Did he love her enough to protect her money even if she never returned to America? She started to dial. She thought he did. Hadn't he said he'd convert to the Islamic religion? She had to put her faith in him. He was her only hope for a future beyond complete subservience as a Muslim woman.

Jake answered on the third ring. For that, Addie thanked Allah. She didn't want the department secretary announcing this forbidden call for all ears to hear. "Drug Evaluation. Immunology. Jake Harter."

"Jake, this is Addie," she whispered.

"Not a good time," Jake said, automatic, perturbed. Then in a more concerned tone, "Is something wrong? Are you okay? I mean, calling me here?"

"I need you to come here, Jake. Right away." Still a whisper. She checked her watch. One fifteen. He could make it here in fifteen minutes. Another hour to get to the courthouse she'd chosen.

"Why are you whispering? I can't hear you. Is somebody there? Addie, are the police with you?"

Addie glanced at the note she'd made about marriage license requirements. Jake would have to stop home on his way to her place. He'd need his wife's death certificate. What about a birth certificate? No, the form said a driver's license is okay. He'll have that in his wallet. "No," she spoke in her phone voice, a bit louder than her normal face-to-face voice. "But go home and get your wife's death certificate." She glanced again at the specifications. "A certified copy," she said. "That's very important."

Should she tell him what she wanted now, on the phone? Or wait and do it in person?

"What? Addie, I'm in the middle of a major issue here. Can we discuss this later? I can't believe—"

"Jake, you have to do this for me. For us. If you love me."

"There's no question I do, but I can't leave." He hesitated. In a low voice he said, "It's about Immunone. Tell you about it when I see you. I'll try to get out early."

All week she'd been begging him for information and now he offers to share. If they didn't get the license today, for her, there would be no Immunone.

"I no longer care. Jake, if you don't come to my house with what I asked you for, I will not be here tonight. I'll be out of your life forever." There it was: the ultimatum. If he wouldn't do this for her, he certainly could not be trusted to protect her money. She held her breath. She'd either be leaving the United States single, or she'd be married with access to a fortune when she finished whatever task Saddam Hussein's sons wanted her to do.

Voices in the background, Jake calling, "I'll be right there."

Addie breathed, then gulped as she realized he'd not been addressing her, but whomever was on his side of the line.

"Addie, I don't know what's going on, but you have to promise me no police are involved."

"No police," she said. "Hurry, please."

CHAPTER THIRTY-SEVEN

What did Addie's threat mean, she'd never see him again? Addie was a grounded woman, not a drama queen. She'd never pressured him before. He hoped he could trust her and that this wasn't some kind of trap to link him to Karolee's death. He was still a person of interest and he would be for some time. The spouse was always in the cops' crosshairs, even a disinherited spouse.

How could Karolee cut him out? Was it even legal? Could he risk a legal challenge without incriminating himself? He was facing enough complications. And suddenly, this Addie emergency. What could this possibly be about? He had to go to her. She was his life. All these problems traced back to his need to be with her. The old doctor's death. Karolee's fate. All so that he and Addie could have a life together. And they would.

He cursed the streak of shitty luck that know-it-all woman doctor was bringing down. What had she meant by "she had the data in Tampa?" Did it mean she simply had to hop on one of Keystone Pharma's jets, drop into her former office, pick up the files, fly back, dump them on Sid Casey's desk, completely discrediting Jake? No way she could accomplish this in time for the meeting Casey had called for tomorrow morning. And he'd put the fear of God into the woman about proper FDA protocol. All bluster, but she wouldn't know that.

Jake had been thinking about ways to deal with Dr. Nelson when Addie called, all frantic.

He pulled the Jeep into his driveway and started to get out, preoccupied with why Addie would want to see Karolee's death certificate when the details of his wife's murder had been in all the papers—

"Hey, Jake!" His neighbor bolted out of his door, pulling a knit cap on his balding head. "Cops were here again, man. Dogs this time. First time they brought the dogs, far as I can tell. Didn't go inside. Just had them sniff all around. Came on my property too. Didn't ask permission, but hell, I don't care. Anything to find the guy who killed Karolee. Right, Jake?"

Dogs? Two weeks after the attack? Shit, could they track all the way back to Mack's garage where I left the Jeep that night? No way, not with the snow. But why come with the dogs?

"Thanks for letting me know. I have no idea what they're looking for, but yes, whatever it takes to find the bastard that killed my wife."

"You gonna keep living here?" his neighbor asked. "In the house? Alone?"

"Yeah," Jake said. Not at all sure where he'd be living. "Hey, I've got to get moving. Just stopped to pick something up. Gotta go." Without waiting for a reply, Jake let himself into the house, headed toward his study where he kept the important papers. There it was: Karolee's death certificate, a certified copy. Why would Addie insist he bring it with him? Without further thought, he jumped back into the Jeep and headed to her place.

***

Addie had given him a key to her apartment so he let himself inside. She wasn't in the living room, but as soon as he called her name, she came flying into his arms. He hardly recognized her. Her eyes were ablaze, puffy red circles surrounded them. Even the thought of her crying wrenched his heart. What could have happened?

"Please, Jake, we don't have much time. We have to make a decision. Today. Now."

"What's wrong, Addie?"

She all but pushed him into the living room.

He nudged her briefcase aside so they could sit next to each other on the sofa.

"Let me explain, then we need to decide."

"Okay." He turned toward her, taking both her hands in his. "Tell me."

"Orders from my father to return to Iraq. I leave on Friday. We have only two full days. Tomorrow and Thursday."

"He can't just force you to go," Jake blurted.

"Yes, he can. I must go. Do not waste our time discussing that. I will go. No questions."

"I won't let you," Jake stated.

"This is America. You can't stop me," she said. "If this were my country...but here's the thing."

Jake squeezed her hands tighter. "No!"

"Listen to me. What if we were to get married? Now. I mean, not today. But Thursday. Get our license today. I worked it all out, looked up courthouses. If we leave now, we can be in Ellicott City in an hour. There's a courthouse there—Howard County Orphans' Court—that specializes in marriage licenses. Nobody will know us. It's far enough away from Rockville and all the recent publicity about your wife." She jerked her hands out from under Jake's, pulled a sheet of paper from her shirt pocket. "Here's the address." She stuffed the paper into Jake's hands.

Jake glanced at it as she went on, "Important thing is that we have forty-eight hours. Say we can make it there by four o'clock, we get the license." Addie took Jake's face in both of her hands. "We could be married on Thursday. When I go home, I'll be your wife."

That's why she wanted Karolee's death certificate. Did what she was saying make any sense? Jake sat stunned, unable to process this. Yes, they'd be married, but she'd be in goddamned Iraq.

A marriage two weeks after Karolee's death would condemn him in the eyes of the public and perhaps the law—but without proof, so what?

"And here's what I was thinking," Addie said, jumping up, grabbing her purse. "Make sure you have your driver's license." She reached inside her wallet and pulled hers out. "Come on, I'll tell you in the car. About how I'll get a leave of absence, so I can still get the money when Immunone gets approved."

So, she had a scheme that did involve $7.5 million. And as her husband—

"Come on, Jake. Do you think I picked the right courthouse?"

Jake nodded, stood, and extracted the keys to his Jeep.

"Addie," he said, "I'll do anything for you." And he would. And he had. And it had not been about the money, he reminded himself. But $7.5 million didn't hurt. His job? Who cared anymore? Immunone's approval schedule and all his manipulation, had that been all for nothing? It didn't pay to think about that right now. Concentrate on getting to the courthouse before those lazy county bureaucrats close up shop for the day.

CHAPTER THIRTY-EIGHT

Tim's operating room team at CHOP was ready, the room set up, blood ready for transfusion, Gore-Tex patches on hand, the works. Two-month-old Malika Halabi had arrived yesterday from Riyadh, Saudi Arabia. The pediatric cardiac surgeons there had refused to operate. The little girl was born with tetralogy of Fallot, a congenital heart disease involving four heart malformations: a ventricular septal defect, an overriding aorta, right ventricular hypertrophy, and pulmonary stenosis. The father, a member of the royal family, insisted Malika be transferred to CHOP—the trusted surgical site for children of Saudi royalty.

Tim had met the baby and her parents on the rooftop helipad at their arrival from Riyadh via New York City's JFK airport. Cyanotic, edematous, struggling for each breath, the cardiologists needed the night to stabilize her for what would be emergency surgery as the morning's first case, but the child literally died on her way to the OR. Tim knew the chances of the baby making it through the long and difficult surgery with such large defects at this late stage had been next to none, but when it came to children, he never gave up. Never.

Watching children so ill and trying to quell the devastation of parents of the kids who didn't make it—like Malika's—so drained Tim that he'd never even contemplated being a parent himself. Exposure to such depths of agony was torture he could not accept. The closest he'd ever come to caring about kids of his own had been with Laura's. He'd lived through health crises with two of them: Patrick, when he'd had major cardiac surgery at CHOP as a nine-year-old; Natalie, when she'd caught a drug-resistant bacteria during a bioterrorism attack in Tampa. Each time, he'd been scared beyond imagination, and he'd felt so inadequate.

After the news came down about baby Malika, the surgical team had gone off to commiserate over coffee. Tim had excused himself, his emotions still too raw, needing the solitude of his office. He needed to process the baby's death in the context of his new life. Yes, he'd avoided parenthood, but what about grandchildren? Wouldn't he be a grandparent to Laura's kids' children? Would he be able to handle...this? What if...?

Stop it, Tim. With Laura, you can get through anything.

Laura had a bad night last night. Was it her hand or something else? To the disbelief of her hand surgeon, she was only taking Motrin for it now. He hoped she was faithful to her physical therapy. The therapist went to Keystone for the sessions. Made it easy for her but harder for him to monitor. He felt so protective of Laura; always had, even back when she was in med school, but his protective instinct had skyrocketed in the weeks since her devastating fall on black ice.

The crisis with Patrick consumed her, he knew. The story about David Monroe—Patrick's father—thoroughly perplexed him. Tim remembered Doctor Monroe as the God of Surgery in Detroit. The house staff all but bowed to him. Laura and Doctor Monroe? Tim could not wrap his head around that. But each time he looked at Patrick now, he saw Detroit City Hospital's revered chief of surgery. Paradoxical that Patrick never was interested in medicine; nor were Mike and Kevin. Laura's daughters would be the next generation of doctors in the Nelson family.

Tim hoped Mike's call this morning would push Laura to set things straight with the other kids. He'd observed Patrick closely during Laura's disclosure. Yes, her son had been upset, but he hadn't exploded in hateful anger. Laura needed to reach out to him. Should he urge her to, or just stay in the background, ready to pick up any pieces? Laura had so much on her mind now with the injury, the new job, and that incredible business about Keystone Pharma withholding key data.

Just as Tim reminded himself that he couldn't spend all day hiding out in his office, the intercom buzzed.

"Dr. Nelson on your line," the secretary announced.

"Laura, guess who I was just thinking about?"

"Tim, you're in your office. I called to give you a message, knowing you had that tetralogy surgery."

"The baby didn't make it," he said. "Didn't make it to the OR."

"Oh, Tim, I'm so sorry. Are you okay?" One night he'd confided his dips into despondency whenever he lost a child.

"I'll be okay. Feel shitty right now. The case was going to take all day. I think I'll make early rounds and come home mid-afternoon."

"What I was going to tell you was that I need to fly to Tampa later this afternoon to retrieve that Immunone data."

Tim didn't care if Laura could detect the note of disappointment in his voice. "If you can't avoid it, babe, but your hand! Are you supposed to travel?"

"Company plane. None of that airport security. I'll—"

"Laura," he interrupted, "I'll miss you tonight. I can't believe how much I need you—"

"Quick turnaround," she said brightly.

"Laura, that's too stressful. You are pushing too hard."

"I only need a couple of hours on the ground. To collect the documents I need. My secretary will have them ready."

"Stay overnight, Laura. I'll miss you, but—"

"I want those reports in the FDA's hands tomorrow. Mel and Louis will meet me at the airport tonight, take the documents. Their teams will work all night to collate them with their in-house documents and have them ready for submission in the morning. Lots of folks at Keystone aren't happy with me for keeping them up all night, but that's tough—as we surgeons well know."

"Bet they've never dealt with a whirlwind like Dr. Laura."

"Seriously, Tim, don't wait up. I'll just crawl in bed beside you."

"Be safe, Laura. I know my limits. I can't dissuade you from this...madness."

"Oh, in this damn Keystone maelstrom, I almost forgot to tell you. I talked to Patrick. Caught him between classes."

Tim took a deep breath. So much of Laura's happiness pivoted on her youngest son's response.

"He was polite, Tim, even pleasant. I got up the nerve to suggest that family pow-wow—to talk about, you know, this weekend. And whew—he said okay. Just like that."

"I do think he wants to clear the air."

"Do you think they will forgive me? All five of them?"

Tim caught Laura's tone change to dejection. He had wondered the same thing. If he had to predict, the girls would have a harder time than the boys. But how to know?

"Dear God, I want this to be done," she said. "And, Tim, thanks for being there for me, again."

"I love you, Laura. I'll always be here for you. Count on it."

After Laura hung up, Tim drew a large heart on his desk pad. Inside he inscribed: "Laura + Tim." Yep, just like a teenager.

CHAPTER THIRTY-NINE

Howard County Orphans' Court in Ellicott City, Maryland. Marriage license applicants: fill out a white form, stand in line *E,* have your documents ready. Eleven couples in front of Jake and Addie. The clock was ticking. Now 3:45. The court closed at 4:30. "Do you think we'll make it to the front in time?" Addie whispered in Jake's ear.

Addie's mind had been reeling with thoughts of her future in Baghdad. Would she ever be able to get out? To join her husband? Would he take proper care of her money, or would he steal it, find a new woman, and disappear into a life of Western opulence?

She could imagine his thoughts. Paranoid by nature, he'd be worrying about what the FDA officials would say about their marriage. And he certainly seemed much too concerned about what the police would do to him when they found out he'd married so soon after Karolee's death. They would find out, wouldn't they? She wanted to ask, but not now. During the ride to the courthouse, Jake had seemed on edge, shaken; not the public image she knew, the confident government official.

"Yes." Jake's single word response came out like a hiss. Addie looked around. All the couples in front of them looked star-struck happy. Except one who seemed to stare at each other in open hostility. At least she and Jake did not repulse each other. Addie thought of her fate should she not marry Jake. When she returned to Iraq, her mother would fly into a frenzy to schedule a marriage. Or did her parents already have a husband in mind? Addie would have no say. None. That's why she and Jake had to get this license now. Today.

"Jake," she said, tugging at his arm. "Are you okay? I know this is sudden."

"Yes, Addie," he pulled her to him. "I want to marry you. I can't live my life without you. That's why..." he stopped. Addie turned to look at his face, her heart breaking when she saw a lone tear. *He really loves me. I will be safe with him.*

"Then smile," she said, leaning in to kiss him chastely on the cheek. "Be happy, my wonderful Jake."

There were three couples ahead of them and two behind. Someone had blocked the end of the line with a chain. "Should we schedule the marriage while we're here? Would it be good to get married here?" Addie asked, sniffing the stale air. "Or could we go somewhere else? A more romantic someplace?"

"We have to wait forty-eight hours. I think we could find a nicer place, but Addie, we have almost no time. Once we are married, you said you had to leave, that going to Iraq to see your father was nonnegotiable." Jake pulled her in tighter to his body. "We'll only have one night before—"

"Don't think about that. As soon as I see my parents, I'll tell them about us. They'll be happy for me," she said. Addie knew they would not. There would be hell to pay for her and maybe her parents too. The punishment for marrying an infidel varied according to officials' moods. Perhaps, if her father needed her for important research, the regime would go easy on her. They may even honor her Western marriage and allow her to return once whatever mission they had for her was accomplished. But what would be the state of the world with all the talk of nuclear, chemical, and biological welfare?

The clock ticked, the queue moved, and Addie and Jake walked out with a Maryland marriage license.

CHAPTER FORTY

The FDA was requesting from Keystone Pharma documentation on the thirteen patients in the clinical trials who had died. Four on Immunone; nine on placebo. Laura, as lead investigator for the trials, had her own simplified records system. She had every record on every patient, and she could access them. Not only in computer databases but in hard copy. She had every scrap of data on each patient death, had pored through each case, had documented that the drug had not contributed to any of the deaths.

But after meeting with her staff about the alleged missing information at the FDA, Laura was less than confident that by tomorrow morning they could find all the needed documents. Apparently, Keystone's files were stored in different places, in different formats, under different protocols.

Prior to the Advisory Committee Meeting, she'd had an extended teleconference with the two Immunone medical reviewers, FDA Doctors Ridley and Hayes. The clinical trials had convinced the FDA reviewers that Immunone was lifesaving. Even though twice as many patients in the trial took Immunone versus placebo, the Immunone patients had less than half the number of total deaths. And an efficacy rate of 90 percent rejection-free on Immunone, versus 60 percent on placebo. Clinical data, they agreed, does not get any better than that.

Rather than hope the Keystone staff would locate their records in time, Laura would go to Tampa, get her records, load them on the plane, and personally deliver them to the FDA head of drug approvals tomorrow. No more dealing with Jake Harter. The bureaucratic wimp, whining about being unable to find documentation of blood electrolyte levels and QT intervals on the electrocardiograms. Ridiculous. She knew right where they all were in her old office, which her former secretary had assured her still was unoccupied, intact.

An ulterior and opportunistic motive competed for Laura's attention as she set up a meeting with Ed Plant, now the senior pulmonary surgeon in Tampa. Whether the administration would make him chief of surgery was doubtful, but hierarchical medical politics were no longer her problem. Her intent: secure Lonnie Greenwood's son the top spot on the lung transplant list. But would this be the first of unending demands from someone who could unravel the fabric of her life? He'd sounded pleasant, articulate, a caring father, but... But, she had to get on with her day.

The company plane was reserved, set to fly Laura to Tampa, but she'd have to skip her hand rehab. The throbbing pain had diminished to a low growl, except when put through the excruciating exercises devised by physical therapy. For these sessions, she only took Motrin, and even they were getting more bearable.

She'd been packing up her briefcase with her good hand when her secretary buzzed. "Driver's waiting to take you to the airport, Dr. Nelson, but there's a Philadelphia detective to see you. I told him you're on your way out of town. But he insists; says he'll be quick." In a whisper she added, "I think it's about Dr. Minn."

"Okay, then," Laura said, "as long as he's already here."

The door to her office opened and a middle-aged man in a rumpled flannel suit and an old-fashioned hat strode inside. "I'm already here," he said, taking off the hat, revealing a perfectly round bald spot. "Thank you, Dr. Nelson. Detective Simon Smith. I just have a couple of questions. Mind if I sit down?"

"Sure," Laura said, snapping shut her briefcase, ready to go whenever Detective Smith finished.

"I'll come right to the point. Your predecessor, Dr. Minn. Could you go over step-by-step what happened the night he was killed? We know you were the last to see him alive."

Laura felt a surge of guilt. Fred Minn had been so kind to her throughout her work on the clinical trials, and then he'd guided her through her prep for the FDA presentation. On that last night, he had tried hard to recruit her as his successor. How could anyone have foreseen what catastrophes finally would result in her sitting in his chair? She had been so focused on the pain of losing her profession, the physical pain, and now the challenges of a complex new job—his old job. The hit-and-run had slipped to the back of her mind.

"Almost three weeks," the detective was saying, "and we're no closer to finding the vehicle that struck him. My partner and I tried to interview you the day after he was struck down."

Struck down. She thought he'd say something in cop-speak like vehicular homicide.

"Thought you'd returned to Tampa...and then, well, we learned about the accident." Smith nodded toward her arm, in the sling-like device that kept the hand at the level of her heart to prevent edema. "And we never followed up."

"If I thought I could be helpful, I'd have called," Laura said, hoping this interview would be brief. She had a plane to catch. But she realized with a smug sensation, this plane would wait on her.

"Could you review the evening for me?" Smith requested, his tone respectful. "Everything from your arrival in the dining room until when you left Dr. Minn by taxi right outside the hotel?"

"Yes," Laura confirmed. "I asked him if he'd like to share the cab. He said 'no,' he only had a block to go." Laura glanced at her injured hand. "Now I know I should have insisted."

"You were not staying at the hotel?" Smith prompted. "How did you meet up that evening?"

Laura told him how Minn and Parnell had already been

seated at an alcove table in the Fountain Room. How they'd had a pleasant business discussion over dinner, and she and Minn had left the dining room together, collected their coats, and headed out the main door into the bad weather.

Smith nodded. "Did you see anyone lurking inside or outside the hotel? Anyone who could've been observing you?" he asked.

Laura had not. She'd been totally in the moment, intent on fending off the employment pitches both men were lobbing at her. She searched for any memory, but found nothing out of the ordinary. "No. Nothing that I noticed," she said.

"Please, Dr. Nelson. Take a moment. Go around the dining room in your mind. Did you see anyone out of place?"

Laura dutifully squeezed her eyes shut. So much had happened since that Sunday night when she'd left the Four Seasons, leaving Fred Minn to trudge to his death. Her hand broken to bits, her surgical skills obliterated, challenges in her new job because some incompetent at the FDA couldn't find critical documents, a long-ago nightmare revived... "Nothing. I'm truly sorry," she said, opening her eyes, seeing Smith's anxious expression; sorry she couldn't provide even a glimmer of information.

"Okay," he said. "But will you describe in the greatest detail possible the scene at the hotel front door as you waited for and then left in the cab?"

"Sure." Laura concentrated hard to remember the chill of the air as the doorman signaled the cab. The burly cabbie's pleasant demeanor. The scrunch of the tires as the cab left in the early snow of the evening. Then she remembered the noise of a vehicle engine. "There was a Jeep parked across the street that started up after my cab arrived. An older model, so I wasn't surprised by the loud rev of the engine."

"Did you see where that vehicle headed?" Smith asked.

"It pulled out onto the street across from the hotel, but then I jumped in the cab and thought nothing more of it." Laura was horrified. "Do you think that Jeep hit Dr. Minn?" She'd been so close. If only she'd turned to look. If only she'd insisted the elderly scientist ride with her...

"Tire impressions are consistent with a Jeep. Unfortunately, your cab driver had just pulled in to the Four Seasons, so he got just a cursory look, but he, too, reports seeing an older model, dark-colored Jeep. What we need right now is a tire match. If he's smart, the driver could have destroyed the tires."

"Sorry, Detective Smith. I wish I could have been more helpful. Dr. Minn was such a gentleman and so accomplished. He told me he was looking forward to retirement, going to sail his boat, spend time with his grandchildren in New Zealand."

"Yes," Smith said. "Everybody liked and respected the guy. Well, thanks for your help, Dr. Nelson. I know you're off to the airport." Smith pushed back his chair and reached into his pocket for his business card. "Call me if you think of anything else." He set the card on her desk. "Whoever killed Dr. Minn needs to be brought to justice."

Laura saw the detective to her office door and stepped outside to pick up her itinerary from Dr. Minn's longtime secretary. On seeing tears in the older woman's eyes, she went to give her a supportive hug. "I know you miss him," she said, "and I hope they find the person who did this to such a wonderful man."

CHAPTER FORTY-ONE

When Jake had proposed to Addie on Sunday—just two days ago—she'd seemed hesitant. And now, she was insisting they get married right away. Why the sudden change? Something to do with her father? His health was bad; she wanted to see him before he died. Understandable, but why so important that she return as a married woman? Was that an advantage? Would marriage enhance her image at home? Give her some kind of protection? Jake had no idea. Her culture and religion remained mysteries. What did make sense: marriage to him would secure her immigration status.

"So quiet, Addie. Are you okay?" he asked.

"Just thinking about all the things that have to get done," she said. "There's so little time. I'm worried about the legal things. I don't understand the American way. The laws here are so different from the ones in my country. I'm a scientist, and I never had to pay attention here to business or legal matters."

"I can worry about all that," Jake assured her. "Once we're married. I can handle your affairs. And that will be the day after tomorrow."

Immediately after they'd secured the marriage license, they'd arranged to come back to the same courthouse for their ceremony. Just the two of them; the court would provide witnesses.

"American law considers women equal. Sharia law—the basic

law of Islam—does not. Woman are rated as 'half a man.' Islamic law is just so different—in almost every way."

Jake noticed that Addie shuddered. "Addie, are you sure you want to go to Iraq so soon? You could wait, speak to your father on the phone, maybe plan your visit for later. Your family will understand you're newly married. Just postpone leaving for a while."

What about Immunone? As Jake waited for her reply, he flashed back to the drug approval—was the timing still critical for him and Addie? Or now that their marriage was scheduled—

"No." Nothing about Addie's response seemed to leave room for negotiation. "Jake, there's so much you don't know about Islam. Once I get back there—"

"Sharia? Isn't that some kind of banking thing? About charging interest?"

"Much broader, more complicated," Addie said. "It's a whole set of laws. I wish you'd learn more about my culture."

Jake was too obsessed about Immunone to worry about culture right now. Scenarios kept mixing in his mind. He had to get them straight. Scenario one: Immunone is approved very soon; that would be okay. Addie could leave for Iraq on Friday, he'd have power of attorney, and could manage her affairs. She would return as soon as she settled her father's issues. Scenario two: the Immunone approval drags on—thanks to his intervention—but now the tables had turned. They'd be married; the sooner she had her hands on the money, the better.

"Okay," Jake said, not sure what she'd asked for. He'd zoned out. Addie's hands were trembling, and he reached to hold one. "I will miss you terribly. How long do you think your father will need you?" He almost said, "your father will live?"

"I don't know, Jake," she said.

They'd arrive at Addie's place and Jake planned to go inside so they could prepare. So much had happened. And so much had to be done. After they were married on Thursday, they would go to see a lawyer to finalize the power of attorney. She would show up at Replica, distraught, needing to travel immediately to her dying father. With a parent dying, surely they'd approve a leave of absence. Or would they give her a hard time? Only as an employee of Replica would she be eligible to collect the money from Replica's sale of the drug. Would they be happy to have an excuse to renege on that agreement?

"Addie, I love you," Jake said, as he led her out of the car. "I will wait forever, but please, don't make me wait long. I need you so."

And he did. So much so, that he'd already killed two people. As much as he wanted to tell Addie, to prove to her how much he loved her, he had to keep that secret. For now. Maybe someday, when they'd been married for many years, he'd feel comfortable telling her.

As he and Addie entered her building, Jake had an eerie feeling that something was not right. When they stepped into the elevator, he turned as the door closed, but not before he caught sight of two figures he definitely recognized. Jake felt his stomach tighten as he followed Addie to her apartment and waited as she unlocked the door.

Once they were inside, Addie rushed to him, her arms outstretched, then hesitated. "Jake, are you okay?" she asked, taking a step back.

"I just saw the two—"

The doorbell interrupted, loud and harsh.

"Nobody ever drops by at this time," Addie said, reaching for the doorknob. "Maybe it's Dru."

Dru, the Iraqi guy who insisted she leave for Iraq immediately because her father was ill. Not that he didn't believe the story, her father was getting up in years, and Iraqi living standards weren't that good. Made sense that life spans would be shorter there.

But her company was not Dru. When she opened the door, a familiar voice announced, "Dr. Abdul, you may remember me, Detective Booker. My partner, Detective Finley? Mind if we come in?"

Shit. Shit. Shit. Those asshole detectives. Addie had told him they'd been there before asking questions about the night Karolee died. Now they find him here with the woman. "Gotcha." But, so what? Their marriage would soon be public information. Jake started to feel his heart hammer. He reminded himself that the detectives had nothing. They were on a fishing expedition.

Jake turned to face the detectives as Addie led them into the apartment. Had they been waiting for Addie? Or could they be looking for him? Do they know about our relationship? Best to tell them outright. Claim you and Karolee had been planning an amicable divorce before she was so horribly murdered. Wouldn't the fact that Karolee left him totally out of her will back up that scenario, that they'd been planning to end their relationship, both preparing to move on?

"Mr. Harter." Booker extended his hand as if was selling door-to-door insurance policies.

"We meet again," the younger, pudgier Finley said, moving across the living room. "Nice and convenient to get you both. Nobody home when we dropped by your place, Mr. Harter."

"We have a few questions about your relationship; handy that you're both right here," said Booker. "Mind if we sit down?"

"Okay," Addie mumbled.

Booker motioned for Jake and Addie to the two chairs opposite as he settled next to Finley, already seated on the overstuffed sofa.

"Dr. Abdul," Booker began, "We know you called the Harter residence the night of Mrs. Harter's murder. And you told us you needed information about a drug Mr. Harter is working on at the FDA?"

"By the way," Finley broke in, "what about FDA conflict of interest regulations? I had a case once—"

"Fin, let's not get distracted," Booker said.

"Just wanted to make the point that if the agency doesn't know yet what's going on between you two, they—"

Jake glanced, alarmed by the stunned look on Addie's face.

"Please," he said, "don't scare my fiancée. She's from the Middle East, where law enforcement officials at your home can mean torture, deportation, that kind of thing."

"Fiancée?" Detective Booker's expression did not change. "You two are engaged? As in, to be married? That kind of engaged? Not what we expected to hear. Huh, Fin?"

Finley rumpled his already rumpled hair. "This better be good. Mr. Harter, explain, please."

And Jake did. How he and Addie had met when she'd represented Replica at the FDA. How they'd carried on a secret affair. How he had been working out a divorce with Karolee. How they'd talked about it for years. How they agreed they'd both be happier apart, but until Addie, he'd had no motivation to go through with it. How he'd told Karolee about a woman in his life. How that meant nothing to her. How he'd agreed she keep all interest in her business and her investments. "And then," he said after a pause, "tragically, she'd died."

"Was murdered," Booker interjected. "But go on."

Now that he was a widower, Jake explained, there was no reason for he and Addie not to be married. They'd applied for the license. They would be married Thursday. No ceremony. Simple affair.

"And you chose to lie to the authorities about your marital situation," Booker stated. "Fin, you got the notes where Mr. Harter tells us that bullshit about 'just the usual married people stuff.' Why is it you didn't tell us about your 'impending' divorce?"

They caught you in a lie. Suck it up. Say you're sorry.

"I regret that, I truly do, but I just didn't see the point. I was in shock for days after Karolee's death. I wanted to protect her. Didn't want to air our dirty laundry. She was a proud and private woman—"

"We'll deal with all that bullshit later," Booker said. "And you, Dr. Abdul? You never thought to mention your relationship to the dead woman's husband?"

"I didn't want to get either of us in trouble," Addie said, lowering her head. "Everything Jake says is true."

"Didn't want to get either of you in trouble," Finley echoed. "So you lie to the police. You think that won't get you in trouble. You're supposed to be a smart woman." Finley leaned forward, shaking his head. "Where are you from?" he asked.

"Baghdad, Iraq," Addie said. Americans were not too happy with Iraq these days with suspicions of weapon of mass destruction secreted throughout the country. Jake knew it was just media hype. The UN had been over there and came up empty how many times?

"By the way, Dr. Abdul," Booker said. "Are you an American citizen?"

"No. I have a green card." Jake could deal with these bastards, but it killed him to see the fear in Addie's eyes. They were scaring the shit out of her.

"You still have family in Iraq?"

"Yes. My parents and—"

"Names?"

Addie looked confused, and Finley clarified, "Your parents' names."

"Jamail Abdul, my father. My mother—"

"What kind of work do they do?" Finley continued.

"My father is a medical scientist and my mother stays home," Addie said. Jake recognized the note of pride that had crept into her voice when she talked of her father.

"Yeah? What kind of a scientist?" Finley persisted.

Where was he going with this? What did it matter what Addie's father did for a living?

"A microbiologist," Addie said.

"Now, isn't that interesting. You don't know where they're keeping that anthrax shit over there, do you? The UN's tearing the country apart, trying to find that poison. Your old man's in the middle of all that?" Finley shot a look at his partner. "Booker, remember that briefing we got from the CDC? You think we might have stumbled into a State Department matter?"

"No way," Booker said. "She said her dad's a scientist, that doesn't make him a terrorist, Fin."

"He's very ill," Addie protested.

"Doubt the State Department cares much about his health," Finley remarked. To Addie, he said, "Give me your father's contact information at the institution where he works—or worked if he's too sick now. Can't be too careful. Your country is a mess. Can't believe the way they treat women. I just read the other day that if you're caught in adultery, you get stoned. You get caught filching something, you get your hand chopped off. Somebody doesn't like you, somehow you disappear."

"Quite the speech, Fin. Now, if you're done, let's get back to the murder of Karolee Harter," Booker said. "Mr. Harter, you are a person of interest in the murder of your wife, a more interesting one than before. Your affair with Dr. Abdul makes it much more interesting."

Booker then turned his attention to Addie. Asked her again about the phone call she'd made to the Harters' house.

"I told the truth," she said. "I called to inquire about Immunone. I needed to know. I had never, ever called Jake's home before."

"Why then?" Booker asked. Jake congratulated himself for getting rid of his answering machine. "Why the night his wife was murdered?"

"At the request of a friend who was interested. I told you that before." Addie's mysterious friend from Iraq. Who was this guy, and why is he interfering in Addie's life now?

Finley flipped through his notes. "Yes, Badur Hammadi. Your alleged alibi, Dr. Abdul. We've tried to find him. No success. No response at the Dearborn number you gave us. We need his work contact information. One of the reasons we came tonight." Finley actually grinned. "Besides wanting to extend our congratulations on your engagement, of course."

Jake remained quiet as Addie got up, walked across the room to a desk, and picked up a black address book. From it she read a phone number which she said would connect to Chase Manhattan Bank, the Cadieux Harper branch in Detroit.

"You still claim he'll alibi you for the night of Karolee Harter's murder?" Booker asked.

"Yes," Addie said, sounding a bit more composed.

Composed, Jake thought, until she realized the implication. The small address book fell to the floor, and her body started shaking so violently that Jake was afraid she might be having a convulsion. With tears flooding her cheeks, she managed to whisper, "*Me?* You think *I* killed Jake's wife?"

Jake jumped to his feet, flung his arms around Addie, and tried to ease her back into the chair. "I think you've terrorized her enough," he said, turning to face the two detectives, still sitting on the sofa.

"Maybe so," said Booker. "Dr. Abdul, would you give us some privacy, please, so we can talk to Mr. Harter—your fiancé—alone? We'll let ourselves out when we're finished. Perhaps we'll speak to you again. A lot depends on finding this Hammadi, and on what he has to say about your whereabouts the night of the murder."

Addie leaned against Jake as he helped her out of the chair and into the bedroom, waiting as she settled on the bed. "Don't worry, Addie," he promised. "This is just routine police work. Please, don't worry." A flicker of reassurance seemed to cross her tearful face. He gave her hand a quick squeeze, then returned to the two detectives in Addie's living room.

The interrogation that followed lasted two hours. A minute-by-minute accounting of his time on Wednesday, February 19th, the night Karolee met her fate. And then a repeat. And then a third round. Had he fucked up? He didn't think so. The timeline held. He'd rehearsed it so many times. How he'd left the FDA, how his car broke down, found out it was a broken belt; all corroborated by the Good Samaritan, Frank Barker, whom the detectives obviously had interviewed. Jake's time at the garage was well documented. There could be no doubt he did not kill his wife. Funny, Jake thought, even I'm beginning to believe I couldn't have done it.

The detectives, in Jake's opinion, didn't look encouraged. As they left, Finley said, "Do not leave the area. We're not finished, Mr. Harter. Giving misleading information in a murder investigation is a felony."

"On a happier note," Booker couldn't seem to resist a smirk, "congratulations again on your engagement to such a beautiful and exotic young woman."

CHAPTER FORTY-TWO

Laura had flown with two pilots and an attractive steward young enough to be her son. Thank goodness for his help unloading a dozen boxes of heavy documents. Maybe she'd transported more than she needed, but why not? She had the whole plane to herself, may as well take advantage of it. The Keystone Gulfstream landed at the private plane terminal at Philadelphia International Airport at 1:15 a.m.

Eileen Donovan, Laura's efficient longtime secretary, had met her at Tampa City around six that evening. She had each of Laura's file requests selected, ready for her approval, and packaged for travel. Laura hoped her new Keystone secretary would adjust to the workload once Laura got up and running in the job.

Laura had asked for the file for each of the patients who had died while participating in the Immunone study. She'd provided these documents to the FDA in advance of the FDA advisory meeting, having also reviewed them in advance in teleconference with the two key FDA reviewers, Doctors Ridley and Hayes. During the call, Hayes seemed to be tracking the data carefully, asking questions, clarifying. On the other hand, Ridley, the more senior of the two, sounded bored and uninterested.

Didn't matter now. Jake Harter, who, as project manager, was supposed to make sure the medical reviewers had all relevant data at their fingertips, now said the FDA didn't have the records. Harter either was incompetent or a liar.

Well, Laura did have it. In duplicate, it turned out. While in Tampa, she'd had a call from her staff. They'd located, organized, and packed up the documents on their end too. Protocol be damned, tomorrow, Keystone Pharma, led by Laura, would hand carry the data into the agency. Infuriated by her conversation earlier that day with Harter, Laura had requested a meeting with the deputy director of the FDA himself—Dr. Sid Casey. In less than eight hours, FDA management would be shown the proof of Jake Harter's blunder.

Exhausted though she was, Laura couldn't stop thinking about Lonnie Greenwood. How much did he know about that summer night in 1967 when she'd pulled the trigger that shattered Johnny Diggs' brain? One of Johnny's friends, Ray—aka Snake—Rogers, had figured it out, and successfully blackmailed her to keep him from going to the police. But Snake was dead, and she had dared to believe her secret had died with him. Until Lonnie Greenwood had called her office in Tampa, claiming he was a friend of the Diggs/Jones family, insinuating he knew something she'd rather no one else knew—but did he? Why had he waited twenty-five years? Would he be satisfied once Laura arranged a lung transplant for his son with cystic fibrosis?

If so, that was a motive she could understand. She would do anything for her children. And, she would do everything in her power to help young Johnny Greenwood. She'd already secured the transplant board's commitment to push him to the top of the list for a coveted lung transplant. She had procured his medical records, assessed him an appropriate transplant recipient, and arranged for Ed Plant to do the surgery. Her recent notoriety as the lead investigator in the studies leading to the approval of Immunone, and the generous donation of Paul Parnell to Tampa City Hospital, as well as her vice presidency at Keystone Pharma, put her in the ideal position to meet Lonnie Greenwood's demands, but would Greenwood stop there?

Laura tried to shut off that part of her brain when her limo dropped her off at Tim's—soon to be their—apartment at one forty-five. Tim was still awake, reading in bed. As she undressed, careful not to disrupt the layers of gauze wrapped around her right hand and forearm, he suggested a glass of wine or a cup of tea.

"Too tired, but thanks. You don't know how wonderful you are to come home to."

"All those wasted years." Tim put aside his book. "You look beat, babe. Just join me in here and be comfortable."

"Won't be for long," Laura said, reaching to set the alarm. "Leaving for DC at six o'clock."

"Success in Tampa?" Tim asked.

"Yes. I have what I need to debunk this 'can't find the data' crap."

"Remind me never to cross you, my dearest." Tim pulled up the covers on her side of the bed. "How's the arm?"

"Not much better. No worse." Laura snuggled up next to Tim and was asleep in an instant.

***

Tim must have been up by four o'clock. By the time Laura's alarm went off, she could smell the coffee. Tim, proving himself as husband material, she realized with a smile. Only two-and-a-half hours of sleep, but Laura felt a surge of energy for her day of vindication. She had what the FDA needed for their Immunone final approval, and damn the agency's stonewalling or blundering, she wasn't sure which. How could losing reports be anything but incompetence? And the way Jake Harter had carried on, you'd think his mission was to block approval of the drug. But why? Immunone would help so many patients who needed organ transplants, was much more effective than anything out there, and had fewer side effects. So what was his game? Could he have invested money in a competitive pharmaceutical company? Always a possibility, but the FDA did have conflict of interest laws.

As Laura taped a plastic bag over the wrappings on her injured hand and lower arm, she marveled at how quickly she'd jumped into the big pharma fires. She'd taken on the threat to Keystone's most promising drug, no holds barred. She'd asked no one's permission—or even advice—about her decision to ring up the top echelon on the drug side of the FDA and demand to be heard.

When she'd announced her plan to Louis Sigmund, her regulatory VP turned seven shades of white, but he'd simply said, "As you wish."

Her staff would support her, at least for a while. She was in that honeymoon phase of employment, when they gave your rope enough slack to get the job done or let you hang yourself trying.

***

Tim wore a tattered bathrobe as he served Laura scrambled eggs, bacon, toast, and coffee at the kitchen counter. "You look too good for two hours' sleep," he said, sliding into the hightop chair beside her.

"Wish I could do something with my hair," she said.

Tim ran a hand though her hair, fluffing the blond curls that fell to about even with her collar. "Most women would die for your hair, my dearest." Laura noticed a shadow cross Tim's face. "And your hand? You will have time for your therapy, right?"

"I hope so." Laura really didn't hope so. Those sessions were painful beyond belief. Necessary, she knew, but brutal.

"You coming home after your meeting or going in to Keystone?"

"Not sure. Depends on this dog and pony show, how long it runs. Hope I don't get thrown out. I'm going over a lot of heads. And, I've been warned that ignoring protocol often backfires, but who can stand on etiquette when the FDA pulls such an outrageous stunt?"

"Okay, oh righteous one," Tim said, reaching over to pour them each another cup of coffee.

"Thanks for fixing me breakfast at this ungodly hour, Tim. What's on your schedule for today?"

"We surgeons don't let lack of sleep deter us—" Tim stopped.
Former surgeon, Laura thought, *in my case.*

"Laura, I had a disastrous day yesterday. Lost that little Saudi girl. If only they'd gotten her here sooner. Even a day earlier may have made a difference. Every time that happens, I feel a bit of myself die too."

With a surge of guilt, Laura realized she'd been so absorbed in her corporate world she hadn't even thought to commiserate with Tim about the baby with tetralogy of Fallot, baby Malika. How Tim could deal with infants and children with major heart malformations was more than she could comprehend. Before she could think of something comforting to say, Tim continued, "Two procedures today—a mitral valve replacement, pretty routine. And then a cardiac tumor in a four-year-old. The imaging and echo for the kid look a lot like Patrick's. Just hope this little boy has such a happy outcome."

"Yes, Patrick," Laura said, starting to get up. Her limo would be here any minute to take her to the airport, to the sleek Keystone Gulfstream she now thought of as hers. "If only I could prevent the hurt I'm causing him now. I've been thinking, Tim. Let's go ahead and invite the kids for dinner Friday night, and tell them about Patrick, let them in on my shameful secret. I know I have to do it. Maybe the other kids won't be as gracious as Patrick. But I have to do this."

Tim walked with her to the door. He pulled her toward him, kissed her, then picked up her briefcase and placed it in her left hand. "Yes," he said. "Now you go do battle with the government. I'm betting on a Keystone victory. Do those Keystone people have any idea how lucky they are to have you on their team?"

"Bye, Tim, wish me luck. And do you know how lucky I am to have you on mine?"

CHAPTER FORTY-THREE

Every nerve in Addie's brain jangled. Her life was imploding around her. Her Middle Eastern roots clashing violently with the Western lifestyle she now preferred. In America she had a dream job, prestige with her PhD degree, a secure position in a hugely successful start-up. Highly respected, treated as if she were a male professional, not a half-person, as Islamic law defined females. And, she was about to come into more money than she could even comprehend—if she could keep her job long enough.

And then there was Jake, whom she'd always thought of as a convenient boyfriend, married and safe. But now, not married, and maybe not so safe. He'd dragged her into a police matter, and Addie knew what that meant. She could be arrested and never heard from again. But she wasn't in Iraq. America has courts of justice, and so many loopholes even the worst criminals could avoid arrest. In this web of disaster, she couldn't think straight.

Thankfully, Jake had been up and out early. He'd needed to prepare for an important FDA meeting. He hadn't told her what it was about. When she'd asked if was an Immunone meeting, he'd ignored the question. And if it was about Immunone, why wouldn't he tell her? What did that mean for her future? Marrying a man who refused to be honest with her?

As Addie went about making her morning tea, she felt her hands shake. Just thinking about Jake brought to mind the shocking visit from the police. They suspected her of killing Jake's wife. Why else would they insist on talking to Dru to confirm her alibi? And where was Dru? He'd needed to tell her how she would get her new documents and tickets to travel to Baghdad once she got to London. And why did she need false documents? She was an Iraqi citizen, living legally in the US with a green card. At this moment, she was desperate to find him. He must go to the police and back up her story. Would he do that for her, or would he be scared out of his mind too?

Her kitchen smelled like coffee, a smell she'd never grown accustomed to in this country. She rinsed out the carafe before she sat to drink her cup of tea. She'd allow herself a few calm moments, and then she'd reread the letter from her mother that had arrived yesterday. She'd grabbed it out of Jake's sight, before she realized he couldn't read Arabic. *Torn between two cultures,* she thought.

Dear Daughter,

You are to return home to us your father says. So very good. There is much for me to do. First, I have found you a husband. I have cultivated several, but most could not wait even though I tell them you are the most beautiful. The most good tempered. The most obedient in all ways of Allah.

Mother, you are so far off the mark there.

My friend Anah has still an unmarried son. And, Adawia, you will respect him. Maybe you remember Gabir. Gabir Rahman. Three years older than you. You used to see him at the mosque. Do you remember? Tall. Heavy now with the big belly. But lots of curly black hair. He fixes electric things. Sorry to say he did not go to university. So I am trying not to say much about how important a doctor you are. I just told Anah you are in America and you don't like it and want to come home and marry a Muslim man. Anah needs grandchildren and, of course, I want more too. So that shouldn't be a problem. And you and I know you have to work at the research like your father, but if Gabir likes you, he won't care too much.

Oh Mother, do you have any idea of how nauseous this Gabir person is making me?

So, I am going through the preparations so when you get here, all will be ready. Father has been so ill he hasn't been much help. And even being so sick, he still has to go to work every day. When you come, you take his place. That's what he tells me, but a woman? How can you take the place of a man like your father? But not my place to question. I have a lot to teach you about being a good wife. I taught your sister and I will teach you too.

You might find me a bit more difficult than my sister Farrah, Mother. Perfect Farrah, with her dictatorial husband and her two darling little boys.

Don't worry, Adawia, you and Gabir will be a good marriage, not as high-level on his side, but there are not many men left without a wife, my daughter. You are thirty-four years old. You have been away too long. Your father and your sister are all so happy you will be home with us. This will mean so much to your father. My darling Adawia, your father is not doing well. He's sick and needs you, but don't worry about anything. We will have all ready for you.

I can't do this. I just can't go back to that kind of life. A life without respect. A life as a half-person.

Your loving mother

Addie finished her cup of tea and fixed a piece of toast. This was going to be a long day, maybe the most important day of her life.

Dipping her toast in honey and sipping her second cup of tea, Addie mentally listed her options.

If she obediently went to Baghdad on Friday; did not get a leave of absence; did not marry Jake: she'd be working in bioterrorism; she'd be stuck with Gabir; she'd not have $7.5 million that could buy her way out of anything.

If she went to Baghdad on Friday; did get the leave of absence approved today; did marry Jake tomorrow: would she ever be able to leave Iraq? Would Islam accept Jake as her husband and let him join her in Iraq? Could she trust Jake to take care of her money, to not start a new life without her?

What if Replica did not give her the leave of absence, and simply terminated her on Friday? She'd never see the money, but would she still marry Jake tomorrow? What good would it do her?

And, what if she did not get on that plane Friday, two days from now? Married to Jake or not, her family—mother, father, sister, and nephews—would be killed. Could she live with that? And herself, the target of an Iraqi death team even in the United States for her insubordination...

Addie checked her watch. Time to go. The Human Resources office opened at eight thirty. She'd be their first customer of the day. Her hands shook more as she rinsed the cup and saucer before placing them in the dishwasher. Dishwasher. No such luxury in Iraq.

Mentally, she reviewed her decision tree. The first branch would be leave of absence or no leave of absence. Next would be marry Jake or not marry Jake. The last: return to Iraq or put at risk all whom she loved.

***

Addie wore a conservative, burgundy-colored suit for her unscheduled meeting with Human Resources. On a normal day, she'd be dressed casually in slacks and a sweater. Most days, she wore a long lab coat, so it didn't matter how she dressed up or dressed down. She arrived just as official working hours started and told the receptionist she needed to speak with the vice president. Replica was a small company. Everybody knew everybody, but as their most successful researcher—Immunone's creator and champion—she knew Priscilla Fabre would see her immediately. She was offered coffee, requested tea, and sipped her third cup of the morning.

"Come in, Addie." Priscilla stood at her office door, holding it open for Addie. Dressed equally as professionally and definitely more expensively, Priscilla greeted Addie with a wide smile, as she patted her gray curls in place.

Replica didn't have a separate public relations department, so Priscilla's responsibilities as a vice president included human resources and public relations. Addie guessed the stylish designer suit in shades of gray and matching Italian shoes had something to do with the imminent approval of Immunone. Should the approval happen today, Priscilla was dressed for television news.

Addie liked Priscilla and admired her determination. Recruiting Addie to Replica had been Priscilla's doing, and Priscilla had been the architect of Addie's employment agreement. Replica could not afford the escalating employment packages offered by the larger pharmaceutical companies, so they'd offered a modest salary, considered low for a scientist of her training. But to sweeten the pot, they gave her 5 percent of the selling price for her Immunone project, should it be acquired by another company. Contingent on Immunone's approval and contingent on Addie being a full-time employee of Replica at the time of drug approval. Since Immunone had been sold to Keystone Pharma for $150 million, her share amounted to $7.5 million. When the deal had been struck, the drug had been in an early phase of development. A risky venture, but now Immunone's approval was a sure thing—almost. Why hadn't Dr. Nelson called her back?

Priscilla was practically jumping up and down as Addie walked into her office, mug of tea in one hand and briefcase in the other. "Good news? So early in the day?" she asked expectantly.

"No, Priscilla. Not good. I have a request. For you, for the company."

"Sure," Priscilla said. "What is it?" The older woman took a seat across from Addie and leaned forward.

"My father is gravely ill. I have to return to Iraq to be with him." Addie's eyes started to tear and she reached into her briefcase for a pack of tissues.

"Here, Addie," Priscilla already had a handful of Kleenex which she pressed into Addie's hand.

"I may need to be away a while. I don't know how long. And I came to ask about a leave of absence. I still want to be employed, but I can't be physically here."

"I see," Priscilla said. "And I appreciate the timing of this request. When do you plan to leave?"

"Friday," Addie said. "I can't wait. He is desperately ill. I need to be there. I'm sure you understand."

"I lost my father two years ago," Priscilla said softly. "I still miss him terribly. I do understand. Problem is, this is not my decision. I recall your employment contract well. As a matter of fact, now that we are so close to having to pay you such a huge sum, I'm taking some flak for 'giving away' so much of the company's money. But I keep reminding the board, 'a contract is a contract,' and we wouldn't have Immunone at this phase without you. But I can tell you, they're not likely to cut you a break here."

"Can you ask them? Now?" Addie had to know. This was branch one on her decision tree. The tree that would mean life and death to many. Her family, yes. But what about future victims of mass bioterrorism? Isn't that where they want her to dedicate her research?

"I'll try to get our legal counsel if it's that important to you." Priscilla dialed, got passed through to the outside counsel Replica used. "But you should consider delaying—" She put her finger to her lips and whispered, "He's on."

Addie listened with an out-of-body sensation as Priscilla argued her case to the attorney on the other end. The attorney whose mission was to protect Replica. Addie could tell by Priscilla's body language and her end of the conversation that the request for a leave was being denied.

When Priscilla hung up, she faced Addie and shook her head. "The contract is clear," she said. "You need to be full-time employed in good standing. Of course, you could hire an attorney."

"Work with an American attorney from Iraq? Communication there is nonexistent." What Addie did not say was, *as a woman, I'll have no rights. No rights whatsoever.*

"When would you like your last day to be? Or do you want to reconsider?" Priscilla looked crestfallen. "We'll really miss you, Addie. You're a brilliant scientist and a lovely person. Everybody on staff loves working with you. I'm so sorry about your father, but maybe..."

What should I tell her about my last day? I have so many decisions to make.

"I'm sure you understand if you are going to be leaving as early as Friday—two days from now—there's paperwork that needs to be processed."

No leave of absence. No millions of dollars.

"I will reconsider, Priscilla. Thanks for trying to help me. I will think it through and let you know."

***

Addie all but shuffled back to her office, pulled down the window shades, and sat. She looked at her diplomas, her certificates of achievement, the trophy-like tokens she'd collected. They reflected her professional career, the years at the University of Michigan, the years at Replica. Now, all coming to an end. Would life be easier to accept if she'd never been sent to the United States? If she'd finished her training at Baghdad University, never having experienced the freedom and the pleasures of the Western world? Probably so. Wasn't her sister perfectly happy? And she'd never been outside of Iraq.

Back to the here and now, her decision tree. Addie had the answer to her first question: no. Now she had to address her second one: whether to go through with her marriage to Jake. Would being a married woman prevent the arranged marriage her mother was negotiating? From any perspective, being married to Jake— even if they never saw each other again—would be better than life with Gabir Rahman. But would Jake want to marry her now that she'd not have the money? She was quite sure he would. Until now, money never seemed to be a factor in their relationship.

"Well," she said aloud. "I'll put that to the test when he finds out I will lose the Immunone money."

CHAPTER FORTY-FOUR

FDA Deputy Director Sid Casey managed the drug side of the agency. The humongous agency consists of six product centers, one research center, and two offices. Of the six centers, the Center for Drug Evaluation and Research regulates over-the-counter and prescription medications. This was Casey's bailiwick and he took it seriously, agonizing over any trouble, basking in any success.

Susan Ridley and Karl Hayes were already in the deputy director's conference room when Jake arrived.

"You bastard," Susan seethed. "Jake, you fucked us over."

"What are you talking about, Susan?"

"You know goddamned well. Immunone. All that shit about missing data about the death cases. Well, Jake, there is no missing data. As we speak, the Keystone Pharma folks are presenting the missing data to Sloan and to Casey himself. They started at seven thirty this morning, did not invite us. Told us to wait here. What kind of shit are you trying to pull?"

"And the cops were here yesterday, asking questions about you and the woman scientist at Replica," young Karl added. "You been seeing her, I mean, romantically? Giving her confidential information?"

Okay so the shit's hit the fan. How am I going to play this? Jake had been so distracted by Addie and marriage and her Iraqi plans that he'd not formulated a credible story; how had the data gone missing? What was he going to tell them?

The conference room door swung open as his boss, Charles Sloan, entered with Deputy Director Casey. A stern-faced Casey took the seat at the head of the table as two Keystone representatives marched in, wordlessly taking chairs. His adversaries. That obnoxious new vice president, Dr. Laura Nelson, and Louis Sigmund, Keystone's regulatory affairs director, whom Jake had thought he could trust.

"We have an issue to resolve today, ladies and gentlemen," the deputy director announced. "I am here to relay to you how urgently we want resolution. I want you all to solve this matter before you leave this room. There will be no minutes or record of this highly confidential meeting. Sloan, get this debacle corrected. The agency can't tolerate negligence."

Jake tried to look straight ahead, but his gaze met Karl and Susan's hostile expressions. His eyes started to blink in rapid spasms so he squeezed them shut. Only when he heard Casey storm out of the room, did he open them to see the department's secretary enter, pushing a cart with three stacks of thick reports.

"I'll distribute," Sloan said, dismissing the courier.

Jake's eyes continued their involuntary blinking while Sloan handed out one report from each stack to each of the remaining attendees.

"I trust no introductions are necessary," Sloan began. "Dr. Nelson?"

"I'm familiar with Doctors Ridley and Hayes and Mr. Harter," Nelson said, with a nod to each in succession. "Although the last time we met, I was not yet a Keystone executive."

"And you've spoken with Mr. Harter as recently as yesterday?"

Nelson nodded.

What was this, a fucking deposition?

"And what about Doctors Ridley and Hayes?"

This time she shook her head. "No, Dr. Sigmund in regulatory affairs advised me that FDA-industry protocol frowned on the vice president of R&D calling a medical reviewer directly." She seemed to grimace, adding, "That was after I'd gone ahead and called Mr. Harter." Nelson paused to adjust the cast-like appliance on her right arm. Her transparent bid for sympathy, of course. "I thought my problem was simply an administrative error and he, as project manager, could solve it."

"How did your conversation with Mr. Harter go?"

"Keystone had received notice of missing information relevant to the deaths that occurred in the Immunone trials. I wanted to clarify with Mr. Harter directly, to assure him all required data had been provided. We sent the complete file package well in advance of the February 14th Advisory Committee meeting."

Jake forced himself to stay in his seat, to control his input. He wanted to leap up and strangle this impertinent woman. Who was she to put him down? She didn't know shit about how the pharmaceutical business worked. That when you dis' the FDA, they bury you and your company. And with this bitch, bury was not just an expression. He would *bury* her.

"And Mr. Harter told you?" Sloan prompted.

Jake kept his head up, didn't want to show weakness, but he did let his eyes wander to inspect the reaction of the medical reviewers. Would they back him up? Or would they throw him under the bus? Susan, usually so apathetic, looked alert and energized. And perky Karl, quite agitated, squirmed in his seat, eyes dilated.

"When I offered to have it hand delivered, he said normal channels would be sufficient, and it would take some time for him to get to it so..."

And right now, I don't give a fuck about whether the drug gets approved in the next minute or if it takes forever. Addie will go back to Iraq either way. Damned ironic, the sooner the approval, the better now. If I hadn't interfered, Addie would have her money, we'd be married, and I'd never have to worry about another job.

"Rather than wait, this morning we delivered two packages

of reports: one from Keystone's files, the other from my files at Tampa City Hospital, where I was the primary investigator for the clinical trials. These documents are identical to those that already had been provided to the FDA for the Advisory Committee."

"Mr. Harter," Sloan said, his tone chillingly formal, "after we spoke yesterday, I asked Doctors Ridley and Hayes to assemble the data you'd declared missing. They did and I inspected it with Keystone's representatives this morning." Sloan gestured to the piles of documents on the table. "In front of you, you have three packages. Each contains the exact information you found missing: ours, Keystone's, and Dr. Nelson's from Tampa. I want you to review the reports, side by side. We want you to review each, personally. Now. While we wait. So there can be no misunderstanding."

"You want me to what?" Jake asked. "You mean, right here with all of you watching?"

"Exactly. I want this settled here and now, so there will be no cloud over the approval of this drug. If you find a discrepancy, or a missing data point, inform us now and we will deal with it. To make it easy for you, we developed a checklist of the components you could not locate. You check them out to your satisfaction. Take as long as you like."

The room remained silent except for the clinking of coffee cups on saucers.

Options? Did he have any? Five pairs of eyes focused on him as he opened the FDA report, cross-referenced it with the checklist, and started checking off the boxes. Thirteen patients: four on Immunone; nine on placebo. EKG reports and lab values.

"Yes," Jake spoke after thirty-five minutes of pretending to pore over the report. "The data I'd been unable to locate are here. I see no need to go over the Keystone version or the Tampa version. I don't know how this had gotten misplaced, but I'm glad we found it. Thanks, Susan and Karl."

What else could he say? He'd tried to deep-six some of the

reports, but the FDA has an amazing backup system. But what the fuck. The approval of Immunone right now, today, would now be of benefit to him.

"Indeed," Sloan said. "Doctors Ridley and Hayes pulled this together very efficiently. So, Mr. Harter, as project manager, you are satisfied we have no problem with missing data, our records are intact?"

"Yes, sir," Jake said. He almost added, "Cover Your Ass." At the FDA, even the lowliest employee could blow the whistle about anything that smacked of impropriety.

"Then let's get this drug approved," Sloan announced.

Jake wanted to slap the smile off of Nelson's face. A violent slap, one that would teach her never to fuck with Jake Harter. Instead, he directed a menacing gaze at her lackey, a man he'd worked with in the past, a man who should not have betrayed him, the sycophant, Louis Sigmund.

"Mr. Harter, please prepare the documents for approval. The commissioner will sign the approval in the morning, and we'll have a press conference in the lobby at noon tomorrow. Doctors Ridley and Hayes, thank you very much for your extraordinary efforts in bringing this to resolution."

The Keystone duet, all bubbly with smiles, had already pushed their chairs back, anxious to report to their buddies in the company and start the celebration. On their way out, they shook the hands of Sid, Susan, and Karl, ignoring Jake. "Ignore me at your risk," he mumbled, before realizing he'd no longer be a risk to Keystone or any other pharma company. He'd be basking in wealth with his gorgeous bride. Wait until Addie heard the news! How could she leave for Iraq at the pinnacle of her success?

As the jubilant pharmaceutical executives filed out the door, a shadow of a storm crossed Jake's face. He'd always paid his debts, be they financial or otherwise. And he owed Dr. Laura Nelson a debt of retribution.

"Jake, don't leave yet," Sloan said, once the others had cleared the room.

Jake remained seated as his boss took a chair across from him.

"I don't know what kind of a game you tried to play with that missing data claim, and I really don't care. You're either losing it or you have an ulterior motive. No matter, you have a bigger problem. The police have been by to ask about you and the woman doctor at Replica. They say they have evidence you were having an affair with her during the time you were responsible for Immunone. Since she has a substantial financial stake in that drug, you've got a major problem with conflict of interest. When Casey found out, he decided—"

"Well, you tell Casey," Jake interrupted, "that Adawia Abdul and I are getting married. And, I will be leaving the FDA."

Sloan's face registered shock. "So soon after Karolee...?"

"I can't bring my wife back," Jake said, delivering the lie effectively, he hoped. "Karolee would want me to get on with my life."

"Twenty-five years at the FDA," Sloan leaned back in his chair, the surprised look replaced by one of relief. "Hate to see you go, but your resignation will make life easier. We were going to have to put you on paid leave until this conflict of interest situation was investigated."

"You'll have my resignation."

"And Jake, the FBI came to see me."

"What?" Could this have to do with Minn or Karolee's murders? Both local police matters. So why the FBI?

"Apparently, your bride-to-be has some scary stuff in her background. That's the impression I got. Iraqi connections that have them scrambling."

Scrambling? More like his brain was scrambling.

He made an effort to come to Addie's defense. "She's a wonderful woman, very smart—obviously, as her discovery of Immunone proves."

Jake was finding it hard to make sense of what he'd just heard. What could the FBI want with Addie? Could she be in some kind of trouble? Is that why she wants to return to Iraq?

"I have to say, Jake," Sloan went on, "I'm shocked by your affair with the Replica doctor. And your sudden marriage to her? Does your son know about this?" Sloan did know Karolee left all her money to Mark. Jake had confided that during a weak moment.

Now Jake was up and at the door. "No, Mark does not know, and I don't intend to tell him. After he screwed me over with Karolee's money, I don't need him or his miserly wife."

Without a good-bye to Sloan, Jake left. He needed Addie, wanted to hold her in his arms, to help her if she was in some kind of trouble. What was all that about the FBI? Plus, he would tell her the confidential news: Immunone would be approved tomorrow.

CHAPTER FORTY-FIVE

"The name Badur Hammadi mean anything to you two? NSA Deputy Director Mack Long asked his two direct reports in the NSA's Information Assurance Directorate—IAD."

Long ran stubby fingers through his steely-gray, close-cropped hair. A Stanford-trained, mathematical-computer genius, Long had served his country in the navy as a vice admiral. Now, he headed up the domestic arm of NSA's surveillance—eaves-dropping—and supercomputer mission. He found it suited him. More pressure, maybe, but of a more intellectual nature. Following his daily briefing at the Pentagon, he'd called to his office his two closest aides.

He watched as their two heads—one blond, the other black—shook in unison. These two not only fascinated him, they'd won his respect: the lanky, former special service agent, Tommy Mintner, and Paula Sharkey, the African-American mi-crobiologist from USAMRIID. Long's brownish skin reflected his own biracial genes, and he did all he could to promote racial di-versity in the agency.

"Should we?" Mintner asked, perplexed.

"CIA's had an interest in him for a while," Long said, draw-ing a photo out of a manila folder. Both heads shook again as they scrutinized the photo of a young, tan-skinned man in stylish Western garb.

"Iraqi?" Sharkey guessed.

"Yep, and seen recently in the vicinity of an Iraqi scientist, Dr. Jamail Abdul. Abdul has close ties with—"

"I know Dr. Abdul by reputation," interrupted Sharkey. "Saddam Hussein. His name comes up in scans for anthrax-related intel as well as other organisms with mass destruction potential. What's the connection?"

"Turns out Abdul's daughter has been in the States right under our noses for twelve years. She got here via the University of Michigan. Got a PhD and went to a start-up drug company in Bethesda. The one in the news lately with a new drug for transplant patients that's about to hit the market."

"So, she's been under surveillance," Mintner said, "by what agency?"

"Negative. Best not to make assumptions when it comes to the silos of our intel systems. Abdul's daughter has avoided NSA radar. She's used her own name, filed all the necessary paperwork, the connection just never surfaced."

"Why now?" Sharkey asked, twisting a black curl in her hand.

"Four hits just yesterday," Long reported. "Random pickups. One, Abdul's daughter, was questioned by the Rockville cops about a murder that occurred a week or so ago. She needed an alibi, as the dead woman turned out to be her boyfriend's wife. She gave Badur Hammadi as her alibi. His name crossed our links, got flagged. From the same Rockville cop report, we intercepted her father's name. When the cop asked for her father's name, she readily gave it up."

"Strange," Sharkey said. "It's like she has nothing to hide?"

"You said four hits," Mintner prompted, anxious for the meeting to end, the action to begin.

"When we intensified the cyber web over the DC corridor, we found a marriage license application for Adawia Abdul, the daughter, and Jake Harter, an FDA employee, the boyfriend whose wife was murdered. And we found an airline ticket issued for Adawia Abdul from DC to London for this Friday."

"So she's going to Europe? A honeymoon?" Sharkey suggested. "That FDA guy traveling with her?"

"Back to Badur Hammadi. Last week, satellite surveillance picked him up in Baghdad at the entrance to one of the palaces where Qusay Hussein and Hussein Kamel are holed up, presumably masterminding weapons of mass destruction beyond the reach of the UN inspectors."

"Airline evidence of travel?" Sharkey asked.

"No record of Hammadi leaving the country. Must have an alias," Long said. "Sharkey, what do you know about Dr. Jamail Abdul? Rumor has it, he's being treated for severe heart failure."

"He's a respected scientist. Heavily into the genetics of microbiology. Rumored to deal with organisms such as anthrax and botulism. I'd half expected the UN inspection teams on the ground in Iraq to unearth sites of materials he's bioengineered."

"What's our role versus the FBI at this point?" Mintner asked the prickly question. NSA was a super-spy agency. The FBI, the enforcer—within the boundaries of the USA.

"We are consultants to our FBI brethren, but let me make this clear. The president, our commander in chief, wants those WMDs found. We're into the tenth round of IAEA inspections and, so far, zilch. Reputations and national credibility are on the line. These connections were made solely by our intel, but I'll have to brief the FBI. Meantime, you two get to the bottom of Badur Hammadi's relationship with Saddam's regime, and find out whether there's any connection to what the Abdul woman is doing in the US and her father's role in Baghdad."

Mack Long didn't linger for his agents' reactions. They wouldn't be pleased about working with FBI agents, considered them infinitely inferior in both intelligence and patriotism. Reaching for two packets in an accordion file, he handed one to Mintner and one to Sharkey.

Long stood. "Update here first thing tomorrow."

CHAPTER FORTY-SIX

Fighting tears, Addie walked out the front door of Replica, heading for the FDA. She had to tell Jake she'd been denied a leave of absence, she would not be getting the $7.5 million Replica owed her. How would Jake react? In her own mind, she still hadn't decided if she'd be better off arriving in Iraq married to Jake or as a single woman, the earmarked bride of Gabir Rahman.

She felt a jab of reality as she approached her car. Would she ever drive again? Not a privilege enjoyed by Iraqi women. A key to independence, an independence she'd come to cherish. She needed to relish Western culture during her last few days here. As she pulled out her keys to the sleek black Audi, she noticed a tall, striking-looking black woman in a chic burgundy-colored suit. The woman seemed to be looking directly at her. Beside the woman, a white man in a dark business suit was speaking into a walkie-talkie.

Addie with her dark skin, black hair, and black eyes often attracted curious looks. More frequently now after the Gulf War—or the American War as they called it in her country. In America now, all signs of Middle Eastern roots attracted the silent scrutiny and covert mistrust of a populace obsessed with weapons of mass destruction. For the first time, she realized these suspicions may not be so misplaced. What would she be doing when she returned to Iraq? She had to remind herself that she looked no different. You are just Dr. Abdul, a scientist, not a terrorist. Not yet. What had Jake always said about those glances, if not outright stares? "People think you are exotic—and the most beautiful woman they've ever seen." She gave the couple no more thought, climbed into her Audi, and headed for the FDA.

The outdoor parking lot for the FDA at the Parklawn Building in Rockville was situated across the street from the massive structure. An elderly security guard sat in a small, controlled-access booth. When Addie pulled up, she stated she had a meeting with Jake Harter. The guard found Jake's name on a computer and motioned her to enter. She'd expected him to call to confirm that meeting, but he had not.

As Addie walked toward the crosswalk, she again saw the black woman and white man pair she'd seen in the Replica parking lot. How could this be a coincidence?

"Dr. Abdul?" A woman's voice made Addie turn, taking her eyes off the suspicious pair.

She recognized the blond woman stepping away from a man in a pin-striped suit. "Dr. Nelson?"

Addie hiked up her shoulder bag and held out her hand to Dr. Nelson before she noticed the woman's right hand was in some kind of bandaged cast.

"Call me Laura," Dr. Nelson said, offering her left hand. "I know you've been trying to get hold of me. I've been out of the office a lot."

Addie couldn't help but stare at the woman's right hand, the bulky bandage. "I heard about your injury and I'm so sorry. And will you please call me Adawia—or even better, Addie."

"Okay, now we're on a first-name basis. You know, Addie, I so much appreciate what you've been able to accomplish with Immunone. As the lead clinical investigator, I have first-hand knowledge of its promise for transplant patients, but it wasn't until I took over as Keystone research VP that I realized just how innovative your early research was. Replica and Keystone, and an endless number of transplant patients, owe you so much."

"Thank you." Addie was touched by Laura's genuine gratitude. Had Replica shared this sentiment, they'd have let her keep her job. But, no, greed had taken over. This was America, after all.

"Once we get the approval, I'd like to organize a joint celebration, some of us from Keystone and your colleagues at Replica. And how about connections from the University of Michigan? Isn't that where you began your research on the Immunone class? One of my sons went to U of M. Kevin graduated in 1989, but you would have been long gone from Ann Arbor by then. He loved the university. 'Go Blue!'"

"Yes, 'Go Blue!'" Addie smiled, recalling with a thrill the game Dru had taken her to in the Big House. The roar of the crowd when the Wolverines scored against their enemy, Notre Dame. The acrobatic cheerleaders, the University of Michigan Marching Band. Not that she understood the game, but the excitement had been intoxicating. "I loved Ann Arbor." All this Michigan talk reminded her of Dru. Where was Dru? Addie's elation faded to fear when she thought of the Rockville police visit to her apartment.

Then she remembered the suspicious couple following her. Trying to look nonchalant, she checked her surroundings. Right by the security booth at the parking lot entrance, and their attention was openly directed toward her.

As Addie focused on the lingering couple, Laura turned to her companion. "I'll just be a minute," she called. The man nodded, and Laura gave her attention to Addie.

"I'm sorry to keep you," Addie said. As anxious as she was to talk to Jake, she wanted to avoid walking by the suspicious couple if she could.

"No problem," Laura said. "My colleague's anxious to get back to Keystone. We have very good news. News that you will be—" Laura stopped midsentence as an olive-green Jeep careened around a row of parked cars, heading for the exit.

"Jake," Addie yelled. "Excuse me, Dr. Nelson—Laura—I need to see Jake Harter. That's his car. Darn. Looks like he's leaving."

"That's Jake Harter's car?" Addie saw Laura's eyes widen as they followed the Jeep out of the parking lot. "That greenish Jeep? Are you sure?"

"Yes, and I need to talk to him and—"

"I think I've seen that Jeep before," Laura said, her cheery mood changing. "How well do you know Jake Harter?"

What to say? Addie attributed much of her success to instinct. And on instinct she trusted Laura Nelson. Maybe it was the straightforward way she'd presented the Immunone data. When the committee threw out tough, challenging questions, Laura had answered directly, honestly, not hesitating.

"Maybe I shouldn't say this, I hope it does not jeopardize Immunone's approval, but I know Jake well. He and I are..." Addie hesitated, knowing that if her skin tone were lighter, she'd be a bright red. "...lovers."

Laura—now she thought of the older woman as Laura—turned back to her companion, calling, "I'll be a few more minutes." Facing Addie, she said, "Did you know that's considered a conflict of interest?"

"Jake told me we had to keep it a secret, but if we get married, then it'll be okay?"

"Look, I'm new to this industry. And since the approval of Immunone is imminent, I'd hate to be the one to blow the whistle. Does the FDA know?"

Imminent? Blow the whistle? Addie slumped against the nearest vehicle, a red pickup truck.

"Addie, are you okay?" Laura stepped up, steadied her with her left hand. "Maybe we should go inside, sit down."

"No, I have to find Jake." Her glance followed the Jeep out of the lot—in the direction of Replica. Addie managed to stand almost upright, and withdrew her hand. "What did you mean by 'imminent'?"

"Well, Addie, I think you're going to like this. It's not yet public knowledge, and, if you promise not to run to the press or to your bosses at Replica..."

Like she'd be talking to "the press," and she'd no longer have bosses at Replica. But will I have a husband? So preoccupied by her primary dilemma, she hardly listened to what Dr. Nelson was saying about Immunone.

Addie risked a glance at her observers. They'd eased up closer. But within hearing range? She didn't think so. Who were these two people?

Laura's companion waved back at her, respectful. Here men treated women as equals. When she returned home, things would be different. Could she adjust? She'd been homesick for so long when she'd arrived in America, but now...

Laura waited for the answer, but Addie was so distracted, she struggled to remember Laura's question. Oh, yes, she wouldn't...

"Jake Harter knows," Laura prompted, "but not the general public. And they cannot know before the press release. I'm not much into finance, but it's all about the stock market response. And, don't do any insider training. A week ago I didn't know a thing about it, but insider training is a crime."

Too complicated. Addie needed to concentrate on her $7.5 million. Was it back within her reach? Hope crept into her brain until she recalled Laura's original question.

"Dr. Nelson, I will speak to no one about this. I am so confused about American laws—what's legal and illegal. But it's okay to talk to Jake because he knows?" She needed clarification. Her elaborate decision-tree thing was crumbling.

"I'm Laura, remember?" Laura smiled and patted her shoulder. Addie stood straighter, feeling stronger. The next two days would determine the course of her life.

"We at Keystone had a meeting this morning with the FDA about Immunone. Jake Harter had reported missing clinical data. Data the FDA clearly did have, but for some hard-to-explain reason, claimed they couldn't find. I know that data backwards and forwards, and I flew to Tampa last night to retrieve it. Keystone, too, found the data." Laura paused. "I know you've been calling me about the progress of Immunone's approval process. Do you know Jake had misplaced the data—his claim was the reason the approval was delayed?"

"What?" Addie asked, resisting dizziness again. "He said there were problems. He never said what." She'd asked him so many times. He'd evaded her time after time. What kind of game was Jake playing? He knew how important it was to her to get Immunone approved before she had to go back to Iraq. He knew she'd have to sacrifice the money if she walked away from Replica. There must be a logical explanation. She needed to ask Jake, confront him if necessary. Was there something she didn't comprehend about American men? What they seemed to want, they didn't want? Where did that leave her?

"We couldn't figure out what was going on at the FDA, but as of this morning, I think it's cleared up. We and the FDA are having a joint press conference on Friday just after the approval is signed. We may want Replica to participate too. Your company may even ask you to represent them. But, I'm getting ahead of myself. We have many details to work out. This'll be big news on Wall Street. And most importantly, we'll save the lives of so many that need organ transplants. We started on lungs, but we'll be doing trials on hearts and livers and kidneys—"

"Friday," Addie interrupted. "Immunone will be approved on Friday?"

"Yes," Laura said with a wide smile. "Remember, you have to keep it a secret for another two days. But now I must go, my colleague is getting restless."

Laura started to walk off, but before she did, she turned back. "Addie, I want to make sure I understood what you said about the Jeep we saw pulling out of the FDA parking lot. You said it belonged to Jake Harter?"

Addie shifted her gaze to the man and woman couple still observing her before answering, "Yes. That was him driving. It's urgent I talk to him."

"Where does he live?" Laura asked.

"Rockville," Addie said. "Not too far from here."

"Does he have any connections in Philadelphia? I think I've seen that Jeep before. I remember because my son Kevin had the same model before he collided with a deer on a Pennsylvania mountain road."

"Philadelphia? I don't think so." Addie's eyes again panned to the stalking man and woman. How long would they lurk? Once Laura left, should she head back to her car, or walk inside the FDA building as if she was proceeding to her planned destination?

"Hmm," Laura said. "Well, I've enjoyed talking to you, Addie."

Uncertain where to turn, Addie lingered a moment too long as the observant pair approached her, the woman calling her by name. "Dr. Abdul, please give us a minute with you."

Addie stood transfixed. What could she do? Run away? Hardly, in three-inch heels.

"We're from the government. On a joint task force." The woman spoke, but both showed her ID cards that looked official. Addie was too shaken to read the name of the agency. Did it matter? The government was all-powerful. What would they do to her? Lock her up? Torture her? *Stop it. Find out what they want.*

"Come with us, please, to the Pentagon. We need to talk to you." The man spoke, after introducing himself as Agent Mintner and his partner as Agent Sharkey. Strangely, they'd both offered their hands to shake and she did, but her hand trembled.

"Now's not a good time." Her voice sounded small, terrified. The Pentagon? She knew it was military. Was it a prison? She didn't know, should have paid more attention to American institutions.

"It's very important, Dr. Abdul." The woman spoke, her voice firm, deep for a female.

"Okay, but can we go inside here and talk?" Addie gestured to the looming FDA building. "They must have a small conference room." She knew they did, Jake had escorted her into one the day she visited him.

"Please, just come with us. If you ride with us, we'll bring you back here to get your car."

"The Pentagon—why?" Addie got up the nerve to ask.

"Because our headquarters are forty-five minutes farther— Fort Meade—and timing is essential," the blond, good-looking man said.

They escorted Addie between them to their waiting vehicle, a black sedan, maybe a Lincoln. All three sat in the back seat, Addie in the middle.

The man told the driver to proceed to the Pentagon. The woman said she'd like to inspect the contents of Addie's purse, please. Addie nodded her permission. What else could she do? In her wallet the agent would find her driver's license, green card, Replica ID, credit cards, and her car's registration. And in the side pocket she'd see the airline ticket to London. Addie's worst fears played out. Under arrest in a foreign country, privacy violated, co-erced. What everybody said about American freedom was false. She had so much to figure out, but panic and a piercing headache precluded any logical thought process. She needed Jake. And she needed Dru.

CHAPTER FORTY-SEVEN

"Was that Dr. Abdul from Replica?" Louis Sigmund asked, when Laura joined him at the stretch limo waiting to take them to the airport.

"Yes," Laura said. Should she mention that Adawia Abdul and Jake Harter were having an affair? No, she decided, best to keep her mouth shut. Laura had no way of knowing what would happen if Addie's affair with Jake Harter, the FDA project manager, came to light. Would Immunone's approval be compromised? She didn't think so, but the last thing she wanted was an obstacle to the drug approval so important to her employer. How different this job was from the practice of surgery and the management of a hospital.

"Interesting discussion. She's a very bright woman."

"Attractive too, exotic," said Louis. "So what did she want? A job with Keystone? If so, I think she'd be great for our Pharmacology Department."

"No, not a job." Laura said, "But while I was talking to her, I saw Jake Harter drive off in a dark-green Jeep. Do you know whether Fred Minn knew Jake? I mean, on a personal basis?"

"Highly unlikely," Louis said. "Why do you ask?"

"I thought I saw a similar vehicle outside the Four Seasons the night of the hit-and-run. When the police questioned me, I forced myself to recall everything I remembered from that night but—"

"Lots of dark-colored Jeeps out there, Laura. Don't let your imagination run away with you."

Laura realized how silly she must have sounded and shrugged her shoulders.

"You've got something real important to do, Boss." Louis held out the car phone to her. "I'll dial, but you get to tell Paul Parnell the good news—we got the approval! Customary that the VP of R&D delivers the news."

"My pleasure." Laura smiled as Louis dialed Keystone's CEO.

"And we have champagne on the plane for the trip back to Philly," Louis announced. "Another tradition. You know, Laura, we all felt you were making a grave mistake, breaking protocol and going up the chain to the deputy director, but damned if it didn't work!"

Laura immediately was put through to Paul Parnell, and once she'd told him they could expect approval on Friday, she could sense his elation though the phone line. He put her on speaker phone, and gathered all her department heads to hear the good news. Amid their cheers, she emphasized the approval was because of their efforts, and how proud and honored she was to share in their success.

Once she and Louis settled into the plush seats of the Gulfstream, champagne was served. Laura took a token sip, then handed her flute back to the attendant. "I was up all last night," she explained. "Any more of this will knock me out. In fact, Louis, I hope you don't mind if I close my eyes? Suddenly, I realize how tired I am." Laura started to recline the plush seat, but stopped midway. "I'd like to make one more call before we take off."

"Of course," Louis said, accepting a refill of champagne.

Laura leaned over to pull a card out of her briefcase. She dialed, waited as the call went to an answering machine. Lonnie Greenwood was not available. She left a message for him to call her tomorrow at her office. She'd tell him about his son's optimistic chances for a lung transplant. Worry about the repercussions later.

Then Laura leaned back in the seat, closing her eyes. Too tired to rehearse what she'd say to her kids Friday night when she faced them all to finally tell them the truth. Would she stretch to the breaking point the bonds with her kids that had always been so strong? And would Patrick *really* be okay?

***

The next thing Laura remembered was Louis tugging at her arm. She needed to raise her seat to the upright position for landing. She checked her watch, two thirty. Then she turned her attention to the throbbing in her hand. She'd neglected to elevate it and the swelling had put enough pressure on the dressing to turn her fingertips blue. She'd missed her physical therapy yesterday, and since she had to put in an appearance at work on such a celebratory day, she'd miss it again today. Once she reached her office, she'd loosen the bandages, lessen the pressure, take more Motrin.

CHAPTER FORTY-EIGHT

Immunone would be approved on Friday. Jake had to tell Addie. He sped out of the FDA parking lot, heading for Replica about ten minutes away. They would be married tomorrow—Thursday. Naturally, she'd postpone her visit to Iraq by a few days. That way she'd be here for the actual approval and there'd be no question about her employment status. And they'd take a few days for a romantic honeymoon. The two of them. Married. Extravagantly rich. Immensely happy. At least for a few days—then he'd have to let her visit her family, break the news of their marriage. After that, he'd leave it to her. Jake honestly didn't care where they lived, what customs they adopted, or what religion they followed. All he cared about was holding Addie in his arms, every morning and every night.

Addie had planned to request a leave of absence today, and Jake wanted to get to her before she talked to Human Resources. He hoped against hope she hadn't rashly resigned outright. He checked his watch. Eleven o'clock.

Parking in a handicapped space in the visitors' lot, Jake bolted for the front entrance to the small company. In the lobby, he found a group gathering. All smiles. Had the news of Immunone's approval already reached them? It wasn't supposed to, there was a news embargo until the press release, but since Immunone was Replica's discovery, maybe their management would find out in advance. If not, now that he had confessed to being Addie's fiancé, the FDA would probably assume he was the leak. So what? He'd quit. Nothing they could do to him now.

Jake introduced himself to the receptionist, a thin, twenty-something girl. He asked her to call Dr. Abdul.

He waited as a circle of Replica's management headed toward a small conference room off the lobby. Among them, he recognized Priscilla Fabre, the human resources director. Had Addie already spoken to her?

"Sorry, Mr. Harter," the receptionist set down the phone. "There's no answer."

"Is she in the building?"

"I have no way of knowing. She did come in earlier this morning. She may have left without my seeing her. Sometimes I have to step away, deliver packages, that sort of thing."

"I'll just go up and check. Maybe she's in the middle of something in the lab."

"No one's allowed beyond Reception today," the girl said, tucking her long brown hair behind her right ear. And in a lower voice, "Something's going on." She pointed toward the conference room, its door now shut. "The management board—all in there."

"Surely, that can't mean me." Jake pulled out his now defunct FDA credentials. "I know how to find her office."

"Oh, we have a protocol for FDA visitors," the girl said, and started to thumb through a file on her desk. "I need to interrupt their meeting." She nodded toward the conference room with the closed door.

"Don't worry, Lisa," Jake said leaning a bit closer to read her name tag. "This is not official business."

The receptionist appeared flustered, and Jake gave her a quick wink. "Personal," he said. "Let me surprise her."

"I'm sure Dr. Abdul would like that," Lisa said. "But not today. The head of security gave me strict orders, in person."

He wasn't getting anywhere with Lisa.

Should he knock on the conference room door, ask for Priscilla, find out if Addie spoke to her—

No, Jake decided. Why make assumptions? Head to Addie's house. If she wasn't there, keep calling her at work. One thing for sure: he had to talk to her. Immunone's approval had changed just about everything. And to think he'd done all he could to stop it. Even killed an old man. "Fate is unpredictable," he mumbled as he unlocked his Jeep. Just a week ago, he wanted that drug approval delayed to keep Addie here. Now, at the most perfect of moments, the FDA would approve it. He patted his faithful vehicle before climbing inside. He would miss his Jeep, but moving up to a Mercedes wouldn't be so bad.

***

Jake unlocked the door to Addie's apartment. Calling her name, he passed the kitchen and headed for the bedroom. Empty. All normal. Bed made. Dishes in dishwasher. So, she must be at work. He called her office. Voice message. The normal one, she'd call back as soon as possible. He called the receptionist. No, Lisa had not seen Dr. Abdul leave, and she'd been at her station ever since Jake had left Replica.

Where could Addie be? Yesterday, he'd asked her what she planned to wear at her wedding. She'd seemed depressed at the question, and he had not understood why. He'd figured she'd be missing out on some Muslim ceremonial ritual that might have triggered a surge of nostalgia. Had she gone shopping for a wedding gown? Not really a gown, he knew, but a new—maybe white—dress. Was white the custom in Iraq? He had no idea. But Addie did love to shop, so she could be gone for some time. If so, she must have submitted that request for a leave of absence. How had it been received?

Eventually, Jake made himself a ham and cheese sandwich, wondering if he'd be allowed to eat ham when he visited Iraq. Muslims didn't eat pig; that much he knew; Hindus didn't eat beef. He hadn't realized how hungry he was and he made himself a second sandwich, this time adding tomato, lettuce, and mayo. He felt better when he'd finished, and let himself contemplate his luck, how it was all coming together, how this was his last day as a single man—rather, a widowed, single man—how tomorrow afternoon he and Addie would be man and wife. That's all he wanted in life. Nothing else mattered. Not the money, not the actions that circumstances had required of him, not the probability that they'd have to spend time in her country. He'd upgraded 'possibility' to 'probability,' but he'd not conceded to 'reality.' Not yet. Surely, in the course of their American luxury honeymoon, she'd decide they'd be happier living in the United States—somewhere warm, like California or Florida. Or maybe a Caribbean island.

As he finished his second sandwich, Jake realized with a jolt that he kept his passport in his office. While Karolee was alive, he felt it was more secure out of her way, lest she go on an angry rampage and decide to deep six it. After her death, he'd never thought to retrieve it. Now, with his and Addie's new plans, he'd need it. Besides, he wanted a few other personal items from his office, accumulated over twenty-five years, that he cared enough to keep.

"One more call to Addie," Jake said aloud. "If she's not there, I'll get my stuff at the FDA and stop by Replica again." He sighed. "Just in time for rush-hour traffic."

Picking up the phone to dial Addie's direct line at Replica, Jake noticed the blinking red message light. Had it been on before? Must have, or he'd have heard the phone ring. He pushed the message button and listened: "Addie? It's Laura Nelson."

Jake almost dropped the phone. Oh yes, he knew that bitch's voice. The one that ripped him into a million little pieces just this morning. But calling Addie at home? Calling her by her nickname like they were *girlfriends?*

"I enjoyed chatting with you this morning. Don't worry, I'll keep everything in confidence. But I have a question about the Jeep. Can you give me a call? I believe you have my office and home numbers. Take care."

In confidence? The Jeep? Home phone number? Addie, what have you been up to?

Jake slammed down the phone, grabbed his keys, and headed out of Addie's apartment building. He'd check again whether she'd shown up at Replica. Either way, he'd next go to his office, pick up his belongings. Then what? Figure out Addie's connection with Nelson, and why she had mentioned a Jeep in her voice message. A sickening thought—could Addie be with Laura Nelson now? No way. Impossible.

Just drive, Jake told himself, as rage directed at this evil woman surged. Accelerating, foot pressed too hard on the gas, he tried to stop at the light before it changed from yellow to red, but failed. Impact with the dark-green pickup truck was immediate and violent. Metal on metal, a rain of chunky, shattered glass. By the time Jake could release his seatbelt and stumble out of his car, he saw the burly driver of the truck, swiping at the oozing blood on his broad forehead and coming at him, menace in his eyes.

"Shit!" was all he could blurt out before a beefy fist slugged him in the face. In the background, screaming sirens pierced the air.

CHAPTER FORTY-NINE

Dru never had signed on for espionage. Back in 1971 when he came to America, the United States was on much better terms with Iraq. He'd been welcomed as a business school grad student in Ann Arbor. At first he'd had assimilation problems, but as foreign students do, he soon fell into Western ways. While studying for his MBA, he began to appreciate the principles of capitalism and even democracy, always defending them when he felt he was safely with a Western crowd.

From the beginning, he'd had no illusions about his role; why the regime had supported his education and allowed his lifestyle. They needed Iraqi citizens on the ground in America to provide them with the real facts, not the propaganda they thought the press fed the world. In America, what was reported in the media was pretty much reality. Not all, but most of what appeared in the international news covered by US media was factual. That could not be said for media in Iraq or most countries in the Middle East.

Dru's career in banking had served the regime well. He'd been compliant to his country's request for inside information; he'd shared with them processes and procedures used by his employer of nineteen years, Chase Manhattan; he'd given them lists of clients, even inside trading tips. What he'd done over the years was illegal, but he'd never come under scrutiny. He dressed like a

US businessman, spoke with no accent, attended business-related social affairs, followed sports, drank alcohol, ate pork. His colleagues often remarked that he was more American than the average Joe.

He lived in the Muslim-populated—mostly Shiite—section of Dearborn, but never invited Western coworkers to his home, something that had frustrated his wife. Iraqi-born Shada was attractive, totally Westernized—following their arranged marriage—and an excellent cook who loved to show off her skills. Dru loved her dearly, and they were devoted parents to Ali and Sam. When Dru was called to a foreign country to meet with his Iraqi contacts, Shada was understanding, asked no questions, welcomed him home with affection and trust.

But for each routine, there is an exception. For Shada, that exception was Adawia Abdul. Dru had been assigned as Adawia's mentor when she came to the University of Michigan twelve years ago in 1980. That had been the year he'd been summoned to Baghdad to marry Shada, the sister of his brother's wife. Shada had not been pleased when Dru spent evenings and weekends with the beautiful, young doctoral student. Adawia still was a sore subject in the Hammadi family, even though Shada had gone to Eastern Michigan University and earned a bachelor's degree, her English now flawless, her beauty a challenge to Adawia's.

Upon return from his recent trip to Baghdad, Dru made a decision. He moved Shada and the boys to a remote area in Alberta, Canada, a place he'd identified years ago for a worst-case scenario. Shada had vigorously objected, but finally relented when he told her as graphically as possible about Qusay Hussein's and Hussein Kamel's threats. To make matters worse, Shada's trust in him had radically eroded when she'd discovered his recent renewed interaction with Adawia. Shada and Dru had not parted in a loving manner.

Right now Dru couldn't find Adawia. He needed her under his direct surveillance until she boarded the London flight en route to Baghdad via Jordan. He was quite sure he was being followed and that did not bode well. The same car he'd seen when he stopped at the gas station, he'd seen at the curb outside Adawia's apartment building. Nervously, he checked his watch. Three o'clock. He had only forty-eight hours to get her out of Washington, DC. He'd secure her as soon as she came back to her apartment and stay overnight with her. Tie her down if he had to. If her old-man boyfriend gave him a hard time, he'd deal with him too. Dru had no doubts as to his proficiency with his Spyderco knife, a four-inch steel blade with an Emerson opening hook. His training back in Iraq hadn't been just academic.

As he paced, Dru decided to call Shada from the pay phone just outside Adawia's building. He had to talk to her, to make sure she was okay. To his dismay, the suspicious car was parked on the street about half a block away. Dru placed the call to the Canadian exchange, thinking how Shada would go ballistic if she knew he was calling from outside Adawia's residence.

"Dru, I'm so glad you called," Shada answered.

"Is everything okay? The boys?" he asked, trying to quell the panic in his tone.

"They're okay, but I'm so worried about you. Dru, why do we have to be hiding like this? The boys miss their friends. What are you doing, Dru? Are you okay?"

"I'm fine, Shada. I don't want you to worry."

"But I don't know how to contact you. What if something happens to the boys and—"

Dru let the phone slip when he felt a heavy tap on his shoulder, and turned to face two men in dark suits.

"Mr. Badur Hammadi?" the burly one asked.

"FBI," the trim, dark-skinned one said. "We need to talk to you."

Had Shada heard? If so, she'd be frantic. He had to terminate the call now so the Feds didn't catch on. But...he fumbled for a name as he retrieved the phone: "Okay, Fred," he said, "I'll take care of it tomorrow." He hung up, faced the men and said, "My boss." Once the words left his mouth he realized he'd screwed up. A simple matter for the Feds to track this call, and it wouldn't be to Chase Manhattan in Detroit. They'd know he'd lied. That's how they trap innocent people. For the first time, Dru came to realize America was just as much a police state as Iraq. Freedom was nothing more than an illusion—just as his teachers had told him when he was a little kid in school.

"We'd like you to come with us," the burly one said, as the other grabbed his right elbow in a not-so-subtle move.

"Why? What did I do?" he said, refusing to budge.

"All will be explained," the thinner one said. "Once we get to the Pentagon."

"Pentagon? Isn't that the army?" Dru said, needing time to think, to decide. Go or resist?

Not that there was a choice, as the agents escorted him to a dark-colored sedan. Before opening the car door, the larger of the agents told him to spread his legs and lean forward, hands against the car. The one with the dark skin felt inside his jacket pockets, finding only gloves. When he moved to his jeans pocket, he found the knife.

Dru's heart accelerated, sweat breaking out on his forehead despite the chilly air. He'd been told by a colleague at the bank that the four-inch blade was technically illegal, but the guy at the gun show where he'd bought it had said, "No problem with the carry."

"Mr. Hammadi, we're going to take the knife," the burly officer said, removing a clean handkerchief and handing it to his partner before continuing his search for weapons around his waist, the length of his legs. "Not an automatic release," the officer reported to his colleague. To Jake, he said, "We'll hold on to it for now. Give it back when we're done, unless..."

Unless, circulated over and over in Dru's brain as the knife went into a plastic baggie. Then he was ushered inside the Feds' vehicle. Alone in the back seat of the car, Dru asked again, "Why are you taking me to the Pentagon?"

"A matter of convenience," he was told. "The agents wanting to talk to you are from the DIA. They normally work out of Fort Meade. The Pentagon is closer. Plenty of interrogation rooms."

Dru had never made it his business to follow the various alphabet soup of agencies of the American government. "What's the DIA?"

"Defense Intelligence Agency."

After that he asked no more questions, and the two agents in the front seat chatted about the formation of the "Dream Team." In normal circumstances, Dru would have jumped in, offering his projections for the first American professional-player team to compete in the Olympics in Barcelona that summer, plugging Isaiah Thomas of the Detroit Pistons. But these were anything but normal times, so Dru kept his mouth shut, worried whether he should call an attorney, wondering whether that American privilege extended to this Defense Intelligence Agency?

Dru had driven by the Pentagon on several occasions over the years Adawia had lived in the DC area, but he never could have imagined being taken there. Now he was on his way, escorted by agents who had found a knife in his pocket. He had failed. His fate was sealed. His family was doomed.

Once they'd arrived, the same two agents took Dru to a conference room located within the maze of the huge, looming, white building. Maybe he'd never leave the Pentagon. This was a military establishment; this is where the Americans did their torture. Once they got what they wanted, they simply eliminated their victims. Not dissimilar to Saddam's regime in Iraq. Just more secret. After all, they did have to maintain the pretense of justice.

The burly agent asked Dru if he wanted water or coffee. Dru nodded a reflex response.

"Okay, Mr. Hammadi. Which? Water or coffee?"

Water or coffee. Was this it? Poison in the drinks? No, too easy.

"Coffee," Dru mumbled. He was a caffeine addict. Would get a blistering headache if he didn't have any soon.

"Be back."

Both agents left, locking the door behind them. He was trapped, would never get out of this behemoth of an institution.

Dru waited for twenty minutes before the two agents returned with a mug of steaming coffee. The aroma filled the small room, and Dru eagerly reached out for the drink.

"Sorry it took so long," the skinny one said. "Freshly brewed."

"Nothing but the best for our clients," said the other agent. "We're saying our good-byes now. Depending on what the DIA guys determine, we may turn you over to the locals for illegal possession of a weapon. Have to see how it all plays out. Lots of jurisdictions in play here."

Jurisdictions? Like, if they eliminate me, who cares about the knife?

"Wait here. The DIA agents will be in shortly. Enjoy your coffee."

When the FBI agents left, Dru was even more scared. They'd treated him humanely. No telling what these clandestine DIA people were about.

Alone in the drab conference room, sipping his coffee, feeling more clearheaded, Dru assessed his options. Qusay Hussein himself had ordered him to deliver Adawia. She was vital to their escalating bioterrorism program. If he failed, he and his family would be executed. Of this, he had no doubt. Imprisoned here, he could not get Adawia out as ordered. He needed to tell her how to access the fake documents that would get her from London to Jordan and on to Baghdad. Without them, she'd have to use her own passport and her own money to get to Baghdad. Would she do it on her own?

Dru knew he must appear to cooperate with these Feds, but he could tell them nothing about his link with Jamail Abdul and the Iraqi regime. He had to protect Shada and the boys. Once Adawia was back in Baghdad, he'd join Shada in Canada. Right now, Canada seemed a safer place to live.

Dru finished his coffee, wishing he'd asked to use a restroom before the two FBI agents had left. How long would they keep him here?

CHAPTER FIFTY

Addie sat rigid in a straight-backed chair at a conference table somewhere in the Pentagon. Her interrogators sat across from her. Agent Tommy Mintner, a friendly-appearing, youngish blond guy, and Agent Paula Sharkey, equally young, African-American, and eager to convey that she was a trained microbiologist. Mintner's questions focused on Dru; Sharkey's, on Addie's father.

They'd asked about her alibi for the night Jake's wife was killed. She'd given them Dru—Badur Hammadi. They knew about the Maryland marriage license. They asked about marriage plans. She told them. Friday, same courthouse. Nothing more. They'd asked her about her family, her father, what he did, about his research. She'd been honest, explaining he was a research doctor in Baghdad. She had no one but herself to blame for exposing Dru and her father by her honest answers. She should have been more evasive.

About Dru—Mr. Hammadi—they wanted answers about how long she'd known him. Where they met, how often they saw each other? Why he'd visited her recently? Why was she traveling to London in two days? Wasn't she still a suspect in Karolee Harter's murder investigation? Had the police confirmed her alibi with Mr. Hammadi?

She kept answering the Dru questions truthfully, with one exception. She denied having any knowledge about his travel. As for her trip to London? "Just a holiday," she said, and "no, no one told me I couldn't leave the country. The police were going to talk to Dru, Mr. Hammadi, to confirm my alibi, that I was with him the night Mrs. Harter was murdered. I don't know whether they did or not. I've not seen him."

As the questions kept coming, Addie began to realize the Americans must have some kind of high-tech listening program. Where they monitored phrases and names and places and who-knew-what for key words. The agents wanted her to know that her father's name was a key word, a word linked to the most dangerous names in Iraq: Hussein Kamel, Qusay and Uday Hussein, and Saddam Hussein himself.

Addie—as well as the whole world—knew the Bush administration was frantically looking for "weapons of mass destruction." Ever since the Gulf War ended a year ago. There had been ten different inspection teams sent by the United Nations, each with a specific agenda. The focus was not only nuclear, but also chemical and biological. That's where her father came in. He was Iraq's top microbiology scientist. Who else would Saddam trust with his bioterrorism initiative? Addie's father had never divulged this secret, but she'd figured it out when Dru demanded she return to "carry out his research." The American spies must have figured it out too, and now she was in the Pentagon, being interrogated. As if she had no other pressing problems.

Addie struggled not to break out in tears as she answered questions. Not knowing what her father had been doing helped. She could simply say, "I don't know," "I haven't been back home in four years," "My research is antirejection science; his is microbiology—two different fields." She did not reveal that the underlying biomechanism for Immunone for antirejection was similar, very similar, to chemical entities with the potential to resist certain organisms—anthrax, to be specific. With her know-how, Iraq—or the United States, if they were interested—could have an antidote to newer, more lethal anthrax strains, and could operate with impunity in an anthrax bioterror attack.

"Yes, I realize that," Sharkey said. "But you are his daughter. What do you know about his research?"

"Nothing," Addie had to repeat, as the question was asked over and over.

Mintner, the more human of the two, asked if she wanted water. She said she did, and he went to get it.

Alone with Sharkey, the woman said, "You and I have a lot in common. We both graduated from the University of Michigan Medical School. Both at the top of our class. So we're both smart. Look at us, even our suits are the same color." Sharkey pointed to her trim suit and to Addie's, the same shade of burgundy. "I don't buy that you're not playing into your father's hands. He's brilliant. As a microbiologist, I followed his career until your country stopped sending scientists to international meetings. My experience at USAMRIID tells me he could cook up an anthrax plan as easily as most can boil water. So even if you don't know diddly about microbiology, it would be easy for him to pass along to you what he knows. Wouldn't it?"

Yes. That's exactly what I think is going on. He's ill and the regime wants someone well-trained that they can trust.

"Is that what you want, Dr. Abdul? To produce toxic organisms that will kill indiscriminately in the most horrific of ways? Have you ever seen an anthrax death? I have."

Addie shook her head and, finally, a tear trickled down her cheek. "No, of course I don't. I want to heal, not hurt...or kill. Why are saying this to me? There already have been ten inspections throughout Iraq; nothing has been found."

"There are still places we—the UN—cannot go. Places where your father has ready access. The Presidential palaces, for instance."

"I don't know," Addie said. What if they knew Dru had been at the Radwaniyah Palace only recently? And there were many other palaces where her father could move freely.

Agent Sharkey had leaned across the table to fix her with an intimidating stare.

Addie slumped in her seat, lowered her head, and let the

tears flow. Sharkey reached over to a shelf for a box of Kleenex, passed it across the table to Addie.

Addie was blowing her nose when Agent Mintner returned with her glass of water. "What...?" he started.

"Dr. Abdul knows more than she's telling us," Sharkey said. "Dr. Abdul, I'm a microbiologist, and I get it that your antirejection drug Immunone has similar properties to newer antibiotics, those effective against evolving resistant organisms such as anthrax."

Addie was stunned. This woman had figured out the link between Immunone and the discovery of related chemicals that would protect against bioweapons of mass destruction. Chemicals the West would want to develop. What would they do with her? Could they force her to work with them? Keep her here against her will?"

"You are free to go," Agent Starkey was saying. "But we may have further questions."

Addie nodded, needing to get out of this oppressive building. She was an Iraqi citizen.

She needed to talk to Jake, but first she needed to get to Dru. She'd told the Feds all she knew about Dru, but truthfully, she didn't know much. He was an Iraqi who'd befriended her in college, who helped her navigate Western ways. When that agent asked if Dru had visited Iraq recently, she'd said, "Not to my knowledge." A lie, but a safe one, she thought, unless they interrogated Dru and he told them otherwise.

She was worrying about just this possibility as Agents Mintner and Sharkey walked her to the exit.

"A driver will take you back to your car," Sharkey said. That's when a familiar figure rounded the corner to her right, his back to her. Dru, wedged between two men in suits. The Feds had Dru. Here. Now. What would he tell them?

***

Only after the agency driver dropped Addie off at her Audi in the FDA parking lot did she begin to shake so violently that she had trouble inserting the key. She'd held herself together in the back seat of the FBI car, having not said a word, not shed a tear, but once alone, she slumped over the wheel of her car, her body heaving with gulping sobs.

The sun was setting by the time Addie sat up and started the car. She didn't know what to think, what to predict, where to go, whom to trust. Those DIA agents hadn't actually threatened her, she realized, with a slight sense of confidence; as a matter of fact, they'd been quite cordial.

Her main focus was on Dru. What had he told them? Had the Feds meant her to see him? She didn't think so, but in a secure building that massive, could it be a coincidence their paths had crossed? She didn't think that Dru had seen her, but his presence there changed everything. Would he contradict what she had told the agents? Didn't law enforcement everywhere try to play one suspect against the other? Would Dru use her to his own advantage? Would the DIA agents let him out as easily as they had her?

Dark enough for headlights now, Addie switched them on and drove out of the parking lot. She'd head home where surely Jake would be waiting. She'd tell him all about today. How she'd left her request for a leave of absence up in the air at Replica. Good thing, as Immunone's approval had been confirmed for Friday, as Jake well knew. She'd tell him about being picked up by the FBI and about the DIA interrogation. Maybe he could explain to her about the different agencies and the task force they kept referring to. But would he still want to marry her now that she was a target of the federal government? If she was married to Jake, an American, would it give her protection under the American laws? She presumed it would. He did love her, but would he marry a woman under government surveillance?

Addie found a parking spot and, as she walked the short block to her building, she wondered where Dru's loyalties lay. With Iraq, where his parents and brother still lived? Or with the United States, where his kids were born and his wife seemed happy? How long could he walk the line of dual allegiance? He'd told her, hadn't he, that he was scared for his wife and kids, and had sent them off somewhere? Did that mean that he'd made his decision? He was choosing the West, sacrificing his family in Iraq? Leaving them to the horrors of torture by Qusay Hussein?

And what about her family? If she was not on that London flight on Friday, her parents, her sister, would be arrested, maybe tortured, even killed. What would happen to her two little nephews? Would they take Farrah's husband too? Leaving two more orphans among the thousands of Iraqi children who'd lost their parents to war or torture?

Addie could not let that happen. She'd comply with the orders handed down to her through Dru. Married to Jake or not. As she turned the key in the door of her apartment, she planned to tell Jake everything, let him decide.

CHAPTER FIFTY-ONE

Tim's surgical case had run for ten hours. Laura had called him six times during the day, but he had not been able to take any of the calls. Later, she missed him at home because he'd stopped at the grocery store on his way. At each failed connection, she'd left a message, upbeat, bubbling over with excitement at Immunone's imminent approval. Except for the last one, just before she'd left Keystone. She'd sounded exhausted. Well, who wouldn't? Tim tallied the reasons. Laura had less than two hours sleep last night. She was only sixteen days post extensive surgery on her shattered hand. The pressures of her new job were even greater than expected. She'd taken it upon herself to divulge a deep, dark secret of her past to her kids, risking a lifetime of their respect and loyalty. She'd not allowed herself time to deal with the psychological trauma of losing her cherished surgical career. Other than that, no problem. Or so Laura would have you believe.

On the way home, Tim had stopped to pick up steaks, potatoes, salad makings, and a bottle of champagne. Laura would have had a glass of the bubbly with her colleagues at Keystone, but when she got home, he wanted it for just the two of them, a simple dinner, sipping champagne before a glowing fire. She'd been self-sufficient for so long that he wanted to shower her with attention, to protect her—as much as she'd let him—from overexertion, from overextending herself.

As Tim seasoned the sirloin and set it aside to prepare the potatoes, he couldn't help but chuckle. *Who am I kidding? Laura thrives on hard-core work and responsibility. Why the hell would I want to change her?*

But his smile turned to a frown when Laura came through the front door. Tim wiped his hands on the nearest towel and rushed to her side. She was struggling to remove her coat, all but strangling herself with the scarf caught in the left coat sleeve. The dressing on her right arm and hand was too bulky to fit in the sleeve, and when the coat fell to the floor, Tim noticed the edema and discoloration in her right hand. Last time he'd checked, the color was pink, and there'd been no swelling whatsoever.

"Laura, my God, your hand—let me see it."

"It's okay. I just have to get it elevated."

Tim led her to an oversized, upholstered chair in the living room and immediately began arranging pillows to raise her hand to a position higher than her heart. "Didn't you go to therapy today?" he asked.

"I wanted to, truly, but with all the hoopla over Immunone's approval, I couldn't get to it. I took some Motrin. It'll be okay."

"Laura, you have to take better care of yourself. My God, so soon after surgery. What would you tell your patients if they disregarded everything—"

Shit! Wrong. Why did I have to bring that up? Of all the things to say—

"Sorry to be such a nag." Tim leaned over, kissed her on the forehead, and was rewarded with a tired smile.

"I'm going to pop the potatoes in the oven," Tim said, bending to slip off Laura's two-inch heels and lifting her feet onto the ottoman. "I'll redress your hand, take some of that pressure off, then you can get out of that suit into something more comfortable. Champagne dinner will follow. Sound okay?"

"Tim, I so don't deserve you," Laura said, leaning back, starting to relax. "I haven't even asked about your day. How did the double valve replacement go?"

"Difficult, long, but I think the kid is going to be okay. I'm glad we got started at six this morning, or I wouldn't be home yet to tend to my favorite patient. Really, Laura, you have to take better care of that hand."

"I know, and I will, I just had to get today behind me. We got the approval. There'll be a lot of public relations activity, but then my department can get back to work on the next big breakthrough. I just wish I could continue my surgical transplant program now that Immunone's on the market; the prognosis for heart-lung transplant will be even better. We'll still have the organ shortage issue though."

What could he say? How could he help Laura mourn the loss of her hands-on career? "What docs Keystone have in the pipeline?" he asked, hoping they had something that would fully engage Laura's talents.

"Cancer," she said. "Keystone's new frontier is cancer. And the most promising lead is for lung carcinoma, so that's right up my alley. God knows I've operated on enough lung cancers. So now, I'll be trying to cure them with drugs."

"Sounds good," Tim said. The potatoes in the oven, he went to get Laura's medical supplies.

When he returned, Laura looked more relaxed. He wondered whether he should disturb the ambiance of the evening by asking how she wanted to handle dinner with the kids, to bring them into the Patrick paternity loop. She'd decided to do it sometime, somewhere, on Friday night; she'd told Mike she would, okayed it with Patrick, but mustn't this be weighing on her mind, with so much else going on?

"I need to ask you something, Tim," Laura said, interrupting his quandary. He'd just cut through the thick layers of bandages, loosening the pressure, watching with satisfaction as the color improved in Laura's hand.

Here it comes. "About dinner with the kids?"

"No, though we do have to talk about that, too. This is about something weird that happened to me today."

"Okay," Tim said, peeling off the final layer, exposing raw flesh in various stages of healing. Laura's wound was healing by "primary intension," that is, openly—no stitches, staples, or other closure devices. An ugly option, but the one that would prevent infection following extensive debridement surgery. "Can I get you a couple of Motrin?" he asked, before applying antibiotic ointment.

Laura winced, held her breath for a moment, and said, "No. I'm okay. What I wanted to ask was whether or not I should call the police?"

"What?" Tim stopped his rewrapping, and stared, clueless.

Laura chuckled. "Oh, I guess I forgot to tell you. The other day, a Philadelphia detective stopped by my office to ask me about the night Fred Minn was killed outside the Four Seasons where we'd just had dinner." She paused, Tim nodded, and she continued, "They wanted to know whether I'd seen anything that night. You know, the 'anything at all' line. Naturally, I wanted to help them. And I did think of something. I saw a dark-colored Jeep that night. Pulled out, headed the way Dr. Minn was walking. I actually did a double take because, at one point, Kevin had a Jeep that looked very similar, a Jeep Cherokee, I believe."

Tim heard a timer in the kitchen and jumped up. "Just a sec. Let me take the steak out of the marinade." When he returned, he picked up where he'd left off in the bandaging process, as Laura went on. "Today, I was standing in the FDA parking lot with the woman doctor at Replica responsible for the discovery of Immunone. Adawia Abdul. And I saw what seemed to be a really similar Jeep—dark green. I found out this Jeep belongs to Jake Harter, Immunone project director at the FDA, the one who supposedly 'couldn't find' that missing data. And, guess what?"

"What?" Tim was not quite following the logic of her account.

"Dr. Abdul, or Adawia—during our conversation we got to a first-name basis—said she and Jake Harter were getting married."

"So?" Tim asked. "Any law against that?"

"Conflict of interest," Laura said. "I'm getting steeped in

all this corporate-government intrigue. Life was much easier in academia."

"So her fiancé is in the position to push her drug through. But wait a minute, why would he claim data was missing if that was the case?"

"Beats me," said Laura. "I may have said something I shouldn't have, but I did tell her I'd just come from a meeting and the drug would be approved on Friday."

"She didn't know?" Tim asked, still not sure where this was going.

"She tried to get Jake Harter's attention when he tore out of the FDA lot, but he didn't see us. So, back to the Jeep: should I call the police and tell them?"

"Sounds far-fetched to me, Laura. Must be a lot of dark-colored Jeeps. Philly's a long way from Rockville, Maryland."

"You're right," she said, reaching over to the table for her purse. "The detective gave me his number just in case I thought of something. He did say they had a tire imprint from the car that had been parked where I saw it, the Jeep. I just wonder...but, you're right, it sounds crazy."

"Sleep on it, Laura. It's late, you're exhausted, and I'm about to serve you champagne. Just a sip before you change. By then I'll have dinner on the table."

Laura set down her purse. "I wish I could put off Friday night with the kids too."

"Let's talk about that during dinner," Tim said, helping Laura stand, supporting her right arm. "I have some ideas."

Tim had given Laura's problem much thought. Based on his own shock when she'd told him she'd had a brief affair with the chief of surgery when she'd been a medical student, he wondered how her kids would respond. They were the "younger generation." How important was marital fidelity to them? In general? With respect to their parents? He was too out of touch with twenty-year-olds to know.

Patrick, himself, had reacted better than Tim would have

predicted. Likely, based on his deep respect for his mother. And Patrick wanted this secret over and done with. And soon it would be. Friday night.

Tim had taken the initiative and arranged for a private dining room at the Barclay Hotel. A public place would discourage any histrionics on the part of the kids. Tim wasn't so worried about the boys, they seemed to take everything in stride. Case in point, Patrick did not go crazy on Laura. But the girls? To him, they seemed much more judgmental when it came to their mother.

What am I getting into with Laura? She's a handful herself— and her five kids? Tim smiled at how much meaning she'd added to his life.

CHAPTER FIFTY-TWO

Jake had crashed his Jeep into one mean bastard. Bad enough being shaken up at the impact, chest hurting like hell each time he took a breath, and a freaking bump on the head, but the man in the green truck knocked him out cold with a sucker punch. Jake woke up in the ambulance, oxygen tubes connected around his ears, a blood-pressure cuff on his arm, and a pulse oximeter clamped to his finger.

He'd tried to sit up, but found himself strapped to a gurney, the EMT sitting beside him, forcing him back down flat with a heavy, knuckled hand.

"I'm okay," Jake told the big man, his temporary caretaker.

The only reply, "Tell that to the ER docs."

"What about my Jeep?"

"It'll be towed."

That was it for chitchat on the way to the hospital. When Jake tried to move again, the broad strap across his abdomen held him back. When he struggled against the restraint, his caretaker's big hand reached over to press him back. The combined movement and pressure on his chest made him moan in pain. He fell back prone, helpless and alarmed.

Arriving at Suburban Hospital ER, his attendant and driver jostled him inside, lined up his gurney against the wall, filled out some forms, and left without saying another word.

Still strapped down, now unplugged from the oxygen, Jake

glanced around the busy ER. What could he do to convince them he did not have to be seen? He was awake, conscious, and could leave without the need for any paperwork.

When a young female intern approached him with her clipboard, he told her he wanted to sign out. Go home. He was fine. "Just unstrap me." But his demand seemed to fall on deaf ears.

"I have to take a history," the woman said. "And then examine you. With that head wound, we'll need an MRI."

"Take off the strap," he repeated. "I can't breathe with that damn thing tying me down."

The young doctor hesitated, glancing around as heads started to turn toward them. "Sir, I can't," she said, looking up as two police officers in uniform approached.

"You the guy involved in the altercation at Norbeck and Baltimore?" the stockier one asked. "Ran your Jeep into a guy's truck? He knocked the shit out of you? We got you for reckless driving. You gonna press charges on the guy who punched you out?"

Jake tried to take a deep breath to steady himself, but the pain in his right side stopped him short. Maybe he did need X-rays of his ribs, but so what if they were broken? There was no treatment; they just had to heal on their own.

"Officers, I don't want any more trouble. I'll give the guy who hit me a break. I just want to get out of here. Where's my car, anyway?"

"Jeep's been towed to city impound. Your insurance adjusters can check it out there. Front end's a mess. You been drinking?" Both of the men leaned in closer to catch a whiff of Jake's breath. "Don't smell any," the slimmer of the two said.

"I'm feeling okay now," Jake said. "I don't need to be seen here. Leave the doctors for the real emergencies."

"Up to them," the slim cop indicated the intern who waited at the foot of the gurney. "Right now, looks like Detective Booker and his partner are on their way here."

"Yeah, what's that all about?" the stocky cop wanted to

know. "You in some kind of trouble with the law? Ran you through, nothin' came up."

"No, I work at the FDA. I admit, I was going too fast. Distracted, I guess. I'm getting married tomorrow."

The detectives, however, did not show up. Must've been called to work another crime. The young doctor did proceed with her plan, subjecting Jake to a brain MRI—negative—and to a chest X-ray—two cracked ribs. Five hours later, now nine p.m., he left the hospital in a cab and headed to Addie's apartment.

***

Addie was home now, but not alone. She appeared to be in deep discussion with a Middle Eastern-looking man. Could this be Dru? Her friend from Detroit, originally from Iraq, the one who'd helped her out when she first came to the States as a university student in Ann Arbor. The one who was now acting as a liaison between her and her parents in Iraq.

The man's loud voice sounded angry, but he stopped talking when Jake entered the room.

"Jake, this is Dru," Addie said, hastening across the room to meet him. "He's here to help me with my travel plans for Friday."

"Dru, this is Jake." *Not, this is Jake, my fiancé.*

Jake had so much to discuss with Addie. Immunone's approval. Her status with Replica. Their wedding plans tomorrow. And why the hell had she been talking to Laura Nelson.

"Glad to meet you, Dru. Addie's told me about you. But now's not a good time. We have—"

"Jake, are you okay?" Addie had noticed the bruised left side of his face and the discoloration settling in his left eye socket.

"Adawia, tell your guest to come back another time," Dru said, dismissing Jake as if he'd just delivered a pizza.

The pain in the back of his chest—the site of two fractured ribs—had escalated on the jostling cab ride. Jake now figured he should have taken the Percocet, but hadn't, wanting to stay clear-headed as he sorted out this Addie-Laura Nelson relationship.

Right now, he didn't have the patience or the intention to deal with Addie's friend.

When Dru walked to him, placing the heel of his hand against his chest, Jake only wished he had his Glock. Pain or no pain, it'd be fun to scare the hell out of this creep.

"Move," Dru said. "Now. Out."

Jake was about to shove him, when Addie stepped between them.

"Dru," she said, tugging at the guy's arm, "we're about finished, aren't we? I understand the urgency and the timing. I'll be there."

"Be where?" Jake interrupted, taking a step back. Why was Addie having this cryptic conversation, now, when he needed her undivided attention? He had his own questions and concerns, and they didn't involve this Iraqi dude from her past.

"No." Addie's appeal had failed. "Get rid of him. Now." Dru yanked his arm out of Addie's grasp.

"Jake, could you give me and Dru a few more minutes? Alone?"

What was all that shit about the man's dominance in Muslim relationships? Addie's lack of deference to him, her future husband, was both startling and unacceptable.

Jake faltered. His woman. He desperately needed to talk to her. This Arab creep had to go.

The flashing of a knife, an extended four-inch steel blade, made his decision. It appeared so fast, demonstrating the user's obvious expertise. If he'd had his piece, Jake wouldn't have hesitated. He'd have taken out this bastard in four seconds. When the cops had been all over him in the ER today, he'd been grateful not to be carrying, but now—

"You get the fuck outta here, man. And I mean forever. You and this woman are through. Forget you ever met her."

"Dru, this is Jake. I told you about him. About—"

In a swift move, knife in one hand, Dru turned and slapped Addie. Hard. "You shut up and do as I tell you, Adawia."

Addie fell back against the arm of a sofa, a moaning sob

escaping, breaking Jake's heart. He may have shot a woman dead, but he'd never, ever, hit one. This asshole would pay.

Dru bolted toward Jake, still hovering close to the door. The knife gleamed as light played on the steely surface. Jake recognized the fight stance and the determined, yet desperate, look in the eyes of his attacker. He backed to the door, his hands finding the knob. An easy twist and he all but fell into the opening door, sending a current of pain throughout his chest. He did not hesitate. He was gone. Out of Addie's apartment, hustling down the hall to the elevator. Once on the street, he gingerly raised an arm to hail a cab to take him to the Budget Car Rental in Bethesda.

CHAPTER FIFTY-THREE

Dru flinched as Adawia fingered her bruised cheek. A unexpected pang of shame for striking a woman.

"Sorry, Adawia, I didn't mean to hurt you," Dru said, closing the door to her apartment, bolting it. "I had to get rid of that man."

"That's Jake, the man I'm going to marry."

"Sit down, Adawia. I have a lot to talk to you about. I got picked up by the FBI and they took me to—"

"The FBI? Dru, I saw you at—"

"Come, please," Dru interrupted, gesturing for her to take a seat on the sofa. When she complied, he continued, "They took me to the Pentagon. Left me there with agents that were more like the CIA, but they go by DIA. Defense Intelligence."

Dru paced as he let her absorb this. She seemed less shocked than he'd anticipated.

"They know I'm connected to you and to your family, specifically, to your father. You see why I had to get rid of your friend Jake?" Dru stopped mid-step to stare at her. "Shit. Did you tell the bastard about your father? His connections in Baghdad?"

"Of course not," Addie said. "Nothing. Maybe after we're married. Dru, do you share everything with your wife?"

"Of course not," he said. *Especially not that I'm with you in your apartment tonight.*

"Oh," Adawia sounded deflated. "We're getting married tomorrow. I think being married will give me some stability with my family. Plus, an American husband will give me some protection."

"Are you out of your mind?" Dru couldn't believe the woman's naiveté "Your family has a husband picked out for you. Your father told me. Arrangements have been set."

"That's exactly why I want to be married before I get there. I can't stand even the thought of being married to the repulsive man they picked out for me."

"Gabir Rahman. He's not so bad." Dru considered the man a bastard, but this was not the time to share that opinion.

Adawia jumped up and glowered at him. "You knew about Gabir?"

"Let's get back to reality. You're not marrying Harter. And now that the American government is involved—"

"Tomorrow, Dru. We have a Maryland marriage license. Jake and I are getting married tomorrow. That way, when I get the Immunone money on Friday, I will have someone to take care of my affairs over here."

She turned away, sat down again on the sofa, and pulled up her knees.

"You're getting the money Friday?" Dru spun around, incredulous. "Since when?"

"The FDA will approve Immunone on Friday. There'll be a press conference. They may even want me to participate. Since my flight to London isn't until 11:00 p.m., I should be okay."

Dru was trying to figure the implications of this distribution of money when Addie said, "I was at the Pentagon today too. Agents picked me up in the parking lot at the FDA. Same as you, DIA agents."

"What?" was all he could say.

"They know about my father. They know about you. I saw you there when they were taking me out. What did you tell them?"

They'd questioned Adawia?

"What did you tell them? About me?" Dru could feel the

sweat start to bead on his forehead, in his armpits. If she'd told them he'd been in Baghdad last week... Dru's hand fingered the knife, now tucked into his pants pocket. If they'd known he'd lied, they surely wouldn't have returned the knife. "Adawia," his voice raised in an angry fear, "what did you tell those agents about me?"

He had to leave the US. Join Shada in Canada. Get a new identity, a new life.

But as Adawia repeated the agents' questions and her answers, his desperation abated. She had not betrayed him. If she was telling him the truth, and he judged she was, their stories lined up perfectly.

Although his priority was getting Adawia to Iraq as ordered, Dru found himself distracted by that $7.5 million coming to her in just two days. Friday, the day she was to leave for the homeland. Could he manipulate his way into at least of piece of that money? He could use it to establish a new life for Shada and the boys in Canada.

Dru's mind started to spin. Now that Immunone's approval and Adawia's payout were scheduled, could he, as her banker, handle the funds? She'd be in no position to invest the money from Iraq. Of course, she'd need to assign him power of attorney. Who better to trust? But first, he had to eliminate Jake Harter.

"Okay, here's what you're going to do," he told her. "Break off with Harter. You are not to marry him. With your father so high up in the regime, with you replacing him, do you think they'd allow an American husband? So get over that stupid idea right away."

"I thought my parents would adjust—even if they consider Jake an infidel, but—"

"They will not tolerate him. Period. Before you leave Friday, you sign over power of attorney to me. That's the important thing. I'll invest your money somewhere safe."

"Somewhere like Switzerland?" Adawia asked.

"Wherever is safest. You know that's my expertise."

"If only—"

"Adawia, they will kill you and your entire family if you don't leave for Baghdad. First leg, London, Friday night."

"I guess I've always known my family wouldn't accept an American," she said, starting to cry, "but Jake makes me feel safe, and he says he'll become a Muslim—"

"Jake doesn't know shit about Iraq, about Islam, about sharia law. I'm not saying he's a bad person, but he doesn't deserve the trouble you'll bring down on him."

"I never thought of it that way," Adawia said with a sniffle. "I do think he loves me. Enough to—"

"It doesn't matter. You have to leave the United States." Dru went into Addie's small bathroom, brought back a box of tissues. "Here. Stop crying."

Adawia blew her nose. "I forgot to tell you. The DIA agents know I told the detectives from Rockville I was with you when Jake's wife was murdered. They knew that I need for you to give me an alibi."

"That's bullshit. They think you killed that man's wife?"

The telephone rang. Dru told Adawia not to answer it.

When it rang again, he got up and disconnected it.

"Look, you're out of here in two days. I'm not volunteering to talk to the cops. Besides, the Feds never mentioned that to me. If they did, I'd admit I was with you that night. So don't worry."

"What if that call was from Jake?" Adawia asked, standing over his shoulder now, still sniffling.

"You're done with him. So forget about it."

Adawia would never talk to Jake, Dru assured himself, *because I will not let her out of my sight.*

CHAPTER FIFTY-FOUR

Jake rented a charcoal-gray Chevy Blazer SUV with 4-wheel drive. Not as tough a ride as his Jeep Cherokee, but sturdy, dependable, with only 600 miles on the odometer. He tried to concentrate on his plan, but his head pounded, and his anger surged, and every bump he took felt like hell. First, that Dru pal of Addie's would pay. Tonight. Next would be Addie's new girlfriend, Dr. Laura Nelson.

Jake stormed into his house, barging into the walk-in closet off the hall, stopping at the hidden compartment in the rear where he kept his guns and emergency supplies. Just a few steps from where his wife had died, and the police hadn't even found it. Karolee hated guns, one of their many differences. As for Jake, his thing for firearms had begun in the Marines, and over the years, he'd collected some nice ones.

The closet was packed tight. It contained food items, water, cash, first-aid supplies, flashlights, but, by far, most space was taken up by guns and ammo. Handguns hung from hooks; twin Glock 9mms sharing the same hook; the Browning .22 caliber fitted with a six-inch suppressor on another; the Beretta, a third. All were loaded. His long guns rested in the corners: a Mossberg 12-gauge tactical shotgun, a Bushmaster .223 outfitted with a Zeiss scope, and an AK 47 he'd won playing cards. Jake loved his guns, and felt an instant of nostalgia for the Smith & Wesson .38

that had terminated the life of Karolee—his Saturday night special now rusting in Croydon Creek.

Jake considered his strategy. Should he take only the two weapons he'd need tonight: the Browning with the silencer, carried in his jacket pocket, and the Beretta for backup in an ankle holster? So far, the cops had not discovered his arsenal, but his instinct told him to take them all. Survival mode. *Once a Marine, always a Marine.*

He went to the basement to retrieve his large fishing cooler, backed up the Blazer to the garage, placed the cooler in the back, and started loading. Any deep breath caused stabbing pains in his chest, so he panted small but rapid air intakes as he made multiple trips from his hall closet and basement to the garage. Except for the guns he'd carry tonight, he was able to pack his firearms into the cooler with little problem, except for the shotgun, which he needed to break down to fit inside. He could only take about half of his ammo, but that would be plenty. He threw in a fishing pole next to the cooler for disguise. He figured with the ammo, the loaded clips, and the guns, the cooler would weigh about 300 pounds. He'd have to reconfigure the load into multiple containers soon. Too bad he didn't have the Jeep, where he'd had hidden compartments installed for just such an occasion—traveling armed.

Jake was breathing hard, despite the intensified pain from his broken ribs, by the time he stuffed a large black backpack—his bug-out bag—on the floor of the Blazer's front seat. Ready to go at all times, the bag contained water, protein bars, Tylenol, oxycodone, bandages, antibiotics, an assortment of knives, his Glock 17, a powerful flashlight, leather gloves, and twenty thousand dollars in hundreds and twenties.

Jake locked the hidden cabinet, leaving only extra ammunition. In the closet of the guest bedroom, Jake had at the ready a duffle loaded with warm clothing, extra underwear, a comforter, and a pillow. Karolee had never mentioned it, likely never noticed it. He carried it to the Blazer, throwing it into the backseat. Going to his bedroom closet, Jake selected a suit and a more casual outfit, a couple of dress shirts and other items, placing them neatly in a garment bag. He carried the bag as he took a last walk through his house, not knowing or caring if he'd ever be back. He locked the house, not activating the alarm. The garage door was still open and he retrieved his sleeping bag, camp kit, and an ice chest from the garage, put them in the backseat, the garment bag on top, and went back to lock the garage.

Once in the Blazer, he headed back to Addie's. He'd deal with that Arab on his terms and with his weapon of choice. Jake patted his jacket pocket. Jake's job at the FDA may have been pushing paper, and he was a damned good planner. But most important, he was a Marine.

On the road, Jake wondered what Addie must be thinking of him right now. Jake, the coward, slinking away from that asshole Dru's knife, abandoning her to a guy who'd hit her. Back in Vietnam, Jake had killed another bastard who'd hit a woman, and he'd kill Dru too. He'd prove his commitment to Addie, make her proud of her man, and tomorrow, they'd be husband and wife. The following day, Friday, Immunone would be approved, and Mr. and Mrs. Jake Harter would be a wealthy couple, free to travel the world.

Jake thought of Mark's voice message. Thought of the baby Amanda. Chuckled at the thought of Addie as a grandma. Then he sobered, realizing that he and Addie had never discussed the possibility of children. He remembered hearing that Laura Nelson had kids. Tough, with a job like hers, but Addie seemed to idolize the woman. But not for long. Addie might be deluded into hero worship, but Nelson had screwed him, and he would make her pay.

As Jake approached Addie's building, a parking spot opened up directly in front of the door. He swung into it, feeling a surge of luck. Still in the darkened interior of the Blazer, Jake patted his right jacket pocket, assuring himself his primary weapon was at the ready. He reached down to his right ankle, felt the Beretta in place, at the ready for backup.

Jake drew no attention as he entered the lobby of Addie's apartment building, as he had done so many times before. He glanced about for security cameras, tried to keep his head down. No one took note of Jake as he strode through the lobby and headed to the elevator.

Outside Addie's door, Jake took a calming deep breath and turned the key. Without hesitation, he charged into the room. Addie was sitting on the sofa across the room, still wearing her business suit, legs tucked up under her. Jake saw her eyes widen and he heard a choked, "Jake!"

The man he had come to kill was standing in front of a fake-leather chair, only three feet from Jake as he stepped inside. Jake swung the gun toward him, aimed at center mass, and pulled the trigger, the resulting sound a muffled pop.

Addie's friend Dru fell backward into the chair, his white shirt already soaked in blood. A messy kill. Should have tried for the head, a trickier shot, but much cleaner.

"Addie, get a blanket," Jake ordered. "Do you have any plastic sheets?"

Jake hadn't given any thought about how to deal with the body. The man must weigh 160. Chopping him up in pieces was not an attractive option, but he realized it might come to that. He did have one of those battery-powered chain saws in his escape pack.

Addie had not moved other than to place her feet on the floor. Her mouth was open but silent. Her black eyes were huge, unblinking, as she stared at the man he'd shot.

"Help me, Addie. We have to get him out of here."

"You killed him, Jake," Addie's voice was so quiet, almost inaudible.

"I had to, my sweetness. You saw him attack me with a knife."

"Go check him," she said. "See if he's dead."

"He's dead all right," Jake knew what a bullet at that range would do. "We have to deal with him. Don't want his blood all over your place."

Jake shoved the gun into his pocket and walked across the room to Addie. He reached for her arm to ease her up. "We need to clean this up right away. What about a plastic sheet?"

"No," Addie said, as Jake pulled her to a standing position.

"Plastic bags then. Big ones." Once he got the body wrapped, the rug would have to go.

When he let go of her arm, Addie stood, frozen.

"I'm going into the kitchen to get them. Addie, I'll need your help here."

Jake crossed the living room, disappearing into the kitchen, searching for the large plastic bags he knew she used for her trash. Bending down to peer under the sink, he found a full package of them. They'd have to do. He'd drag the body over the polished wood floor into the bathroom. Contain the blood to the extent possible, and figure out how to get it into the dumpster outside the back door to the building. He'd use the battery-powered saw he had in the trunk of the car if he couldn't carry out the body in one piece. Get rid of the rug and the towels he'd use to clean up. Turn the Blazer rental in tomorrow after picking up his Jeep from the impound lot. Then he and Addie would drive to the courthouse to be married, right on schedule. Friday, she'd come into her inheritance. From then on, they'd be free to live wherever they wished.

Pulling out a handful of black plastic bags, Jake headed to the living room. The throw rug under the body would make it easy to drag it across the floor into the bathroom. The tough part would be getting the body into the bathtub. Then he realized he could just as easily use the separate shower enclosure. Drain out as much blood as possible to make the body more manageable. His clothes would be a bloody mess, but they'd go into the dumpster.

His garment bag had a couple of changes of clothes and a new pair of shoes.

When he returned to the living room, Dru lay slumped in the chair just as Jake had left him. The room was agonizingly silent. Where was Addie?

CHAPTER FIFTY-FIVE

"Laura, I know you're awake," Tim said. "You had a bad night, but it's time to get up. You have to be at the airport at nine. Right?"

"Yes." Laura started to roll over to face Tim, but of course, she couldn't. That was her injured side. One glance at the bandaged hand told her the swelling was excessive. She should keep it elevated, difficult with all she had to do today. Once this Immunone approval extravaganza was behind her, she'd get back to a therapy schedule. Post-op rehab was vital to a patient's functional healing—she was no exception.

"You okay?" Tim asked, helping her into a sitting position. "I'd suggest you take the day off work, but this is no ordinary day."

With Dr. Minn dead, Paul Parnell wanted a scientist-doctor to speak for the company at the press conference announcing Immunone's approval. Thus, Laura would be the face and the voice of Keystone Pharma. She knew that billions of dollars rested on her performance. But most importantly, thousands of lives would be saved by this remarkable drug. To prepare her to step into this major public role, Keystone's public relations machine had scheduled a prep session all day today for the Friday event.

"I'll miss you tonight, Tim. I wish you could join me at the Hay-Adams."

"I might, if I can juggle my schedule to free up Friday morning. I have a six-year-old, coming from Brazil. If she's stable enough, I'll switch her to Monday."

"Tim, I'm sorry for being so selfish. You take care of your little patient. I'll be fine. But I will miss you."

Tim took Laura's left arm and helped her out of bed. "I hope our nights apart are few and far between. And speaking of our life together, Laura, we need to set the date. Sooner rather than later, babe."

"Sooner works for me. But let's get Friday night with the kids over with first. I have no idea what to expect from my family, how they will react."

"Your kids will be fine. So it's a deal. We'll set the date this weekend."

"I'm off to take a shower and get dressed while you're still here to help me button and zip."

***

Laura had not slept well last night. Not because of her role in the press conference, not even because of Friday night's encounter with her kids. Weighing on her mind was Lonnie Greenwood. She needed to talk to him. She hoped it could be face-to-face, but since he was in Detroit, how could she justify a trip there? She needed to find how and what he knew. What he planned to do. Right now, it seemed he cared about his son; she was able to get the young man jumped to the top of the lung transplant priority list in Tampa. But would Lonnie demand more? She'd fallen prey to blackmail before. Would history repeat itself? She didn't know. If the Detroit Police find out... If Tim and the kids find out...

Tim now knew about David Monroe, but could he accept an even worse transgression? That she'd killed a man and had gotten away with it—so far. Laura had told only one person about that night twenty-five years ago. Not her husband, but David. And now there was Tim. Did she love Tim and trust him enough to tell him—regardless of Lonnie Greenwood's anticipated threat? Would confessing her lethal act that horrific night change everything between them? And what about her children? What was best for them: leave the skeleton in the closet, or let them know their mother had killed a man? On top of the other guilty secret she had promised to disclose to them tomorrow night?

***

Wearing a teal-blue suit and white silk blouse, Laura stood while Tim arranged the shoulder of her cashmere coat over her right arm. The limo had arrived, and Tim was ready to walk her to the car, carrying all her stuff. Laura couldn't help but wonder if he would ever again let her leave the apartment unaccompanied.

"What's this?" Tim asked, picking up a business card from the coffee table.

"Remember I told you about the detective that came to my office to ask about the night Fred Minn was killed?" Laura remembered the shiny, bald spot revealed when the rumpled detective took off his hat. "Simon Smith. I've decided to call him."

"Okay," Tim said, a skeptical frown signaling his opinion.

No matter how stupid it might sound or how irrelevant, Laura felt she should pass along the information about the Jeep that Jake Harter drove. But only if they promised her anonymity, so she wouldn't come across as a lunatic.

CHAPTER FIFTY-SIX

"Abdul's got a clean record," Mintner was saying. "Model grad student at the University of Michigan."

"Go Blue," Sharkey inserted.

Long looked up from the report he was studying and grunted. The boss was a die-hard Ohio State fan, Sharkey knew.

Mintner pressed on. "Made important discoveries about a new class of drugs to treat transplant patients. Got hired by Replica. Small bio start-up. She's well liked. Respected. Due to make a not-too-small fortune when this drug is approved. Which it will be—confidentially—tomorrow. Company wants to showcase her during the press conference."

"Communications with her father?" Long asked.

"What you'd expect," Sharkey responded. "Mother with family matters. Father is ill. They want her back. That's what she's telling us. Maybe we'll find something on her home or work hard drive to connect to bioweapons over there."

"Lot of pressure from the Bush administration to find any trace of bioweapons," Long stated the obvious.

Sharkey again, "Denies knowing anything. But when I made the point that Immunone analogs have potential in anthrax protection, I saw a spark of validation."

"Her air tickets to London?"

"Holiday," Mintner said. "I don't believe her. About to marry a guy and she doesn't say 'honeymoon.' She and Badur Hammadi must have something going. Our surveillance has them both in her apartment. Came in last night and haven't left yet."

"They're sleeping together?" Sharkey asked, her eyebrows arched. "Intel is that Hammadi is devoted to his wife and kids. Wouldn't be the first time."

Long glanced from the wall clock back to his papers. "Abdul woman and Jake Harter, the guy works at the FDA, applied for a marriage license on March 3rd. Two days ago. Marriage scheduled in the same courthouse March 5th. That's today."

"I thought Muslim women were more...what's the right word?" Mintner said. "So, she's sleeping with Hammadi and marrying this other guy?"

Long ignored the comment. "Harter's name goes into our surveillance genies. And guess what? Gets picked up on both ends. A query from Philadelphia PD to DC regional PDs regarding a vehicle owned by Jake Harter. Had to do with a hit-and-run in Philly a few weeks ago."

"We didn't push her on her relationship with Harter," Sharkey mused. "She didn't even mention him. Wonder why she didn't tell me?"

"Really, Sharkey, you think women open up to you because of gender allegiance?" Mintner asked with a rare chuckle.

"That puts an interesting spin on Abdul and Hammadi spending the night together." Sharkey ignored her partner's dig. "So, what is this hit-and-run?"

"When Rockville PD responded to Philly's inquiry," Long scanned the report in front of him, "they were able to tie it to a recent accident involving Harter. City impound still had the suspect vehicle." He smiled. "Working tire-impression comparisons as we speak. If there's a match, this adds another element to your investigation. Beats me what the connection could be though. What are your next steps to either clear or connect Abdul and Hammadi?"

Mintner shook his head. "Go for warrants for Abdul's and

Hammadi's computer drives, warrants for phone taps, bring them both back in here. Sharkey and I don't think we can justify the manpower for ongoing surveillance."

"Okay, go for the warrants. Coordinate with Detroit for Hammadi."

"Yes, sir," Sharkey said, getting up to leave as Mintner stayed seated.

"You can go now," Long prompted.

"Just thinking about this Harter guy. Why the tie to a hit-and-run in Philly?"

"Find out, Agent Mintner. Now go. I've got a ten o'clock in here."

CHAPTER FIFTY-SEVEN

Thursday, March 5

Was there something going on between Addie and the dead guy? Jake was quite sure Addie wasn't fooling around, but what if they'd been lovers in the past, or had shared some religious or cultural bond? She must have been more freaked out than he'd expected when he'd shot and killed her Iraqi friend. Obviously self-defense, she'd been there earlier when the guy came at him with a knife. What did she expect Jake to do, turn tail and run away?

He'd kept the television on, volume low, all last night to help him cope with Addie's absence, and now with the introduction of *The Morning Show,* he knew he had to come up with a plan. Where had she gone? And how was he going to find her?

There was no more dead body, and Addie's apartment appeared normal. Jake had been very lucky last night. When he realized she had left, he immediately went in search for her. Right outside her apartment door, he almost tripped on a phone book. Not thinking, he picked it up and carried it toward the elevator. He hopped on the elevator and took it to the ground floor, hoping to find Addie in the lobby. He didn't. He didn't go outside, but he did stand at the door, looking up and down the street. No Addie. Still carrying the phone book, he took the four flights of steps to her floor. Did she have a friend in the building where she could hang out? Addie was a very private person, and he thought not.

As he approached the long hallway from the stairs to Addie's apartment door, Jake all but ran into a thin, fifty-something man emerging from a door. The guy's bald head was down, and he was struggling to pull a large roller suitcase as a computer bag slid off his shoulder.

Holy shit. No lights were on in the silent apartment. This man was leaving for some time, judging by the big, bulging piece of luggage.

"Let me assist you, sir." Jake set the phone book down in front of the door and turned inward to grab the handle of the luggage. Instead of trying to roll it, he hefted it up and swung it into the hallway.

"Thanks, man," Addie's neighbor said. "I'll be away for a month, several climates. I should have used one of those carts they keep downstairs. I'm getting too old for this much travel, but it goes with the job."

The man adjusted the strap of his computer bag with one arm and reached to pull his suitcase with the other. "Damn thing keeps sliding off when I wear this coat. Well, thanks again."

The man left without a look back at Jake or at the gap in the door where the phone book kept it propped open.

Jake had not found Addie, but he had found a place to store the Arab's body.

But now it was morning and Addie had not come home. He climbed out of bed, his jaw aching, each breath a stab of hurt, but he was a Marine, trained to work through pain.

For one sick, fleeting moment, Jake wondered if Addie could have called the police. In her eyes, would she think she'd witnessed a murder? Would she think it her civic duty to report it? Even if it meant turning in her fiancé? Certainly not. Addie came from Baghdad, where murders were everyday occurrences.

CHAPTER FIFTY-EIGHT

Shouldn't there have been more blood? Addie wondered, recalling Dru's body splayed on the floor, unmoving. Jake's bullet hit Dru in his chest. She could see the hole between his breasts, blood coming out of it, spreading in a circular pattern, staining his nice white shirt, but not pumping out enough to drench it as she would have expected. Addie was a PhD, not a medical doctor. She'd never seen a gunshot wound, never anticipated she would. She remembered with surprise that the gun had made only a popping sound, nothing loud enough to alert neighbors, attract police.

She remembered asking if Dru was dead. Jake's answer: "Yes."

Dru was dead. In her apartment. Jake had shot him.

She'd bolted out her door, not bothering to close it, ran toward the stairs, hurtling down all four flights, heading toward the back door of the building where maintenance unloaded the daily trash. She worked her way under the cover of dark dumpsters to the shadows of the alley that would lead her close to her car. She knew Jake would try to follow her. He'd convince her to tell the cops it was self-defense. Or, she thought with horror, would he try to blame her? No, Jake loved her. Isn't that why he shot Dru? Jealousy? Must have thought she and Dru were having an affair, that she was going home to be with Dru.

Cringing in the dark alley, Addie knew she must escape Jake. He had taken himself out of her life. He was a murderer. Because of him, the comfort of knowing Dru had looked out for her over the years was gone too. She was on her own. She could identify just two objectives.

First, her family. She needed to show up in Baghdad, or Saddam Hussein's regime would kill her family. Dru had made that clear and she knew the threat to be real. Second, she needed to protect herself. A woman in Islam was nothing more than an inert possession. She did not want a life of subjugation. Neither would she make herself a pawn in Saddam's biological weapons program. She had to find a compromise, a way to save her family but a solution that also would save her.

Addie moved cautiously along the back alley beyond the foul-smelling dumpsters. The black, moonless night both protected and terrified her. As she neared the dimly lit street that ran perpendicular to hers, she breathed a sigh of relief. Her car was parked a short block away. She gripped her handbag, thankful for the reflex that had made her grab it as she fled the apartment.

She often parked on this street, and tonight saw no one whom she recognized. She reached into her bag for her car keys as she approached her Audi. Before pulling out of her parking spot, she hesitated to listen carefully for signs of police or emergency vehicles.

All she heard were the usual sounds of the night—traffic at its usual cadence, a few stray voices. No pounding footsteps, no sign of Jake, or anyone else, behind her.

On impulse, Addie made a three-point turn and headed away from her house. Would she ever return? How could she, after seeing Dru's body lying dead in her living room? The horrors of the night had left no room in her mind for the DIA investigation. Till now. Would the agents be looking for her with more questions? Did they have the right to search her apartment? Of course, they did. Would they find Dru's body? Or would Jake get rid of it? Was that why he didn't come after her? What about Dru's wife and young sons? Hadn't he said they were hidden away somewhere? How would they learn of his death?

She felt faint and pulled into the lot of a convenience store, leaning over the steering wheel, taking deep breaths. "Addie," she finally heard herself say, "stop it. You need a place to spend the night. Somewhere no one can find you. Start driving." On the highway toward Baltimore, she chose a dumpy motel, paid with cash.

During the night, a startling idea had crossed Addie's exhausted mind. Was there any way agents Sharkey and Mintner could help her? She'd heard of witness protection... Would the US government help an Iraqi woman escape with her family?

Now in the clarity of morning, Addie scolded herself for even thinking such stupid thoughts.

She knew she had only one real option: try to get through the day. Avoid Jake; avoid her apartment; maintain her employment until the Immunone money was committed to her. How to actually take possession of the money, she did not know. Dru was to manage that for her. But now she had no one.

CHAPTER FIFTY-NINE

THURSDAY, MARCH 5

Jake waited until nine o'clock. His head and jaw throbbed, and each breath shot a knifelike pain into the right side of his chest. And still no Addie.

In the car, he removed the Beretta from his ankle holster. He put it in the backpack with the extra ammo. Getting the contraption off his ankle felt good. He headed for a nearby deli where he indulged in a three-fried-egg breakfast with bacon, sausage links, whole wheat toast, and lots of coffee. When he would next eat pork, he didn't know. Eating pig's meat was against Addie's religion and he should probably respect that when they were together—which would be all the time.

All had appeared normal when he'd exited Addie's building. No sign of excitement or suspicion in the lobby. No sign of cops in the area. So far, the dead man in the apartment on Addie's floor must not have been discovered. It would take a while before the body decomposed, creating a telltale odor.

The city garage confirmed he could pick up his battered Jeep. It was drivable, his insurance appraiser had declared, despite the damage to the passenger side fender. Jake would feel comfortable once he was back in his own vehicle. The Blazer he'd rented did not have the security he required. Once he transferred his survival supplies—including his weapons—to the Jeep, he'd head to Replica. Addie should be there. They would drive together to the courthouse in Ellicott City. This afternoon, they'd be man and wife. Never to be separated, no matter what.

By the time Jake arrived to claim his vehicle, his head felt better, but the broken ribs would take time to heal. He would just have to suck up the pain. As much as he loved the Jeep, Jake figured this would be a good time to sell it. He and Addie would get a new Lexus or maybe a Mercedes. He'd let her choose it; the color too. He'd fit it for a security compartment and—

Something caught Jake's eye as he was about to turn into the impound garage. Cop cars, several of them, but even one cop car was too many. He decided to drive by slowly, get a better look. Hovering by the entrance, he saw the two detectives who were investigating Karolee's murder. Booker and Finley. Why the fuck were they hanging around the impound area where owners could retrieve their cars? Jake drove on. He didn't need to tangle with them. He still was their favorite suspect in Karolee's murder, but they had no proof. These two clowns had nothing to do but hassle him. Today, he had no time for hassles.

CHAPTER SIXTY

Addie found Replica in a festive mood—a small start-up realizing its dream of a huge cash infusion. Millionaires would be made tomorrow and she'd be one of them. A dream she'd never thought would materialize.

But festive was at the other end of Addie's emotional spectrum. Last night, she had witnessed the murder of Dru, her oldest friend in America, her Iraqi mentor, the one tasked by Saddam Hussein's regime to get her out of the US and back to Iraq—for good. She was numb from trauma, plagued by questions without answers. How could the person she thought she'd been in love with, kill Dru outright? What had Jake done with Dru's body? Had anyone found it? What if the police were now in her apartment? And when would the agents reappear who had interrogated her yesterday? Agent Sharkey said they would have more questions.

But Addie knew she must be present today at Replica. To be a part of the team, with her colleagues. To arrange for her money. Once she had the $7.5 million, she could at last decide. Go back to Iraq? Or disappear, and risk her family's lives by defying Saddam?

She wended her way through the Replica employees hanging out in the lobby, accepting congratulations with as much grace as she could muster. Once in her office, she closed and locked her door. She simply sat, getting up only once, leaving her space to make a cup of tea, returning, locking the door. She must stay in close touch with Replica, but she must evade everyone else, the DIA investigators, and mainly, Jake. How to elude Jake? He'd be looking for her here, at Replica. What if he still expected her to marry him? That would be like Jake. Last night, after he shot Dru, he acted like nothing of import had happened. But she'd seen him shoot Dru. She was a witness. What if he decided to get rid of her too? She shivered when she remembered Jake's wife. Could he have killed her? She had to get out of here. Now.

She was about to pick up her purse and a few personal items when a knock at the door interrupted the silence. Her body froze. They must have let Jake in. With his FDA credentials he could enter any pharmaceutical establishment.

"Addie?"

Priscilla Fabre. Addie slumped back into her chair. Alarmed, she realized she had not informed Priscilla that she did indeed plan to stay with the company. That she would forgo her request for a leave of absence. As required by her contract, she'd be here on payout day.

"Yes, I'm here."

"Can I come in?"

Addie unlocked and opened the door to an ebullient Priscilla.

Priscilla stepped toward Addie for an intended embrace, but then pulled back. "Addie, are you okay? I know you're worried about your father, but with Immunone's approval tomorrow..." Priscilla frowned. "Well, you don't look too good."

"I didn't sleep well," Addie admitted. Doesn't everybody use that excuse for an off day?

"You do know, don't you? We got the Immunone approval!"

Addie wasn't sure how to answer. Laura Nelson had told her in the parking lot yesterday, but said the news was confidential. Would Priscilla assume Jake had told her?

"I...heard it would happen tomorrow." Addie couldn't control a stammer. "I am thrilled because I'll be a full-time employee."

"But you don't look too happy," Priscilla said. With a frown she added, "Isn't that the same suit you wore yesterday?"

"I'm worried about my father," Addie was quick to respond. "But I can put off going to him. Work something out with you. I just hope so much that he lives long enough."

"Next week, once this thing gets approved, we can talk about your leave of absence. Take whatever time you need for your family. I do understand. I felt awful when the lawyers denied you yesterday."

"Thanks, Priscilla, you've been so kind to me." Addie was about to say, "I'll miss you," but no use going into that right now. Just get through until tomorrow's approval.

"The reason I'm here right now is that we want you to play a role in tomorrow's press conference. Our biggest ever. For the medical and scientific press and the financial media. Television, *Wall Street Journal, Washington Post...*"

"Why me?" Addie wanted to disappear, attention from the media was the worst scenario she could imagine.

"Replica hired you because you discovered the drug. You developed Immunone to the stage we could sell it to big pharma. Tell me, who could be a better choice?"

"I was not born in this country. My English—"

"Your English is fine. The board has discussed this, Addie. This is not a request. They want you out there, standing next to Keystone's media choice, Dr. Laura Nelson."

"Laura Nelson," Addie repeated. A woman she'd only met twice, but a woman she felt she could trust. And she had to trust *someone*. In ordinary times, she'd be honored to share a press conference with Laura Nelson. But these were not ordinary times.

"The Year of the Woman Scientist." Priscilla grabbed Addie's hand. "Two beautiful, smart, incredibly successful scientists—the human interest angle is almost overwhelming."

"Overwhelming," Addie repeated, slumping back, resigned.

"Now, we have to get you the proper clothes. I'll call in my personal shopper," Priscilla said, with a glance at her own perfectly tailored gray suit with just the finest of pinstripes. "I'll arrange for a hairdresser to do your hairstyle in the morning." After a glance at Addie's hands, she added, "And a manicurist."

Addie noticed only now that Priscilla was carrying a leather folder, offering it to her.

"This is for you," she insisted, but politely. "Your talking points. You'll make a brief statement. It's all in here. Take a good look at all the possible questions, and the answers you need to have at your fingertips. A media consultant will go over this with you this afternoon. The idea is, no matter what they ask you, you answer with one of these points. You're okay with that?"

What could Addie say or do but nod her head, "yes," accept the folder, and try to keep her hand from shaking?

"I'll leave these with you then. Really, Addie, you're perfect for this role. You'll do just great."

When Priscilla closed the door behind her, Addie locked it. She went back to her desk, sat down, forced herself to breathe in and breathe out. *She must calm down.* Then she reached into her purse, found Laura Nelson's business card, dialed.

"Dr. Nelson is out of town, Dr. Abdul," the kindly voice said. "I can leave her a message."

"Just tell her Dr. Adawia Abdul called. It's important. Could she call me at my office?" She provided the number, speaking so fast she was asked to slow down and repeat it.

Hoping for a quick response from Laura, Addie opened the talking points folder. She read the remarks she was supposed to deliver. Easy. No practice needed. She moved to the Questions & Answers section. As Priscilla had warned, the questions varied, but the answers were all pretty much a variation of a list of a dozen responses. Addie found this baffling. Distracted, she left her office to make another cup of tea. Jake would be coming after her soon. She had to leave. But she'd try Laura's office one more time.

This time the kindly woman who answered advised her to contact Laura at the Hay-Adams Hotel in Washington, DC.

The clock on her desk, a graduation gift from her faculty advisor at University of Michigan, told her it was 10:10. Grabbing her purse, her briefcase, and the folder Priscilla had given her, Addie rushed out of her office, down the corridor, and out to her car.

CHAPTER SIXTY-ONE

A knock at the Hay-Adams boardroom door introduced a bellman, presenting a cream-colored sheet of paper on a small silver tray. "A message for Dr. Laura Nelson," he announced.

"Over here," Laura said, getting up to accept the note.

For the last hour and a half, Laura had focused intently on instructions offered by her Keystone colleagues and their public relations consultants.

She welcomed any distraction, any excuse to end the rehearsal for tomorrow's press conference. The room went silent as she read the handwritten scrawling script: "Dr. Nelson, I am here in the lobby. I need to talk to you. I will wait." Signed: "Adawia Abdul."

"Okay, team," Laura announced. "I'm ready for the reporters tomorrow. I thank you all for such diligent coaching. I have something I must attend to." She stowed her documents in an Immunone press kit folder specially designed for the event. "So let's call it quits until the real deal in the morning. I think we're at the point of diminishing returns, anyway."

"We're in good shape," the senior media consultant said. "If a journalist asks anything we haven't gone over, Laura has her talking points for reference."

Laura just hoped that tomorrow she would achieve the right balance of accuracy and spontaneity.

***

During the lunch break, Laura had slipped away to a desk in the hotel's business center to make some urgent calls. Her parents were delighted to hear her voice, but worried about her hand injury recovery. She'd called Tim, but he was still in surgery. She left a voice mail message, upbeat and encouraging, ending with "Love you, Tim." To be able to say that, meaning it so deeply, felt right to her. Why had it taken so long to understand what she felt?

Out of old, ingrown habit, Laura had thought for a second about calling her kids. All adults now—not cool for Mommy to call in the middle of their day. She smiled, but the smile wilted when she remembered the family meeting planned for tomorrow night. Nothing she could do about that now. Stay focused. Compartmentalize.

At Keystone, her secretary had chatted about the cartons of champagne piling up in Paul Parnell's executive suite. But there was one message she had wanted to bring to Laura's attention, "From that woman doctor-scientist at Replica. Dr. Adawia Abdul. The callback number I have is her office at Replica." Laura scribbled the number on her Immunone notepad. "She's anxious to talk to you. She sounded, well, distressed, even about to cry. I figured she should be upbeat with her drug being approved, but she definitely did not sound that way."

"Okay," Laura had responded, thinking about her early morning call about the Jeep to the Philadelphia police detective. Adawia Abdul had been the one to confirm that the suspicious dark-colored Jeep was Jake Harter's. "I'll try to reach her, but if she calls again, tell her she can get me here."

"Will do. And, Dr. Nelson, have you seen anybody famous there at the Hay-Adams?"

"Not yet. This has not been a glamour gig—at least, not so far."

Laura's left hand shook as she'd dialed the next number. The woman in Mayor Young's office sounded perky, "Mr. Greenwood is in Washington, DC, today. I know he wants to talk to you, Dr. Nelson. He has meetings with former DC Mayor Barry at the Hay-Adams today and tomorrow." Laura had hesitated before starting to disclose that she was at the same hotel, but, in the brief silence, the woman disconnected. Relief, if only temporary. Can't think about it now.

Next, she had called Replica and asked for Dr. Abdul. But Addie's line just rang and rang. And now, the note saying she was here, in the Hay-Adams, she said.

***

Laura got off the hotel elevator and scanned the grand lobby. All but hidden in a remote corner, Addie perched uncomfortably on a hardback chair, bent forward, head in her hands as if she were crying. "Addie?" Laura managed to get her attention from several feet away.

The young doctoral research star looked disheveled. Not her usual, stylish self. When she raised her head, the red-rimmed eyes, smudged mascara, and uneven makeup left no doubt that she had been in tears. But why, on the eve of her monumental success?

"Are you okay?"

"Dr. Nelson—"

"Laura, remember?"

Addie seemed to struggle for words, so Laura prompted, "My office said you called, but—"

"Yes. They told me you were here. I'm sorry to interrupt, but I need some advice. Desperately."

"You're not interrupting. Actually, you saved me from another twenty minutes of grueling preparation for the press conference." Hadn't someone told her Addie also would be on hand tomorrow, representing Replica, the little start-up company that beat tremendous odds against success in the pharmaceutical space?

"Replica wants me to be a part of that conference, too, but I don't think—"

"Addie, you'll be fine. If you wanted to go over your part with me, I'd be happy to—"

"No, Dr. Nel—Laura," Addie said, seeming to anxiously scan the lobby before lowering her head back into her hands.

"I am in terrible danger. I don't know who else to turn to. You've been so kind that I—"

"Addie, let's go to my suite. We'll have privacy there. We can take the elevator up to the fifth floor."

"Thank you," Addie murmured, letting herself be guided. Laura kept the pace efficient, but she couldn't help glancing around for a man whom she presumed to be black and in his forties—wearing an expensive suit, probably. The Hay-Adams clientele, although diverse, looked upscale. What did Lonnie Greenwood look like?

CHAPTER SIXTY-TWO

Jake stormed through the outer doors into the lobby of Replica. Security had been augmented. A plainclothes agent stood beside Lisa, the same receptionist he'd encountered before on his visits to Addie's office.

"Mr. Harter—sorry, no visitors admitted today," said Lisa. So she recognized him, knew he was from the FDA.

He looked around the modest lobby, noting how festive it looked. Flower arrangements decorated a rectangular table draped in white linen. Next to it sat cases of champagne. Getting ready for the Immunone approval party.

"It's critical that I see Dr. Adawia Abdul," he said. "As you know, I'm from the FDA."

"She's not here. She's supposed to be, but she left. Sick, I imagine. Not a good time."

The receptionist glanced about the room. Immunone's approval tomorrow was confidential, could disrupt the financial markets if leaked. "Well, since you're from the FDA, you must know—about tomorrow."

"I most certainly do. That's why it's mandatory I speak to her. Who would know where she is?"

"Home, most likely," said the clueless woman.

No, Addie is not home, wasn't home all night.

"Let me in. I need to talk to the department secretary."

"Mr. Harter, I'm sorry, but I can't let anybody in. We're preparing for..." She hesitated.

Jake noticed the security grunt step closer, a beefy specimen with "inept" written all over his pudgy face. He still had the Browning in his jacket pocket, and the sudden urge to shoot this clown almost overwhelmed him.

"Lisa—" Jake said leaning closer.

"Sir, back off," the guard said, edging closer.

Now was not the time for confrontation. Jake took a deep breath and complied. Changing his tack, he asked, quite politely now, if she would simply call Dr. Abdul's department. The department secretary would know where she had gone. Addie was meticulous about informing her employers about her whereabouts. She wouldn't simply disappear on the day before her drug's approval.

"I can do that," the receptionist said, as Jake noted the guard ease back to his original position.

A few clicks later he was connected to the woman who juggled the clerical needs of all the scientists in the pharmacology department. He was told that Addie had been in, but left shortly after ten, not telling anyone where she was going, even though she had to practice for a press conference. "She did seem a bit upset," the woman offered, "and looked, I don't know, different. Not herself."

Jake was about to ask whether she'd left any messages, when, by some instinct, he swiveled to face the lobby door. He froze. Set down the phone. His other hand went to the bulge in his right jacket pocket.

Backing up, Jake moved toward the revolving door at the lobby entrance. He needed to time his exit to the exact second. Detectives Finley and Booker stepped in tandem though the door as Jake, his back to them, slipped out.

He'd parked the Blazer on a nearby side street. He could only hope the detectives had not ID'd the rented Blazer. Jake's assumption: they'd found the body; connected Dru to Addie; they were looking for Addie.

Jake spun the Blazer around, heading away from Replica. He needed to find Addie before the cops got to her. Her sense of ethics might entice her to tell them what happened last night. As he made the next right turn, he passed a bridal shop. "Of course," he said aloud, slapping the steering wheel. At four o'clock that afternoon, he and Addie were to be married. Of course, that's why she skipped out on work. He admired Addie's sense of fashion. She'd want that perfect dress. The dashboard clock flashed 2:00 p.m. Plenty of time to get to Ellicott City. He had imagined them driving together, sharing the romantic interlude, but Addie must have learned about the American custom—the groom should not see the bride on their wedding day until the ceremony begins.

Jake thought about his own attire, not happy with the drab brown suit with a spindly pattern, but he'd been too preoccupied this morning to consider his wedding apparel. But he looked okay, a white shirt and decent striped tie. The one thing Addie and Karolee had in common—the only thing—they admired his style.

Jake found the moderate traffic comforting. All was normal, no sirens, no apparent surveillance. From now on, until after he and Addie left the country, he considered himself a hunted man. He was prepared, his survival pack loaded with provisions, enough cash to buy his way to a safe place, enough firepower to make it happen. And his wife at his side.

On the road, heading toward the Howard County Orphans' Court in Ellicott City, Maryland, Jake considered the risk he was taking now that the police were looking for Addie. But surely, Addie would not have told them when and where they'd be married. He'd be on alert, his piece loaded. He pulled the Blazer into a side street just south of the courthouse.

He checked his watch. In exactly one hour, Addie would arrive. He'd positioned himself in a recessed doorway across the street, giving him a view of the courthouse entrance. As soon as he spotted Addie, he'd join her and, fifteen minutes after that, they'd be man and wife. Twenty-four hours after that, they'd be multimillionaires on their way to their new life.

CHAPTER SIXTY-THREE

The word sumptuous came to mind as Addie followed Laura into her suite. She'd never been in the Hay-Adams, and she glanced about in awe as Laura went about fixing them a cup of tea. She'd offered to call room service for snacks, but Addie declined, despite having had nothing to eat since she'd fled her apartment last night.

The two women sat, sipping their tea, mostly in silence. Laura didn't push her, and for that, Addie was appreciative. She needed to trust someone. With Dru dead and Jake a cold-blooded killer, her support system had collapsed.

During a prolonged lull as Addie struggled with what to say, the hotel phone rang and Laura got up to answer it. Addie heard her say things like: "Sorry you're not here; I hope the child does well; I'm trying not to think about tomorrow night." And finally, "I love you, Tim."

Addie imagined herself saying to a man "I love you" and meaning it. She'd come close to sort of loving Jake before last night, when she realized he was a dangerous psychopath.

"Laura, let me ask you what you'd do," she said, once Laura had returned to sit down across from her.

Addie told Laura her story. How her father was ill and the Iraq government wanted her to return; more than wanted, threatened her family if she didn't proceed immediately—as in tomorrow; how she was coming into a lot of money from Immunone, but had no way of securing it if she had to leave for Iraq so soon; how she and Jake Harter were to be married today, but she had not shown up at the courthouse; how she now realized he couldn't be trusted and might even be dangerous. She told Laura the Rockville police had questioned her about Jake's wife's death. She told her of the DIA's interest in her Iraqi background.

Laura interrupted to ask about Jake. She told Addie how Jake had deliberately jeopardized the Immunone approval. "Why would he do that?" Laura asked.

"I don't know." And she didn't, but right now that was a problem from the distant past. "But I'm glad it'll be approved. What's really terrible is that I have—had—a friend who could help me deal with the money I will get. Invest it, that sort of thing, but...he died suddenly."

"How terrible," Laura responded, her tone sincere.

Addie stopped short of telling her that Jake shot Dru in her apartment. Neither had she dared confide in Laura about Iraq's plans for using her and her expertise in their bioweapons program.

"What can I do?" Laura asked, when Addie paused to wipe tears from her eyes.

"I can't let Jake find me," Addie said. "He'll be very angry. I'm afraid of him. He has a very bad temper."

"I'm not surprised to hear that," Laura set down her tea cup. "Now, back to you. Would you like to stay here tonight? I was expecting my fiancé, but he can't make it. Early and urgent surgery tomorrow morning. You can sleep over there." Laura pointed across the parlor to the oversized sofa laden with fluffy, decorative pillows.

"He's having surgery?" Addie gasped. "Shouldn't you be there? With him?"

"No, he's the surgeon. Pediatric cardiac surgery."

"Oh," Addie said, "that's nice."

Had Laura actually invited her to stay here in the hotel? Could she stay here, undetected, attend the press conference tomorrow representing Replica, and then...then what? Leave for London, then make her own booking to Baghdad? She had enough cash to do that, but she needed to get the Replica money secured. How would Replica pay her? A check? A money transfer to her bank? And when? Tomorrow? Or would it take days? Or weeks?

"So, do you want to stay here overnight, Addie?" Laura was asking. "If so, do you need anything? A change of clothes? Makeup?"

Addie looked down at her wrinkled skirt. "Do you think I can wear this for the press conference tomorrow?" she asked. "I left my apartment so suddenly. I didn't bring a change of clothes. I did pick up a few items at a drugstore."

Laura looked at her appraisingly. "That suit is perfectly appropriate. The hotel can press it and launder your blouse and your bra and panties. I've got an extra nightgown and panties in the meantime. But, we'll have to get your things to housekeeping soon."

"I don't know how to thank you, Laura," Addie said.

Laura had gone into the bedroom, returning with a fluffy, white bathrobe monogrammed with the Hay-Adams logo. "Why don't you put this on in my bathroom and, while you're in there, check out my makeup? I'm happy to share, but frankly, I doubt you need any. Your skin is perfect."

"I use a little eye shadow," Addie said, "but right now, that's the least of my worries."

"I have shades in blue and taupe," Laura said. "I'm going to call for the bellman to pick up your clothes—"

Laura was interrupted again by the phone.

Addie lingered by the bedroom door long enough to hear Laura say, "Hello, Mr. Greenwood." Then, "I'd be happy to meet you here in the hotel."

She was putting on the bathrobe when Laura called, "I'm going to the lobby to meet someone. Stay here. Do not open the door to anyone except the bellman to pick up your clothes for the laundry. Do not answer the phone."

"Are you sure that's okay?" Addie asked.

"Yes, and when I get back, I'm going to call my son Mike. He's a lawyer. Maybe he can help you deal with some of the money issues around the Immunone payout."

"He'd do that?" Addie asked. She knew American lawyers were powerful and expensive. And now that Dru could help her no more—

"My kids *usually* do whatever I ask them," Laura said. Then Addie heard the door to the suite close and she was alone.

CHAPTER SIXTY-FOUR

"What we got on Abdul and Hammadi?" Mack Long directed his question to the two agents seated across from him at the rectangular table in a nondescript Pentagon conference room. "Shit, six thirty already. Supposed to be at my kid's basketball game. Play-offs started."

Agent Mintner took the hint. "We got Abdul's hard drive from her personal computer, techs working it; nothing yet, sir. Replica's more of a problem; pharma companies are paranoid about confidentiality. We'll get it, but it's unlikely she would use it for bioterrorism. We searched Hammadi's hotel room, didn't find a computer. We've got Detroit searching his home, which by the way, is vacated. His wife and kids are not there. Left a week ago. She took the kids out of school. Said nothing to the neighbors."

"When we picked him up," Agent Sharkey said, "he'd been on a pay phone. Call traced to Alberta, Canada. So maybe—"

Long cut off Sharkey. "Did you find Hammadi?"

"We didn't." Mintner's scowl demonstrated his frustration.

"We do know Abdul did not show up for the scheduled marriage in Ellicott City," Sharkey said. "Neither did Harter, who's wanted for questioning in that Philadelphia hit-and-run we told you about."

"The connection?" Long asked, with a glance at the clock.

"Don't know," Mintner said. "Anonymous tip this morning

that linked his vehicle—a Jeep Cherokee—to a hit-and-run on an elderly doctor, employed by Keystone Pharma. Turns out they have a tire-impression match."

"They have Harter in custody?"

"No, but there's a bulletin out for him. Security images show Harter leaving Abdul's apartment this morning. And, they show him entering last night. Twice, actually. He'd been there, left, and returned. This morning, we know he showed up at Abdul's office at Replica. We know he hasn't tried to pick up his Jeep."

"Couple of things, though." Sharkey used a ballpoint pen to push an errant curl from her face. "Surveillance cameras did not pick up Abdul leaving her apartment, though she did show up at work this morning; acted 'odd' her coworkers said, then left early and abruptly. Hasn't returned to her apartment."

"You said a couple of things," Long said. "What else?"

"Badur Hammadi," Sharkey said. "He also showed up at Abdul's place last evening. Went in, recorded on security camera, but no evidence of him leaving. When our guys were in there to pick up her computer, they did a quick inspection. Nobody home. Nothing out of order."

"So what you got," Long summed up, "are three *don't knows.*"

"Only a matter of time, sir," Sharkey said, starting to get up, knowing her boss wanted to leave.

"When you do find Hammadi," Long asked, "any basis to keep him?"

"Guy's got a clean record. Naturalized citizen. Good job in a bank—Chase Manhattan."

"What about Dr. Abdul?" Long consulted his notes. "Adawia? That how you say it?"

"Yeah, she goes by 'Addie,'" Sharkey said. "Didn't get anything out of her except acknowledgment that her father was the Doctor Jamail Abdul, and her father is ill. She's concerned about him. Her last trip home was four years ago. Hasn't seen him since then. And don't forget, she has a ticket to fly to London on Friday."

"All things considered," Long said, rising from his chair, gathering his papers, "we have more important threats to worry about than these two. Follow up on the hard drives. If there's nothing there, let the woman leave the country, but have Immigration pull her green card so she's not coming back. Hammadi is another story. He needs to tell us about that satellite image the NSA pulled up in Baghdad. As for Harter, let Philly take care of him."

"We'll grab Hammadi, sir. He'll tell us what we want to know."

"Hands off, hotshot. Leave the shady stuff to the CIA. Now, I'm off to see my kid's game."

CHAPTER SIXTY-FIVE

Laura tried to disguise her trepidation as she headed to the table in the far corner of the lobby where a middle-aged black man sat alone. Fashionably dressed in a navy-blue suit, white shirt, striped navy-and-white tie, he appeared the epitome of a successful business man, except for his hair, worn in an old-fashioned Afro. Lonnie Greenwood stood up as she approached. Taller than Tim, maybe six-foot-three, lean but muscular.

"I'm Laura Nelson," she said, extending her hand.

"Lonnie Greenwood." He took her hand, shook it with a firm grasp. "I've been curious to meet you for a long time, Dr. Nelson. Thanks for meeting me here on short notice. When my secretary found out from your office you were here... Well, I do believe in serendipity."

Laura didn't know what to say. She remained silent as she sat in the chair he held for her.

"I work for Detroit Mayor Coleman Young," Greenwood said, "and happened to be in Washington to go over some matters with former DC Mayor Marion Barry, a gentleman who's gotten himself in hot water, as you may know. But he's determined to make a comeback, and he's got friends who will help him."

To say something, Laura asked, "You said you know Mayor Freedman from Tampa, my hometown?"

"Yes. I know Sandra. She's the person who told me about

you. She speaks highly of you. But I hear your new hometown is Philadelphia. I know Mayor Green too. But never mind mayors. I want to talk about my son. You've looked into his case?"

Laura sighed with relief as Greenwood moved into familiar territory. "I know about your son," she said. "I reviewed his records. I agree he needs a lung transplant, and I was able to move him to the top of the list in Tampa. When Dr. Plant—who's taking my place at Tampa City—gets a lung with a favorable match profile, it will go to your son. And, of course, I'd recommend Immunone therapy. The clinical trial results are—"

Greenwood reached over and took her hand. "Bless you," he said. "Johnny is my only child. Maya, his mother, moved from Detroit to Tampa in 1969 before he was born. I know you were in medical school in Detroit during that time."

"Yes," Laura said. She didn't like his familiarity with her history. But the man did seem genuinely grateful for what she'd done on behalf of his son. Waiting lists for lungs were long. In Tampa, there were thirty-eight qualified candidates, and a healthy lung from a compatible donor came along rarely. No telling how long it would take to get a match for young Johnny Greenwood, but he would get top priority.

"I told Lucy Jones I'd be seeing you." The man's Afro bobbed as he spoke. "She was pleased. She's a big fan of yours. Made me promise to give you her best wishes. More than any human being on this planet, I respect that woman. Losing two sons, raising four daughters on her own. Well, you knew her back then."

Laura nodded, wondered if she should pull back her hand, but didn't.

"Did you know she credits you for 'saving' her daughters? When Stacy started to drift into the gangs, you befriended her. And now she's a brilliant doctor. Making a name for herself in Atlanta at the CDC. You know, I saw you at her medical school graduation party at Lucy's house. I couldn't help but notice how all the Jones girls looked up to you. Frankly, I was dumbfounded—under the circumstances."

Where was he going with this? Does he know I killed one of Lucy Jones' sons?

"And little Katie is a psychiatrist. You didn't know Anthony, but that boy was going places—until he got mowed down by the cops. I was there that night. I was in 'Nam too, but I never saw anything like that July night in 1967 when Detroit burned."

Anthony had been in a vegetative state when he'd been assigned to her—her first patient. That's how she'd met Lucy. How eventually she had found herself cornered one disastrous night in a deserted parking lot by Anthony's brother Johnny. And, ultimately, how she'd come to kill Johnny. How much of this did Lonnie Greenwood know?

"The Detroit riots," mumbled Laura. "Terrible times."

The man let go of her hand, and now sat with his head bowed in contemplation. "You seem like a nice woman," he finally said. "But I gotta tell you that I know. I know it was you who shot Johnny. Snake told me. Snake also said he was shaking you down for drugs. Would have kept it up too, if he hadn't gotten himself killed. Bet you didn't know that it was my gun he used to kill that doctor at the graduation ceremony."

Laura felt her heart stop. The weapon that killed her beloved David, Patrick's father, belonged to the man now sitting across from her?

"Learned a lot about guns in 'Nam. Got shot up there too. Still got a gimpy leg."

Still, Laura said nothing. Her breaths were shallow, she felt faint, but she met his eyes, questioning.

"I was down, and Snake took the weapon off me so I wouldn't off myself. Wasn't until I got into rehab that I even cared enough to look up Maya. Found out I had a son. He was four years old then. Had a lot of breathing problems, pneumonia, things like that. Eventually got diagnosed with cystic fibrosis."

Laura couldn't hold out any longer. "Why are you telling me this, Mr. Greenwood?"

"Please, call me Lonnie."

"Okay, Lonnie. And I'm Laura."

The man reached into his pocket and pulled out a three-by-five-inch faded photo. She recognized the background as Detroit, but not the exact location, somewhere around the medical complex. "See that mural on the building in the background?"

Laura nodded, then gasped. She recognized four out of the five faces: Johnny and Anthony Diggs, Ray Rogers—aka Snake—an unknown young black man, and Lonnie Greenwood with a very large Afro.

"Snake painted that mural. Then the city tore down the building. He was enraged with the world." Lonnie pushed the photo closer. "We called ourselves the Alexandrine gang," he said. "All dead now, except me." He pointed out the three boys she'd known back then: Anthony, Johnny, Snake. "There's me and Willie, poor kid overdosed on heroin."

Laura stared at the photo, then pointed out Lonnie. "I've seen you before. I was a medical student when they brought you into the ER that night. Was that Maya with you?"

Lonnie straightened, his eyes widened in shock. "Yes. So you know—"

Laura cringed at the memory. "I was with the chief of surgery for an orientation. He took me into your treatment room. So yes, I know. There'd been a television crew filming in the ER that night." *And I was injured that night too.* Nothing she intended to share with Greenwood.

"Then you're only one of a very few who know about my infirmity. With my buddies all dead..."

Laura wondered what it must be like for a young man to go through life with his penis destroyed by his girlfriend's firearm blast. Maya must have been pregnant at the time. Laura wondered if she'd spent time in jail.

"Son of a bitch." Greenwood grimaced, set his glass of water down, and leaned in closer to her. "So I know your secret and you know mine."

"What do you want from me?" Laura asked.

"I wanted help for my son," he said. "Once your Tampa mayor mentioned your name, I made the connection, remembered what went down in Detroit."

What went down in Detroit. The focus even now of Laura's constant nightmares. If only it had been just a nightmare.

"Thought I'd use what we call—leverage," he continued. "That's the main reason I contacted you. But I always planned to let *you* know *I* know what happened all those years ago. When I first started working for the mayor, I used to plot how I'd expose you, make you pay." Lonnie leaned back, picked up his water glass, drained it. "But you know what? I see all the good you've done. Now you've jumped in to help my son, I don't want to harm you." Lonnie's lips curled up in a crooked smile. "And now you have something on me."

Should she say more? Should she tell him how Johnny had raped her? Threatened to kill her? That what she'd done was self-defense? Or just leave it at this between them? A sort of truce.

Laura met his gaze and, for a long moment, neither moved.

"Thank you," she said, having made her decision.

Could she trust him? Would the truth always hover over her life like a shadow?

And the haunting question: should she tell Tim? Did she have the courage to tell Tim?

She didn't think so.

CHAPTER SIXTY-SIX

In daylight, Jake surveyed his surroundings. He'd chosen well last night, camouflaging the Blazer in a remote clump of dead trees on Maryland farmland, well off the beaten track. Small chance some farmer would detect the vehicle before he was long gone. The weather wasn't bad for early March, the temperature in the mid-forties.

Despite the cramped quarters, Jake had slept well. He'd changed into sweats, folding his dress clothes carefully. With the Blazer seat reclined, covered by his comforter, and the firm pillow he preferred, he had no complaints.

After stepping outside to urinate, he rummaged through the backpack for water and a protein bar. Clumsily, moving as fast as he could in the chilly front seat, he changed into the same suit he'd worn yesterday, but he pulled a clean shirt and a different tie out of the garment bag. Before heading off, he needed to select his carry weapons. Sadly, the sweet Browning had to be tossed in the Potomac last night, after he'd used it on the Arab. He'd take one of his Glocks as his primary, tuck it into the pocket of his bulky winter jacket; the Beretta would go in the ankle holster. Using a gun was not part of the plan for phase one of this mission: pick up Addie. Definitely, he'd need a firearm for phase two: assassinate Nelson, and it wouldn't be a handgun. Jake prided himself on his diverse skills: he could be mountain man; hard-core assassin; city slicker. By the end of the day, he'd show the world all three.

When Addie hadn't shown up at the courthouse yesterday, he blamed Nelson. Addie idolized that woman, and Nelson would stop at nothing to get back at him for losing the Immunone data. So she played up to Addie to try to discourage her from marrying him. Well, this was a game she would lose, terminally.

Jake fired up the Blazer, appreciating the on-demand heater, and pulled onto the rural road, heading toward Rockville. He turned on the radio, then flipped it off, hearing only news and morning talk shows. He was not interested in the news. Hell, he'd be making the news today. But first, he had to put a few things in order.

He'd have to rearrange the gear in the Blazer into more manageable containers to prepare for the likelihood of changing vehicles. He cursed the asshole who had smashed his Jeep. He'd created the perfect compartments to store guns, ammo, camping gear. Now all that was out in the open. He'd gone to the trouble to download his eclectic collection of music onto a set of CDs, which he kept by his side in the Jeep right next to his assortment of maps. At least the Blazer had 4-wheel drive, but would the tires withstand the rough back roads?

Jake didn't like feeling scared, and he may never admit it even to himself, but he was scared to go back and reclaim his Jeep. Those cop cars spooked him. But how could the cops possibly have anything on the Jeep? The Philadelphia hit had been a few weeks ago. Nobody could connect it to him. Or could they? Nelson's voice message on Addie's phone did mention a *Jeep.*

On his way to Rockville, where he knew he'd find Addie at the Immunone press conference, he stopped by McDonald's, using the men's room to clean up and shave. After today, he may let his beard grow. Arab style. Addie would like that.

Heading toward Rockville, Jake forced himself to consider a worst-case scenario. What if that Arab's body was traced back to him? Lots of people would know that both he and the dead guy were linked to Addie. Thankfully, he'd disposed of the gun. But if they did connect Mr. Arab to Addie, they'd check her apartment and find trace evidence everywhere. His and Mr. Arab's. No problem. He and Addie were to be married, of course he'd have left DNA and fingerprints. And she had a history with the Arab. So what?

His worst worry: her trust and her confidence in him. How badly had it been eroded by Nelson's influence? As soon as the Immunone approval was final, he'd take her to a justice of the peace, finalize their marriage. Then to a lawyer for power of attorney. After that, he had in mind a remote campsite in the West Virginia mountains. Hang out there until the coast was clear, then off to the island paradise of Addie's choice.

Laura Nelson was a loose end. He'd vowed to eliminate her and he would fulfill his vow. She'd screwed him at the FDA; she'd contaminated Addie, posing as her soul mate. Nobody screws over Jake Harter. Nobody. Jake's mind flew back to the list of those he'd killed and the reasons why. He'd been justified. Yes, he was an assassin, but a discriminating one.

Nelson would be a participant at today's press conference. And Addie would be there too. Replica would require her to be there. When he left the press conference, Addie would leave with him. But what if she didn't go willingly? What if he had to subdue her? She could be headstrong. She had run from him Wednesday night. She hadn't shown up at the courthouse yesterday. She seemed to be under the sway of Laura Nelson. His first impulse had been to punish Addie, but he knew he wouldn't. He remembered the torment he'd felt when Addie's Arab pal slapped her that night. No, he, Jake Harter, would not strike a woman.

He'd decided to bring a syringe of ketamine, a sedative he'd once evaluated for its weird psychological side effects, but only as a last resort to put her out for as long as it took to take control.

Once he had Addie secure, he'd go after Nelson. Should be easy. The bitch was now a part of the Keystone limo convoy. She'd be traveling in style to the private terminal at National, boarding the Gulfstream. He'd done his homework, scouted out positions, found the perfect ambush spot on a small knoll with a direct visual to the tarmac. Armed with his prized Bushmaster, long-range and fitted with a scope, and his superior marksmanship, he'd pick off the lady doctor. Quick and easy. With his escape route precisely mapped out, he'd be out and away and untouchable.

Jake noted the clock on the dash. Eight thirty. Perfect. Enough time to clean up, get to the press conference by the scheduled ten o'clock start. Immunone was big news. There'd be a crowd, science reporters and business reporters. But after twenty-five years, he knew the FDA Parklawn property: where to park, where to stand, where to disappear. The three Cs would be working for him: crowd, chaos, crime. Jake had to chuckle at his clever new slogan. The Three Cs.

CHAPTER SIXTY-SEVEN

Laura had the best sleep she'd had in weeks, not having woken until her alarm sounded. Her hand hurt less. Her mind had slowed down. She felt profound relief after the conversation with Lonnie Greenwood. Last thing before falling asleep, she'd called Tim. She now knew she needed to tell him what had happened in that desolate parking lot in Detroit twenty-five years ago. He deserved to know. She hoped he'd still love and respect her. But first, she needed to tell her children about David Monroe and Patrick's paternity. For as long as she'd known Tim, she'd been trapped in a web of interlocking secrets. Before he married her, he had a right to know what she'd kept hidden for all those years.

Laura called Tim from the phone in the hotel bedroom at seven o'clock. No answer. He'd be scrubbed at CHOP by now, reviewing the operative procedure with his surgical team. He was the senior pediatric cardiac surgeon, a source of pride for him, as it will be for her as his wife. Fourteen years ago, Tim had operated on Patrick, when Laura's youngest child had been nine years old, with a cardiac tumor. A benign tumor; to this day, Laura still felt the flush of relief on hearing the miraculous word *benign*.

And today, Tim would save the life of another young child. As much as she'd like him with her in Rockville to share her moment in the spotlight, he was the real hero back home in Philadelphia. *And yes,* Laura thought with a smile, *Philadelphia was now her home.*

Laura had ordered room-service breakfast for her and Addie to be delivered at seven forty-five. Before Laura headed for the shower, she peeked into the parlor where Addie slept on the ample sofa.

"Seven o'clock," she called out, even though Addie was already up, reviewing her notes at the small table. "I'm going to shower."

"Okay, Laura," Addie said. "I figured I'd better at least read through what I'm supposed to say."

That's the least of your problems, Laura thought. To Addie she said, "You'll be stellar."

"I can't tell you how much better I feel after talking to your son Mike last night, and signing the papers that he faxed. After the press conference, I feel comfortable leaving, knowing my Immunone money will be secure."

Laura worried about Addie leaving the United States to return to terrorist-oriented Iraq. But had her own father been ill, she knew she'd risk considerable danger to go to him. Still, Addie's safety concerned her. Was there anything more she could do for this charming, bright young woman?

By the time Laura appeared, showered and dressed in a trim turquoise suit, breakfast was being set up in the parlor. Addie remained in the bathroom until the bellman left, then emerged, looking fantastic in yesterday's clothes, now laundered and pressed.

Together, in near silence, the two women sipped coffee or tea, nibbled croissants, and drank orange juice, as each reviewed her own press conference prep notes one last time.

CHAPTER SIXTY-EIGHT

Tim's flight landed on time at Washington National Airport, leaving him a scant hour to get to Rockville for the Immunone press event. He'd known Laura wanted him there—but she'd never ask him to postpone a critical surgical procedure on a child. He grinned at the thought of surprising her.

He'd arrived at CHOP to find his small patient had developed an ear infection. Not a big deal in a kid—except for a kid facing surgery. A bacterial infection in a patient posed an unacceptable surgical risk. Treat for twenty-four hours with intravenous antibiotics, Tim's team of doctors agreed. Then reassess the risk—other complications that can arise from a bacterial infection could mean serious cardiac risk—and tomorrow morning, a difficult decision. But for now, Tim was free to catch the eight o'clock flight out of Philly to DC.

After the excitement of the press conference, Tim knew, Laura's attention quickly would shift to the revelation to her kids planned for tonight. She'd obsess, he feared, consider each kid, try to predict each reaction, try to predict her reaction to their reactions. But obsessing only would confuse matters. She must simply speak her heart. Her children loved and respected her, Tim judged. They'd be shocked, yes—but vindictive? Not their style.

But what if he misjudged them, and they deeply hurt her? As

much as he wanted to protect Laura, he felt helpless. After her press conference, he'd be there with her, try his best to keep her distracted. For Laura, it was, and always had been, about her devotion to family. Realistically, he still felt like the outsider with his nose pressed to the glass, wanting Laura's love, and coveting the privilege of joining the family. But tonight, would a twenty-year-old secret be the death of the close-knit Nelson family unit? Finally, he had to admit, he couldn't predict.

CHAPTER SIXTY-NINE

Riding with Laura in the Keystone Pharma limo to the press conference site, the FDA Parklawn Building, Addie steeled herself for
a conversation with Priscilla Fabre. Once they arrived, she searched
for Priscilla among the group of milling employees. The tall woman
was easy to spot, and to Addie's great relief, Priscilla seemed genuinely glad to see her. Didn't even mention that she'd disappeared
from work yesterday, and never called. Replica's press materials
highlighted her appearance. Had she not shown up, they'd have
been embarrassed. Or, maybe, a smart lawyer would have made her
presence a condition of giving her the money. Didn't matter. She
was here.

"Priscilla," Addie had to take a breath, "I must leave for home
tonight. Since I am technically an employee as of the date when
Immunone was approved, I want to make sure the money set
aside, as per my contract, will come to me."

"I know how worried you are about your father, and I'm so
grateful the timing worked out for you. I've been in touch with
legal. I've confirmed that the funds due you will be distributed
shortly. But if you're going to be out of town, you should give us
instructions. Would you prefer a direct deposit, or to have the
money wired? It's a very large amount."

So, Replica was not going to give her a hard time. Addie could
almost relax. After talking to Laura's son, Mike, into the late hours

last night, she knew her rights, but, nevertheless, it was gratifying to know a lawsuit wouldn't be necessary. An American court would always favor a big company over an individual. Last night, she had signed her power of attorney relative to all financial affairs involving US dollars to Michael Nelson. He was a lawyer with a big firm, and she had Laura's assurance she could be confident her contract would be honored. Michael had confirmed the $7.5 million total would be diminished by whatever taxes were due, but no matter how Addie looked at it, she was a wealthy woman. Would she ever come to need or appreciate that wealth? She didn't know.

Addie had always assumed Dru would manage her finances, and then Jake after they were married, but now she was on her own, her financial life delegated to Laura's son. The relevant documents all had been faxed or e-mailed back and forth through the hotel's twenty-four-hour business center. Addie reached into her purse and removed an envelope.

"Mr. Nelson has prepared my resignation letter." She handed the envelope to Priscilla: "It's effective tomorrow."

Priscilla accepted the envelope. "We'll miss you," she said, stepping up to hug Addie. Then Priscilla turned to the podium. "Time to shine…"

When it was her turn, Addie went to the podium, adjusted the microphone, and spoke directly into it. She'd memorized the script Replica had given her. As she paused at appropriate intervals, she glanced around the crowd. She'd never imagined so many cameras and video recorders. As she concluded her remarks, she stepped back as planned. Laura, representing Keystone Pharma, and the FDA commissioner would follow her. Questions and answers would come at the end.

To save her family, Addie now knew she would return to Baghdad to take her father's place. Knowing her mother's wishes would be fulfilled, could she still get on the plane? She'd have to marry Gabir Rahman. But in her new scientific role, Addie would do all she dared to sabotage bioweapons of mass destruction, to limit the impact of terrorism. Her father was a kind and gentle man. Could he covertly have had the same intentions? She'd never even considered that possibility. Maybe taking his place could extend that legacy—

Addie's thoughts were interrupted by a question addressed to her. She hadn't even registered what Laura and the FDA had said. It must be time for the Q&A. And the first question had been directed at her. The FDA staffer coordinating the conference asked the reporter to repeat the question.

"Dr. Abdul, when you first discovered the Immunone chemical," a reporter asked, "did you know how important it would be in transplant rejection?"

One of the anticipated questions on her list from Replica. The answer: "No, but she's so gratified," etcetera.

The Q&A continued with only one further question directed to Addie. "What new medications is Replica working on?" Addie had the easy answer: "Antibiotics for resistant bacteria, and growth factors for hematopoietic bone marrow cells—to treat leukemia."

While the press packed up their equipment, Addie and Laura stood talking to the FDA staff. As long as she stayed in a cluster of people, Addie felt safe. So far, she'd not seen a sign of Jake, but she kept scanning the periphery. Maybe she'd get out of the building without him finding her. As the crowd dwindled, the Keystone Pharma attendees, including their CEO, Paul Parnell, gathered in a circle around Laura. Addie felt marginalized and vulnerable. Time for her to thank Laura and say good-bye.

Addie planned to take a cab to Washington National. She had tickets to London Heathrow, booked under her own name. Dru had told her that after the United Nations had imposed restrictions on Iraq following the Gulf War, the United States and the United Kingdom established a no-fly zone for the country. Dru's solution: fly Royal Jordanian Airlines from London to Amman, Jordan, and then on to Baghdad. That's how he'd done it.

He warned her not to use her own name when traveling to Jordan or Iraq. If she did, she might not get back into the US. She had no alternative now, other than to buy her own ticket revealing her true identity. But did that still matter?

Of course, Addie dreamed the United States and Iraq would one day become allies, and their citizens would travel freely between countries. Only a dream, but if her dream came true, she would be a very rich woman. Michael Nelson had explained how her money would grow in value.

Inching closer to Laura to say good-bye, Addie remembered the DIA agents saying they still might need to talk to her. Were they following her, she wondered? Agent Sharkey had seen her airline ticket to London. Would they show up at the airport? Had they checked her apartment? Found Dru? She could not answer these questions. She'd follow her plan; go to the airport.

Laura turned to hug Addie when she approached. "We're all headed for the airport, Addie. How about you? What did you decide?"

"I have a flight to London, early evening," she said. "Laura, I can't thank you enough—"

All of a sudden, Laura rushed out of her embrace toward a tall man with red hair walking straight toward them, a wide smile on his face.

"Tim!" Laura pulled him into a hug, kissing his cheek. "You came? What about your patient?"

"Had to postpone," he said. "You were great, Laura. I watched it all."

The man turned toward Addie, "And, Dr. Abdul, you were fantastic. Laura's been telling me a lot about you."

"Tim, meet Addie—Doctor Adawia Abdul. Addie, this is Tim Robinson, my fiancé."

Tim looked ecstatic to see Laura and slung his arm around her left shoulder. Pointing to the Keystone contingent, he said, "I wanted to say hello to Paul Parnell. Thank him for convincing you to stay in Philadelphia."

Laura grinned. "Okay. Come on. Addie, you come too."

Again, Addie looked around, expecting to see Jake, fearing having to face him. Maybe she should ask Laura for a ride to the airport. There'd be room in that stretch limo. Once she got to National, there'd be plenty of security, and she could blend in with the passengers at the crowded airport.

CHAPTER SEVENTY

Jake watched the press conference from the seclusion of the small utility closet off the lobby. The acoustics were perfect, as was his angle of vision to the podium. He heard each of Addie's words. He realized her remarks would have been written by her superiors at Replica, but even so, he was extremely disappointed that in her acknowledgments, she hadn't mentioned him. An easy matter to just slip his name onto the prepared list. But she hadn't. While she'd been speaking, every nerve in his body screamed for him to go to her, to stand beside her, to gather her up, and to escort her to the waiting Blazer. But he'd grasped the edge of the door and held back. Soon. *Very soon,* he told himself.

Jake scoured the crowd for Detectives Booker and Finley. He knew they were looking for him. Why else would a cop car be stationed outside his house on each of the two occasions he'd risked a drive by? Cops hanging out around his Jeep and his home were not a good sign. And if they'd found that Arab's body where he'd stashed it in Addie's apartment building, all the more reason for Jake to be cautious. The cops knew about him and Addie, and they knew about Addie and the Arab; they must be close. So far, Jake hadn't spotted them, but he did notice a man and a woman lingering close to the podium, their attention on Addie. After she completed her statement, he noticed the dark-skinned woman take a step toward Addie, but the man's hand shot out to pull her back. Those two did not look like reporters. They looked like law enforcement.

Jake glanced at his watch. This would be all over in a half hour. Tonight, he and Addie would be bundled up in their campsite, eating dinner by an open fire.

Next up was Dr. Laura Nelson. The source of his grief. *Just let it go,* he told himself. Don't let the Nelson bitch alter your focus. Concentrate on Addie. Yes, he'd vowed to make Nelson pay for humiliating him and for trying to turn Addie against him, and he had already had decided on a time and a place.

Nelson droned on about what a wonderful job her predecessor, Fred Minn—God rest his soul—had done, and so on and so forth. The wonders of Immunone— She put on an air of false modesty, but self-promotion was her game. Couldn't fool him. His hand reached into his jacket pocket, felt the Glock, ached to pull it out, aim at the bitch, and pull the trigger. "No, not now. Wrong place." When he heard his own whisper, he realized he'd spoken aloud.

After Nelson, it was time for the FDA Commissioner to do his own version of self-aggrandizement, and then the FDA public relations machine fielded press questions and answers. Never once in the entire press conference was he, Jake Harter, mentioned, the project manager for the wonder drug Immunone. Kudos to Sid Casey, his boss Charles Sloan, acclamation for the medical review officers—the obnoxious Susan Ridley and the wimpy Karl Hayes—but none for Jake, who'd directed the entire prolonged process, from the drug's Investigational New Drug submission to today's approval of the New Drug Application.

Again, his hand went to the Glock. This time, he clutched the handle. Laura Nelson had taken his job, his dignity, besmirched his reputation. He should be sharing the podium, but here he was, cowering in a closet.

Then the press conference ended and the bright lights extinguished. Jake stayed put, letting the media trickle out. Naturally, the speakers were surrounded by their supporters. The big shots at the FDA were accustomed to the ass-kissers, wanting a word, a chance to push their causes with the upper echelon, not understanding that at the FDA, the project managers were the real seat of power. Nothing goes anywhere unless the project manager gives the green light. Except this time, when Laura Nelson had stepped all over him. "Fuck it," he muttered, as he stepped out of the closet and moved with the crowd toward the lobby exit.

Jake hung by the exit leading from the lobby, through a short hall to the outer door of the building. Since the FDA staff would head inside toward offices upstairs, he wasn't worried about being recognized. Monitoring the diminishing circle of well-wishers still at the podium, Jake saw a tall, redheaded man in a brown suit approach Nelson. When she noticed him, Nelson rushed to hug him, and then to Jake's dismay, she turned to introduce him to Addie. They appeared to chat, then the three of them made their way to the Keystone group gathered around the guy Jake recognized as the company CEO. Jake fumed at the sight of Addie with Laura Nelson. What kind of pull did Nelson exert on her? Whatever it was, the woman soon would regret it. Five minutes later, the three of them left the group and strode together toward him and the exit, talking, but not loud enough for him to hear. Not wanting to intercept Addie while they were still inside the building, Jake stepped out the door ahead of them. This was where he had decided to take Addie, but according to his plan, she should be alone.

"I appreciate the ride to the airport," Jake heard Addie say as she stepped through the door.

The sight of Addie with Nelson, acting chummy, like girlfriends, so infuriated Jake that he yanked the Glock out of his pocket. Driven by a white rage he could no longer subdue, he pointed the barrel at Nelson.

They were so busy chatting they hadn't seen him, walked right past him. Wearing a bulky jacket, a black knit cap pulled down close to his eyes, and wearing dark sunglasses, he'd not so much as caught Addie's eyes as she passed within six feet of him, where he'd stood on the sidewalk, just off their path.

"The driver can drop you at the main terminal just after he leaves us by the private jets' field," Nelson was saying, "but won't you come back to Philly with us? You can meet my son and..."

Jake passed the trio as they walked toward a black stretch limo. With the gun trained on Nelson, he stepped in front of them, blocking their path. Not seeing the gun at first, not recognizing him, they came to a stop.

Gun in right hand, now held behind his back, Jake grabbed Addie's arm with his left. "Let's go, Addie."

Jake's plan hadn't included the use of weapons on the street, but the notion of Addie going anywhere with Nelson incensed him beyond tolerance. "Now!" he repeated.

"Jake?" Addie looked up at him, her eyes clouded with something he feared was betrayal.

"Addie, come," Jake said, catching her coat sleeve.

"No." Addie tried to free her arm. "Jake, I can't go with you. I'm sorry."

"Mr. Harter," Nelson said, "Addie's with us. Come on, Addie, just keep walking."

"You are coming with me." Jake's heart beat faster now. He meant to keep his tone normal, but his words came out a command. "You are with me."

"The lady doesn't seem to want to leave with you," the redheaded man butted in. "So—"

In an instant, Jake swung the gun toward Nelson, who didn't seem to flinch. *What, she wasn't afraid of bullets? Didn't think he'd have the balls to terminate her worthless life? Well, she was about to—*

The gun in his right hand, within point-blank range of Nelson, Jake saw the redhaired man start to move. He had to kill the bitch, now. He pulled the trigger, but not before Addie pulled out of his grip, flinging herself in front of his target. As the bullet tore through his beloved's chest, Jake felt his life implode. His body started to fold, the gun almost slipped from his hands, but within a millisecond, a surge of adrenaline restored his strength. Again he took aim at Nelson, who now was on the ground beside Addie, kneeling in a pool of bright red blood. *I can't let Nelson's be the last face Addie sees.* Aiming at Nelson's chest, Jake pulled the trigger just as a force hit his knees. The gunshot reverberated as Jake hit the pavement, landing on his side. On top of him now, the man with the red hair delivered a powerful blow to his jaw. He felt bone shatter. When he looked up, he no longer faced the redhaired man, but looked into the faces of the black woman and the white man he'd made as law enforcement. Each held a firearm inches from his face. "Federal Agent," the woman said, "Jake Harter. You are under arrest."

Jake's garbled, "Addie?" was drowned out by a man's shout. "Laura, no! Get an ambulance! Now!"

Pinned to the ground, facing away from Addie, tears flooded in Jake's eyes. "Addie? Are you—"

"Mr. Jake Harter." The familiar voice of Detective Booker. "We've been looking for you. Been wanting to pin a murder charge on you. Doctor Fred Minn? Name sound familiar? Outside the Four Seasons Hotel in Philadelphia? And maybe we could make the case for your wife too. But hey! Now we got you cold. Killin' your fiancée. Didn't you say you and the beautiful young doctor were planning to marry? And so soon after losing your wife Karolee?"

"Addie?" Jake called in anguish through the pain in his busted jaw. As the handcuffs went on, he struggled for a glimpse of Addie. What had Detective Booker meant? "Addie!"

Jake's head throbbed as he kept trying to turn and look at the spot where Addie had fallen. Sirens screamed, the sound closer and closer. "Hurry," Jake yelled. "Addie, you have to be okay." He wanted to call out to Nelson, a chest surgeon, to beg her to help Addie, but when he tried to talk, his efforts were thwarted by blood flooding in his mouth. That guy had hit him hard, very hard.

Despite the cuffs, despite the searing pain in his jaw, the thumping in his head, despite a pair of guns still trained on him,

Jake managed at last to turn far enough around to see the ground where Addie lay drenched in blood. But she was not alone on the blood-soaked pavement. Beside her lay Laura Nelson. The red-haired man leaning over her, talking to her. Jake's field of vision was not clear enough for him to see whether either Addie or Nelson were moving, whether they were breathing, but the intermingling blood where they lay was profuse. Onlookers stood around, mostly wringing their hands, waiting helplessly for the ambulance that was now screaming its arrival.

"I need to be with Addie," he begged.

"Too late," pronounced Detective Booker.

CHAPTER SEVENTY-ONE

When Tim leaned across the gurney to kiss Laura's forehead, she saw dark red stains on his pale yellow shirt, and an irregular pattern of darkness on the dark brown suit jacket. So much blood had soaked his jacket she could smell the acrid odor.

The Georgetown University Hospital doctors wanted her admitted right there, right then. Laura intended to keep her appointment with her children that evening in Philadelphia. She would not take no for an answer. The compromise: Georgetown ER physicians would stabilize her. The Gulfstream, which Keystone Pharma often volunteered for medevac missions, would take her immediately to Philadelphia. She promised to remain at the Hospital of the University of Pennsylvania until doctors there signed her medical release.

She'd been shot through her left shoulder. A lucky shot, if a gunshot wound could be considered lucky. Damage to muscles and tendons, but they would heal. Among the doctors, including Laura, no one could agree whether, given a choice, it would be better to be shot in her bad arm or her healthy one. Fate picked the good arm. When she went down, she'd landed on the site of her injury, but Addie's body, already bathed in the blood of her mortal chest wound, absorbed much of the impact.

An ambulance had taken Addie to Georgetown, too, but she

had been dead on arrival. The first bullet had torn into her friend's left ventricle, destroying it on impact. The second time the gunman took aim, he might well have killed again, if Tim's tackle had not deflected the bullet. Just before Laura's morphine injection, her last conscious thought was grief over the loss of a promising young medical researcher and a charming friend.

***

Having slept four hours, Laura awoke in a hospital room. Tim sat in the chair next to her bed, still wearing the brown tailored suit he'd worn to the press conference. While in the emergency room at Georgetown, they'd removed her contact lenses and, without her glasses, she couldn't make out much detail.

Lost without them, she asked Tim, "Do you have my purse?"

"Funny question. You need cash? I'm sure the hospital will accept a check."

"My glasses," Laura said. "Can't face the world—or my family—without them. What time is it?"

"It's five thirty." Tim reached into her bulging handbag, fumbled around, and pulled out the case with her glasses inside.

"This is better," Laura said.

She attempted to rise to a sitting position, but the pain in her bandaged left shoulder made that maneuver impossible, and she still couldn't put any pressure on her right hand without reinjuring the healing bones. She felt helpless, not to mention a mess. "Can you elevate the bed, or, if there's a button, I can push it."

Tim found the button, raised the bed to a comfortable angle, and sat down beside her in his chair on the edge of the bed. "Seriously, Laura, how are you feeling?"

"My new bad arm hurts like hell, and my old bad arm is not about to let me forget, but overall, I'm okay. Most of all, though, I grieve for Addie. I didn't know her that well, but I really liked her. She's not that much older than Natalie and Nicole. What a loss to medicine too."

"This may not be the right time, Laura, but I have something to tell you." Tim paused, took a deep breath. "While you were asleep, Mike came to see me."

Tim had said *me*. Why Tim?

"What did he want?" asked Laura, a panicky note in her voice. Tim had changed the venue for the planned meeting with the kids to a conference room here in the hospital, rather than the restaurant at the Barclay Hotel. They should be here in two hours. "Was it about tonight?" Had Patrick already told his brothers and sisters? Was her family already shunning her?

"No, Laura." Tim reached for her left hand, held it gently. "Mike came to me about something else."

"Everything okay for tonight?" Laura verified, trying for a neutral voice. *What I really want is to put off tonight until never.*

"Yes, if you're up to it. Each of the kids called to check that it's okay to come. Patrick called three times. I told them all a tentative yes, knowing you, how stubborn you are. Said I'd let them know if you decided to postpone. You know the shooting at the FDA has been all over the news. You're reported as 'stable with minor injuries.'"

He had told her in the Keystone Gulfstream flying back from DC that Jake Harter was in custody. Thanks to Laura's tip linking Harter's Jeep to the night Fred Minn was killed, the Philly police had arrested Harter for that hit-and-run. And they still suspected him of killing his wife.

"Good thing I showed up today, huh?" Tim said. "I'm coming off like a hero in the news. I just wish I could have acted before Harter shot Addie. He was aiming at you—Addie jumped in the way. She's the real hero."

"You are a hero, Tim. My hero, always will be. And Mike? What did he want?"

"Mike told me about last night. How he'd worked into the early hours to pull together the papers Dr. Abdul needed to secure the money Replica owed her. And to put the funds into safekeeping until she felt free to access them. She also did not want her family in Iraq to come into this money unless she so requested. Mike put it in a trust."

"Yes," Laura said, "Addie seemed fine with Mike as her trust-ee. Not that she wasn't worried about going back home—"

"Mike told her she needed a backup plan." Tim had cut her off, and Laura wondered why he seemed overanxious. "What if something happened to Addie before she could use the money? She had seven and a half million dollars in the US. She didn't know what to do." Tim paused to take a really deep breath. "So Mike advised she assign it to a good cause. When she asked 'what good cause could you recommend?' he said, 'CHOP.' So, Laura, now that Addie's dead, that money will go to CHOP to be used for whatever programs I recommend."

"Tim, that's wonderful. If anything good could come from losing Addie, this is it. You save so many lives. You know, after you called last night saying you wouldn't be able to make the press conference today, I told Addie about you, about your patients, about how CHOP had become the surgical hospi-tal of choice for children with congenital heart disease from the Middle East." Laura hesitated as tears slipped down her cheeks, "But I was just bragging about what you do. You're my hero."

"I'm still in shock," Tim said. "I wanted you to know about Addie's legacy. No one at CHOP knows yet."

"Addie was conflicted about her Western and Middle Eastern lifestyles," Laura said. "I think she'd want this kept anonymous. Let's go over that with Mike."

"Speaking of Mike, the kids will be here at seven thirty."

"I need to get cleaned up. Tim, how will I tell them? I have no words."

"Go with your heart, babe. Use the words in your heart to reach them."

A knock at the door interrupted. "You have a visitor," the cheery nurse announced. "Go on in, Mr. Parnell."

Again, Laura attempted to sit up and, again, was thwarted

by pain in both arms; throbbing in her right lower arm and hand; sharp and searing in the left shoulder.

"Laura, I can't tell you how distraught I am." Paul Parnell's cheeks did, in fact, look a bit less ruddy than usual. "All of Keystone Pharma, actually. Instead of popping champagne corks, we're mourning Dr. Abdul, and praying for your quick recovery." He walked up to her bedside and stood by Tim.

"Thank you for coming," Laura said. She wished he hadn't. She knew she looked awful. She had a lot on her mind that had nothing to do with being shot or with Immunone's approval or her boss. "Sorry, neither of my arms work now."

"No work for you, period, for a while," Paul said. "We do hope you recover fast, but when you feel better, please take a break?"

"Laura, I think you absolutely should take your boss' offer." Tim turned to Paul. "I've been trying to get your new employee to settle on a wedding date, and with your considerate offer, I think we could even fit in a honeymoon. How about that, Laura?"

Unless my kids reject me tonight. Decide that the mother they'd grown up respecting all their lives was a phony. A deceitful slut who'd indulged in an extramarital affair, who'd betrayed their poor father. Tim, if my life became a wasteland, I couldn't marry you.

"We'll see." Laura tried for a smile, but managed only a grimace.

"I'll be running along," Paul said. "I can see you're in a lot of pain. Any idea when they'll let you go home?"

"We're hoping for tomorrow or Sunday, at the latest," Tim said.

"Just keep us posted at Keystone, Laura. In the meantime, we'll keep that champagne on ice. You were brilliant at the press conference. We all thank you. You take good care of her, Tim."

Paul Parnell left, looking more robust than when he arrived.

Laura rang for the nursing staff, requested a sponge bath and help with her hair, refused any mind-numbing pain meds, but accepted a tray of finger sandwiches, grateful that she could at least pick them up with her left hand and lift them to her mouth; likewise, she could lift the glass of water and drink through the straw.

***

Tim pushed Laura's wheelchair into the conference room he'd arranged for the Nelson clan meeting. A far cry from the private room at the Barclay. The hospital had provided soft drinks and the same little finger sandwiches they'd given Laura in her room. Not much, just a few munchies to create the illusion of a social occasion.

Tim had said to go with her heart. Laura's heart was with her kids, always had been. Had she been a good wife to Steve? Probably not. Had he been a good husband to her? In some ways, but not at the end. Had he been a good father to her children? Yes, for the boys. No, for her twin daughters. Were her children old enough to even remember Steve? Definitely Mike, he'd been fourteen years old when Steve died. Maybe, for the others; Kevin, eleven; Natalie and Nicole, ten; Patrick, nine.

Patrick now knew Steve was not his biological father. She'd told him about her involvement with David Monroe. Patrick was twenty-two, he deserved to know. He'd taken it well, or at least he appeared to have. How would the other four react: their brother Patrick, in reality, a half-brother?

She would know soon enough. Thank goodness she had Tim. Tim had become her strength. Why, she wondered, had it taken so long to come to realize she and Tim belonged together. More than she and Steve. Even more than she and David, although that realization still stunned her. For all these years, Laura had remained true to the memory of David Monroe. She and David had spent only one night together. And David had died in her arms.

Laura had no clothes of her own at the hospital, so she had to meet her family in one of those open-from-the-back hospital garments under a gray-striped robe. She looked pathetic. Her hair hung limp and her nails were broken and she wore her clunky glasses.

She insisted that she sit at the table in a normal chair. Tim dutifully did as she'd requested; parked the wheelchair outside the room. She was ready. Tim sat beside her. They simultaneously checked their watches. Twenty after seven. Tim had gotten up to get her a glass of water when Natalie arrived. Still in green scrubs, her daughter explained that one of the other residents on her team wanted to surprise his wife for their anniversary, and she'd offered to take his call since she'd be in the hospital anyway. That was Natalie, always looking out for others. Would her generous spirit prevail tonight?

Natalie sat down on Laura's left and, after an air kiss, inspected Laura's left shoulder. "Bullet missed the scapula," she said.

"Right." Laura hoped for a clue about Natalie's choice of specialty. "You thinking about orthopedics?"

"Me? Wrong daughter," Natalie said. "But I wouldn't put it past Nicole. That field is dominated by men."

Mike arrived next, still in his business suit. Probably came right from his office. He swooped down to kiss her cheek. "You okay, Mom? Did Uncle Tim tell you I stopped by earlier? Gosh, Mom, you sure gave us all a scare."

"Am I late?" Kevin arrived within minutes. He looked business-like in a suit of muted greys, except for his loosened tie. Must have been meeting with clients. In the field he wore khakis, a t-shirt, and work boots. "Traffic from Princeton was heavier than usual." He headed toward Laura, pressed his cheek to hers, instead of doing his usual bear-hug routine. "You okay, Mom? You've been all over the news. Wish you'd stay out of harm's way. You need another bum arm?"

Laura watched Kevin playfully punch Natalie's shoulder as he settled in the chair next to her. "Looks like you didn't have far to travel. How convenient that Mom comes to your hospital. Where's your better half?" Laura could only hope their camaraderie would not shatter by the end of the evening's discussion.

"I talked to Nicole about an hour ago," Mike said. "She went home to change. Wanted to look good in case Mom decides to hold her second press conference of the day."

"She's on Dermatology this week," Natalie said. "Ridiculously easy call schedule. Maybe she's got a big night planned. It is Friday night. But I won't be going anywhere."

"I'm betting Nicole becomes one of those dermatologists to the stars," Kevin said, his mouth stuffed with a sandwich. "The kind that rips people off and makes billions—"

"I heard that." Nicole barged through the door. Her brainy daughter wore a black cocktail dress that came well short of her knees and displayed too much cleavage for Laura's taste. Nicole wore more makeup than usual and her hair was pulled into a classy updo. *Not a child anymore,* Laura had to remind herself.

Nicole approached her, aborted a hug halfway, planted a kiss on Laura's forehead with a simple "Hi, Mom." She sat down next to Tim. "Okay, Uncle Tim, what's this powwow about? I can tell you, I wasn't happy having to come back to this place when we were all set for a sumptuous meal at the Barclay."

"Uh, Nicole," Tim said. "Your mother..."

"Oops, I'm sorry. Mom, that came out wrong. Not your fault you got shot. You are okay, aren't you? I mean, you're sitting up. No respirator. Not even an IV line going. Can you imagine when I walked into the Derm waiting room and saw *you* on TV? I did a double take. That was *you* they were putting on a stretcher. Then they showed the woman who was murdered. My God. Did you know her?"

"Yes," Laura said, blinking back a tear. "Adawia Abdul. She went by Addie, and she was lovely."

"Yes, beautiful," Nicole agreed. "I'm so sorry, Mom, You must feel really bad."

"I do," Laura admitted. "And we lost an exceptional scientist."

"Were you scared?" Kevin asked. He got up, went to Tim, and said, "Uncle Tim, we all have you to thank. You were the hero today. We know Mom's fearless, but you saved her from that FDA maniac."

"Thanks, Kevin—" Tim would have said more, but Kevin cut him off.

"Hey, what are we going to call you after you and Mom get married? 'Uncle Tim' sounds odd, but familiar. 'Dad'? I don't know."

"Just Tim will be fine," Tim said as Patrick stepped into the room.

Her youngest son hurried to her bedside, carrying a huge bouquet of yellow roses, her favorite.

"Shit, Patrick," Kevin said. "Just like you to show us all up with the flowers. How do you think that makes the rest of us look?"

"Just so you all know, I sent flowers to Mom's room already," Mike said with a big-brother grin.

Tim took the yellow roses from Patrick, and set them on the credenza that held the tray of sandwiches. Laura made a mental note to ask for a vase.

Patrick did not sit. Rather, he stood behind Laura. She couldn't see his face, wondered if his stance was protective or defiant.

Then he spoke in a master-of-ceremony voice. "Bet you all want to know why we're gathered here tonight?" Laura realized that as the youngest of five, he'd had little opportunity to preside over family matters.

"I think it's a bit dramatic for a wedding planning session," said Nicole, "but, hey, I'll go along with it."

"Wrong," Patrick said. He put his hand on Laura's good shoulder. "Mom, let's get right to it. Do you want to tell them or should I? I don't mind—really."

Since her decision to confess to the kids, Laura had watched this moment in her mind, tried to foresee how this would play out, but now, with Patrick offering himself as spokesperson, she was stunned, speechless.

Laura didn't know how much time passed in silence—seconds? minutes?—before Patrick spoke.

"Okay, I'll handle this. Siblings, this communiqué is for you. Tim and I already know."

Laura couldn't breathe. Her soul left her body, she knew it did.

"I am an illegitimate child."

"Aren't we all, in one way or another," Kevin said, loosening his tie.

"Bro, I'm not kidding. Your dad, Steve Nelson, is not my biological father. So there! Back me up on this, Mom."

Again, a room full of silence. No one seemed to breathe. Laura still wasn't sure she could inhale.

Patrick still stood behind her. She felt his fingers tighten on her right shoulder, but she couldn't see his face. Still no one spoke. With a tiny pan of her eyes right and left, she could see four stricken faces.

Nicole, the first to speak, "Patrick, what are you f-ing talking about? Our dad, your dad, died fourteen years ago. You were young. You had just had heart surgery. You must have weird memories. Anesthesia can do that to you. But why are you bringing this up now? My God, Mom's just been injured, almost killed—"

"Because she wanted me to," Patrick said, voice calm, tightly controlled. "And be assured, my brain hasn't suffered any after effects from the drugs you doctors use to put kids under."

Laura heard strength in Patrick's response. She had to jump in and take over the narrative. If only she could see his face, read his emotions, but he still stood solidly behind her.

She'd avoided looking directly at any of her children. When she ventured a glance, she felt weak, woozy, like maybe she was having a stroke. If she were ever to be struck down by a catastrophic illness, this would be the time. *I have to speak to them, make them understand.*

"Mom, we know something happened regarding Patrick when he had that emergency heart surgery," Mike prompted. "Dad never told us the details, but something—"

"Yes," Laura finally breathed. She looked at Mike, over to Kevin, then at her twin daughters. "I had always intended to tell you, but there never was a good time. And Patrick—" Laura shifted in her chair, turning as best she could to face him, "I needed to explain everything to Patrick first."

"Mom, are you sure you want to go on? You don't look good. You're in the hospital. You were *shot* today. Couldn't we hear this later—whatever you want to say? You know, like when you're out of the hospital?" So like Natalie, wanting to avoid emotional trauma.

"No," Nicole said. "Patrick, could you come sit down with us? You're making me nervous standing over Mom like you're going to take her into custody if she doesn't say what you want."

"You okay, Mom?" Patrick asked as he complied, and came around to sit next to Nicole.

Laura looked at Tim. When he gave an almost imperceptible nod, she shifted a little to sit up straighter. "Here's what happened," she said. "Your Dad and I had a pretty good marriage until we moved to Detroit. After that, not so good. And by the time we moved to Tampa, we stuck together mostly because of you kids. And then he was... Well, he was killed." Laura hesitated. No one came to her rescue so she continued. "There was a time, a very short time, when I became involved with another man. He was on the faculty." She did not divulge that she and David had spent only one night together. A very fateful night. A night she would never regret.

All but Patrick and Tim stared at her. Big eyes. Open mouths. An audible gasp from Nicole.

"There, I've said it," Laura paused. Her eyes were dry, she'd always feared she'd cry when she revealed her transgression, her unfaithfulness to Steve.

"Oh, my God," Nicole turned to stare at Tim. "Is Uncle Tim...the one?"

Tim's redhead complexion turned pink. Laura could see him shake his head just slightly.

"No," she said, "not Tim. The man's name was David Monroe.

He died when Patrick was just a baby. He never knew he had a child." Here, Laura was lying, but she could not bear to relate the tragic circumstances of David's death, how he'd been holding Patrick, how—she believed—he'd instinctively known Patrick was his son.

"Mom, how could you?" Natalie asked, tears starting to flow. "After all these years, we find out? I mean, Patrick? What about Patrick?"

"Natalie, I don't care," Patrick said. "Sure, I was shocked and hurt at first, but the guy's dead, died many years before the death of the man I have, and always will, consider my dad. After that Mom was on her own, and we kids had a great life, right? Hey, just look at all you American success stories. And Mom's happy now that we have Tim in our lives. Let's just move on, okay?"

"If Patrick's okay with moving on, I am," said Kevin. "Do the rest of you think we can just forget about this? That'd be my vote."

"Sounds good to me," Mike said. "I'm glad this all came out. Remember, Kevin, when Dad got all weird when Patrick got sick? He kept saying Mom had done something bad, but he refused to tell us what 'until we were older,' and then he died soon after."

"Vaguely," said Kevin.

"He'd just found out," Laura said.

"I can deal with this," Nicole said. "Now we know Mom's not perfect. She's like one of us. I, for one, appreciate that. Natalie, stop crying. Let's give Mom a big hug. But watch the arms."

All five kids jumped up, went to Laura and hugged her, gently, murmuring, "I love you, Mom. It's okay, Mom."

"Okay, kids," Tim said once they'd all settled down. "I'll get your mom back to her room with her new flowers. Sorry we won't be having that big feast we promised you. Nicole, you look like you've got places to go. Any of you want to stay in the apartment, there's plenty of food and beer."

They all stopped to give Laura one more kiss before they left, Natalie now dry-eyed.

Mike was the last one out and he turned at the door. "So that's the only bombshell you want to share, Mom?"

Laura forced a smile as she nodded, yes. Just the thought of her remaining secret sent her heart into triple-beat. That secret she would never reveal to her children. But she would tell Tim. Tonight.

After all her children had left, apparently in decent spirits, Tim stood behind her chair to help her up.

"Tim, would you mind sitting down, staying a little longer? I know you've had a few shocks today, but I have one more story I want to tell you."

And Laura told him about that night that had hung over her life like a shadow of death.

31901067040834

CPSIA information can be obtained at www.ICGtesting.com
Printed in the USA
LVOW08s0319140116

469371LV00004B/6/P